This book belongs to

_____

FROM   DATE

By Jennifer Haskin

For information contact: www.jenniferhaskin.com

Cover design by SeventhStar Art/Inside cover art by ABlueEyedMamasShop

ISBN: 9798842437535

First Edition: January 2023

10 9 8 7 6 5 4 3 2 1

TABLE OF CONTENTS

DEDICATION

This book is dedicated to my girls.

I see so much of myself in you, and I see you in my characters' best moments.

I pray you create the stories of your lives with love, ambition, creativity, and joy.

My Jayna Grace, Emmy-Kate, and Addie-Girl.

Your mama loves you.

CHAPTER ONE

THE LOTTERY

MOST PEOPLE ARE HORRIFIED WHEN SUDDENLY faced with their imminent demise, and Marishel was no different. The day death called her name—literally—began like any other. After classes in the caves, she toiled through her afternoon at work, then left to pick up Yolenie—her best friend since kinder school—to walk home together.

Marishel waited for Yolenie in Ulu's Metal Repair shop. Cords of pulsing electricity arced from Yolenie's tool and screamed through a steel plate.

"Oww. Watch it with those sparks." Marishel slapped her sleeve a few times, tamping the glowing orange ring around a new hole in her shirt. "Are you done yet?"

"You're standing too close." Yolenie's small voice competed with the sounds of machinery. "I'll be right there."

"No problem." Marishel headed toward the doorway and called, "I'll wait outside." She'd battled a strange feeling all day—a certain wrongness enveloped her. Feeling foreign—like she didn't belong in her own surroundings—unnerved her. She hurried out the door.

The glacial air of the cavern inside the rocky dwarf planet sliced through Marishel's sinuses, and a tear slid down her cheek. She dabbed at the corner of her eye, careful not to disturb the wireless contact currently playing the season finale of *To Venus with Love*. She wasn't watching the show though; her mind drifted to a warmer climate where she lay on her back next to a silver-haired boy. *Two more years and I'll be done with school. Once I have a secure job, I suppose we could build a home together.* She sure didn't have any other prospects, but she wouldn't even allow herself to look for love until she was firmly established on her own. She'd promised Grammy.

Her shoulder lit where it pressed against the living concrete wall outside the shop, its bacteria glowing at her touch. A plastic basket of mending, crooked in her elbow, cut off circulation to her already swollen fingers—more work she hadn't gotten finished at the clothiers—although a long afternoon of sewing numbed her fingertips. Her stiff joints ached in the cold, and she flexed her fingers.

Yolenie swept through the doorway. "You ready?"

"Yeah. I'm so tired, I'll be lucky if I make it to a reasonable bedtime." She laughed, but her stomach clenched like a knot of yarn—tighter, tighter.

"Then let's go," Yolenie said, and they strode toward their neighborhood.

Marishel minimized the feed with a flick of her eye, and a light blinking out far above them caught her attention. She reached behind her ear and muted the show with her cochlear dial. Tech was still available, but the once-proud Outerlimits of Haumea had been crumbling for several generations. Carved out of solid rock and minerals, the remnants of art took shape above them—centuries of chiseled stone, like the ancient frescos on Earth.

She hugged her sweater closer to her body. Her fingers were thin icicles, brittle and frozen stiff. Oftentimes, Marishel couldn't shake the chill. One day she'd move to the Summerlands, beyond the farms and their temperate climate, nearer to the core of the planet, where Haumea was always hot. The rich lived in a massive cavern there, with swimming pools and homes with open arches and fluffy furniture.

The shells of her ears tingled with early frostbite, and she rubbed them to get the blood flowing. Her father claimed to hate the cold as she did, though—like her—he'd grown up in the Outerlimits and was "used to it," he said. Even visiting the Farmlands made him feel as if his bones were melting. She knew expense was part of the reason they were stuck in the Outerlimits, but not how much. Her future would soon begin—when she finished school and could escape the Outerlimits—dependent on no one. She shivered.

"You cold?" Yolenie asked, her haggard expression full of empathy for a moment. Yolenie didn't mind the crispy coolness of the Outerlimits. She quickly covered her concern with an unaffected mask that was often modeled by the work-weary adults of their society, emotion found as distasteful as weakness—positive or authentic emotions, at least. She rubbed Marishel's arm briskly as if that was all it took to defrost her.

Marishel nodded. "I can't wait for next week. Classes are done, and I'll be so warm."

"You going to your aunt's farm?" Yolenie coughed.

Marishel chuckled. "Like every other school break we've had in the last ten years." She bumped her friend's shoulder.

Yolenie coughed again, so Marishel patted her friend on the back.

Yolenie choked, then wheezed out, "Stop. You're making it worse."

"Sorry." She worried that Yolenie might have the sickness. The mining kicked up dust. No matter how hard they tried to purify the air coming out of the mines, they never caught it all. Miners like her father breathed it all day as they created a new cavern for expansion. He coughed in his sleep. Mostly, miners got it, but the dust settled in the Outerlimits and covered everything in a filmy grit. Of course, the miners lived in the Outerlimits, so naturally, many of them were sick. The dim chill didn't help.

Another light flickered from above like a blinking warning sign.

Electricity cost a substantial portion of the workers' salaries, and the Outerlimits couldn't afford to pay much collectively, so they lived in perpetual dusk—or what she'd heard of dusk. She'd never seen the sun. Told it looked like a small star from here, she'd never been outside the dwarf planet to see what stars actually looked like. Just the videos in school.

Marishel noticed the time on her *Eye* screen and quickened her pace, pulling her friend by the sleeve. "We've got to hurry. We're going to miss the announcement."

"The lottery? Ah, who cares? It won't be us." Yolenie scoffed.

"I'm worried for my cousin. Our last name was chosen for this lottery. You didn't get called this time?"

"Nope. My surname isn't in this pool." Yolenie grabbed her arm again and threaded her hand through Marishel's elbow, squeezing it. "Don't worry Risha. She'll be fine. They only choose sixty girls out of the whole planet."

She chuckled nervously. "Right. Bigger odds." Marishel couldn't swallow the lump of anxiety that clogged her throat. Their leader's son, the Ambassador, would soon be the winner when all those seventeen-year-old girls were chosen to compete—to the death—for the title of Ambassador's Bride on his eighteenth birthday. Jilly—her cousin on her father's side—was eight months older than she and so her name was destined to represent the family if their surname was drawn. But Marishel believed in the one percent—if there was one percent chance it could happen, it would probably involve her. So, she said a little prayer that Jilly would escape the dreaded fate.

They turned the corner of a row of rocky homes, stacked one on top of the other, and reached Marishel's street. More of a ten-foot-wide path, it crumbled in the middle, the edges showing remnants of a once-smooth walkway—the streets weren't self-repairing, like the buildings. Definitely an oversight. The girls waited for a hunched man with stick-like limbs to push a cart loaded with metal scrap.

"See you on Monday," Marishel said. They continued to use the old times and dates from Earth, though Haumea made a complete rotation every four hours. Days and nights were only a concept here. She couldn't imagine walking on the *outside* of a planet and being warmed by a huge sun in the sky.

Yolenie smiled. "See you Monday."

When Yolenie's coat disappeared, Marishel kicked up the dust and ran.

15

"I'm home," Marishel called as she slid the front door closed and dropped her basket on the floor.

"Hi, honey. Good day?" Her mother stepped out of the nook they called a kitchen and wiped her hands on a towel. Her gaunt face wore the stress of her nights as an Outerlimits nurse, and Marishel noticed lines at the corners of her eyes and her forehead for the first time.

"Mmm hmm." She frowned, then absent-mindedly tossed her mom a smile. "Nex, turn on the vid screen." The wall screen lit up, and she plopped onto the threadbare loveseat.

"Hey!" her sister Madigan shouted, spread out on the floor among her school tablets and touchpads. "Don't step on me."

"Missed you by a mile." She leaned forward and tugged her sister's braid. "Nex, volume up." Each home's housebot was named by its inhabitants. Her father had originally named theirs *Calanets* after the current "Political Intercessor" for their sect of the Outerlimits (called The Needles)—a joke to himself about his *lack* of political discussion—but Madi was often frustrated as a little girl when all she could say was "Nex," and couldn't turn on the lights.

"You nervous?" Madigan asked. "They could pick her."

Marishel opened her mouth to answer.

"Of course not, Madi," her mother interjected, going back to the kitchen. She called out, "Supper will be in half an hour."

Marishel smiled at her little sister's innocent question and shrugged. *If anything goes wrong…*

A sweet floral scent surrounded her in its soft essence and worked to ease her jittery heartbeat. *The candles were lit.* That meant there was news. "Why'd you light the candles?" she called over the couch.

Her mom peeked around the wall. "I met with Granny Elspeth. She was all in a tither because Sootsie's daughter eloped last weekend with a boy from the Summerlands who put her in,"—she looked over at Madi—"a family sort of way."

"What's that?" Madi asked.

"Wait." Blood drained from Marishel's head, and the back of her neck prickled like she was a pin cushion. "Aunt Sootsie? That's Jilly's mom."

"What is it?" Madi repeated.

"That's right. Jilly's gone off to the Summerlands to start a new family. That's what it means," she said, a little too brightly.

Marishel turned around and faced the screen, effectively dismissing her mother. Fuzzy numbness covered her body—no, not *lacking* feeling. In fact, her skin buzzed with electrified energy. If Jilly wasn't in the lottery, that meant it was possible *her* name could be in the pool. She concentrated on the breath she pressed out her nose and inhaled deeply to inflate her lungs.

Nothing could interrupt her plans. Not now … not yet. Before Grammy died, she had lived with them in a closet space, converted into a sparse bedroom off the kitchen, and taught Marishel about the coldness of adult life. Grammy had passed up her schooling at an early age—and getting a job—for love. She'd been quite happy to raise Marishel's mother and sister, but when Gamps was crushed in the

17

mines, she was forced to rely on the charity of relatives to survive. And she hated every minute of it.

"I'm too old to go back to classes," she told Marishel when she tucked her into bed as a little girl. "I'm too weak to learn a skill or get a job. It's humiliating to be so worthless. Promise me, little Risha, promise me you'll do it the right way. You must learn all you can and get a job to support yourself. Then, you can look for love. It's the only way to be happy. You can make everything fair if you are the one in control of your destiny."

"I will, Grammy. I promise. I'll follow the plan and be useful. Then I'll be happy, right?"

"Yes, bright girl. I knew you were going to be brilliant the first time I saw your tiny face." She brushed Marishel's hair back from her forehead.

"That's why mama named me after you." Marishel yawned. "So I would be smart."

"Much smarter than me."

Colors flashed on the screen when the program began, framing the show's host—she couldn't remember the guy's name. "Welcome," he boomed, "to this generation's Blood Match coverage. I'm your host—"

"Why do they call it that?" Madigan asked.

"Sshhh!" Marishel didn't have time for silly questions—*especially ones she didn't have answers to.*

"A blood match is like a soul mate, Madi," their mother called.

The scene shot to the ruling family of Haumea—the Leader himself, Karthik Porter; his wife Gioia, known as The First; his oldest son Quinlan, called the Ambassador; and his younger son Canon. They sat with stoic poise, except for Quinlan, who looked like he'd rather be surfaced without a suit than sitting on a televised sofa with his family.

18

Marishel thought he might have looked excited or at least *pretended* to be, but he glared at his father and the camera. *The other girls think he is so handsome. He could be—but his attitude sure isn't attractive.* She sniffed.

The First was draped in a sparkling gown of indigo sequins. *It must have been brought ready-made from Earth,* she thought. Nothing Marishel ever sewed was that fancy.

"Good evening. I thank you all for watching as we play the lottery." She gave a little chuckle. "As you all know, the Blood Match honors The First, and I am *very* honored to be the mother of this generation's Blood Match. The contest for the title of Ambassador's Bride has been carried out for centuries. Though it began as a silly pageant, when Analiyah the First came to power, she won by proving her *true* worth in a battle against the other contestants. Wanting nothing less for her own son's bride, she carried on the competition, and her daughter-in-law did the same. On and on we've honored the old traditions." She clasped her hands. "So exciting! One month from now, one young woman will prove herself worthy of being the Ambassador's Bride, in the most romantic, self-disciplined, show of bravery … and she shall be the future First."

"Yeah, and all the rest of them die," Madigan said, coloring a page with her stylus on the floor. She lay on her stomach, swinging her feet back and forth.

"Hush." Marishel leaned forward to the creak of the furniture.

"This year's contest—"

Bang… Bang. Marishel's father shoved the door aside and slammed it shut. She turned around to look but didn't dare "shush" him. She valued her life. She grinned at him; he wouldn't hurt an atom.

"Hello, family," he mumbled absently, coughing as he plopped down in a chair at the table to kick off his boots. He unbuckled the straps of the exoskeleton across his muscled thigh and then began pulling on the other leg's strap. "Nalyn! You aren't going to believe this." He coughed into his fist.

Her mother came out of the kitchen. "What? What happened?"

"They pushed through a new decree." He slammed his hand on the table, his still-mechanized fist nearly cracking the surface. "They're taking corporate ownership of the mines."

"Who?" Madigan popped up and kneeled on the loveseat next to Marishel, facing backward. "I thought *you* were going to own it, Baba."

On the vid screen, the show's host was going on about contests of the past and flashing pictures of girls in fancy dresses and pony-tailed contestants training with state-of-the-art weapons. Past contestants stood up to the podium before the match, showing the symbols of their individual family heritage—an East Asian peace-sign, a Middle Eastern sign of power, a West African salute, an American hand symbol of goodwill with her thumb pressed vertically to her breastbone. Marishel wanted to watch but she also knew what a crisis this was for her father.

"That was the plan, Madi. The mines have always been owned individually ... must have been something they forgot when Haumea was divided into community property. But now they've realized the mistake and want to make it corporate." He put his face in his hands and Marishel's mother laid a hand on his shoulder.

"We were almost there," she whispered.

20

Marishel s father had worked his way up from the bottom to become the name on the mine's lease. It was almost paid off and he planned to sell it once it was his outright, and that would be his ticket to the Gentry—what the rich called themselves. It was his dream—to choose where to live, to have what he wanted, to leave the mines. It was all over now. *The hoping.* The plans for a home in the Farmlands next to her aunt. They'd be stuck in the Outerlimits forever now. A chill danced over her skin. She'd never escape the cold.

A set of parents sat huddled together on the screen and attempted to smile bravely. "We are so proud of our daughter's patriotism," the father said.

His wife echoed, "She fought heroically and made the family proud."

"And now for this generation's contestants!" the screen rang out.

Her family stopped and watched the screen as names scrolled from the bottom to the top and photos of girls flashed one after another. The announcer called out twenty names and some of her apprehension eased. Marishel's eyes were crossing, and her sight was blurry while reading all the text. After forty names, a blanket of calm enveloped her, and she watched to see if she recognized anyone who was chosen. But she couldn't release her grip on the armrest yet. Kindel, a girl she'd seen at school, was chosen and didn't live too far away. That eased the last of her tension. They wouldn't choose girls who lived so close together, right?

"Number forty-nine is Marishel Vance."

The announcer's stentorian voice echoed in her ears, and the letters of her name appeared bigger and bolder than the others—they seemed to scroll up the screen more slowly. She sat, motionless. Had she really seen it? Her family was not reacting. It must have been a trick of her senses.

She looked around the room at her family, each staring at her with open gazes, and Madi's mouth hung open.

Oh no. No, no, no.

CHAPTER TWO

THE SUMMERLANDS

THIS ISN'T HAPPENING. THE NEXT DAY, MARISHEL vibrated from the motion of the speeding aerotrain, the scene of her family's shocked expressions lingering in her head. After the names were announced the day before, her mother had been the first to rush to her and wrap her in a warm hug, as she stared numbly at her father, and her sister began to cry softly. The program had continued well into suppertime, instructing contestants to be at the aerotrain station this morning.

So Marishel had mechanically followed her mother as her suitcase was packed. Her square, blue, Lucite case was already packed for the farm, but her mother tsked as she removed plain clothes and replaced them with the finest garments Marishel owned. She didn't think about what her mother packed, she didn't care about doing it, or if her dresses looked too "outer-limits" compared to the other girls, she didn't care about any of it. She did manage to

23

shove in a few of her favorite garments, though—worn pants and soft cotton tops. She needed the comfort of home where she was going. A fog of disbelief crowded all activity from her brain. The only thought reverberating through her mind on repeat was, *this isn't happening. This isn't really happening.*

Marishel sat in a cylindrical suction-based train, speeding along inside a pressurized tube from one side of Haumea to the other—just another day to everyone else. They flew through the long tunnels using the planet's swift rotation. Haumea's rotation was so precise that colonization was required to be evenly distributed, or else the potato-shaped dwarf planet would have become barbell-shaped and eventually split in two. So, they made equal settlements inside both ends of the oblong planet, around its heated core. Both sides had hot Summerlands nearest the core, balmy Farmlands further out, and cold Outerlimits. The current mining for expansion had to be completed in mirror fashion for both communities.

The Leader's compound of buildings, as well as the arena, was located in the capital, on the other end of the planet. Technically, as the colony lived on that side first, where the main dock was, *she* lived on the *other* side. But perception was paramount.

"Make a good impression," her mother said at the platform with a hug.

"You make us proud," her father added with shining eyes. "You always make us proud."

"I don't want you to go!" Madigan shouted and ran from the boarding platform to the building.

"Aw, Madi. Don't leave like that," Marishel called, but the door closed.

24

Her mother had dressed her in her fanciest kaftan. Though the people lived interspersed among each other, their ancestral heritage was especially important in Haumea, and Marishel's father, Yami's, family had originally hailed from Morocco. Their finery was all Moroccan flair. She'd been too preoccupied to notice that the kaftan she was wearing was new. It must have been something her mother had been working on, and it fit with perfect proportions. The peach gown was gauzy and full-skirted—ivory beads created a stunning pattern on the bodice and ivory roses scooped along her neck, to the wide ornamental belt, and down both sides of the split overskirts. She suddenly felt very overdressed.

"You look like a true princess," her mother said while Marishel sat vacantly in front of the mirror, allowing her to thread delicate drops of ivory from her ears and pin her hair in a mass of auburn curls at the back of her head. Though her father's skin was brown, Marishel favored her mother's lighter coloring and auburn hair.

Marishel stared into the mirror without answering. The shock had her limbs pinned, her muscles taut, and she gritted her teeth. She was floating—but tethered.

"You can do this." Taking Marishel's face in her hands, her mother's eyes filled. "You are a good girl, always thoughtful, obedient, honest, and so clever. Keep yourself protected—" Her voice broke on the last word, and she went back to fussing with Marishel while she waited in a daze.

As the sidecar burst to full speed after another platform stop, she jolted from her state of absence to realize her true situation. First, she wished she could go back and say a proper goodbye, but that thought led to her going home, and she needed to get that fantasy out of her mind right away.

She couldn't afford to hope that she'd ever go back there again. The heavy gray feeling pressed against her chest and made it hard to breathe. The point of no return was passing her by. She put a hand on her ribcage and focused on her breath. She peered out the window and watched the fields of her Farmlands speed by.

They were *hers*; had been since she was seven. Every year, when classes were through, she spent the season at her aunt's farm with her best guy friend, Trae, the boy she dreamed of. They would lie by the lake for hours without saying a word, but each knew the other's mind. His grandparents' farm was next to her aunt's. Marishel and her cousin, Prester, did chores and at night, music filled the fields. It was the only time she ever got to sit in the grass.

Grass didn't grow in the Outerlimits. Madi didn't care for it, but the green, freshness of it, and the way it tickled the back side of her knees, drew Marishel to lay in it and ponder. The mineral composition of Haumea was almost the same as the Earth's crust, so growing plants had turned out to be surprisingly easy. As a child, she imagined the air as colors and she inhaled the icy blue air, breathing out red gas that the grass and trees greedily sucked in, spewing more of the blue she desperately needed. Laying in the grass under the VitD lights, she would watch the colored air swirl with the fibers of cotton on the man-made breeze.

Marishel considered jumping off the train and running to her aunt's to beg clemency. But there was no way out of this. *Maybe I could win?* If she somehow won the contest, it would elevate her family's status. The winner's family was moved up to the Gentry. Baba's wishes would come true. Maybe she could be happy without her life plans? She wasn't used to having her choices abolished. Fairness was controlling the outcome.

26

She wasn't going to win, though. She was going to lose. Her need for escape gripped her shoulders and punched her gut. She panted, and water rushed to her mouth. If she dropped out—left the competition—her family would lose everything they had. And the government would find her and bring her back to the Match anyway. *I can't do that to them*

Her heart thumped. Maybe she was *generally* brave, she was often outspoken, and she wasn't stupid—in a game of skill, she had a chance—but a fight to the death? Who was she kidding? She was going to die.

She was so stuck in her melancholy that she jumped when she noticed a girl standing next to her, clearing her throat.

Marishel swung her head to gape at the girl. "Yes? Am I in the wrong seat?"

"No, oh my, no." Her voice was tiny as a whisper. "You're—going to the Summerlands—right?" The girl stuck out her hand. Her blushed skin was a lovely golden brown and she wore a traditional Mexican *poblana.* Marishel had sewn a few at the shop and loved the color patterns. She took the girl's hand hesitantly and wondered why this girl would know anything about her. "I saw your picture on the program last night."

Ohhhh. A drama-lover. Well, it was a public train. She smiled graciously and said a cool greeting, looking longingly out the window as the pools of the Summerlands began to flash by, pulling her like a magnet. When the girl plopped down in the seat facing her, Marishel's hostility ignited. *Doesn't this girl know that I am off to face my death, sans friends or family?* Didn't she know that the last thing Marishel wanted was to meet someone *now?*

"I'm Shalise." The girl smiled with a shy tilt to her head, green eyes sparkling. She lowered her voice conspiratorially. "I got picked, too."

Marishel's gaze darted to Shalise, probing for falsity, but all she found was an innocent barely masked fear. "I'm sorry," she said. It's what she wanted to hear—from *someone*.

"Papi says I have a chance. Are you a fighter?" Her calmness was part balm and part irritant, but she had an honest openness about her that made Marishel feel like she could trust her.

"No. I am far from a whiz with weapons. I'm a seamstress." She mimed sewing with a needle and thread.

"Everyone says it's so romantic for a girl to prove her love in the Match." Shalise thought a moment and whispered, "How can we be romantic with someone we've never met, someone we don't love? I mean, that's why he dates—us: looking for compatibility ... and great TV. But what if there's no love there? Will I fight as hard, or sacrifice myself?"

Her honesty loosened Marishel's tongue. "I used to think so too—that it was so romantic. I've never had an unfavorable opinion of the contest in my life. That's how things are done—the way they have been done." She looked around them. "But not for me. I'm no 'chosen one' from a story. I already know what I want to do with my life, and this isn't in my plan. Besides, the Ambassador doesn't seem really interested in it at all. I have one option—to pour myself into training and hope for a chance to live. That's what I'm resolving to do."

Shalise smiled. "Me too. I can teach you a few things. I grew up with big brothers."

Marishel returned the smile. "Thank you."

"We're going to be great friends."

Marishel evacuated the tube, heaving her suitcase onto a wide and brightly lit platform. She was a mole emerging for the first time, but to a hot desert sun, or what she'd heard of it. Her lungs shriveled like dry sponges. Great cavern walls rose behind Marishel, to the dome of the ceiling burning with VitD lamps, too bright to see the area around her. She put a hand to her forehead to shield her eyes and stepped down the stairs to join a group of girls her age, who all appeared to be looking for instruction from a tall, thin woman with short blond hair.

"Girls. Girls! Your attention please." The woman clapped her hands, frowning. The tendons in her neck were stretched as she stood on tiptoe to look over the group. She poked her index finger to the buttons shining on her forearm from a uBand. "You will all follow me!" she called to the girls in the back. Marishel marched with purpose, though still on autopilot. Reality hadn't kicked in yet. As they moved en masse, Shalise edged up next to Marishel until their shoulders touched.

"Where do you think we're going?" she asked.

"I dunno," Marishel mumbled back, looking around them, estimating the number of girls. "I've never left the Needles, except for my aunt's farm."

"The Needles?" Shalise cocked her head.

"Yeah, we live in the Outerlimits, near a cave of stalactites that are long, thin, and deathly pointy."

"Ah, I know that cave. I guess I never thought of it having a name. I live on the edge of the Farmlands, not too far from you—well, I guess I *used* to…"

Marishel would have told her *it's okay, everything will turn out fine*, but then she realized it would be a colossal lie and stopped herself.

About twenty girls followed the blond woman hauling bags and suitcases from the aerotrain station. Marishel held her suitcase handle in both hands, and it bumped against her knees when she walked. They'd arrived in the hottest part of the Summerlands, and she wished she had a suit to swim in one of the sparkling pools. She'd never been so close to Haumea's core before. Inhaling the heated air through her nose, she shivered as the VitD lights helped to warm her skin and the muscles underneath. She pulled off her wrap and folded it over her arm, then shivered again as dots of heat prickled her skin and warmed her from all sides like an oven.

They stopped in front of an opening in the railing at a sidewalk terminal. Marishel had never been on a moving sidewalk before and looked on, amazed. It wasn't like she'd never heard of, or seen the fast-moving sidewalks, but they didn't have anything similar in the Outerlimits. The safety arm barred their entry as passengers sped by. At a bell-like sound, the sidewalk slowed to a crawl. The light turned green, the arm raised, and the bell dinged once.

"Hurry, ladies! Hurry! Let's all get on as a group. Hurry, now." The woman rushed to herd their group through the gates before the light flashed red. Marishel stepped onto the sidewalk belt and looped her elbow through a stabilizing strap that glided in a track under the railing. After about thirty seconds, the bell dinged twice, the arm came down, and the sidewalk began to speed up. She strolled along with the group and watched the scenery as it flashed past them.

Vibrant ochre plastered walls, scarlet-tiled roofs and the admiral blue splashes of pottery and pools surrounded her with color. Everything was so … *bright*. It hurt, but it was like having someone switch the lights on, for the first time in her life. She marveled at the beauty of the saturated hues alongside green plants and high domes with art in every shade. Potted cacti of every shape and color lined windowsills of gated homes. It was almost as wonderful as she'd dreamed it would be. Each house she passed, she longed to go into—to plop down her suitcase and yell, "Hey everyone, I'm home!"

Soon, they came to a bridge for the cross street. Marishel held onto the strap as the grade raised, but the sandpaper grip of the sidewalk belt held her shoes and kept her from slipping as it gradually pulled them over the heads of passengers going under them. After a bit, they changed direction and traveled past the arena. It stood like a fortress.

She watched the ball games regularly as they were televised, and she'd seen footage of previous Blood Matches here. But she wasn't prepared for the strength, the steadfast structure standing sentinel, the place of their death. Her life would end in that arena. Marishel turned forward in disgust. She had a lot of work to do before the Blood Match. *Will I be ready in time?*

Even with the sidewalk's help, Marishel's fancy shoes—a pair of her mother's—rubbed blisters into the backs of her heels by the time they finally reached the leader's estate. The group passed through an arched gate, gazing at the impressive cluster of honey-colored buildings. Gioia, The First, rose from a nearby bench, holding a small tablet.

"Welcome, contestants!" She attempted a gracious smile, but the practiced expression didn't look right over her cool mask of indifference. "I insist on greeting the girls myself. You are the last group to make it. We have finally all arrived." She clapped the device in her other hand. "Sayra will lead you to the training center where you can get settled. Dinner will be in one hour. Please dress accordingly." She looked pointedly at a few of the girls who wore plain, but colorful, woolen shifts in lieu of cultural finery.

Maybe mother was right.

They trod a paved walk through an expanse of short green grass, toward a tall building with open, arched windows and doors. Marishel marveled at the formal security guards scrutinizing the estate's perimeter wall. She glanced at the outbuildings and a guard station to her left, noticing a camera pointed toward the gate and felt momentarily claustrophobic.

As they crossed the massive lawn, the woman they were following, presumably Sayra, threw words over her shoulder. "This month will bring lessons on the etiquette befitting an Ambassador's bride." This caused a few murmurs that Sayra frowned at and continued, "You must show the ability to deal with pressure, hardship, humility, attention to authority, obedience, skill with weapons, and strength of will. Winning this contest will show true strength and worth."

The fact that they kept calling it a mere "contest" grated on Marishel's nerves; but the idea of having value and worth, and being able to *prove* her strength of will, appealed to her somewhere in the place where her mind met her will and emotions—the very place where she became who she was. She surely wasn't going to lay down and die. She would fight her way through this. The pilot light to her anger flared. Oh, she would fight if she had to. She didn't hear what Sayra said next as they entered the building.

Inside the hall, freshly cut flowers bloomed in vases sitting on half-tables pushed up to the walls—which were papered a warm cream on the top half, a cool navy satin on the bottom. The halls were richly carpeted, and her shoes sank into the fibers. Soon, they reached a long open room, tiled in stone, with sixty oval-shaped twin beds lined up six feet from one another down both sides of the space. A soft-looking cream coverlet lay on each bed and sported a card with one young woman's name.

Two-thirds of the beds were already surrounded by girls meeting, chatting civilly, and unpacking items into the bedside cabinets.

"Find your beds and meet your bunk mates. No, you may not trade. Don't ask. I don't care who your daddy is. The answer is no," the woman said with hands on her hips. "I'm Sayra, your trainer. This"—she pulled a smaller woman with translucent skin and piercing eyes to her side by the elbow—"is Sobia, your allocated attendant. Not your slave, understand?"

She waited with a frown for the multiple murmurs of confirmation from around the room. "The doorman is Icen," she said, though Marishel saw no man in the room. "Tonight, you'll meet the show's producer—I'm sure you've heard of him—Sarver Bello. He will be at dinner along with the members of the Ruling Family. Please conduct yourselves with behavior becoming of polite young ladies. You must dress for dinner. We have extra clothing available if you did not come equipped, and you will all be pleased to know that there will be a fitting and you'll all be outfitted for the Blood Ball, taking place the night before the match."

A few of the girls actually looked enthused, as though they were on a holiday shopping spree. Maybe they were in denial? In a way, she envied their ignorance and wished for a moment to forget that she had one month to live. If she could forget it, she could have fun and enjoy all the festivities. How many people got to dine with the Ruling Family? How many people would get to know what they would know? But she couldn't forget it. The looming date of her death was an asteroid tied around her neck—orbiting her and pulling the string tighter as it went around.

"Sobia and I will be coming around the room to disable your *Eye* feeds for the duration. You were instructed to bring your cases." Sayra waved them into the room.

Marishel found her bed close to the door, between two occupied bunk mates putting their personal items in their cabinets. Marishel woodenly opened her suitcase. She was unpacking her toiletries when she bumped into the girl behind her.

"Oh. Sorry. I didn't mean to knock you over," Marishel said and smiled at the girl whose *cheongsam* reflected pink in her golden cheeks, tinting her white-blond hair, cut in a blunt bob. She was gorgeous.

"Oops. That was me. It's okay." The girl stuck her tiny hand out. "I'm Valorena, but just call me Rena. I was hoping to take this dress off, but it looks like we have to stay fancy. *Ugh.*" She rolled her eyes. "I just want my comfy clothes back on."

Marishel laughed. "Well, you look beautiful in your cultural wear. I guess I don't mind mine so much." She touched the ivory roses at her neckline and felt a sentimental wash of emotion realizing that her mother had made it in secret, and she never even said thank you. It pricked the back of her eyes. She felt them getting wet.

Rena held her hands up in terror as soon as she noticed the tears. "Hey. I'm sorry. I didn't mean to, ah—insult you or whatever. I just meant—I mean, you look beautiful, too. I'm ah, I—"

"It's fine. I'm okay. I'm just going to put my stuff away."

"Are you gonna be okay?"

"Haven't you heard? We're dying next month." Marishel gave a half-hysterical shout of laughter. "I don't feel like I'm ever going to be okay."

"Kerse it, girl, don't lose it on the first day. I gotta bunk next to you." Rena bumped her with an elbow, giving a chuckle. Marishel echoed her.

"What are you guys laughing at?" The girl on Marishel's other side placed a manicured hand on Marishel's bed, disrupting her things, leaning toward them in interest.

She didn't look genuinely interested, though. She had the sharp look of a true gossip—someone who measured people for their weaknesses, to exploit them. Exuding confidence, her lips curled into a sly smile that seemed to make her blue eyes even frostier. Blond ringlets fell over her shoulder, and she flicked them back. "Well? What's so funny?"

"Nothing, really," Marishel stuttered. "We were just meeting. Hi—I'm Marishel." She stuck out her hand.

Looking at her hand with disdain, the girl took it with her fingertips and squeezed it, letting go quickly. "I'm Lonna. I'm generally the queen bee—"

"Itch." Rena disguised the word in a cough behind her and Marishel wanted to roll on the floor laughing, but she settled for a welcoming smile.

"Nice to meet you—Lonna."

"I'm sure," Lonna said. "You're from the O.L. Bet you've never seen anything like this before." She gestured toward the end of the room where two sets of glass doors stood open, curtains blowing from the fans.

It wasn't a question, so Marishel just nodded. "So, you guys are from around here? Are you also in school?"

"Ha. I finished my learning long ago—tutored, of course. You still go to *school?*"

"Well, I finished childhood learning two years ago, and began a collegiate program." She couldn't resist the jibe.

"Oh, brains *and* poor taste in fashion," Lonna said with a chuckle and turned back to the girls on her other side.

Marishel frowned, but Rena merely rolled her eyes.

Sobia arrived at Marishel's bedside with a handheld device that looked like a pricing gun. The woman was probably around twenty-six. She was slight and looked like she'd fly away in a stiff gust of wind.

"It won't hurt," Sobia said softly with a Slavonic accent—most likely Russian—as she held the gun up to Marishel's head, and both her *Eye* feed and volume were cut short.

"Thank you," Marishel said, and Sobia looked shocked. Wasn't anyone being nice to her—at least, polite? Sobia smiled gratefully at her and Marishel felt sad for the shy woman, but in an oddly protective way.

As Marishel peeled off the epidermal VR-sleeve covering her hand in a breathable glove, she wondered why a middle-aged woman would want this job. The low life expectancy in the harsh climate of space, especially with the mining, was what Marishel had been told was once young. The oldest woman in generations was alive now at nearly sixty! Many of Marishel's former classmates were already knee-deep in their life plans or growing new families. She was waiting to finish school, though seventeen was considered a median age for marriage, hence the Ambassador's contest for a bride. If still unmarried by twenty-one, it wasn't uncommon to hear whispers of "spinster" floating around.

Pressing her thumb to the oval on her case, her print popped the lid open, and she put in her contact and glove, then snapped it closed.

"If you disable our feeds now, what proof do we have that they'll come back online?" one of the girls asked Sayra.

"Only one of you needs to worry about that. And I don't think she will have a problem," Sayra said sharply.

The girl nodded with tear-filled eyes and Sayra continued in a softer voice, "Get used to the facts, or you'll be overwhelmed at the end." *How could these girls just accept this? Where is the rage? Even so, what good would my anger do?* It certainly wouldn't change the situation, which was what she really wanted. But why was the outrage non-existent, and the horror so readily accepted? She'd never given the matter thought until this morning.

Over the generations, the people of Haumea had hardened and cooled, like lava. Public emotion was considered distasteful, except disdain. They were bored of the endless cycle of life inside this inescapable, spinning rock. The Blood Match was anticipated for the irony, the sport, the camaraderie, and ... the blood. Most people played the game's lottery to win, and used the Match for its best purposes, whether they gambled to gain new wealth, played for distraction, or reached for a better status. They guarded what was theirs jealously, and for all society's virtue signaling, contests like this just didn't faze them. It was a fact of their desolate life in space—more death meant a greater portion of leeway, supplies, and food rations for everyone. And like stone, they were heavy and set in their ways.

Marishel and Rena decided to save their wardrobe for other days and wore what they had on to dinner. Lining up at the door, they passed Shalise. Marishel grabbed her and introduced her to Rena. Like a herd, the girls exited the training center, crossed the lawn, and moved reverently down the opulent halls of the manor. It was the biggest single home in all of Haumea. As the girls gazed enviously at the detailed art and curtains, contrasting with stark white plastic-looking walls and floors, they whispered and gasped. It was easy to see, some could imagine themselves living here. *Only one of us.*

When they entered the dining room, every girl who could, flocked to sit next to the Ambassador who, though he looked awfully sharp in that jacket, appeared flustered at the attention, and civilly ignored them. He had prominent bone structure, his dark skin hollowed between high cheekbones and a sharp jaw—brown hair cut short, but long enough to style. Not the worst thing to look at—if you like your guys pompous. Those who didn't win a spot near him, clustered around the show's producer, Sarver Bello; the First; or the Leader, Karthik Porter—a proud-looking man with dark skin, a full, frowning black beard, and clear eyes; confident, discerning eyes. He smiled once, graciously, at the admiration, and the First looked delighted in the adoration of her enthusiastic followers, though as removed as royalty.

Marishel chose a seat farther away, next to the leader's other son, Canon—also known as the Second. Merely thirteen, he smiled genuinely when she asked, "May I sit here?"

"Sure." He resembled his mother, who sat poised in a powder-pink sari across the room, with about a hundred silver necklaces, and her black hair pinned up off her neck in an impressive coif. Canon had her cinnamon coloring and easy smile, but his eyes were a soft brown and not her shrewd green. She looked like she could spot a lie a mile away—she looked not *at* the girls but straight through them, seeing the secrets they tried to hide. Marishel instantly wanted to cover herself.

The oval pad at her place on the table was familiar to her and Marishel placed her finger on the oval and pressed. Through a microscopic amount of blood, the device read the nutrients she needed and anything she was lacking along with her anti-radiation supplements, to be injected into the food made by the Nutrition Interface Printers. Marishel listened to the conversations taking place around her. The girls near her were politely meeting each other and asking one another's common likes and animosities, did they have someone back home, their skills, what they dreamt of, and what they were afraid of. Surprisingly, no one mentioned being present as a fear, and Marishel found that dishonest.

After about five minutes of waiting for her food, she asked Canon, "Why does your printer take so long?"

He laughed just as the tabletop in front of her split down the middle and slid inside itself to reveal a plate of food on a tray that rose to the surface of the table.

The First stood as the plates were rising in front of the attendees and clinked her utensil on her glass. The room abruptly silenced, and she flashed her camera-ready smile. Of course, this dinner was televised—all their training would be. It's why they took the girls' newsfeeds—so none would know anyone else's ranking in the winner's pool.

The cameraman crept around as if he feared missing a spat or catfight, or the one girl who always loses it. It took Marishel's concentration not to notice the man lurking around the periphery of the dining hall, nearly hiding in the folds of the diaphanous gauzy curtains that covered arches to the patio. The camera was a floating black sphere mounted on a prosthetic base, implanted high on his temple, catching essentially everything he could see and hear in a 360-degree radius. The other giveaway that he was a reporter was the notebox he held and continuously scribbled on with a fancy, feathered stylus. Marishel made a mental note to keep her mouth shut around that man.

The First was speaking about her pure elation to have the girls all under her roof. She was to be their mother for the next month. *But what about my mother?* Surely her family was right now hunched over the table, shoveling mouthfuls of couscous and greens, facing the vid screen, and watching for glimpses of her. As the reporter turned his head in her direction, Marishel made an effort to smile as she toasted the words of the First and dug into her food. The textures weren't right. She screwed her face as she chewed the unfamiliar consistency.

Canon chuckled again.

"Why are you laughing at me?" She frowned.

"Something's not right with your printer."

"It's not a printer. That's real food. That's why it took longer. They still inject it with what you need, but it's grown, not printed."

"Wow," she whispered, taking another bite.

She'd never had real meat, the little meat there was to have, was given to the Ruling Family first, and then whoever bought it in the Summerlands. The overstocked ponds did have to be thinned, so she'd had flakey white fish, but never this pink thing on her plate. It was chewy, almost buttery, and so juicy. The accompanying sauce danced on her tongue.

Do they eat like this all the time? It was a wonder the First was so thin. Rena and Shalise talked softly on her right, so she turned away, to give them privacy. She studied each member of the Ruling Family. The Ambassador looked like he'd thawed a bit and was talking to Lonna next to him. That girl knew she was going to win. It was written all over her face. She hung on his every word. *Great. Give him a big head. That's all we need.*

Maybe *she was* worthy. But worthy or not, fifty-nine young people in their generation would be deprived of a wife because the Ambassador needed the "best." Marishel wasn't ugly, but she wasn't the prettiest one here, she may not even catch his eye. He was supposed to date them all and get to know them for the show, but how much time would he spend with those who were obviously not in the running?

How could he be okay with this? On his behalf? She wondered about the Ambassador's conscience. Was his whole family short on compunction? She peered at Canon next to her, silently eating in miniature bites, mostly shoving wilted greens around his plate. He didn't appear to be listening. He wasn't talking, and no one had spoken to him since she'd been there; he appeared completely vacant.

His face blushed and he turned to glare at her with brows raised. "Always stare at people?"

CHAPTER THREE

THE ROUTINE

CANON'S QUESTION SURPRISED HER. SHE HADN'T realized she was staring, and heat flooded her face and neck. "Oh. I'm sorry."

His brows returned, he smiled quickly, and it disappeared. "It's okay. I won't bite." He chuckled wryly. "Sorry—really. Something else is bothering me, it's not your fault."

"You haven't been the center of attention in quite a while, have you? Anything to do with your brother being the bachelor of the decade?" She smiled softly.

"I haven't been more than a topic of conversation since Quinlan was born."

She squinted her eyes. "But he's four years older than you."

"Badum pum psss."

It took her a second to realize he was joking with her. He raised one eyebrow, pursed his mouth comically, and rolled one index finger in a circle. "Now you're getting it."

She laughed. "I'm sorry. It's not really funny, but your expression—"

"Have you met anyone yet? Made any friends?" he asked quietly, picking up limp spinach with the end of his utilitarian utensil and dragging it around his plate.

"I've made a few. You?" Her eyes twinkled with mischief.

"Just you." He smiled conspiratorially.

After they'd eaten, the First said to mingle and have coffee or tea while the plates were removed, and dessert brought out. It was like they were in a witch's cottage and the witch was fattening up the girls before putting them in the oven. Maybe Marishel was inside the most messed up fairy tale yet.

Dinner guests milled around with demitasse cups and little saucers, dresses swishing the floor. Lonna's dress draped over one shoulder and the fabric presented her tanned decolletage like an open treasure chest, then wrapped her small waist and dropped from her hips in sheer yellow like rays of sunshine; a slit traveling higher up her leg than was necessary. She embodied the Summerlands and obviously came from Gentry with the golden bracelets clinking on her wrists and delicate chain around her sun-kissed neck, clasping a yellow gem.

Canon repeatedly clicked the end of his utensil, switching from the prongs, to a bowl, and then a blade, over and over, as they watched the procession of colored dresses swirl through the room like curlicues. *Click. Click. Click.* Marishel loved to people watch. *That's when you see who people really are.*

43

The girls flocked the Ambassador as he strode regally about the room, chatting with those who looked like good prospects, or the ones who forced his attention. Marishel sat patiently. Apparently, he found her beyond common courtesy, or maybe she—obviously not a winning contender—wasn't worthy of it? A flame of indignation sparked as he passed her for the third time without even glancing her way. It wasn't like he hadn't stopped to speak to more than one seated person. She snorted and shook her head in wry amusement.

"Don't pay any attention to him. They're doing it for you, anyway." Canon motioned to the girls trailing him, Lonna vying for the lead.

"I'm noticing a distinction between the girls who feel they can make it and those who know they can't." Marishel squinted one eye.

"It seems they're either fearful or they're bullies."

"It does seem so." She thought about it. "I imagine everyone's operating in a mode of unreality and presenting their best personalities through the lens of their coping mechanisms."

"Indeed." He smiled at her.

"I'm here to risk my life for him—he could at least say hello. It's not like I asked to be here." She knew her voice bordered on petulance, but she was irritated by his disregard for her.

"Like I said, don't pay any attention to him. He's so full of himself right now. He can't see beyond his own pains."

"Oh? What would cause pain to someone cushioned here?" At his frown, she amended, "Not like there aren't pressures and problems everywhere. I just figured your family had all you'd ever dreamed of."

It was his turn to snort. "What *I* want? Nobody cares what I want."

"I do," she said quietly.

He shook his head. "It doesn't matter. There are lots of things I want, but I'll never have what I want the most. Never. It's not possible."

"What would you ask for, if you could have *anything?*" She imagined he'd want to live on his own, maybe buy a farm, have a pet, own a company. Or have a shipment bring him all the Earth or Mars items he wanted…

Embarrassment reddened his face. He ducked his head and spoke so softly she could barely hear him. She leaned close and their shoulders brushed. "I want to go to Africa."

"Africa?"

"Yeah. On Earth. It's a continent with oceans and deserts and animals and these flat trees that giraffes eat. Can you ride a giraffe? Like, do they have saddles?"

"Beats me. You want to fly back there? It would take years. Besides, everyone says it's a junk heap—the planet ignored to the point of its own destruction. By the time enough of them cared, it was too late to reverse all the damage they'd done." She drained the last of her bitter brew. "That's why they colonized Mars to begin with."

"I could handle the flight. I mean, you could go hybrid and stay awake a few years, then go into cryostasis. Right? And they always say that about the planet, but it's the same place our ancestors left from. It has to be. I've seen all the pictures…"

"From what I know, your choices are to stay awake and risk going crazy, or cryo-sleep for the next six years and wake up feeling old—and that's at hypo-sonic speed. But … people on the Earth do live longer. Maybe if you left when you were forty-five, after a full life, then it wouldn't matter. If you got extra years ... bonus."

"Hmmm. It's worth considering." He looked thoughtful for a moment and said, "You know, he's really pretending." He reminded Marishel of her little sister when she had the inside scoop on the latest gossip.

"What?"

"My brother. He only pretends to be like them..." Canon nodded to the adults, who responded to conversation with removed emotion, bordering on disdain. "The robots."

On the Ambassador's next passing, Canon's long arm shot out across the table and grabbed him by the jacket.

He stopped like he'd been yanked back and scowled at his brother. "What?"

"This is—what's your name again?"

"Oh." Marishel was a little uncomfortable being singled-out, but she might as well meet him now. "I'm Marishel. It's nice to meet you, Ambassador."

He sighed and put out a hand, looking at the people passing him. "I see you're entertaining my brother?" He said it like a challenge, but the question was there: *Why aren't you following* me *around?*

She lay her hand on his long fingers, and he bent to brush his lips across her knuckles. When he looked up at her, his eyes widened. *Hmph.* Now *he notices me?* Not happening.

"It's Quinlan." He smirked quickly as his breath bathed the back of her hand in heat and peered through unfairly thick black lashes. *His eyes are green, like his mother's.*

"Are you from the capital?" he asked, still bent over her fingers.

"No." She snatched her hand back and tucked it in the skirt of her kaftan. "I'm from the other side … in the Needles."

"Ah. Haven't heard of it. Well, what do you think of *our* Summerlands?" He stood.

Marishel paused. Of course, he would assume she hailed from the Summerlands on the other side. Hadn't he at least heard of the Needles in business? It's not like she was tanned. What ruler didn't know the districts in their own jurisdiction? She judged him unworthy of the truth. "It's lovely. A mirror image of home, I'm told. Have you been there often?"

"I can't say I've ever had cause to visit."

"Surely, meeting the people you rule would be cause enough, would it not?" She raised her brows.

"If I'd known how lovely the citizens over there were—" *Is he flirting?*

She frowned, but Quin stood relaxed in front of her, cool and confident, and he wore it like a fancy tailored coat. Long, lean fingers worked together as he stroked the index finger of his other hand. His eyebrows rose and he flashed even, white teeth in a formal smile—completely lacking warmth—and Marishel realized she was glaring at him. Thoroughly frustrated, her resulting hot blush irritated her. She wanted to duck under the table and melt away. She absolutely did not want to look like a blushing bride in front of—*oh.* Yeah. *The cameraman.* Standing several feet away, the cameraman gleefully watched her humiliating reaction to the Ambassador as he smirked.

Marishel was tempted to flash them both either a broad smile or a sign of bad luck, but the cameraman darted away.

"There you are." Lonna appeared next to the Ambassador and pulled on his elbow. "I have someone you should meet, *Quinlan*."

Marishel lifted her chin at his look of indecision. "Go attend to your other guests, I'm sure we'll meet again, Ambassador."

"Quinlan." He frowned.

"Yes."

She didn't mind the attention of a handsome boy. It would have been fun to flirt, however foreign the action was. Quin's lean physique and bright green eyes *could* make the blood rush through her veins—but she didn't *like* him. He was generally cold and self-absorbed, worrying about whatever "his own pain" was, as the girls were called to sacrifice themselves for him. Loving him didn't even seem like a possibility. Plus, winning his heart wouldn't win this competition. Beating the rest of these girls would.

He had been engaged in their conversation, but from her seat, it looked like he repeated that conversation with all the girls. How could he never find a reason to visit her side of the planet? Still, if she won the Match, she'd be stuck with him. Maybe she could find something good in him? Of course, the alternative was dying, so how bad could he be? As he walked away, she thought he might not be as cold as he seemed, but worth dying for? *Nope.* She hadn't changed her mind on that.

Marishel lay in the dark. Rena snored softly next to her, and Lonna was reading under her blanket, her transparent book screen glowing through the fabric. Marishel put her hands behind her head; she enjoyed the heat. The curtains at the end of the room billowed in on the breeze that continuously blew in the Summerlands from the fans around the core, sweeping the heat through the massive caverns toward the Outerlimits, though it never quite reached that far. The ceiling fans above them spun and little hairs tickled her forehead. Some girls were sweating in their sleep—tossing and turning. She was going to be tired tomorrow, but her mind wouldn't shut off.

A wave of homesickness swept over her, and she wished she was in her room. Normally, when Marishel couldn't sleep, she'd crawl in bed with Madi, and if *she* couldn't sleep either, they'd raid the cabinets and watch tutorials on the vid screen with the volume all the way down; pictures flashing in the dark, throwing light around the room. It was their secret.

Not anymore. She'd never crawl in bed with her little sister ever again. The thought sucked the air from her lungs like a vacuum and crushed her heart with a weight so heavy that the tears came instantly. She covered her mouth trying to silence the great hiccupping sobs that threatened to take over her body. Her abdomen clenched tightly in a spasm, her nose ran, and tears slid from her eyes to gather in the shells of her ears. She cried for her parents, and Madi, she cried for the other girls who would die—and for herself— whose life hadn't begun yet. She'd spent all these years preparing for her future—a future that would never come. What good were all her plans now? She had no control over her own life, even after she'd planned it so carefully. The irony of it cramped her stomach. She'd wasted her life waiting for "the future" to begin so she could *start* living, and now it was almost over.

As the sounds of sniffling echoed throughout the room, she thought she might not be the only one making this revelation. Marishel resolved to rise above this fear and fight her way through this. She didn't know when she fell asleep, but the morning came way too early for her taste.

"Rise and shine, ladies!" Sayra walked the aisle at their feet clapping her hands and occasionally blowing a whistle that Marishel wanted desperately to shove down her throat. "Breakfast is in thirty minutes. Wear your daywear, we'll be training later. If you require appropriate clothing, we can provide it. For now, though, please remain casual." This was what Earthens called "business casual," and would require more than her everyday clothes.

She realized with a mixture of relief and dismay that her mother had packed only her nicest things. Thank the stars she'd shoved her favorite pants in at the end. They were threadbare, which would work well for training, but she'd never be accepted in those.

She dressed quickly in an ice-blue kaftan with white flowers embroidered on the bodice, about a thousand buttons trailing from her neckline to continue down the split in her skirts, and a thin silver belt. The material fluttered from her shoulders as she hurried down the hall with Shalise and Rena to the stairs and the classroom on the third floor.

A buffet set up in the back of the room was stocked with coffee, juice, water, bagels, and fruit—the real kind. She chose her breakfast, and they sat three tables from the front of the room to the left side. Marishel bit into a slice of orange. The flesh burst with juicy tartness, and she swirled it to the back of her mouth. The oranges at home lacked this pop, the sharp zing on her tongue.

Sayra walked down the center aisle with the producer, Sarver Bello, to the front of the room where she perched on a table facing the girls. He sipped coffee as they spoke.

Sayra gave them a few minutes to get assembled and then asked Sarver to have a seat. He sat facing the girls and stretched his long legs out in front of him, crossing his ankles. His confidence did nothing to put Marishel at ease.

Sayra spent the morning droning on about proper etiquette and how to behave on camera. The instructors—who'd watched the video replay of last night's dinner—had plenty of ammunition. And the girls—being replayed on screen in front of everyone—were duly chastised.

> *Rule: An Ambassador's bride shows a constant display of humility and the ability to humbly take correction.*

"You will have free time," Sayra said. "You may roam the estate, and may go anywhere the Ambassador takes you, but you can only leave the premises with permission. Do *not* be unaccounted for."

Marishel's fingers burned with overuse as she wrote down notes after hours of instruction and she made a fist—opening and gripping—a few times.

"My hand hurts, too." Shalise dropped her stylus and rolled her wrist in a wide circle.

"No kidding," Rena whispered back, dropping her head onto her folded arms on the table.

Sayra frowned at them and continued.

After lunch, the girls were divided into six groups. Ten girls made up Marishel's grouping with equal parts humility and haughtiness. She was hoping Rena or Shalise would be with her, but she didn't know where they were. Though the girls milled about together awaiting instruction, they couldn't have been more different. Outfits were made of cloths Marishel recognized, and instinctively knew their feel under her fingers, but the designs and cuts were all distinctive styles.

Everyone spoke the same language, but Haumea's only culture was the passing down of myriad traditional Earth cultures. The pioneers of Haumea didn't want to form a new society that had the same traditions for all—bland and boring. The whole "melting pot" of America never worked the way it should have because people missed their differences. So, all cultures lived in community, dispersed among themselves, and *family* heritage was prized by most. A new bride was expected to adopt the customs of her husband's family if they followed any—so the winner of the Match would traditionally take on the Ambassador's heritage, values, and rituals.

The girls' conversations were stilted, though, as a few of them had accents so thick Marishel could hardly understand them. Children were often raised in their "second" language first, and spoke only their cultural language at home, so their speech was accented. She felt slightly out of place as she'd never been taught her second language—because, in her case, Baba's father married into the family without a cultural lifestyle, so they passed down Granny Elspeth's heritage, but Baba's father didn't want to learn or teach his children any "Moroccan" language. It was like losing a family heirloom. Baba would have passed it on if he could have spoken it, but at least they had the rest of their traditions.

The group followed Sayra to a small ballroom outside the dining room that looked like it hadn't been used since the last Blood Match. Which she guessed *could* be true— what other reason did they have for a small ball? Maybe the

Legacy Games banquet? Every four years they competed in sports and games, vying for recognition within their culture.

There hadn't been a political social gathering since the colonies separated decades ago. But the parties they put on for the Match rivaled any other holiday. The Blood Match brought much-loved sport, and excitement; fancy soirees and viewing parties with neighbors, bets on the winners, bets on the losers, etcetera. Little girls would wear the fashions they saw on their favorite contestants. And the announcers would show their appreciation of the girls' participation—as if they had a choice—and echoed, repeatedly, the dreamy romance of the Match. All for the Ambassador. *Bah!*

The ballroom was mostly lined in wood laminate, which would have been awfully expensive to build on Haumea. That was a lot of heavy cargo. Glass light fixtures stuck out from the walls in half-domes giving ambient light. A layer of dust coated every corner of the room. And because the first Haumeans brought an entire ecosystem with them for nominal living, multicolored spiders and other bugs had concocted homes in all the corners. The girls stood around looking at each other in confusion. Were they learning how to dance?

> *Rule: The Ambassador's bride must handle hardship well and be a servant to the people.*

"Okay ladies." Sayra walked into the room holding buckets. "You are going to clean this room. All of it."

A chorus of groans resounded, and she held up her hand. "Ladies do *not* complain. Those who complain, or work without a smile, get double duty. Am I clear?"

"We have to work with a smile?" one girl with flushed cheeks asked.

"Yes. The winner will be expected to smile at times when she absolutely does not *feel* like smiling. There will always be a cameraman around, watching her expression. This is your training ... and should be practiced regularly." Sayra took a tub of cleaner and a rag and handed them to one girl. "You and you and ... you. Clean and buff the light fixtures. You two, take these brooms and sweep. Start there and work your way across the room. You two take the mops and go behind them. Carry your buckets and don't spill them. You will sweep cobwebs, and you will wipe..."

Marishel looked at the enormity of the job and felt tired. She wasn't dressed for this. Luckily, she'd pulled her hair back this morning into a bun. At least it was out of her face.

"Here." Sayra pushed a scrub brush into her hand and a bucket into the other. "Open those curtains and go through the arches, then scrub the patio." The lemon smell of the cleaner stung Marishel's nose and eyes.

"By myself?" she asked in a small voice. She didn't want to start any trouble, but it was a huge patio.

"Get out there."

Marishel turned and a shove to the middle of her back made her trip forward a few steps.

She gritted her teeth and went to pull the heavy cord to open the drapes, then crossed the patio. From the corner, her attention was pulled to a panel of dimly flashing lights and movement. She peered through a window across from her and saw what must have been the security room behind dark glass. She wanted to see how and where they were monitoring the girls, but the glass was too shadowy. She didn't have any kind of agenda, but she began to form a map in her mind of the estate's layout to get her bearings.

"Aren't we done yet?" Abrielle's blond ponytail swung as she sat back on her heels.

"Should be soon." On all fours for about two hours, Marishel's knees had imprints from the stone, and her arms were limp noodles. The pain in her shoulders mirrored the pain in her arms and hands. Her cheeks were cramping. Wouldn't it be easier to kill them all off and then just train one girl?

Sayra had sent out another helper, Abrielle, and they talked as they worked shoulder to shoulder, pushing and grunting with their effort. Abrielle came from the Farmlands initially, but she'd moved to the Summerlands about a year ago. Something about a medical procedure she needed in the capital.

A shrill whistle sounded, and Sayra shouted, "Bring your tools here. You'll be using them tomorrow."

They both sighed. Marishel was more than happy to hand over her worn-down brush and scummy bucket and hoped they'd get a chance to lie down before supper. She was exhausted. Abrielle was about to wilt against her like a thirsty, cut flower.

Sayra did indeed lead them back to their bunks, but with clear instructions to dress for training. *Rule: An ambassador's bride has stamina, you know.* The girls changed clothes in silence, too tired and apprehensive to speak. The other groups of girls filed in and were told the same. There would be no one with advantages today.

Marishel shrugged on a cotton top and soft wool pants with leather ankle boots her father had made for her as his evening hobby. She ran her finger along the seams, remembering his face. How happy he was to see her wearing them to class, proud to own them.

"Those look comfy," Rena said kindly, sitting on her bed and pulling on her shoes.

"Yeah."

"Hey. You okay?"

"Yeah. Fine. Only tired and nervous. Shalise said she'd teach me some things about fighting, but we haven't had a chance yet. Do you have a weapon of skill?"

"Me? Naw. Never held a weapon. Wait! Yes, I did. I blew a dart gun once." Rena chuckled.

"Really? Why?"

"Instructor brought it to class. I didn't know the guy put an actual dart in it. How was I supposed to know?"

"What happened?"

"I shot my friend." She looked sheepish, and added hastily, "It wasn't a poison dart or anything. Just pierced her butt." She cackled loud enough to get the attention of Lonna—the queen bitch.

"You are so weird." She leaned forward to look around Marishel at Rena. Then, in a matter-of-fact voice, asked, "Have you ever fought before, Marishel?"

Marishel looked at Rena who shook her head in warning. She turned to Lonna. "Sure. Um, have you?"

"All the time. I take extra classes for exercise and mental health." She sniffed. "My father always hoped I'd be chosen. He's been preparing me since I was eight."

Marishel was astounded. "You've been *preparing* for this?" The thought was so foreign to her.

"Daddy said if I was ever chosen, this way I'd win for sure. And if not, I'd be healthy and could take care of myself. He said it was irresponsible for parents of girls my age NOT to train their daughters in case they were picked."

"Who would do that?" Rena peered around Marishel this time. "I mean, other than a bunch of Upper Summerlanders who have time to waste? The rest of us have to *work* for a living."

Lonna's face turned fuchsia. Then, serenely, she straightened her spine and said to Marishel, "I'll help you train today. Show you something you've never seen."

"I wouldn't…" Rena warned in a sing-song voice.

"Shut up, drag." Lonna narrowed her eyes at Rena.

Rena looked shocked and then stormed out of their room to the joint bathroom.

What was that about? The offer from Lonna, though she suspected it was barbed, was bait she needed to take. Lonna knew a lot and she was prepared to win, if she took Marishel under her wing, maybe they both had a shot.

Marishel stepped onto the training grounds and the heat shriveled her sinuses. Sweat gathered around her hairline. It was a dusty open field with sawhorses arranged, posts set up, and an archery range to the left side, with a looming two-story obstacle course at the rear, near the stone estate wall. A set of uniformed men rolled out a big case with doors and when they opened it, there were lines of lances, training—she hoped—axes and swords, throwing items, and things she had no idea about. She recognized a stick she knew would be an electronic shield when held and a few strap-on devices that were weapons for the wearer. One of the men near her, a guy about her age, with deep brown skin turned to her and she gasped at the clear blue of his irises. It was a stunning contrast with his bright smile directed her way.

She snapped her open mouth shut and nodded back at him.

"I'm Icen."

"So, you're the doorman. I wondered if we'd ever meet you."

"I'm supposed to do whatever they tell me. Sometimes I'm a doorman—and other times—" He waved his hand toward the cabinet that the girls were clustered around, awaiting Sayra's next lecture.

"Marishel! We do not fraternize." Sayra gripped her arm just above the elbow tight enough to bruise, but Marishel didn't rip her arm away.

Sayra stood in front of the cabinet, facing the girls, and let go of Marishel. "These are your judges." She waved her arm out toward a group of five men and women holding electronic clipboards. "You will be ranked in skill to be placed on the initial winner's list. The viewers want to know who to put their money on. As you grow in skill, your numbers will change, but today, we want the lowest scores possible for your first test." She looked around at their haggard faces. "That shouldn't be too hard, hmmm?"

"Will we know our score?" a girl with a slick ponytail asked.

She chuckled. "Of course not. It's for possibility and making bets."

"What if we score too low? Will we be kicked out?" A quiet girl with long, fringed bangs had her hand raised and her eyebrows nearly to her hairline. She looked so full of hope.

"No. Don't be silly. You just won't be ranked as one of the winning pool." Sayra clapped her hands together. "Let's get started. We'll begin with ... oh, say, hand to hand?" She looked over at the judges who nodded in agreement.

"Partner up girls! Go ahead and spar with each other, share your knowledge and when we come by you, we will have you fight hand to hand until one gets knocked down." She turned to the judges and walked to huddle with them.

Marishel looked around for Rena or Shalise. Her arm was suddenly in a vice. She spun as Lonna gripped her. "There you are," she said.

"Yeah, so what do you know?" Marishel was wary of Lonna and didn't know what she had planned, but she had to keep the option open that Lonna was simply looking for a friend or someone to help make it through the contest. She had to give her the benefit of the doubt.

CHAPTER FOUR

CHEAP SHOT

LONNA TOLD MARISHEL THAT TO BOX, one had to hop around on their toes. *Haven't you seen a fight before? They always hop around.*

"Keep your arms in front of your body so no one can get to you. Yeah, like that. Jab with 'em. Keep your head up so you can see, yeah. Then, when you're ready to fight, get in front of the opponent. Got it? Then you can stop weaving around quite so much, so you have better aim, and just punch like wild. You want to punch whatever you can. Unleash your fury." Lonna had the look of a serious trainer and Marishel was glad. She had been so worried she wouldn't know what to do. It all sounded like it made perfect sense.

The judges alighted on the first team and blew their whistles. Everyone stopped and turned to watch as two evenly matched girls started to fight. It wasn't a boxing match so much as a wrestle for rank. There was hair-pulling and slapping, anything they could do to try to throw the other one down first. The taller girl kicked out and swept the other girl's feet out from under her and the loser fell on her behind with a thud. She smacked the ground with a shout and raised a cloud of dust.

Shalise and Rena were sparring about ten feet away. Marishel looked over at Shalise and saw her bouncing around on her toes. Maybe Lonna knew what she was talking about. She relaxed knowing that she was making a friend, bonding, and learning how to win.

"Come on," Lonna said. "Practice hitting me."

Marishel hopped around as did Lonna, then they jumped toward each other and practiced fake punches. When the judges arrived at their group Sayra said, "When you're done, you may go shower for dinner. Go."

Again, Marishel hopped around Lonna in a circle facing the girl as she turned around, and the judges chuckled. She kept her arms out in front of her and measured her swing. She approached Lonna and raised her chin, prepared to trade some blows, but Lonna startled her with a left punch. Marishel ducked back and avoided the hit, keeping the hand in her sight, distracting her from Lonna's other clenched fist as she pulled it back and socked Marishel right in the face. Dazed, with stars in her eyes, Marishel didn't see the punch coming toward her stomach and took the hit to her diaphragm, nearly losing her lunch with her breath. Leaning forward with eyes barely open, she swung her arms around with all the intensity she could muster, punching at anything she could. Her fist brushed Lonna's sleeve and she fumbled to grasp the fabric, no longer caring if she played fair.

Lonna gripped Marishel's outstretched wrist and pulled her forward sharply, causing her to lose balance, but as she fell, Lonna kneeled before her. Marishel landed across her shoulders and Lonna stood up, gripping her left arm with one hand and her left leg with the other, then Lonna ducked, heaved Marishel's body over her head, and threw her to the ground. Marishel landed in the fetal position and bounced off her hip bone.

Completely blind-sided, she wheezed as she looked up at Lonna's grinning face. "You'd better use your big brain on the day of the Match because you suck at fighting."

Lonna turned on her heel and marched toward the building, leaving Marishel holding her stomach on the ground and the judges typing furiously on their clipboards.

It was the first time Marishel had ever been insulted for being smart. She wasn't a genius … and she did suck at fighting, but Lonna wasn't going to win that easily. Marishel was naïve and inexperienced, but she wasn't stupid. Maybe Lonna was right, and she would have to use her brain to get through this. But how?

The next day, they were ranked in archery. On Marishel's turn, she stepped up to the line, inhaling great gulps of air. The VitD lights were hot on her head. A target was placed far in front of her. She squinted to focus on the center circle, blew out her breath, and inhaled deeply. She squared her feet, shifted her weight, and pulled the arrow back as far as she could. Letting go of her breath, she let the arrow fly. She squeezed her eyes shut and then looked to see where her arrow landed.

Yes, she hit it! *It hit the target! The last ring!*

The judges were sighing and frowning as they took notes. One man shook his head as he wrote. *But who cares?* She hit it. Maybe it wasn't the smallest target, and it wasn't *really* as far as it seemed, but kerse it, it was amazing that she hit the thing at all, and they couldn't steal her joy at the accomplishment. *Baba would be proud.*

It gave her hope that she might be able to improve enough to stay alive, and that was all she needed. *But what about being paired with the Ambassador?* Her thoughts tormented her. She still thought he was rigid but wondered if he might be hiding a personality as Canon suggested. Her curiosity was piqued, but she was still too angry about having to fight for him to admit it.

She looked up to see him strolling from the labyrinth, his mother on his arm. She stuck her tongue out and made a face just as he turned, and she thought she saw him chuckle, but she was sure it was her imagination. They had to be too away for him to see.

Over the first week, Marishel settled into a routine of learning, cleaning, fighting, meeting with the other contestants, and dining with the ruling family. Each day was a variation of the one before. They would soon be expected to go on "dates" with the Ambassador. Marishel was not enthused, but the other girls often vied for his attention. Her agitation grew daily.

Rule: The Ambassador's bride will be completely devoted to the Ambassador.

"How are you this evening?" The Ambassador looked over her head as he spoke to her in the dining room—his back to the curtains. She might as well have been on another planet.

She stood on tiptoes. "I'm right here."

"What?"

"You keep looking around. I'm standing right in front of you." She frowned.

He did the same.

Though she liked talking to Canon, speaking to Quinlan was like talking to an animal. It listened, and looked at you, but didn't register anything you were saying. It was like he couldn't be bothered to entertain her because she wasn't an obvious winner. At least that was the only reason she could think of as to why he didn't give her attention even when she was speaking to him. She thought about it. If she were in his position, she wouldn't want to have anything to do with knowing the losers, either. Or any of them, really. It would be painful to know the people who lost their lives for you with no choice. Then it hit her. He should *have* to deal with her. If she had to fight for him, possibly *die* for him, he had to carry the memory of her on his shoulders. So how could she make him *feel* it? Could she ethically gain his attention—possibly attraction—and then fling it back in his face?

Well, Grammy used to say that you catch more bugs with sugar ... and then you shut the jar. Right. It wasn't a matter of her ethics. He needed to be responsible for what happened to her. She was worth being remembered. Her life was more than an attendance slash and she wanted him to see it. *Step one: make him feel something.*

She smiled. "You look very handsome in that pattern." Indeed, he did—the material looked shiny and soft, and it had a high collar with a diamond pattern in gold and navy. She didn't know yet if the Match wasn't to his grand design, and she wanted to hurt him. She was so consumed with disgust when she pondered this fate that she never should have had to face—because of Jilly—that she could barely stand to tell him that he looked handsome at all.

"Yeah?" He raised an eyebrow, goading her.

She knew he'd heard it from all the other girls, and he didn't look like he believed her for a minute. She obviously hadn't made that big of an impression the first time they met. Should she break his heart the way hers broke for home? Could she? She wanted to be remembered, but not like that. Not like a heartless shrew. That wasn't Marishel. She'd have to come up with a better plan. For now, she just wanted him to *know* her—know she existed—and care.

She laughed lightly. "You know, I'm no good at this flirting thing."

He wiped the back of his neck and turned pink. "Neither am I. Like, what am I supposed to say?"

"The truth?"

"Touché."

"Good thing we don't have swords, huh?" She grinned.

"Oh, I'm not worried." A mask of haughty confidence slipped over his face.

He wouldn't be. She frowned and he cleared his throat.

"Would you like to walk with me?" He held out his elbow. She figured she'd better grab it before someone else did. The mound of muscle under his sleeve surprised her. Everyone worked on an exercise regime in Haumea, their bones and muscles needed hard activity. She hadn't had the heart to tell Canon that first night that he could never go to Earth anyway. He'd never be able to walk around in their atmosphere with all that gravity. Haumea's artificial gravity kept their feet on the ground, but there was no doubt each generation had been born with lower bone density. The only

65

reason they didn't break bones regularly was due to the calcium infusions in their food and the VitD lights, though they perpetually kept new remedies in trial. Poor Canon was stuck in this rock. It would take the full force of gravity itself to pull his dreams into reality. She ached at the thought of his dreams being shoved aside and never realized. Then she remembered that was her position as well.

The Ambassador led her through the dining room's adjoining dark ballroom, past the cameraman's rolling closet, and onto the patio she'd scrubbed for days. She marveled at the little flecks of olivite and pyroxene in the rock. The VitD lights were dimmed for nighttime, and she imagined them as stars in the night sky. What would it be like to breathe all that open air—to look up and see Haumea spinning in its orbit among the stars, knowing they were stuck inside? Did anyone care anymore? For an unknown reason, she felt peeved. The planet, the contest, the Ambassador—did no one see her?

"You're awfully quiet," he said. "What are you thinking?"

"Stars," she said without thinking. Trying to recover, she grasped for an idea that would appeal to him. "The contest ... and you."

"What about me?" The corners of his lips curled into an inviting smile he'd hidden from them in the dining room. The skin crinkled around his eyes, and she second-guessed her plan, but rushed forward while she had the nerve—and the irritation of being there, yet totally unrecognized.

"I don't know you. But I'm going to die for you. How does that make you feel?"

He jumped back from her as if she'd burned him. His eyes narrowed. "How dare you? You have no idea what you're talking about."

"So, tell me."

"No." He crossed his arms. "You're one of"—he swept his hand toward the dining room—"one of the girls. A guest."

"I think we both know I'm not a guest. You can tell me. Besides, think of it this way: if I don't make it, I can carry your secrets to the grave. I can't imagine it can be that hard, but I won't judge. And I'll even try to be civil." She tried to fake a smile but was sure she failed.

His eyes were slits as he measured her. She wondered if she'd pushed too far, then he said slowly, "I'm not any happier than you about this situation. And the government will do anything it takes…" He whispered, "I hate feeling impotent, being forced into this position and everything it requires, but not having a voice."

"You seem angry. I think you have more impact than you realize. Your brother seems to think you are concentrating on your own pain … and that you're pretending to be unaffected."

"Oh he does, does he?" His voice took on a bite.

She warred with herself, wanting to be cold and hateful but knowing it wasn't her nature. If she wanted him to know her, she needed to take another approach. Marishel laid a hand on his arm. "What are you afraid of?"

"Who says I'm afraid of anything?" He trembled with suppressed emotion.

"Because anger comes from fear."

He blew out his breath and looked around the empty patio, obviously weighing his desire to expand on the topic. "I've been trained over and over to keep all this inside, but I don't like to hide behind the truth…"

"So, tell me. You can trust me," she said softly. "I'm friendly."

"Huh." He smiled wryly to himself. "'Bout time."

"What?"

"I've given up wanting actual friends."

"You don't have friends?" She couldn't imagine a person of his fame, status, and attractiveness wouldn't be inundated with requests for his friendship. "Not even a best friend?"

"I have to be anonymous on all my feeds—for political reasons—so I can't make real friends that I can see or meet up with, no one can know who I am. It's ... lonely, sometimes."

"So, tell me what has you so upset," she said gently. She gazed up at the lights. Not a broken one. So unlike home. She felt like an alien in a foreign land.

"I shouldn't even tell you this." He turned to look out at the lawn, and she waited silently for him to continue. "All my life, my father has been present but unaccounted for. He doesn't know me. In his eyes, I'm just a child at the mercy of his legacy. Nothing I do is important. I know I could make a difference if—"

"If what?"

"Nevermind. You couldn't understand." He offered his arm, and they continued their stroll on the shadowy patio.

"Maybe not. But I could try. You have to trust someone—try me. You must respect to gain respect—you must trust for miracles to happen."

"Why do I feel like you're the only one listening to me?"

Maybe she wasn't the only one who wanted to be seen. She shrugged.

"Who loves you—respects you?" he asked. They'd come full circle around the patio and were back near the arches, soft music wafting outside through the curtains. He pulled her around to face him, placed a hand around her waist, and shifted his weight from foot to foot, leading her in a slow dance to the tune. He was light on his feet.

A shiver ran up and down her body at the heat radiating between them. Despite her circumstances, for an inexperienced girl, it was a pleasant memory to keep. His breath smelled minty as it fanned her cheeks. She flushed, sure that if their skin touched, their bodies would spark. She could feel his hot touch through her kaftan, soft sea green with shimmery gold embroidery.

She didn't have to think about his question, but she couldn't quite concentrate. Who loved her? *Oh right, my family.* But she couldn't think about them now. She wanted to, but she locked into his green eyes, striped like malachite, and realized with finality that she was really here, and this was really happening, and there was no way out. She didn't love this boy. She didn't *know* this boy and he didn't know her. She made a pact with herself to make him feel something for her. He would remember her—she would make sure of it.

"I miss my family," she said in lieu of an answer. Marishel blinked as her eyes filled.

He looked down at her, his face shrouded in shadow. Though he wore a mask of indifference, she heard the emotion in his voice. "I'm sorry. This is harder than I thought."

"Yeah," she whispered.

The sound of polite laughter carried out to them, and she heard Lonna's voice say loudly, "Has anyone seen the Ambassador?" They both took a step back from the closed curtains.

Marishel closed her eyes. "Ambassador—"

"Quin."

"Oh. Okay. Quin… Will you remember me when I'm gone? Will you remember me alive or dead?"

He straightened as though shocked. "What? I—I don't want to think about that."

"You have to. There is no other option. I don't know where I rank, but it isn't the top."

Soft light reflected along his cheekbones, and he looked pained. She continued, "You don't want to think about it, but it's *my* life. The *end* of my life. I don't want to die alone." She gripped his forearms as the realization hit once again; the abomination of the contest, and how terrified she truly was.

He backed up from her, pulling his arms as she gripped the fabric. "I—I don't think I can handle this. I mean, dinner and all is one thing, but I don't want to—I can't—I can't deal with this. I'm sorry," he said and strode inside, straightforward, stiff-backed, and outwardly unaffected.

He *can't deal with this?* Well, he was going to have to. If she had to follow him around every night.

Though she waited a full thirty-ish seconds, the moment Marishel slipped through the curtains to the dining room Lonna glared at her. Marishel waved, though the animosity drove her temperature to boiling. So, as she drank her steaming tea, she scowled at the perfect channel for her anger—the Ambassador—Quin. He seemed uncomfortable under her gaze and kept moving his back to her. But they both knew that he knew she was there. She drank cup after cup of the strong brew, to be one of the last ones to leave. When there were about five girls left, and four of them surrounded him like clucking hens, with Marishel watching his back from her seat, the Ambassador said his goodnights and disappeared. *Coward.*

70

No wonder his father doesn't trust him to rule. He can't handle conflict and runs when things get tough. I don't respect him, either.

She went back to her bunk with the last group of girls. A few of them were propped up in their beds, reading, or chatting in whispers to each other. Rena was snoring like a jet engine and Shalise had succumbed to her exhaustion as well. She wanted to talk to someone about her revelation of the Ambassador's character. The girls would want to hear about it tomorrow—she couldn't blame them for sleeping. She'd be tired too if she hadn't just had about six cups of tea. What was she thinking?

Late in the night, Marishel dozed lightly, when she heard a scratching sound. *There it was again.* She couldn't figure out what it was, but once she was awake, she had to use the bathroom—the other downside to drinking so much tea.

The lights remained on in the bathroom at all hours, though they dimmed substantially at night. As she was going into the room of stalls, Marishel realized that what sounded like scratching out there, was someone sniffling in the bathroom. But she didn't see anyone. She opened the nearest stall and it stopped.

"Who's there?" she ventured, not sure if she'd get an answer. After a moment of silence, she added, "It's Marishel."

A tiny voice squeaked, "Abrielle."

"Are you okay?" she whispered to the wall.

A broken sob escaped the poor girl, and she cried in syllables. "N—no. I'll never be okay again."

"Shhh. You're gonna wake everybody up crying so loud. I understand how you feel, but you've got to pull yourself together. We can do this. If we work together, maybe we can … help each other."

"Really?" the tiny voice asked. "How?"

"I don't have a clue. Maybe we can fight together? I thought if I tried to force the Ambassador to deal with it, he might—well, I'm not sure that's a sound plan. Do you have any ideas?"

The girl started cry-talking again, hiccupping on her words. "I just m-miss my fiancé so much."

"Your fiancé?"

"They said technically, I'm still single. But we've been engaged for six months. What'm I gonna do? I don't wanna fight. I want my Tanner."

It occurred to Marishel that these girls, like her, all had lives, jobs, families, and future plans. It was stupid. The whole thing was stupid. A spark of rebellion glowed like a long-dead fire in her belly. Hot coals of anger radiated her need for justice. But what could she do? She couldn't go up to the First and say, *Hey lady, your contest is dumb. Can I go home now?*

"Maybe we should do something." Marishel thought out loud. "All of us. I don't know how we can help each other, but you deserve your life. Now, if we can help it."

"What can w'do?" *Sniffle.*

"I don't know yet. I might have an idea. No, no that won't work… Don't worry, I'll help you think of something." Maybe if she found a way for Abrielle to be free, she could find a way for herself. "I'll help you."

"Promise?"

"I promise. We'll think of something…"

They emerged from the stalls and Abrielle clung to her. "I can't wait t'tell Tanner we hava future again. What're you thinking for now? What's your best idea?"

72

A new idea struck her. Rather than fighting… "Well," Marishel said, "maybe they shouldn't have this contest at all."

Abrielle gasped. "But—"

"I know, I know. That's the way it's done. But if it's wrong, what kind of excuse is, *we've always done it this way?*" She shook her head. "It'll come to me; I know it will. We just have to figure it out."

"It doesn't matter what it is, I'll do anything t'be with *my* own husband. I don't care t'marry the Ambassador."

Marishel thought about it as she dropped her hands into the machine on the wall. They didn't have these at home. Warm water sprayed her hands, then the tickle of soapy silicone bristles massaged the fronts and backs of her hands; another spray of water and the air jets blew at her wrists. She pulled her hands out slowly to dry them.

Marishel's heart broke for the lost lovers, and she knew that even if she couldn't do a thing to save herself, she wanted Abrielle to be able to have the choice to marry her fiancé, not *dying versus marrying someone else.* It wasn't right. They never should have drawn her name. She heard herself speaking as if she were miles away. "We'll get you out of here. We can do it. Now go to bed. We've got to think of a plan."

CHAPTER FIVE

THE LOST LOVERS

AT THEIR TABLE THE NEXT MORNING, Marishel's eyes were red-rimmed and puffy.

"Ooh, you don't look too good." Rena plopped into the seat next to her and Shalise sat on her other side.

"Did you stay up too late?" Shalise asked softly, ducking behind her curtain of hair.

"You could say that." Then, Marishel whispered to them about her plan to guilt-trip the Ambassador into remembering her, and the episode in the restroom. "She wants to get out of here and meet with her fiancé."

"That's so unfair. Poor Abrielle." Shalise patted her arm. "How are you going to help her?"

"I wish I knew." She thought for a moment and whispered, "The whole thing is wrong. Why doesn't anyone see that? They're always saying our generation asks too many questions, but what if they're the right questions?

Why do we even do this to people? At least Abrielle has someone. Do you guys have boys at home, too?"

Shalise shook her head. "My brothers scare off anyone who tries."

They looked at Rena who shifted in her seat. She said just for them, "I like girls. One in particular." She gazed into space, grinning at the thought of someone else. "I don't even WANT to win. But I definitely don't want to die."

"Oh, Rena." Marishel laid a hand on hers. "This shouldn't be happening to you. I'm sorry."

"It's okay. Hey! What if Quin said he was gay? Then we could go home, right?" Rena said.

Shalise looked hopeful, but Marishel couldn't let fantasy override her senses if she was going to figure things out. "If it wasn't us, it would be sixty boys lost in the same competition. You know that. It wouldn't be any fairer than it is now. It *needs* to change."

"Yeah. I guess it's just too bad the Ambassador isn't a lesbian. I might try a little harder." Rena's impish smirk delighted Marishel. Rena never seemed to lose her sense of humor and Marishel knew she'd made friends with the right girls.

They chuckled and Sayra scowled at them, then barked, "Eat before class starts."

They went back to their hushed conversation. "So, what do you guys think about the Ambassador?" Shalise asked timidly.

"He's a puppet," Rena said, wiping crumbs from her mouth.

Marishel still didn't know him, but that didn't mean she didn't have an opinion. "I think he's a pompous ass. He might be inconvenienced by the contest, but he doesn't even care that it's our lives at stake—just what it means to *him*."

"Oh." Shalise looked down. Softly, she said, "I think he's nice. And sweet. I saw him pick a flower from the greenhouse and give it to the head gardener. He tucked it into her graying hair, right behind her ear. She smiled like it was a game they played." She twisted up her hands and tucked them under her chin. "I like boys who treat old people well."

"We're not on a dating show." Rena spat more crumbs when she spoke. "How did you see him in the greenhouse anyway?"

"Yes, we are." Marishel handed her a napkin. "Gross."

"Well, I, um," Shalise stuttered with a pretty pink blush. "I kind of snuck out on my chores and followed him."

"Shalise! You wild woman." Rena chuckled and they tapped each other's index fingers together and Shalise grinned.

The idea of a sweet and considerate Ambassador didn't line up with what Marishel had seen and so she brushed the image away.

The session began and Sarver spoke of the pomp expected at the ball before the match. It was apparent by his tone and joyful expression that he'd been waiting his whole life to produce the Blood Match this year. He'd be taking on a novice reporter in the future to train as the next generation's Blood Match producer, just as he'd been prepared by his mentor who'd already passed. His moment in the sun was ripe, juicy, and ready to pluck.

Marishel couldn't concentrate. The lost lovers—Abrielle and Tanner—needed to be reconnected. She wished she could stop the whole contest, but at the least, she could figure out a way to get Abrielle home.

"Haumea to Marishel…"

"Huh?"

Rena guffawed and Shalise tittered with her. They sat in the dining room, eating lunch before their chores. (Marishel's group had graduated to the girls' bathroom. At least many hands meant lighter work.) Lost in thought, she had no idea what they'd been talking about.

Rena wiped her eye. "I said—ah, nevermind. Where is your brain?"

"I've got to find a way to sneak Abrielle out to her fiancé."

"Why do *you* have to do it?" Shalise's brow was wrinkled in concern for her friend. "It's dangerous."

"Who else? Do you see anyone volunteering? I promised her I'd help, and the only thing I can think of is sneaking her out. But how?" She squinted her eyes in concentration.

"What about taking a walk around the grounds and slipping her out the gate?" Shalise asked.

"There are cameras everywhere," Rena reminded her. "And we only know of one way in or out."

"Oh. Right."

"It has to be at night." Marishel thought about their bedtime routine. "It would give her the most time to get away." But at what point could she sneak Abrielle out? After dinner, they went back to their room and had downtime in the low lighting. Since they stripped their sheets in the morning, they made their beds daily and after dinner they brushed their teeth, took showers, grabbed a book, threw their dirty sheets in the basket…

The laundry basket gave her the idea. She'd seen the cameraman pushing and pulling what looked to be a very heavy box of equipment on wheels. If she could sneak Abrielle in there before any of the girls got back from dinner... She was fairly sure she knew where he parked it while they ate. Abrielle could be rolled out to the storage building, and if Marishel could block the camera, Abrielle could sneak out the front exit if she stuck to the shadows. Marishel would have to bundle up blankets in Abrielle's bed. Hopefully, by the time she was discovered missing, Abrielle would be long gone. If they got married quickly, would the First put a married woman in the match? She didn't know.

She planned the whole event while scrubbing the tile in their bathroom. The ploy had possibility. She wanted to tell the girls about her plan, but she didn't want them to know anything or be lumped in as accomplices. She didn't expect to get caught, either. It would be up to Abrielle to get through the gate. If she made it, it wouldn't be Marishel's fault. She smiled in confidence.

After training, on their way to get ready for dinner, Marishel grabbed Abrielle's arm and pulled her to the side. She whispered her idea and Abrielle nodded with tears in her eyes.

"Thank you. Thank you so much. We have to do it as soon as possible. Tonight."

"Tonight? But I haven't made a concrete plan—"

Abrielle jumped in, "It can't wait. It must be tonight. Oh, thank you, Marishel." She gripped Marishel's hands in her own.

"Um, okay. Don't mention it. Are you sure we need to do it so soon?"

"Absolutely. It can't go wrong. I'll be home *tonight.*" Abrielle squeezed, and Marishel—though jealous—hoped she was making the right decision.

Once it was final, the plan seemed foolhardy. As she ate dinner, Marishel wondered what she was doing. *I'm fighting back,* she thought. But she knew she was being just as cowardly as Quinlan. If she was *really* fighting back, it would have been *herself* that she was sneaking out. *Coward.*

Maybe if it worked with Abrielle, she could try it herself—but there was nowhere she could hide. And she couldn't bear being on the run and hiding alone—not going home.

The fish, in a cream sauce, tasted like ash on her tongue. Marishel tried to calm her jumpy nerves, but her utensil shook in her hand.

"You seem preoccupied." Canon leaned over and bumped her shoulder with his. "What're you thinking about?"

"Huh? Oh, yeah. Just thinking."

He threw his head back and laughed. People turned their heads and Marishel felt exposed.

"Hush." She looked down.

"You're out of the Oort cloud somewhere."

"Sorry. I suppose I am."

"Anything I can do?" He raised his eyebrows.

"I wish there was—but no." The candlelight on their table threw shadows here and there as it flickered. She was having second thoughts. Maybe Abrielle could do it herself?

No. She needed Marishel's help. *Okay. Get it together. She needs my help. I'll figure out another way for myself.* The idea hadn't fully occurred to her as a reality—escaping herself—not really. But if she did, she'd need to take Rena and Shalise with her, of course... Then the faces of the other girls appeared in the candlelight before her eyes. The shy ones, sweet ones, feisty ones—they'd all be killed. They flashed through her mind, eyes open, mouths dripping blood. She couldn't leave *any* of them behind.

That would never work. *What if we forced our way out as a group?* They'd probably end up in a cell somewhere and then eventually put in the arena anyway. *But there'd be nothing they could do if we all refused to fight...* Although everyone had to agree. If even one person disagreed or told on the plan, it could be all over. The dissenters would be sent into the arena without weapons. They'd been warned, this was the consequence for any "funny business" regarding the match.

Canon bumped her shoulder. "If I was him, I'd pick *you.*"

She smiled at him and whispered, "That's sweet. Though he doesn't *get* to pick, does he? It's pretty much up to us—but you're right, he should have a choice. We all should."

It was the first time she considered how the match might affect the Ambassador. No wonder he was so moody. He didn't get to choose his fate, either. Sure, he'd get to live either way, but he could be endlessly unhappy. Maybe if she could convince the girls to refuse to fight, he *could* choose his mate. Would the idea appeal to him? Would it matter? Perhaps if she got him on her side, he could petition his mother?

The mantle clock chimed seven o'clock—time for action. She would have liked to plan for a day or two, but Abrielle was desperate to flee.

"Excuse me, please. I need to speak to someone." She wadded her black linen napkin in her fist and rose, stuffing it in her pocket.

"Sure. You sure you're okay?" Canon's brow wrinkled.

"Me? Oh, I'm fine. Really. I'm just going to the restroom."

"I thought you were talking to someone?" He frowned.

"Um, yeah. In the restroom." She smiled.

Stupid, stupid, stupid.

"Oh. Okay. See you later." He smiled, but his eyes remained squinted, and it looked more like a grimace.

Abrielle was waiting in the hall when Marishel slid through the doors, barely open. "Everythin' good?" she asked.

"I just tipped off Canon." At Abrielle's look of shock, she added, "He doesn't have a clue. I meant he's aware I acted oddly. He might even be suspicious, but I doubt he'd say anything. Come on, they'll be back soon."

"I can't wait t'see Tanner." Abrielle's smile was broad and eased Marishel slightly.

She felt good about helping, but an underlying fear gripped her by the throat. They hadn't taken time to make sure this would even work. It was foolish at best. She slowed down. "I think we're moving too fast, Abrielle. *Think.* What's going to happen if you get caught?"

"I won't get caught." She passed Marishel and turned around. "What're they gonna do? Kill me?" She gave a short, dry chuckle. "That's already the plan. I hafta try."

"I'm not saying don't try. I just want some time to make sure it will work."

"I don't *have* time, Marishel. I need t'go. I'll do it with or without your help."

Abrielle would get caught without her, so Marishel felt obligated to stick with the plan. After all, it was her plan. She sighed. "Fine. I'm coming."

They took half the sheets out of the laundry basket on wheels and piled them under Abrielle's covers, in a rough outline of her shape. They left her bag tucked under her bed.

"You'll have to leave without your things. It would be too obvious."

"I don't care. It's an easy price t'pay."

The two girls ducked out the side door to the training yard and flattened themselves against the wall. "The camera for the entrance is on the roof of the guard station. I saw it when we first arrived. I'll need your help to get up there," Marishel whispered.

They followed the periphery of the fence closely in the darkest shadows. A pair of guards walked the wall, but Marishel and Abrielle ducked behind the twelve-foot shrubbery, crouched in child's pose.

Decorative architecture protruded from under the slanted roof of the guards' station. Bright and busy during the day, the empty interior—softly lit by a lamp sitting on a desk next to what Marishel assumed was the check-in roster—now lay in shadow. Marishel ducked back behind the building and waved over to Abrielle, who cupped her hands and hoisted Marishel as high as she could. Marishel clung to the scrolled plaster and swung her leg up to catch the roof's edge with her toe. She tried to suppress a groan as she pulled her foot up, then hooked her knee, swung up her other leg, and rolled over the edge, reaching for a place to grip the tile.

She crawled up the roof to its peak and straddled it, then slid herself along the ridge until she was right behind the camera. Marishel gripped the tiles with her thighs and leaned as far as she dared, toward the corner of the building. She flapped her napkin out, holding it by one corner, and it landed on the camera, but slid off to the side. She didn't want to alert anyone, so she leaned farther and thrust the material forward. The black napkin corner landed, barely covering the lens. She leaned a bit further, pushing the fabric over the cylindrical projection, but she lost her balance and threw her weight the other way to sit up, but overcorrected, leaning treacherously to the other side, and she began to slide down the tiles. Quickly she grabbed the peak ridge by her elbows and when her feet flew under her, she dug her toes into the tiles, looking for purchase. The force of her kick broke a tile in half, and it clattered to the ground beside the station.

"Marishel?" Abrielle's small whisper sounded as loud as alarm bells to Marishel.

"Shhh. I'm coming," she hissed back, sliding down the grade until she hung by her palms. "Get under me, Abrielle."

"Go ahead. I've got ya."

Marishel let go and both girls tumbled to the ground with a hard thump, then they skittered back into the shadows. Dinner had to be over, and the girls would be returning soon. They needed to hurry.

Marishel led Abrielle through the lawn, to the patio where Quin had taken her, and they found the cameraman's equipment box inside the dark and empty ballroom. Without waiting a moment, Marishel unlatched the seam and began to scoop out armloads of cords and cables, camera stands, and playback screens. She nodded to the box and whispered, "Grab as much as you can, and follow me."

They waddled through the ballroom to the hall where Marishel knew the security team was. They'd cleaned this hallway, polishing the floors. She waited in the darkness to make sure no one was coming their way. Two doors down, Marishel opened the door to the broom closet, and they deposited their stash as quickly and quietly as possible. A bucket clanged and Marishel froze. No one ran from the security room, so she carefully backed out into the hall.

Marishel felt the ball of acid in her stomach rise in her throat as Abrielle shut the closet door. *What am I doing? This is beyond foolish.* But Abrielle grabbed her hand and pulled her back to the ballroom. The box stood dark and open as they'd left it, and Abrielle climbed inside, hugging her knees.

"I hope I'll be able t'breathe."

"You'll be fine. Just remember. Wait until the caretaker pushes you into the storage shed for the night. I won't turn the lock or pull the latch. Let yourself out and sneak to the gate as fast as you can. There's no telling when they'll realize the camera is only black."

"Thank you, Marishel."

"Sure," she muttered as she closed the box and flipped the latch halfway. She patted the top of the box and whispered, "Good luck."

As decided, Marishel ran back to the dorm, grabbed one of Abrielle's book tablets, and got ready for sleep with the early-to-bed group. When the rest of the girls returned, no one was surprised to see them—just a girl reading and another one fast asleep. She read the same paragraph over and over, but her nerves wouldn't allow her brain to comprehend the meaning of the passage. Her hands shook the screen. *I hope this works.*

Sayra asked about Abrielle, and they said she'd gone to bed before they came back.

"Hmmm. Maybe I should see if she's sick." She took a few steps toward Abrielle's bed.

"She's fine," Marishel said a little too loudly, scaring herself. Sayra jerked her head in Marishel's direction. *So much for not implicating myself.* "I mean, she told me she was just really tired and was getting a few extra hours of sleep."

"You spoke to her?" Sayra asked. "She's well?"

"Yes," answered Marishel.

"Oh." Sayra nodded and turned the lights off, then walked over to the basket, glancing at Abrielle's bed. Marishel prayed she didn't notice anything wrong. Sayra gave the laundry basket a heave, rolling it down the aisle between their beds, and disappeared into the hall. Marishel let herself breathe.

Despite her earlier anxiety, she fell into a deep and dreamless sleep. All was black and quiet. She relaxed.

"You!" Rough hands threw back Marishel's covers. The lights flew on in the room scaring the girls, who sat up to see what was happening. Sayra gripped her shoulders, yanking her out of the bed. "You are going to discover what it means to anger the First."

85

CHAPTER SIX

TURPEN'S SECRET

SAYRA HAD A HANDFUL OF THE fabric at the back of Marishel's neck and propelled her on bare feet out of the room and down the hall. The girls, curious and awake in the middle of the night, followed the pair and their entourage of guards out of the building to the training yard.

Spotlights flooded the training yard with a harsh white brilliance. Marishel tripped on the dusty rock, but Sayra pushed her forward to one of the posts. A guard put a pair of bracelets on her, linked by a short chain, and slid the links over a hook high on the post. She faced it on her tiptoes, her gaze darting wildly around her in search of what would come next.

Confusion reigned and the girls whispered. *What is happening?* Every girl gasped when two guards dragged Abrielle into the yard, her hair stringy and hanging in her face. Each guard had a grip on either of Abrielle's biceps, and her legs dragged limply behind her through the dusty training field. When they came closer, it was apparent that something was very wrong with her. Blood soaked her top. It was impossible to see what injury had befallen her with her shirt's level of saturation. When they tossed Abrielle's lifeless body near her feet, her eyes open and empty, Marishel wanted to scream out of fear. Marishel willed Abrielle's body to get up, but she did not move, half of her face pressed into the dirt and her arms flung out to the sides of her head as if shouting her displeasure at the loss of her life.

"What happened?" Marishel's whispered, her voice shaking. Her whole body trembled. *What was coming?* The fear was crippling; her legs would've given out if she could put any weight on them. She pressed her toes into the powdery dirt to relieve her bloodless hands that burned with a twinge of pins and needles.

"She was shot after running through the gate," Sayra said, walking up behind her. She leaned in close to Marishel's ear, but her volume remained a shout. "Did you think we wouldn't put it together? People know when their things are tampered with. Think we're stupid?" Marishel wasn't sure it was wise to answer her.

From another building, the First stepped daintily outside, surrounded by guards. A satin robe covered her nightclothes, with little slippers on her feet. Her brow was squeezed and her normally smiling face was fixed in a frightening scowl. Thank the stars no one had woken the reporter … yet. This would devastate her parents.

Sayra told the girls with theatrical voice the woe-some tale of Abrielle—and Marishel, whose arms were burning, and legs were shaking. "Their plan was stupid at best. It was stupid to tamper with the Leader's equipment and even stupider for Abrielle to call your name," she sneered in

Marishel's direction. "It wasn't brave or smart, but a foolish failure. You were all told not to leave the premises without permission. There is no way out of your situation—there is no escape from the Match. As punishment, the First will apply the cane."

Marishel could only see a few of the girls, but when all the blood drained from Rena's face and she looked ghostly white, that was all Marishel needed to know about the severity of her punishment.

"For the accomplice," the First said with a motherly tone, "four strokes."

The girls gasped.

"And for the runner? I think she's earned her punishment already. No need to injure the dead."

Their audience erupted in murmurs. *What are* they *so upset about?* She'd heard about caning but didn't know about it personally. She didn't know whether she should clench her muscles tight to steel herself against the strike, or if that would make things worse.

The cane made barely a sound as it sliced through the air. She was unprepared when hot pain zipped up her back like a whole strip of skin and muscle was ripped off her body and she cried out. Pain radiated into her shoulder blades, and she thought of her mom's face. She wanted the comfort that only her mom could give. She cried automatically at the assault. The next stroke hit her across the middle of her back like it was cutting her in half. She pictured the fields at the farm. Long, seed-bearing strands of grass swayed in the wind, bowing, and catching the blowing tufts of fluff. She gazed at the boy next to her with silver-gray hair and longed for the comfort of the hot lights on her skin. Then it was too much, and her organs melted inside her skin. The third stroke felt as if they'd set her nightdress aflame. Marishel's strength gave out and she hung limply by her wrists, her hands long gone numb, and let her toes drag. Somewhere around the fourth stroke, her head felt fuzzy and little pinpricks of light danced before her eyes before it all went blissfully black.

Marishel woke in an unfamiliar room. Curtains were drawn around her bed, and in a chair next to her, the Ambassador slept. His long legs stretched out before him, and his hands were clasped over his stomach with his elbows resting on the wooden arms. His hair looked impossibly soft, laying on the back of the chair. She stared at him in the light of day. His cheekbones were high, and his prominent brow gave him a look of authority. A muscle jumped at the corner of his strong jaw, then relaxed as he breathed deeply. *My stars, he s—beautiful,* she thought reluctantly. She'd thought it a trick of the low lighting mixed with the magic of the evening hour that made him appear so handsome before.

Long-lashed green eyes opened, and they stared at each other without words or expression. She was feeling spiteful, so she tried to think of something nice to say to him.

"That was really stupid," he said as he scooted back, but kept his hands clasped, and his elbows propped on the arms of the chair.

"I can tell you're not mad at me anymore." She huffed out a dry laugh.

"What's your deal? You want me to feel bad for you? I do. Happy?" His voice rose and she didn't know who could hear them.

"Where am I?"

He sighed. "The infirmary." He pointed to the curtain behind him. "Abrielle's in the morgue."

"You know she had a fiancé."

"What was I supposed to do about it?" he nearly spat.

"I don't know. You're the *Ambassador*. Couldn't you do something?" she asked with matching fury.

"No." He glared at her.

"Why not?"

"I already told you. I only have power for the insignificant tasks I'm given," he said quietly.

"Then use what political power you do have *wisely*. You can show them—"

"Don't you think I try?" He ran a hand through his dark hair, and she watched it fan through his fingers.

"You want an honest answer?" She held her hands up.

"I don't think so. I did ask for more meaningful tasks, but I can only do what I'm told—it's just impossible to please them."

"Who?"

He lowered his voice. "The powers that be." He raised his eyebrows.

"Maybe you just need a little help." She smiled. "I can help with politics. I study lots of humans."

"No. You can't. What would you know anyway?"

"You'd be surprised." Grammy always said that to her when she didn't want to answer a question outright. "I might have an idea you've never thought of."

He chuckled to himself. "You probably would."

"It's okay, we can talk about politics later." She waved the subject away. "So … not like I don't enjoy the company, but why are you here?"

"Oh." He sat up straighter and pulled on the front of his shirt, rolling his neck. "I'm supposed to, ah, spend time with 'the girls.' My mother told me you'd be here…"

"And you figured I'd be asleep, so it was a good time for a nap?" She smirked at him.

His throaty laugh was deep, and she felt it in her belly. He put up his hands. "Okay, okay. You've caught me."

"Have you spoken to Abrielle's family?"

"No." He cringed. "Really. Why did you do that? You could get sent—"

"—Into the arena without a weapon. I know."

"Then why risk it?"

"The way I see it, I'm probably going to lose in the fight. There's nothing worse they could do to me. Weapon or not, it's only a matter of time. But if I could help Abrielle reunite with her lost love—her fiancé—and go back to the life stolen from her, I had to try. And to be honest, I was interested to see if it worked."

"Thinking of leaving?"

"No." She sighed deeply. "I have nowhere to go. Nowhere to hide…" She lay on her side in silence for a moment, looking at the blue wool blanket over her legs. She whispered almost inaudibly, "But I'll think of something. I have to."

"Are you always this determined?"

"I guess so. I'm used to having a schedule for myself and working it—my life had a plan. But this whole 'contest' has me out of my element. What do you do with the news that you're weeks from expiring? I've always been able to make things work with my strategy. My world consisted of one list after another—check it off and move on—but I've realized the world isn't as ordered as I thought it should be."

"I don't think it ever is."

"It doesn't matter. If there's a solution, I will find it."

He tried unsuccessfully to hide his grin. "So, since you're stuck here, and since you promised to be my friend the other night, I was wondering what we might have in common."

"First of all, I promised you no such thing. I said I was friend-ly. Secondly, we have *nothing* in common." Marishel looked up at the ceiling tiles and tried to imagine a boy of privilege in her world. *Could he even handle the dark and constant cold?*

Quin frowned. "You know, I *am* trying here."

She sighed. "I know. I just don't think—"

"Do you have a family? A brother?" he pushed.

Marishel resisted giving him the easy route. "Yes, I have a family. But I have a sister."

"I always wanted a sister," he said. "I thought she might be fun, and less annoying than Canon. Anyway, good. You live in a home, I presume?"

"Of course." Marishel rolled her eyes. "And I eat food like you do, too. I mean, some things we *all* have in common here."

"Not everyone has a home, Marishel. You probably haven't seen it because *your* side's Outerlimits don't have a shelter for the homeless."

"No ... I've never seen one." Her interest was piqued. "You have one here?"

"Yes, a few. If someone on your side is found homeless, they travel over here to join our Outerlimits population. We have temporary housing and try to help them find what they need. Some of them are first in line for the new housing that will result from the mining."

"You said, 'we.' Does that include you? What do you do for them? Smile and look pretty?"

92

He chuckled. "Well, you're the one who said I was pretty."

A hot blush traced up her neck. "You know what I meant."

"Yes. A not-so-cleverly disguised insult from the fairest maiden of the Needles—in the Outerlimits."

"Well, you don't have to— Wait, who told you I was from the Outerlimits?" Her eyes narrowed.

"I understand why you were testing me at dinner. And I don't want to argue with you, Marishel. Give a guy a chance. I just wanted to get to know you a little." He sighed. "I'm doing my best here. Just like I try to—well, never mind. But I do help at the shelter. I'm what they call a 'big brother' to families with kids and help the program."

She tried to imagine him, his back ramrod straight, playing board games with little kids, his fingers barely touching his surroundings, his face a mask of coldness. It didn't work. She couldn't see it being a good time—or helping anyone. "Well, I don't want to keep you…"

"You're that desperate to get rid of me?" He looked ready to challenge her. "You'd rather be in here alone than spend time with me?"

Maybe it was a novel idea for him. She didn't really want to hurt him; she just didn't see how relating to him would be a good thing. She wasn't going to win—unless she figured out another way for herself and the other girls. Maybe she could get his take on that? If he didn't agree with the Match, it opened up the opportunity to use him as an ally.

"So, were you ever excited about the Match? I mean, you'll get your mate out of the deal."

"You think I want this? Trust me, Marishel, this was not my idea. They've never even let me talk to a girl near

93

my age, knowing this would be my fate. Kids, I can play with all day, but girls...? Can't you give me a break? I'm not the bad guy here."

She appreciated his honesty, but it didn't help her situation at all. "Who is? Who can I blame for the end of my life, the end of my choices?"

"I don't know. The people? Marishel,"—he sighed—"I could use an actual friend. Especially now. I'm going from no responsibility to the second man in charge. I can't help but fail. They want to shut me out for as long as possible and then heap everything on my plate at once. I have no idea how to do this; how to talk to girls, how to be a leader, how to be a friend. So much will be expected when... I'm supposed to train for leadership after my ... wedding." He cringed. "But I can't do anything with my hands tied. I need to be successful with my new campaigns to prove I can make a difference."

"Why me? Why would you choose to be friends with me? Surely, you've noticed—there are fifty-nine other girls here, all vying for your attention."

"That's just it. They don't care about me, they— I don't know. There's something about you... You're warm and friendly—when you want to be—and you have a sense of humor because I see you make Canon laugh every night, your friends admire you with their loyalty, and you tell it as you see it..." He glanced at her sideways. "Mostly, it's that you don't care about impressing me, or winning me, or acquiring my wealth and status. I don't feel like I need to guard myself around you, though I'm not totally sure you aren't just out to get me ... or use me."

She felt her face grow hot with shame. "Quin—"

"I'm so tired of all the pomp and expectations. When I'm around you, I feel like I can do things—make changes—without all the pressure. No one else talks to me like a real person. There are many reasons... And I'm tired of being *AnonymousPlayer1*."

His plea melted something in her heart—an iceberg that had been in front of her—that let her see clearly. This wasn't all his fault. He could be a pawn just as she was—or he could be playing a game with her. She had to give it a shot. His friendship might be necessary. She let down her shoulders and nodded. "I guess I shouldn't ignore the gift of another friend in my last days. But—whether you like it or not—do you think the *concept* of the Match is a promising idea, though? Is it a tradition that needs to carry on? Be honest."

He squinted. "I've never allowed myself to give it any thought. It was a foreign date looming way out in my future, unreachable, ever since the day I learned what girls were and was told this was my destiny. No way out. Repeated over and over by all those around me, *this is the way it's done.* I suppose if I could have it my own way, I'd meet a person the way the rest of the world does it..."

She nodded.

"What about you? Do you have a boyfriend back home?"

"Oh. No, I don't. I was planning to finish school and take over the clothier business when Harlene retired. She's been teaching me since I was little. I even got my own apprentice this year." She smiled. "I thought I had time. I thought I had every opportunity to cement my career and then meet the guy of my dreams. But apparently, here we are." She chuckled wryly, and he laughed with her.

"Oh yes, I'm dreamy." He grinned and stuck out his hand. "So ... friends?"

She looked at his long fingers stretched toward her. Strong hands. Hands that held her life over a fire. But was it really his fault? Could he be just another marker on the game board as she was? Could they help each other in some way? Her mind warred with itself. She kept doubting him but couldn't give up hope that friendship with the Ambassador might come in handy with her goal of canceling the Match. She nodded and took his hand.

"Friends. Or at least, I'll try. I'm just a little bitter about the theft of my future…"

"But that's not my—"

"But I know it's not all your fault." At his look, she said, "Or your fault at all."

"Thank you."

Marishel yawned and her eyelids felt heavy. A warm blanket of possibility wrapped around her. She had a new friend. And possibly an ally. Maybe they could fight the Match together? She still needed a plan… Maybe she'd have time to think about how to use this new relationship to succeed. She wasn't entirely adept with the other sex, either.

"Well, I guess I'll be on my way. I'll talk to you later." He rose and she sat up. Fiery pain screamed up her back and she sucked air through her teeth. He put a hand on her shoulder and helped raise her mattress. "Sorry."

"It's okay." She looked up at him, bent toward her. His smooth tawny skin, like polished stone, resembled a tiger's eye.

He turned and she felt the sizzle of his stare. To her surprise, he lingered six inches from her face. She cleared her throat.

"Your eyes are grey," he said, and the heat of his breath warmed her skin.

"I know." She gazed at him wide-eyed.

"But I mean, they're silver."

"Yeah." She chuckled, feeling a pull in her back. "Ouch."

"You okay?" His exhale brushed her cheek.

She smiled. "Yeah. I guess you'd better go."

He stood and put a finger on her forehead. "Behave." His tone was comically deep, and she grinned.

"Yes, sir."

Quin slid his finger down to the tip of her nose and tapped it once. "See you later."

"Yeah. Later."

That week, the Ambassador spent time with each of the girls, the cameraman following like the train of a gown. Most of the day Quin was with one or another. He paid attention to those who dined with him at night, taking some for picnics, but during the day, he'd taken girls for private trips around the grounds, library lunches, and afternoon walks. Many returned with some token to remember him by.

"He drew me this picture and folded it into a bookmark!" Rorie said, holding the white, color-flecked paper rectangle to her chest. Her white-blond hair and pale complexion bespoke her Swedish background. She showed the paper around to the group. "It's my profile." It wasn't bad. Marishel wondered what other talents he had.

One girl told everyone that *he loves cooked carrots, but hates them raw, as well as wilted spinach.* Another informed them that *he loves hiking and sports but hates listening to "pretty rock."*

"He loves dancing, and he didn't step on my toes once! Then he read to me from his favorite book—some political thriller." Unity nearly swooned in the classroom one morning. They were each enjoying their time with him. She tried to feel no emotion about it, but when he hadn't spent any time with her, she felt like she'd been looked over. They were supposed to be friends. She contemplated getting angry about it. *Nevermind,* she told herself, *I've got bigger problems to solve.*

"I want to talk to all the girls in the lowest pool. I think we can make alliances with them—" Marishel was in the shower room with Rena and Shalise. Their showerheads were to her left, separated by frosted Lucite panels enclosing them each from about shoulder to knee. She kept the water from pelting her still-sore back.

"What are you planning to do with all these *alliances?*" Shalise's brow wrinkled.

"Well, I'm not exactly sure, but if we can band together, maybe we can fight together somehow."

Shalise gasped. "We can't—"

"Oh yes we can," Rena interjected. "It's that or kill the First."

Shalise looked like she was going to be sick. All the color drained from her face.

"I'm kidding, girl. Don't lose your marbles over it." Rena reached over the partition to pat her arm.

"I just think, if we're all together in agreement—when I *do* come up with a plan, it will be that much easier to accomplish. We can work together to stop the contest."

Marishel quieted her voice. "The thing is, we all have to agree. If anyone sabotages us—"

"But they might just kill us all—call us a bad batch and draw new names." Shalise wrung her hands.

"That can't happen. Listen, I know it feels hopeless— it feels like there's no way out. I hate not having the answer. I've always seemed to know how to fix the problem. But this time, I— I don't know what to do. I hate that I— We need help. Who could help us?" Marishel pursed her mouth as she thought.

"The Ambassador?" Shalise's hopeful face made Marishel feel responsible for her.

"I don't think he has much more of a choice in the matter than we do," she said, creasing her brow.

"Everyone should have a choice," Rena said.

"I agree," Marishel said. "I'll try to talk to some more people. Keep your ears open and hint about joining us. If we sow the idea, maybe they'll consider it. But keep it to the lowest tier for now."

When they came out of the bathroom and went to class, they passed their attendant, Sobia, talking to a man in the hallway. He could have been a Greek god of old, with his muscled physique and long blond hair. He could definitely pose for one of those old-timey romance novels of swash-buckling pirates who prey on young ladies with bodices half-open. Upon second look, he resembled Sobia a great deal.

"Hi Sobia," Marishel said, slowing.

"Hello, girls. This is my brother, Turpen. He is here bringing lunch for his forgetful husband." She spoke lightly in the Slavic-Russian accent they shared.

"Oh? Anyone we know?" Shalise asked.

He chuckled with a wink. "I'm thinking so. You've met Sarver Bello before?"

Marishel's brain lit up. Finally, someone who could help. "Um, do you think I could talk to you? I mean, later? Maybe lunch?"

Turpen looked at his sister, who frowned at him and shook her head.

"I am not contest judge," he said with apparent sympathy. Then, looking at her hopeful face added, "Okay. I'm here for supper tonight. We are speaking then."

If I can get to Turpen, maybe I can get to Sarver. It was starting to feel like her own personal challenge. *Whatever I have to do to end this contest, I'm up for it. I'll win somehow.*

"Do you want to have dinner with me?" Quin stood next to Marishel in the hall as they opened the doors to the dining room. He looked down at her kaftan. The sleeves were sheer as well as the outer skirt, adorned with ribboned rosebuds, that vined up from the bottom, and irises climbed the bodice around her curves up to her neck. "You look nice," he said just loud enough for her to hear.

Kerse it. She wanted to—probably should—but she needed to talk to Turpen more and she didn't know for certain where the Ambassador stood on canceling the contest yet. "I can't tonight." She tried to soften the blow with a smile, but he frowned.

He looked around to see if any of the other girls heard them, obviously worried about appearances. Oh, she could almost hear it in his head. It was certainly written all over his face: *how dare you refuse me?* She could see she was about to start a war.

"Your answer is no?"

"Just tonight. Please."

"Don't let me jam up your schedule. By all means, I'm sure you have something much more important to do," he snapped.

"You're being childish."

"*Me?*"

"Yes, you. I will talk to you later," she said as the doors were propped open and the guests entered the dining room.

She found Turpen, sitting near Canon and next to Sarver, but when he saw her, he waved her over to him. She was going to have to do this delicately. This was her ticket. She was sure of it. If Turpen could convince Sarver to cancel the contest—*that he's waited his whole life for...* *Crap.* No, this had to work. She didn't have any other ideas, and it had to be somebody important to make a change this big.

"Thank you for talking to me," she said, sitting down.

They pressed their fingers to the oval buttons.

"Is no problem. I feel for you." He leaned in close and whispered, "I do not agree with this contest. But that is between us."

"You don't?" She was dumbfounded. This was going to be easier than she thought.

"*Nyet.* My family comes from money—money made from deaths of innocent girls. My *prababushka* won on unlikely bet in a landslide two generations ago. My father grew up in Gentry and us, too—Sobia and me ... and our sister, Tamberlyn. Her name was chosen—and all of our money could not save her." He glanced at the First and her sons. "These would be her children if she'd won."

"I'm so sorry." Sincerity oozed from Marishel. He had the same accent as his sister, but he was more well-spoken. She could listen to him all day.

"It still breaks my heart. I was not knowing if I could talk with you or not." He chuckled, then looked at her knowingly. "I'm sure you did not mean to be talking of *my* family."

The salads arrived in front of each guest and conversation lulled as they ate.

I've got him. She was sure of it. As sure as she was that Quin was glaring at her across the room, she knew Turpen was going to convince Sarver to stop it or somehow wreck the Match.

Giddy with her success, she toasted Turpen's drink, and they ate merrily. When dinner was over and they sipped coffee, people congregated, and he turned back to her. "So, what you are really wanting to talk about?"

"I'd like you to help me shut down the contest," she whispered, grinning conspiratorially. "Throw a wrench in the whole thing."

He gazed at her with a sad smile. "I wish I could."

She instantly deflated and felt an ache in her back. "But … you're married to Sarver. He's the producer. All you have to do is convince him not to do it. You don't agree; I know you don't. Why?" Her voice rose as she spoke, and she realized people were looking. She took a deep breath and asked softly, "Why can't you make him?"

"He is my spouse, not my child. I am not telling him what to do."

"But what about your sister?" She was feeling utterly out of control and had a difficult time keeping her voice down. "Doesn't he care about your sister?"

"I am not agreeing because is personal to me—but is also Sarver's life. Is very personal for him, too. He is being groomed for this job his whole life, and if lucky, is having one more generation in him—no way he will end this."

"But, but—"

He laid a gentle hand on her arm. "You are headed in right direction, though. Find out how to get the people on your side, and you will win. Even Sarver is not having the power to stop the Match. Power belongs to the First, and only one with power over her is the Leader…"

"And he listens to the people!" she whispered loudly.

"*Tochno*. Yes."

"So, I need to convince the people to hate the sport they love and forgo generations of tradition, possibly costing them money?" She cringed.

"But giving sixty girls back to community for your generation—sixty mothers to come."

"Don't you think they'll just consider it thinning the herd?"

"I do not know what people will think—you must find this. I am happy to help if I am able. Sobia can reach me. She came also to help girls, even if giving comfort in small ways."

"Thank you, Mr. Bello."

"Call me Turpen."

Marishel spent the next several days thinking as she scrubbed, and fought, and practiced. Training was going well in that she felt she had more strength and stamina, but her skill with weapons hadn't improved much. Defensively, she was getting better at shielding herself from attack, though. Even then, she was thinking.

She needed to find a way to tell not one, but all of the people in Haumea that this was wrong. The wounds on her back healed faster the more active she was in training, so she thought as she worked. Ideas ran through her mind, and she tossed out each one with growing despair.

The girls weren't doing much better. Marishel undressed for sleep one evening and slipped into her bed, only to find her feet surrounded by a moist, gritty substance that felt scratchy on her legs and oozed between her toes. As she hopped out quickly and briskly brushed herself off, laughter tittered sparsely around the room. She pulled the covers open to see an inch-thick layer of wet sand from the training yard spread between her sheets. Tucked under her pillow was a note that simply said:

CHEATER.

Apparently, her message was getting around. And not everyone was happy about it. How was wanting to live a matter of cheating? They should all be supporting her. They should be thankful that she was trying anything at all. It appeared that everyone else was resigned to her own fate because no one else was jumping up to think of a way out of this. It frustrated her so much, that she ignored the pointed stares and sneers, and poured herself into her activities and thoughts. It grated on her nerves that she hadn't figured it out yet.

The guilt weighed on Marishel. In her old ways, she'd always trusted herself and the agenda. Because of Grammy, she'd believed there wasn't anything she couldn't do. She had not only accepted the fact that she could schedule her own life, but she'd also presumed it would always be so.

Marishel was the only one in charge of her destiny. As long as she was smart, she was in control of the situation, and as long as she stuck to her moral beliefs and master plan, everything would work out fine. How naïve she'd been to think that she would always be in control. How stupid to depend on only herself. But right now, all she could do was hope and pray for guidance while wracking her brain for a solution.

Marishel was weeding the estate's garden when it occurred to her. She'd been ruminating as she plucked out the little green stems that didn't match the leafy plants when she picked out a minuscule yellow flower. Memories flashed before her of a time when she gathered the delicate yellow flowers at Aunt Naide's farm. Sitting in the tall grass, she wove the impossibly thin strands together for a fairy crown.

"What're you making?" The boy lying next to her laced his fingers behind his head and tilted his face toward the VitD lights, eyes closed.

She longed to brush back his silvery hair. "I'm going to be a fae princess."

"Fae?"

"Yeah, like fae-ries."

"Ooh. So, we're pretending today?" He grinned at her. They'd nearly grown up together. They spent the seasons out of class hunting for treasure, or simply sleeping days away in the fields.

"Yes. Today is a fantasy."

He pointed to her fingers. "You're really good at that. The stems are so small."

"I'm used to doing this with thread."

"Right. Seamstress-in-training. Right?"

"Yep. Practice makes perfect." She looped a stem and tied a knot. She frowned. *"Have you decided what you're going to do?"* The apprentice program had dragged the boy through several occupations already.

"I think so. I'm going to be a reporter. Draft stories. Work for the Paper."

A few publications circulated through Haumea. The one most widely read, Haumea Today—which everyone lovingly called "the Paper"—was the only one that had Leader-sanctioned news and was highly regarded as the truth of things.

"That's great, Trae." She surged with pride. Trae hadn't displayed much motivation to work—he didn't need a status change. He—unlike her father—never dreamed of the Gentry, he lived the Gentry life, absent of the mundane, everyday problems they faced. Yet, he always seemed troubled.

He snorted. *"Maybe I'll get to cover the Blood Match one day. The Ambassador will be of age in three or four years."*

Plucking the estate's weeds, her back muscles pulling, she wondered if Trae had, in fact, been tasked to work on the Match. She tried to think of all the things she could do if she had the ear of the people. If she told them to halt the match, they'd just laugh at her—and probably dig in their heels and bet against her. She had to stop it anonymously.

CHAPTER SEVEN

NOTES

AT DINNER THAT NIGHT SHE TOLD Shalise and Rena about her idea. If they could get the people on their side, they could win. They just needed a way to speak.

"He lives on this side—in the Summerlands," Marishel whispered, leaning as far away from Canon as possible. As true creatures of habit, they returned to their seats from the first few nights, and generally she bantered with Canon, but this wasn't something he should be involved in—no matter how sympathetic he may be.

Shalise wrung her napkin and looked a bit piqued.

"Won't they connect him to you?" Rena asked around a mouthful of something yellow.

Marishel cringed. "No. That's the thing. He's from here, I'm from there. When I spent vacations with my aunt, he stayed nearby with his grandparents—we aren't related or anything. They'd never suspect me." His face flashed before her eyes.

He stared at her until she turned to him.

"What?" she asked, plucking the tissue-thin petals from a flower and popping the stem between her teeth.

"Let's get married."

She spat out the stem with her laugh. He stared back with a blue opalescent gaze.

"You're serious?" Her brow wrinkled. "Trae—"

"Well, not now," he said. "I mean later. When we're old."

"What if I find a husband before then?" She smiled a dimple at him.

"Tell you what. If we both get to twenty and haven't married anyone yet, we'll do it." He looked so serious. It made her want to giggle in a way, but she liked him so much. They were best friends.

"Deal." She took his outstretched hand, shook it solemnly, and he broke out in a grin.

Oh well, Marishel sighed, *just an old fantasy between friends.* That had been so long ago, surely he'd forgotten about it.

The long week finally over, Sayra blew the whistle for bed Friday night. "Tomorrow, there will be no lesson or training. You may have the day for activities of your choice."

Many of the girls cheered wearily. Some were reading letters from home, some drawing or sewing. She looked over by the door and sure enough, Icen was chatting with another guard, preparing to end his shift. While Sayra's attention was diverted, Marishel slipped out of bed and dashed to the door in her nightdress. She passed a mousy brown-haired girl, who watched her with eyes wide.

"Icen?" she whispered to his left, bouncing on her toes with anxiety.

He was startled and turned to her; his brow drawn. "Miss Vance? How can I help you?"

"Actually… You're from around here, right?" She glanced over her shoulder and saw Sayra's conversation winding down. "I need an address. Do you think you can find it for me?"

He peered around her. "I don't think that's a good idea."

Desperation flooded her eyes with tears. She didn't know anyone else. Would this all fall apart now? She gazed up at him and prayed. *Make this one thing work and I will find a way to stop the killing.* "Please?"

He looked at her and sighed. "What's the name?"

"Marishel!" Sayra's voice carried. "What are you doing?"

"Trae," she said quickly to Icen. "Trae Skinner."

"Marishel Vance! I demand you return to your bunk this second."

Icen nodded at her imperceptibly and she had to hope that he wouldn't just turn her in as soon as the lights went out. She trudged back to her bed where Sayra waited, lightly tapping her foot. She didn't look at Abrielle's old bed. After Abrielle's death, they brought in a new girl, Veda. In true horrible fashion, as punishment, the First had chosen Tanner Winly's little sister to take his fiancé's place. With Veda as the only fifteen-year-old, Marishel would have bonded with or nurtured the quiet girl, but by the flaming glares she shot at Marishel, it was obvious she knew who had gotten her into this mess. There was nothing Marishel could do, this was a fight, and she had more important things to worry about.

In fact, the whole horror of Abrielle's debacle had only strengthened her resolve to get them all out of this, however she could. She hadn't found it an impossibility, rather, a poorly planned mission. Her father said she could do anything she put her mind to, and she had always taken that for granted without any trace of doubt. Now, she was putting her mind to it. She'd explain her ideas to Trae, but they still needed a concrete plan.

An open breakfast buffet was laid out in the dining room, and Marishel soon sat with a plate of eggs and toast. A girl with twin buns and chocolate brown eyes sat next to her.

"Marishel, right?"

"Yeah."

"We heard—I heard—well, some of the girls say that you have a plan to beat the Match," she whispered behind her hand.

It wasn't a question, it was a statement and Marishel didn't want to implicate herself any more than she already had, so she sat in silence, eating her breakfast. A hook-nosed girl watched them from across the room, her eyes squinted. Getting some of the girls to agree was turning out to be a monumental challenge.

The girl beside her, she'd heard her called Nahli Keegan, wasn't satisfied though. "I mean, after you did that to help Abrielle, we were thinking—"

She hissed, "Thinking what? That you'd like to get me caned as well? I can't sneak anyone else out." Marishel didn't mean to sound harsh, but she had to play this part—for everyone's sake.

The girl jumped back in her seat. "No! No, of course not. We wondered…" She motioned for her friend across the room to sit next to her and another girl with shiny black hair sat down and they leaned into Marishel like a ball players' huddle. "We were hoping we could join you?"

Ah. It was what she wanted. She'd been afraid no one would trust her, but the incident with Abrielle had caused several girls to ask if they could be a part of a rebellion for freedom. One girl found her reading later in the morning, one in the hall, and another in the bathroom…

She was coming back from lunch when she saw Icen. He nodded, then palmed her a piece of brown paper with an address written on it.

"Thank you," she said softly.

"It's in the capital neighborhoods. Be back by seven. Not a minute after, or you'll be noticed."

"What's at seven?"

"Dinner. It's late on the weekends. Then lights out."

"Okay. I'll be back." She smiled at him. "Thanks again."

She didn't have permission to leave, and she was sure no one would agree to turn her loose with her reason being "to find a boy and beat the Match." but this was a desperate attempt to succeed. She didn't want to raise anyone's suspicion, so she couldn't try sneaking out the estate's monitored entrances. She'd have to scout the perimeter behind the training building and look for another way out. But what if she couldn't find anything? She needed a backup plan.

Marishel got an idea and went to find the storage room where they kept the training box. She looked both ways at every junction of hallways, every corner of every building, until she slipped through the door to the dark storage room. Dust motes danced in light rays from tiny windows high up the wall, near a tall ceiling. The heat assaulted her nose. She opened the weapons kit and dug through the drawers until she found a handheld claw and a coil of rope. Marishel shoved the rope under her skirt. The tool, she stuck in her pocket and rushed out, making sure to leave the door closed.

On the far side of the estate, behind the training building, tall, leafy bushes stood in a row like soldiers inside the ten-foot-tall wall encompassing the compound. She stopped at the edge of the stone wall housing the dorm building. What about the guards? Between the twelve-foot-tall bushes, she saw a camera on the wall, the kind that looked like a ball, so no one could tell what direction it was watching.

Even though she saw no guards in sight, the camera would surely catch her in that direction. She backed up a few steps and searched the ground. Marishel chose four stones with enough heft to do damage, but not too heavy for her to throw. She crept back to the corner and threw the first one underhand, but it skittered across the ground almost immediately. She wound up and threw again, trying overhand. This one hit the wall near the camera. The next one glanced off the camera globe's side but ricocheted and flew off to the side. She was going to end up outing herself. *Kerse.*

The sound of static alerted her to a pair of guards coming and she ducked back, looking for somewhere behind her to hide. There was nothing in the training yard to shelter her. Pushing her muscles and holding the rope under her skirt, she took off for the obstacle course. Marishel pushed off the balls of her feet and pumped her arms. Sweat dripped from her temples in rivulets down her cheeks. Hot air whooshed from her lungs as she blew out and Marishel inhaled deeply as she ran. She reached the course and pulled herself behind it with clammy hands, placing her palm on her diaphragm as her breath gusted.

She saw the men round the corner, but luckily, they didn't appear to notice the flash of fabric as she ducked behind the structure. She backed up until her wounds pressed against the stone wall and grimaced at the agonizing throb. It wasn't against the rules to roam the campus, but she didn't want to have to answer any questions about what she was doing and where she was going, why she had bulges in her dress, or generally raise suspicions any higher than they were. She was a terrible liar, and they'd see right through her.

Marishel watched the pair of guards continue toward the labyrinth, then she tried a new tactic. At the edge of the training yard, where the grass resumed, the line of shrubbery began. She could trace the bushes around the side of the building and would be close enough to hit the camera while remaining hidden. She wouldn't have to cross the yard after all. *That camera may be guarding an opening nearby,* Marishel reasoned.

She crept along the wall toward the camera, staying as close as possible, until she came to the tall leafy plants and squeezed between the bushes until they covered her. She crept along the tunnel created between the wall and the bushes. Finally, she was confident of the distance. She wound up and threw the last rock. It soared over the camera and the wall and disappeared. She growled in frustration and checked the ground near her for another rock. The only one big enough filled her palm and outstretched fingers.

Nearly to the camera, she stepped into an overhand throw, aimed up carefully, and let the stone fly.

Crack! She didn't know if the camera was broken or not, but the rock knocked it back on its stand, with only a view of the dome above them. Now how was she going to get out? She didn't know the guards' schedule, so she wasted no time. *There must be other ways out back here; a drain, a hole, anything.* Marishel stayed close to the wall and looked for an opening, or some other way through. Hunched over, she made slower progress. Pokey little sticks grabbed at the sheer fabric of her kaftan and scratched her arms. She sucked in her breath as one broke the skin.

Finally, she came to a tall, hidden, metal gate—once black and now rusty around the edges from disuse. *How many gates were hidden around these walls behind the thick growth of hedges?* The gate was lined with vertical bars and sported a keypad lock. *Great.* No code. Game over. She pulled on it just to make sure it wasn't open, and it didn't move. She'd found an opening, but there was no lock to pick—though she wasn't a lockpick, but how hard could it be—no way to squeeze through, not an easy climb. *May as well go with plan B.*

She pulled the defensive claw from her pocket—it was normally worn on the hand. The rope she wound around between two sharp claws and tied a knot that she tightened with her teeth. Marishel tossed the claw over the top of the wall next to the gate and pulled until it caught on the wall's decorative edge. She stepped onto the wall and pulled on the rope, just to see if it would hold her. *This might work.* If she could stay behind this bush...

She climbed two-thirds of the way up the wall, pulling herself forward, and flexing her budding new biceps. It burned her muscles in a good way. She was proud of her strength; it felt natural to her. When her lower foot gave way, she slid, grasping at the stone with her fingertips, then she fell away from the wall and the ground rushed up to meet her. As she landed hard, the wind was knocked out of her, and she let go of the rope. The weight of the claw pulled it down the other side and the rope flew up the wall until it disappeared. She hit the ground with her fist, exasperated. She'd have to deal with that later.

She stood and hit the gate in frustration. *Hmmm.* If she could get a good grip on the vertical bars and use her toes, maybe she'd be able to climb it. Marishel pulled off her slipper-like shoes and shoved one in each pocket. Again, she began her ascent, holding the bars tightly and gripping them with her toes. It was a slow climb and she slid down more than once, but she finally started to gain some height. If she could get high enough, she could stand on the keypad and use it as a push-off point, though she didn't know how she would make it over the rounded top, nor how she'd make it back in. *Well, the claw is on the other side now. I'll use that.* Her limbs shook and her muscles were on fire and cramping as she inched higher, her palms blistering each time her weight pulled her down a few inches.

As soon as she could, Marishel pulled up her knee and propped it on the keypad, pulling herself up straight. But when she stepped on the slanted box, her foot slipped on the shiny surface and her muscles weren't strong enough to hold her. She slipped off the bars, knocking the pad—that emitted a series of beeps—and hit the latch with her knee on the way down. *Kerthunk.* She rocked on the ground, sucked in her breath, and held her kneecap with both hands, near to tears. When she could stand again, she leaned against the gate until the teeth-gritting pain faded. She pushed away from the gate in disgust, and it eased open a bit. She realized that it wasn't latched anymore. Maybe it had broken, or the lock hadn't been all the way secured.

She didn't know how she'd managed to do it, but she wasn't about to stand there guessing about it. Marishel fished her shoes out of her pockets and put them back on. When she leaned over to put on her shoe, her hip bumped the gate, and it rocked back. She tried to stop the motion, jerking the handle backward, but it didn't fly toward her, it just made the same inch-wide opening it had before. Hoping against hope, she braced her hand and foot on the frame and pulled at the corroded gate with all her strength. It opened slightly with an enormous protesting creak that made her freeze.

Icy tingles ran through her veins. Sure, she could roam, but if they found her leaving without permission, it would be seen as escaping. No one would believe she had any plans to return. It was tempting *not* to come back, but she knew there was no other option. What would they do to her if they caught her now? Would they shoot her as they did Abrielle? Her body shook involuntarily. If they were willing to let her die for this contest's prize, what might they do to keep her here? She didn't want to find out.

She waited while her heart beat in her throat, but when no one came running, she heaved it open just far enough to squeeze through. It was nearly rusted shut. She needed to make it look closed as it was before, but this would be a perfect way in and out of the compound from now on. The gravel under her feet gave her an idea. She picked up a pebble and shoved it in the housing gear so that the gate couldn't fully latch behind her. Marishel slipped through the opening and pulled the gate. It stuck open and she pulled harder than she meant to. Her heart sank when it lurched forward and shut with a heavy *clunk*, but she pushed on it anyway. It didn't budge. Well, she was out now, she'd have to worry about getting back in later. *This had to be done—* she had no choice.

Clutching the thin paper and shaking like a leaf, she thought the address would be easy to find. Homes in the Outerlimits were all attached, and the streets were named alphabetically, the houses in numerical order. But here she could discern no pattern of the numbers; it must require the memorization of familiarity. The first families of Haumea had named the Upper Summerland streets in their clans' neighborhoods. The buildings were separate, and 12 Junot sat nestled between 77 Bergamont, and 23 Yarke. How did anyone know where anyone lived? It was a ridiculously stupid design in Marishel's opinion. Not that anyone was asking what she thought lately.

Her only option was to walk each street in the "Upper" neighborhood and look at the houses. She hopped onto the next moving sidewalk. The crinkled slip of paper read:

824 Harver

She worried the paper between her fingers until it tore. "Kerse it." She pocketed the trash and continued. One street was lined with a row of "8" numbers *08, 84, 813,* and Marishel thought she might have gotten lucky, but there was no *824.* There had to be some kind of rhyme or reason to the system, but she was never going to figure it out on her own. At least she had a general direction.

Not wanting to be recognized, Marishel hid behind her hair and didn't make eye contact with anyone on the sidewalk. Her feet hurt and her tongue was a dead fish in her mouth. The thought of finally meeting Trae's family excited her and she hoped she could clearly ask for water when they met. The lights dimmed to night at six, and ten minutes later Marishel—stomach grumbling, hair a mess, feet hurting—found the right house.

Surely, she was wrong. The house was well lit and full of life—she heard the noise from a house away. A man and a woman screamed at each other, the ruckus emphasized by crashes.

"Where did you get the money?" the man yelled. "Did you steal it?"

"Tawn, he's only a boy—" the woman shouted, then emitted a shrill scream.

"Don't you make me hurt her! Do you hear me! If you make me hurt her again—" the man hollered.

A third voice spoke out forcefully. "I got another job. Okay? Let her go!"

The woman screamed again.

The man boomed, "Too good for the mines, but you got a prissy job. Now what, you painting the First's toenails?"

"The paper is not a prissy job. And they got me a side job with a reporter," Trae said, his voice fresh in her mind, though she couldn't imagine his face. She'd never seen him angry. "Let her go."

There was a bang and the planter fell off the windowsill. Marishel could never grow plants in the Outerlimits. She heard the mother crying.

"Don't you touch her. Back off. She's *my* wife."

"Can I have my money back?"

He was no longer shouting and Marishel had a hard time hearing, so she crept closer to the house. Looking around for any watchers, she ran to the side of the building and peeked in the side window. She supposed it was Trae's mother laying in a heap on the floor, her hair still sliding down the wall. Trae looked ready to tackle the man she assumed was his father.

The man laughed. "You think this money is yours?" The man held up the credit slips like a hand of cards. "Anything made in this house goes in the family till. *Got that?* It takes more than I want to spend to put you up, and feed both you and her. You should start in the mines like I did. Build you a character. Make something of yourself. Not spend your life a spineless mother's boy."

Trae glared at his father with hot rage. Marishel could feel the fire of his hatred from where she stood. "If you hate us so much, why don't you leave already?"

"Oh, you'd love that, wouldn't you? You could be all alone with your *mommy*. I like it here. I think I'm going to stay as long as I want. Besides, who'd provide for you?"

"It's Mom's money—you quit the mines," his whisper was small, but the giant roared.

Trae's father reached back and slapped his face. When Trae lifted his fist to retaliate, his father pulled his mother to her feet by a handful of her hair, and she screamed. He put her face next to his own and grabbed both sides of her mouth. "That money is *ours*. Right, honey?"

His mother nodded with a whimper.

Trae stormed out of the room and Marishel saw a light come on above her. Marishel had never witnessed that kind of brutality and her limbs shook. Maybe she should go. She looked up to the lit window above her. *That must be his room.* With trembling fingers and weak knees, she started to climb the stone wall, reaching for a high plant trellis, but the light flicked off, and a few seconds later, Trae dashed down the stairs and slammed the front door.

"Get back here you little worm!" Trae's father yelled. Marishel dropped to the ground and twisted her ankle slightly. She shook it off and limped around the house to catch him, but he was nowhere in sight. She didn't know what to do. She didn't have much time before seven—but she couldn't give up now. She went back to where she was and climbed up the pebbled stone exterior of the building. Her limbs were weak with fear, knowing that man could find her at any moment. Silently, her hands and feet crawled up and up, until she hauled herself over the balcony railing. Stepping over a few cups and wadded-up papers, it was easy enough to duck in his window. Clothes lay on his bed and the floor, and she smiled—*just a normal, messy teenager's room*. She grabbed a piece of paper from his desk and wrote a note for him. Crossing the room to put the note on his pillow, Marishel tripped on a shoe.

"Trae? You up there?" His father's threatening voice came from the stairs.

Marishel ran to the bed, panic in her throat, and slid the note under his pillow, praying he would find it, then dashed out the window. She threw one leg over the railing and hauled the other one over, then dropped to hang by her fingers. She ducked under the wooden balcony and hooked her foot on the support beam, just as the man's head poked over the sill. She hoped the darkness disguised her fingers on the edge, among the assorted trash. Sweat trickled down her spine, absorbed by her waistband. Marishel held her breath, watching him look both ways through the cracks between the boards. She froze, her fingers slipping, and she fought the desire to reach for a better grasp. She squeezed her legs around the support beam under the porch. Her back ached. When he finally left, she inhaled deeply and climbed down quickly, dropping to the ground. Saying another prayer, she ran back to the estate, hoping to make it in time.

She returned to find the front gate—the only other one she knew about—locked. *No, no, no.* She ran full out, following the wall, searching for another exit. Maybe there were more hidden gates ... wait, surely the vehicles needed a way in and out. She prayed there wasn't just another locked gate. Eventually, she'd end up back at the starting gate and her claw. Searching was her only option, so Marishel raced along the estate walls made of white stone with red bricks interlaid. The bricks were made of the same rock they'd carved to make their colony, but they had been converted into energy-generating bricks, made in all colors, that powered people's homes, these kept the estate electrified. She ran her fingers along the gritty surface as she closed the corner, though it didn't glow like at home.

She came around a corner to see a wide, rolling gate, and skidded as she tried to stop and reverse. She panted as she carefully inched forward and squinted to peer around the corner. Through the black bars, she watched two men walking from the gate to the greenhouse. It was behind the outbuildings, that's why she hadn't seen it before. The gate was nearly closed with enough room for a guard's hand to roll it open, but after all the dinner guests left, they'd be locking it for the night.

Marishel stepped back, blew out a sigh of relief, and wiped her face dry, then glanced around the wall to search for cameras. One lens, mounted on the wall, turned in her direction and she ducked back. She waited a moment and peeked around the wall to see the camera scanning in the other direction. She'd have to time this right. Marishel counted the number of seconds the camera took to turn in both directions. She was ready.

Seven, the camera left her corner and began to swivel away. *Six,* it looked away and Marishel dashed toward the gate, running full tilt. *Five. Four,* the camera was pointed away from her and stopped as she heaved the rolling gate, wrenching it open just enough. *Three,* it was turning back. *Two,* Marishel squeezed through the opening and pulled the gate shut with muscles aching from exhaustion. *One,* she jumped behind the wall as the camera scanned the gate itself. She gave up on dinner and would feign illness. Wasting no time, she flew through the training yard and into the building, cameras be kersed. She prayed the guards weren't watching the shadowy back lawn. No one walked the silent halls—it must be later than she thought.

She ducked into the public ladies' room. The sofa in the lounge gave her an idea. She removed her shoes and tucked them under the sofa and then hurried back down the hall, headed for the dorm. She was almost there. As Marishel reached for the door handle to their room, Sayra thrust the door open and pushed through, nearly barreling into her.

"There you are! Where have you been?" Sayra held the door open and Marishel could see curious heads popping up to see what was going on.

"I went to the library really quick to return a book." She was rather proud of the lie, having designed it on the fly.

"Well, where is it?" Sayra barked.

"Where's what?"

"The book!"

Marishel looked at her pointedly. "I *returned* it."

"Why do you still have your clothes on?"

"I didn't want to go to the library in my night clothes. What if the Ambassador saw me?" Marishel pretended to hide a bit of fake shyness, but she was an awful actress and knew she was pushing it.

When Sayra merely stared at her, she added, "I didn't even take my shoes. I couldn't have gone very far. Right?" She swallowed.

All it would take was one word from Sayra and she'd feel the bite of that cane again. If Sayra doubted, she had only to check the security room. The look in Sayra's eyes said she was thinking the very same thing, but with much more glee than she should. Sayra stared at her, and a slow grin curled the edges of her lips into a sneer. She had her.

They stared at one another. Authority and victim—no. Not a victim anymore. She would show them all, she would be the victor here. Somehow. She knew the fire of challenge blazed in her eyes, but it would do the other girls no good if she was in the infirmary. She looked down.

"Fine," Sayra barked. "Get in bed." She held the door open wide enough for Marishel to duck under her arm and slide past her.

"Goodnight, Sayra," Marishel sang in the sweetest voice she could muster.

"Yeah, yeah. Go to bed."

As the girls around her slumbered, Marishel felt the rush of adventure surge through her veins. She knew that if or when she survived this, she would never be satisfied with finishing school and settling down. This crusade was stirring up something in Marishel's spirit that wanted more and better things. She could suddenly see clearly the problems of her world and wanted to solve them all. She was desperate to continue on. Surely, with Trae's help, they could form a solution—a way out of this mess. She didn't have the first idea if she would actually need to battle to win, but she knew, either way, it would be a fight. And then she hoped the world would open up for her. Hungry for change, she clung to the notion that she could solve her problems, because if not ... she was petrified to even entertain the idea of what failing meant. She clung to the hope.

The next day Marishel received two missives. One in the afternoon from Icen and one he brought with the post from a Tanner Winly. She felt powerful; like she'd accomplished something by getting her message to Trae. She'd made it out and back unscathed. But she couldn't count on getting that lucky again. Plus, the hidden gate was truly locked now.

CHAPTER EIGHT

BLOOD ON THE BALCONY

MARISHEL READ THE NOTE FROM TANNER Winly first. He was desperate for her help in rescuing his little sister, Veda, but Marishel didn't relish the thought of being hooked to the post and caned again. She didn't have any kind of solid plan yet; however, she needed all the help she could get when the plan evolved for their exodus. She'd keep him in mind in case she could use him.

Then she unfolded the other paper.

HEY RISHA,

SAD TO HEAR YOUR NAME CAME UP, BUT IF I KNOW YOU—THERE'S A REASON YOU CAME BY. MEET ME BY THE LABYRINTH AT 10 PM.

TRAE

A little thrill of excitement rushed through her, and she clutched the paper to her chest. Then a quick stab of insecurity engulfed her. "The powers that be" would consider her meeting Trae as being unfaithful to the Ambassador. Not that she felt there was a relationship to be unfaithful to, but it had been made clear that their priority over this month was to please the Ambassador. Her back was still sore, though a few stretches were usually enough to relieve the ache. But it was enough to remind her how dangerous her plans were. Thankfully, the Ambassador was absent from dinner the night before and her friends had answered Sayra saying they assumed Marishel was with him, otherwise, she could have been in even hotter water at this moment. She got lucky. Marishel breathed out her thanks.

"There you are." Quin's voice was soft as warm honey to her ears.

She knelt; one hand holding a dirty, sopping rag to the wall. Bubbles trailed down her forearm and dripped from her elbow. Her other wet hand was on the bucket, and she used her wrist to brush a piece of hair out of her face. She knew how filthy she must appear at this moment, in the hall to the library. Sayra had tasked Marishel and a mousy girl with soaping the paneling in this hallway, it included a chemical that dried to a lacquered sheen. She'd been on her knees for an hour, so she merely stretched out her hand.

He helped her up.

"Of course I'm here," she huffed. "I'm part of the cleaning staff now, you know. What *else* could you need?"

He frowned and the skin bunched between his eyebrows. "Why do you always come at me like that? Like it's my fault and you want to hurt me. You know what? Never mind." He turned and walked a few steps before she shook herself out of shock.

"Stop. I mean, please. Please stop. I didn't mean it like that. Really I didn't."

He turned back without expression. His long fingers rested on lean hips, his muscular legs facing the wall.

"Okay. Maybe I did a little—but I shouldn't have. I'm sorry. What do you ... ah, were you looking for me, Ambassador?" Her cheeks warmed.

"Call me Quin." He turned to face her, suddenly looking unsure. "Um, I thought you said, well,"—he scratched the back of his neck—"you said we could talk. And you might have some ideas on helping me and all. I just thought we could…"

"Talk?" She chuckled. His willingness to be honest with her caused her to see him as a real possible friend for the first time. "Okay. I don't think I can leave now, but we can speak here."

He rubbed the back of his neck. "Sure. Um, do you like picnics?"

"What?" She chuckled. "I guess. Why?"

"No reason. Do you like to read?"

"Yes. Is this like twenty questions, or something?" She laughed.

"No. I just don't know how to be a real friend. I mean, what do you talk about?"

"Just, whatever you want to know, I guess. What do you do with your day when not keeping young ladies from their chores?" She grinned at him, and he returned it.

"Well, I do all the meaningless tasks they tell me to—my father and his assistant, and my mother, and the board of directors, and the maintenance men…"

"The maintenance men rank higher than you?"

"Oh. No. I'm just in charge of the household staff and there's always something that seems to need maintenance. My goal is to work on politics—things that matter, things that help people. My father says the best way to rule the people is to meet their needs—whatever they are."

"Your father is a smart man—serving the people is important. That's one of the things I admire about him."

"Yeah. And one day that will be me. I'm just afraid something is going to happen to him, and I won't be prepared. I mean he *is* thirty-seven, after all. If he doesn't start to train me in the big stuff soon, he may lose his chance. He doesn't think I'm ready. That's why I can't screw up these tasks…"

"Okay. Let's talk about it. First, tell me the new political responsibilities you've been given. If those are solved, you can move to bigger things and show them that you're more than they think you are." She remembered all the things he'd done with other girls and the way they said he behaved, as opposed to the stiff picture she had of him in her mind and realized that she still didn't know him. She'd formed her opinion and not given him a chance to be otherwise. She really enjoyed seeing this informal side of him. It was … kind of adorable.

"You think I can be? I mean, more than they think I am?"

"I think you are."

"Thanks."

They slid down the dirty wall where it was still dry, side by side. Her chore accomplice watched them from the corner of her eye.

"Well, my father's given me a few new tasks to prove myself, but I don't have a plan to go about them. It's not like I'm stupid, or these are particularly difficult, but I'm terrified I'll fail and prove his question of how irresponsible I truly am. I don't want to be … immature." He stopped and she lay tiny, thin fingers on his cuff, rolled up to his elbow, to reassure him. "He thinks our generation may have better luck making peace with the other colonies and—"

"What do you think you're doing sitting around on the—oh, Ambassador! I'm so sorry! I didn't see you—" Sayra emerged from the hall to stand in front of them.

Marishel jumped away from Quin, but he merely waved Sayra away with a flick of his wrist.

She backed away from them then, eyes downcast, with her hands against her chest in the Haumean symbol of peace: the first two fingers of the left hand on the chest, pointing to the right shoulder, nestled in the crook of the other hand, over the right thumb. It always looked to Marishel as though the many were helping the few. She'd always pictured herself as one of the many, but realized she was indeed not. Could she afford to waste her last moments helping the Ambassador—Quin—with things that didn't concern her, when she had so much to do to stop the Match? *Who was to say she couldn't do both?* Maybe she could discover how to help him stand up to the greater powers and stop this thing from becoming another blood bath.

When Sayra disappeared humbly, Marishel sighed. "I wish I could do that."

He chuckled. "What? Send the monsters away?"

"Something like that." She smiled at his grin. "I should probably get back to work. I mean, she left for you, but I'll probably find my toothbrush telling me it's been used on the toilet, instead of the cavity it keeps bugging me about."

He threw his head back in laughter and she watched his adam's apple bounce between the cords of muscle in his neck. She liked the attention. No one else acted like she was this funny—except Canon. It felt, she felt ... buoyant.

"Okay. I'd hate to know your toothbrush was assaulted on my behalf."

She stopped herself from making a snarky comment about how assaulted she would actually be on his behalf.

He poked her forehead. "I know what you're thinking." He ran his finger down her nose and tapped the end. "Stop it."

She blew out her breath with a laugh. That was a little too close. Was she wearing her heart on her sleeve? Was she being too obvious in her rebellion? She could only work on this if the leaders believed she wasn't the ringleader. She needed to shift the focus off herself as a rebel leader and back to a contestant—at least in public.

A pair of girls she recognized from the winner's tier emerged with cleaning gear from the hallway Sayra had gone down. They looked at her sitting next to the Ambassador with barely concealed scorn. *Great.* She needed alliances, and they were going to be petty about his attention? She hadn't asked him to the hallway. Then again, maybe a little infighting over his attention would take the focus off her activities, specifically off her plans for the Match...

For simple, jealousy's sake, she laughed at him in a flirty fashion so the girls could hear. They moved down the wall from the seated pair, near Mousy-girl. Close enough to hear them, but still afford them space.

"I think spies have been sent," she whispered. "You'd better go so I can get back to work. Anything we say now must be benign and boring anyway."

He smiled—his white teeth gleaming. "It won't be as much fun without me here."

"You're right." She chuckled. "When you're here, I don't get any work done at all." She crossed her arms and looped them over her knees.

"Oh, is that it?" He raised a brow at her. "You sure you don't just miss my sparkling wit and conversational talent?"

She grinned in earnest. "Let me know when that starts, and I'll tell you."

"Ooh. You are in trouble now." His eyes sparkled—he was enjoying the moment as much as she.

"What are you going to do about it?"

He appeared to be in thought but then he reached out and pushed her over. Marishel sprawled on the floor, knocking over her bucket of dirty soap water.

"Ah, great," she huffed.

"I'll help you clean it up," he offered with a chuckle.

"You've done enough," she growled. "Go do something important and let me get back to being a scullery maid."

He sighed. "I thought we were past this." He pulled her up by her elbow and helped her to stand. She slipped in the water and slammed her forehead into his solar plexus, knocking the air from his lungs. As he bent over, gasping, she gripped his shoulders and righted herself.

"Quin?" she cried out. "Did I hurt you?"

"No," he wheezed, holding his diaphragm. "It's okay. I'm okay."

"I'm so sorry, Ambassador." She frowned, suddenly aware of the eyes on her from behind. The girls were watching this exchange, she knew, with rapt attention. She didn't have to turn to see.

He tilted her chin up. "No." He panted.

"No?" her voice was small.

"I like it better when you call me Quin," he said, just for her. She felt her heartbeat speed. Could he feel that through the veins in her neck? He stared into her silver gaze.

"Then you can call me ... Risha." She breathed out her name like a secret.

He bent forward as if he hadn't heard, and brushed his cheek to hers, her lips to his ear. She thought he hadn't heard and was about to repeat her name when he whispered into *her* ear, "See you soon. Risha."

He stepped back and she nearly fell forward. He chuckled at her disorientation, but it frustrated Marishel.

"Oh, go," she snapped. "Just go do your Ambassadory things."

She heard his chuckle all down the next hallway and felt her cheeks burn fiery red but didn't turn to see the girls watching her.

"We know what you're doing," one girl said. Marishel turned to see them all nod in agreement.

"Yes?" Marishel asked.

"You're trying to wreck the Match. We've heard the talk." The first girl elbowed her friend.

"Yeah. You're trying to cheat," the other one said.

"That's not—" Marishel was about to deny it when she realized it wouldn't matter what she said, she'd have to just keep her eye on the winner's circle. "I don't know what you're talking about."

She left them and went to find the mop. She still had to figure out how to meet Trae at the labyrinth after lights out. Her last late-night foray didn't go so well. The thought released a ball of tumbling cacti into her stomach, and she wanted to throw up. At least she wasn't abetting an escape this time. Girls were strictly not allowed to leave the dorm after lights out. So, how could she get past the guards? How could she stop every camera on her building? She'd have to pass at least three—that she knew of. There may be many more. With lights and cameras, there was no way she'd make it to the labyrinth unseen, and that would put all the pressure on Trae. She couldn't do that to him. So, how could she disable it all at once?

It was during dinner, as she was scouring her brain, that Marishel realized how she would meet Trae. As she used the little orb-shaped salt shaker on her vegetables, the idea dawned on her—something she'd seen in a science show tutorial—then she cleverly tucked the shaker into her pocket.

After a heavy dinner, many girls were shortly snoring away in a carb coma. Marishel pushed back her covers in the dark. The doors would have at least one guard stationed outside in the hall. If it was just Icen, she might be able to sneak out that way, but if it *wasn't* Icen, or there was a pair, she would be alerting the guards to her plan. She couldn't afford that.

Marishel took the salt shaker into the bathroom. She crept along the narrow hall, to the utility closet that had storage for cleaning supplies and an assortment of buzzing, gray metal boxes that she assumed controlled the electricity in their building. Quickly, she grabbed a bucket and dashed to the showers. She emptied the salt shaker into the bucket and held it up to the faucet to fill it. Marishel swirled the hot saltwater with her hand, then carefully carried the bucket back to the closet. Holding the bucket as high as she could, she poured the saltwater over and into the boxes. One looked like her family's fuse plate, and she poured over it, making a shower of sparks. She flinched, then heard the humming stop. The dim lights stopped glowing.

As quickly as she could, Marishel tiptoed silently to the French doors at the far end of the dorm room and passed through the gauzy curtains onto the half-circle of tiled balcony. She twisted her hair into a bun then grabbed her dark pants from behind the planter and slipped them on, tucking in the end of her nightshirt. Pulling her shoes out, she almost knocked the birdbath over.

"Geez," she muttered, slipping them on.

With both legs over the railing that trailed a mass of curling vinery, she crouched to swing down, when a pair of guards walked right under her. The guards were too quiet, the beep of one's tech was all that alerted her to their presence. Already in mid-motion, she swung, but quickly bent her knees up, and drew her feet to her behind. She hoped she was covered by the viny plants' silhouette. She stopped to breathe out her terror response—heart beating mercilessly. *I almost dropped right onto the guards—what an idiot.* She hadn't expected the night guard so soon. *This might be a bad idea...* It was certainly a bad idea, but what choice did she have? She hung on until they passed far enough, and then kicked her feet to get better purchase with her fingertips. One of the guards turned around, but thankfully he didn't look up quite high enough.

Her arms were shaking when they rounded an archway that led directly toward her destination.

"*Kh'ra!*" she whisper-shouted an oft-used saying of Granny Elspeth's—passed down from the old language—that Granny liked to say when she was frustrated. Marishel dropped to the ground, rolling a time or two, and followed the guards.

When she was near the opening to the labyrinth, no one in sight, Marishel called softly, "Trae?"

Suddenly, a hand gripped her shoulder and pulled her backward into a tall shrub, another hand over her mouth. Her eyes shot wide open with fear. Then a breath near her ear said, "Shhh. Do you *want* them to find you?"

She spun around in his arms to see icy blue eyes crinkled by his killer smile. She wrapped her arms around his neck. "Trae. How did you get in here?"

He hugged her back. "It's good to see you too, Buttercup." He picked up a card hanging from his lanyard and smiled. "Press pass."

The reality of her situation hit her at another, deeper, level. If she couldn't fix this, she was going to lose his friendship … forever. She buried her face in his shirt and let go for just a second, but he held her shaking form long enough to center her and remind them both that she wasn't immune to the perilous predicament she'd found herself in.

"I saw your note. I hope you didn't see—"

"I saw your light come on and then you ran out of the house, but I couldn't catch you. So, I left the note. I didn't see … anything."

The silence said they were both aware she hadn't said what she'd *heard*.

"It's so strange to see you here in my world. I'm so used to seeing you on the farm. How's your family?" He leaned farther back into the bush and with his arms around her, pulled her back with him, chest to chest.

"They're devastated. First, Baba finds out that we're losing the mine, then this…"

"How can I help?" he whispered. His eyes sparked and caught fire with cool blue flames, shining from a light above.

She was here in the arms of her best friend, and she felt so safe. She shook herself. *The Ambassador's bride must not be stupid and keep her head in the sand.* She chuckled to herself.

"So, I guess you did get that job at the paper?" she asked, tapping the card on his chest.

"Two years ago. That's why I wasn't at the farm last year. I wasn't going to be there this year, either, but I had a message for you at my grandparents' farm. Why?"

"Want a controversial story?"

"What did you have in mind?"

"I need to shut down the contest."

"I don't think I—"

"Not you, Trae. Listen, we need the people on our side. If the people rise, the Leader will listen. And he's the only one who has the power to shut it down. The First will never listen. She's ruthless. We have to remember, she's responsible for the deaths of fifty-nine other girls, just to get Karthik. That's got to mess with your ethics and morality, at the least. You'd have to romanticize it in your mind, just to be able to deal with what you've done." She felt like she understood the First a little more. Could she kill even one girl for Quin? She imagined his finger tapping the end of her nose and it made her cheeks heat.

"I don't want that for you."

"Ha." She laughed. "The alternative's not so great. Besides, I wouldn't come close to winning. You haven't seen me on the battlefield. I *am* getting rather good with that shield, though."

He chuckled. "Focus, Buttercup. How do we get the people on our side?"

"I've been thinking of that," she whispered. "Right now, these girls are a sport for the people. They are bets and parties, dress-up dessert clubs, and hopes for a win. But they're also someone's sister or daughter, they have jobs that need them, a future generation of children, future husbands ... and wives. We need to make them people again."

"Humanize the story..."

"Right." She nodded.

"How do you change the minds of a whole group of people who have been rooted in this belief all their lives without ever challenging it? How do we make them see it isn't wrong *now*, it was wrong the whole time?" He twirled a curl near her face around his finger.

She thought for a minute. "Same answer, but in two parts. You make them people again—by getting to know them personally and knowing what will be lost. Don't pressure them to feel responsible for the past but let them know that anything from this point on is on *their* shoulders."

"It could work. We only have two weeks left. With sixty ... we could focus on five at a time ... run a story like we're covering the Match, with five daily features of the girls individually."

"Yes! I can tell you what they like and don't like, they talk about all those things with each other."

137

He tucked the piece of hair behind her ear. "This is dangerous. Getting caught... I don't want you to get in trouble."

"As opposed to happily marching into the arena to my certain death?"

"You've got a point." He chuckled. "How will you get them to me?"

"Don't worry about that. I have ideas."

"I'm not worried. I believe in you."

"And I believe in you. Now let me go, I've got to get back before I'm discovered." She reluctantly pushed away from him and onto the dusty path where tiny plants tried to grow along the edges. She'd probably be out here picking them eventually.

Trae kissed Marishel's forehead, and she let their palms slide until their fingertips touched, then she dashed away.

Marishel noticed none of the cameras on her building were scanning, but she still had to make it back. She snuck around the building, headed for her balcony when she ran into a pair of guards. Before they could see her face, she spun on the ball of her foot as she'd learned in training and took off running in the opposite direction.

"Stop! Wait! Trespasser!" A shrill whistle blew behind her and she looked for a shadowed place to hide in the direction she needed to go.

Marishel circled the building and ducked under the shade from the overhang of the second-floor patios. She was just about to the balcony. A six-foot gap stretched between the shadows she was in and the planters under her balcony. She pulled the breath into her lungs and blew it out. *Ready, set,* go! She ran toward her balcony, just arriving when the pair of guards came back around. She flattened on the ground behind a low, rectangular planter and hoped they didn't notice her feet sticking out in the shadow. Her breath nearly whistled out as she tried to calm her lungs and quiet her breathing. She clamped her lips together and squeezed her eyes shut.

They crept silently down the sidewalk, holding a hand-held device and scanning it around them. *Oh crap.* Where did they get a heat detector gun? She didn't know if they'd be able to see her heat rise behind the planter but couldn't risk it. She grabbed a medium-sized rock from the plant bed. Large enough to make a significant sound, but small enough to travel a good distance. She focused on the end of the sidewalk in the direction they were going. She aimed for the corner of the building. They crept closer and she hurled the rock. *Clack.* It frightened a few birds nestled in the supports under the second-floor outcropping. The birds took off in a flutter of wings and the rock bounced off the side of the building throwing a scattering of pebbles around the corner. The guards looked up, saw the skittering pebbles, and ran around the building.

Instantly, Marishel jumped up and stood on the planter. Her fingers barely reached the floor above. She could hear them coming back. *Kh'ra!* She stretched up on tiptoes, but her fingers only brushed the floor. Her hands began to sweat. *Not now.* She wiped them on her pants.

Knees bent, she sprang up, jumping, reaching for the balcony. She gripped one of the wrought-iron poles that held up the railing. A sharp edge pierced her finger, and she sucked in her breath as she felt the pop of punctured skin, and immediately felt her grip slide in the slick blood that pooled. She kicked hard and strengthened her other hand's grasp. She never would have been able to pull herself up before training. Now, she pulled herself up enough to put her chin on the floor, but that was as high as her shaking limbs would push. She felt, rather than heard the guards coming around the corner. They'd see her hanging here for sure.

She kicked her leg to the side and hooked her toes around a bar and brought her other foot up next to it, so she hugged the outside of the porch railing. She prayed they wouldn't look up. Perspiration gathered under her arms, and she caught a whiff of her own scent ... fear and anxiety. In her mind, she begged the guards to go.

One of the guards' comms went off with a crackle. "Find them yet?"

"No. He's disappeared."

"Not likely." A woman's voice. "Go check the girls. Make sure we don't have a runner."

"Got it."

Don't look up. Don't look up.

She hoped they would come to the dorm themselves and not radio the room's guards. The first guard touched his uBand and a pin pad appeared on his forearm. He held a finger over the buttons and pushed a few when his mate grabbed his hand.

"Let's go shoot da bunk. Mebbe we can *help* check dee girls?" His eyes crinkled deeply in the shadows as he wiggled his brows.

"'Kay. We got time."

When they left, Marishel pulled up her upper body and maneuvered her feet under her, realizing she was leaving a substantial blood trail. *Great. No time for this.* Pulling both legs over the railing exhausted her. All she wanted was to go to bed.

She slipped off her mahogany brown pants and wadded them up, trying to clean up the blood, but smeared it all over the tiles. When Marishel heard the generator kick on, the fans inside resumed their twirling, and she gave up, hurrying inside. Nahli's bunk sat closest to the window, and she bolted upright when Marishel came through the curtains. The girl looked like she was about to cry out but put a hand to her mouth. Marishel put a finger to her lips. Nahli nodded, then lay back down.

Marishel hurried over to her bed, kicked her shoes under it as she pulled back the covers, and jumped in, wrapping her pants around her finger under the covers. She had just closed her eyes when Sayra came charging into the room, throwing on the emergency lights. Each girl sat up, so Marishel made an effort to look surprised and glanced around to make sure she wasn't overdoing it. Sayra walked down the room checking the aisle carefully, and Marishel noticed a drop of blood near the end of her bed. She shoved her pants-wrapped hand in her lap, under the sheet.

"Okay. All ladies present and accounted for. Sorry ladies, we thought—" She stopped a few beds to Marishel's left and looked down. She bent to the floor and swiped a finger over the tile and rubbed it against her thumb. Her eyes narrowed. She turned and silently followed the trail out to the patio. When she emerged from the curtains she asked, "Did anyone see someone come through here? You didn't leave your post at all, Icen?"

"Not recently."

Marishel's heart pounded out of her chest. She glanced at Nahli and found the girl looking directly at her. She shook her head quickly. Nahli nodded.

Once they checked the bathroom and under the beds, a confused Sayra and several guards left the girls alone, switching off the light. Marishel was so drained that she fell asleep instantly.

The next morning, Marishel scribbled a note for Sobia to give to Turpen.

Dear Mr. Bello,

~~I have a way you can help me.~~
~~Supply me with a pretend "job" that~~
~~will give me the excuse to leave the~~
~~compound daily to leak—~~

No. She scribbled that part out.

Please supply me with a job that
will give me the freedom to provide
information to someone at the
paper.

She worried about giving away too much. He would either figure it out, or he wouldn't. That would just have to be enough.

Yours, Marishel

CHAPTER NINE

SHALISE HAS FALLEN

"MAIL!" SAYRA STOOD IN THE DOORWAY to their room and handed out the messages for the day. Without her newsfeed, Marishel felt cut off in a way she had never experienced before. Even as a child, when parents policed the feeds, it was still a matter of *what* she watched, not when … or *if*. It wasn't right to be so disconnected.

"Marishel! I'm not your maid, come get your mail."

That broke her from the reverie. She crossed the room to Sayra and held out her hand. Two envelopes smacked onto Marishel's palm. "Thanks," she said over her shoulder, but Sayra caught her by the arm when she turned to walk away.

Marishel gasped involuntarily at Sayra's expression of raw hostility, worn with a cruel smile like a horrifying masquerade.

"Why does Sarver Bello want you—specifically—to run him an errand?" she asked quietly—ominously.

The fingers that curled around Marishel's arm flexed at the tips, like claws. "H-How would I know? I don't even know what you're talking about."

Sayra let go and snapped suddenly back to a state of normalcy, as her expression registered thoughtful surprise—but she didn't say anything more.

"So… Should I go see Sarver or something?" Marishel encouraged her to elaborate while rubbing her arm where Sayra's nails dug in like little crescent moons.

"Mister Bello needs some files implemented and has asked for *you* to deliver them to his husband." Sayra narrowed one eye. "What are you up to?"

Marishel laughed. "Who? Me? What could I possibly accomplish? I already *learned* my lesson."

Sayra nodded. "Good. Everyone has a moment of panic. I'm glad it's out of your system." To Marishel's surprise, Sayra gave her a playful push. "Get to that errand quickly, we don't want to keep Mr. Bello from anything important."

Marishel grabbed her shoulder bag and strode down the hall. She pulled back one side of her gold-embroidered split skirt as she walked and tucked one envelope into the pocket of her peacock-blue pants. She figured she'd check with Sarver to see if he needed anything for real. On her way to his office, she opened the other envelope and pulled out a heavy, marbled paper with a fancy cursive "Q." She opened the card.

Risha~

Would you have dinner with me? Not in the dining room, just the two of us. If yes, meet me by the labyrinth at six.

~Quin

Of course, he assumed she would say yes. But she wouldn't mind having a real conversation with him— actually get to know him. She smiled. But why did he choose the labyrinth, like Trae? It felt disingenuous to secretly meet two guys in the same place just a day from each other. She let her mind wander, trying to imagine what he might have in mind ... whatever it was, it would be a nice break from all her thinking and planning.

Sarver's office on the third floor was mostly bare of furniture. When she arrived, he sat in front of a desk with an impressive set of virtual screens and holograms. The winner's list was posted on one screen, and she recognized the names. She stood in the doorway and knocked, leaning her shoulder on the sliding door frame. Lonna was listed as number two. She and a girl named Vangie were nearly tied, but Vangie had a minuscule lead. When Sarver saw where her attention was centered, the screen disappeared. It startled her and Marishel looked at his disapproving face.

"I'm sorry—" she started.

"Oh, it's fine." He waved the notion away. "I'd be curious, too. Just don't tell anyone what you saw. It would come back to me."

"I won't," Marishel promised. "Did you need me for something?"

"Yes. Marishel, is it? It seems my sentimental husband"—he tilted his head and shook it with a smile— "has taken on a tenderness for you. I believe he'd like to talk to you but rarely makes it over here without me. Would you mind taking these files he needs and talking to the dear man?"

She smiled. "Not at all. I enjoyed visiting with him just as much."

"He has an effect on *all* sexes." He chuckled. "Just don't lose your heart, he's mine."

She smiled and took the two-inch drive he handed her.

"Tell him these are the First's choices for the Blood Ball. She has instructed down to the place settings. He'll know what to do. And here are the instructions to my house with permission to leave the premises."

She accepted the slip of waxy paper. "Do you work together often?" she asked.

"As often as we can. I give the news, and he does the scheduling and hiring, and well, everything else." It was easy to see they wanted to work together ... be together.

"I'd better go." She held up the drive and made a show of putting it in her pocket, patting it. "I'll see you." She gave the Haumean peace sign and backed away respectfully.

She showed her permission to the guards who patrolled the perimeter and met her at the front gate.

"Do you have an escort?" the taller one asked.

"No," she said. "I'm on an errand for Mr. Bello. He gave me directions."

"You know where you're going?" the other stocky guard frowned, scrutinizing her papers.

"Yes, of course." She laughed lightly, feeling a ball of nerves roll in her stomach. She started to sweat. From the heat or the scrutiny, she didn't know.

"Would you like someone to help you?" the first guard, a pale young man with an unfortunate case of acne, asked with his brows raised.

His partner elbowed him. "You ain't gettin' outta here, and neither is she." He nodded toward Marishel and pocketed her pass.

"What?" she sputtered, "But I have per—"

The guard held up a finger. "We'll see about that. It isn't a usual request."

She waited while he made a call.

"Follow me," he said and took her to the nearby guard station. "Wait here." He nodded toward three chairs against a wall. An even younger man sat at a desk scribbling on a tablet. A box of pagers and uBands sat to the side. An illuminated screen on the wall showed a layout of the grounds with pairs of green dots following the periphery. *The guard schedule.* Several red lines were interspersed around the wall, and she thought they might be gates...

"Ahem." The guard at the desk frowned at her and switched the screen to a saver.

"Can I ask what we're waiting for?"

"The First wants to know of anything out of the ordinary."

Sweat nearly poured from her temples, and the palms of her hands were moist. She wiped them on her skirt. The First would not like this. She felt sick at giving her a reason to punish the Bellos.

The thick guard spoke softly into his device while the nice one brought her a pouch of water. "Sorry," he said. "Protocol."

It won't be when she finds out it's me, she thought.

Marishel heard a man arguing over the connection, and the guard tried to turn from her, but she knew someone was upset. She didn't think she needed to go today, but she certainly would need to see Turpen at some time in the near future if she was to get his help. She was about to give up and try something else, rather than alerting the First, but the guard turned back to her. "Okay," he growled. "Your permission has been validated."

She left the station, and he walked her back to the gate.

"Go ahead," the guard said, opening the gate, his expression glacial.

She tried to gather a full breath to shake off the paranoia and left as quickly as she could. Soon, the heat of the full VitD glare on her head made her hair hot to the touch. The fans weren't always quite enough to make the air comfortable with all the lights on—at least for Marishel. She felt like an ice cube on the hot pavement, melting as it resisted the merciless heat. She had a reversal cloak in her bag. Though she'd used them for heat, the idea of being colder had never appealed to her, but now, the heat was taking her breath away. She traveled a few more blocks to get to the sidewalk with a straight shot to Turpen's home office in the Upper Summerlands.

Once she was settled on the moving sidewalk, she took off her shoulder bag and rummaged through it. Resting the bag against her ankle, she pulled out a square of silky cloth in a champagne color. Unfolded, it resembled a capelet, which she draped over her shoulders, fastening it at her neck. Once she pulled the hood over her heat-radiating hair, Marishel felt the hem of the garment until she found the right button and turned it on. Then pushed again for the cycle she wanted.

Instantly cool and refreshed, Marishel sighed as the electric impulses pushed out by the fabric covering her, fooled her nerve endings into thinking they were refreshed and cool. Once her head and shoulders were comfortable, the rest was easily ignored. Normally she used the cloak to tell her nerves she was toasty warm in the chilly

Outerlimits. Fully happy to ride the sidewalk now, she took the other envelope from her pocket. It was from Madi.

Risha,

I'm so sorry I ran away when you left. I feel horrible about it. I mean, you were being so brave and I couldn't. I didn't want to I was so proud of you. I saw you on vid screen last night. Laughing with another girl, but your eyes looked so sad. You were fighting with a cool laser sword. But then she knocked you down and we turned it off. I'm so sorry. So sorry.

Mom cried all night when you left. Dad has red eyes, too, but I don't know if he's just tired. Yolenie said to tell you hello, and Harlene said not to worry about your work, it will be here when you she can do it. I want to tell you everything, but Granny Elspeth came by and told Mom that she thinks this is why Jilly ran away, and she said not to tell you anything. That's not right.

Mom made pasta soup again. So gross. Like a bowl of glue.

I love you. I miss you. I'll see you when I'll be watching for you. I hate this. I want you to come home. I can't be a sister without you. I'm not anything without you. It's like I'm not here. I wish I'm so sorry. I love you.

Madi

Marishel refolded the page carefully and tucked it into the pocket of her bag. She held in tears as she watched the beautiful façade of the Summerlands go by. She'd always dreamed she'd be here, traveling the streets, cooling herself, but in her dreams, she was a part of it—living the life. Not expiring. Not losing the Match and dying a teenager. Life was already short, why was she dealt this hand?

She walked up to the beautiful home of the Bellos. It had a creamy ivory exterior made of energy-generating brick, with red brick outlining the rounded doorway to the porch. To her left, a deck enclosed by a railing stretched to the end of the building with comfy outside seating, a fire pit, and planters that collected the mist at night. To the right of the door, three arched windows threw light into the family room. She pressed the bell and waited for Turpen to open the door.

"Hello!" He greeted her with a warm smile. "What mischief you are up to?" He motioned her in the door, and she laughed him off with a wave.

When she stepped inside the opulent room with vaulted ceilings draped in gauzy sheets of fabric in jewel tones, Turpen closed the door behind her. She followed him past their modern kitchen—opening to the patio in front—and then turned to the back of the house to his home office. Two walls of the small room were open glass looking out over a huge pool. The other two were touch screens from bottom to top. A clear Lucite desk sat diagonally in the middle of the room, lit with a plethora of dials and buttons. Turpen, too, turned off his screens as soon as she entered.

"Oh. Here." She fished the drive from her pocket. "It's all the First's choices for the Blood Ball."

"Are we *having* a ball this year, oh little devious one?" He smiled mischievously, gesturing to a chair she hadn't noticed.

She smiled and sat. "I don't have the power to stop it. But even if I did, I think the girls would stone me if I took it away from them. It's the only light in the whole thing for some of the less fortunate girls. Besides, I might not be able to pull off … well, to stop it—how could I deny them that spot of brightness?"

"Have you made alliances yet?"

Marishel considered what to tell him. He could turn around and give all this info to the First herself. *No,* she didn't believe that. "Yes. I've made several. They just want to know what to do all the time. But I don't know. I'm already doing all I can to figure it out. I told them to keep training and I'd let them know. I think we should get as many girls as we can to refuse to fight. Of course, any who choose not to join us would be a problem."

She told him about her plan with Trae. He sat at his desk, kissing his knuckles as he listened intently.

"So, what do you think? Will it make a difference?" she asked.

"It must—if the speech is done correctly. You are going in right direction. Even when you have people on your side, what is plan for stopping the Match?"

She hung her head. "I have no idea." She gasped; her brows raised. "Do you? Do you have any ideas?"

"No. I have not."

"Oh."

"Do not give up. The Match did not start in one day, it will take many to end." His brows were raised.

"What do you mean? I thought Analiyah the First had some kind of contest and beat the other girls. Well, somehow killed them. I guess I always thought it was poison—my friend Yolenie heard she killed them in their sleep. My teacher said it was more public than that, but no one seems to be sure what happened. No one who knows will say for sure. Then they continued the tradition, *yada yada yada*. That's not right?"

"When people first came from Earth, not everyone ... handled it well. Being in space for the time to come here, with mining, building, colonizing, plus knowing people are *inside* the planet, so far from home, and no way back, affected people's minds—especially people who came with issues. Is a big problem for a while. This is the time when they are called 'the affected.' People were affected by drastic changes, never being outside or seeing sun again, leaving friends and family forever..."

"I can't imagine it. I can't imagine coming from something so open and free. But what does that have to do with the Match?"

Turpen smiled kindly and continued, "The affected were still mixed with the general population then. When Analiyah was chosen, she should not have been in lottery to be First at all. Analiyah was born to woman who became affected later in life. So, she never learned skills for beauty contest, as she was born affected."

"You said we used to be mixed?"

"Yes, in the beginning, many people were affected at many levels. There was not psychiatric training for diagnosing and helping them all. People were falling through cracks."

"Like Analiyah?"

"Certainly." He nodded. "She did not have abilities of other contestants, but she was falling in love with Leader Tyrick, as Ambassador. He was *not* a man who cared what people wanted, but he did care what people said—and he cared for Analiyah. Is unknown if he knew her plan, but Analiyah did not manage well the thoughts of losing. She refused to give him up and knew if she competed fairly with any of the other girls, she would lose. So, while people were betting for winners and having viewing parties, Analiyah was waiting for the Blood Ball—the night before final runway and announcement of Ambassador's Blood Match. During ball the night before, she systematically"—he cleared his throat—"took them out."

"She killed them at the ball?"

"*Da.* Her mother was an herbalist—a practicing witch—and Analiyah knew which plants to choose from greenhouse. Girls *were* poisoned by food, some by drinks, some left the room with her to never return—found later with throats slit. Her methods were brutal … and effective."

"There's so much speculation, but why does no one ever talk about what really happened?"

"Most do not *know*. Is hidden knowledge. I know because it was taught to Sarver in training for producer. The producer that year was not knowing what to do. People were not happy, but Analiyah cried that her love drove her to action. She was proving in her passion, that she was the only one willing to do whatever it took to gain position of bride."

"Why didn't the people do anything?" Marishel held her hands up. "Didn't they react?"

"*Da.* Parents are then furious and the Leader—Tyrick's father—had two choices. There are many advocates for mental health at these times, and they are happy to be represented as a minority finally seen as worthy. He could not just kill this girl and try again. If Leader denounced her actions, if he called it 'crazy,' people threatened it to be a hate-approach—or he could be accepting the girl as his own and hoping to groom her into one worth following. It also cleared up some infighting regarding inclusion of affected in politics. And not forgetting what he feared the girl's mother could do to him with his own greenhouse…"

"The affected wanted to be in politics?"

"Of course. Many original people are fully functioning when they are leaving the planet, and now they, or their children, were suddenly not good enough to being included—not human enough to have own voices. People spoke of segregation and possibly shipping all affected to one colony. Affected were angry, volatile, generally irrational. Many decided Analiyah's win to be triumph for the affected."

"Wow."

"Fighting lasted generations while Analiyah grew contest. First, many people are disgusted, but the Match satisfied their bloodlust—desires for fighting and war and gambling—and was reality different enough from their own to be entertaining. The Match and bloodshed are sacrifices they are willing to make for entertainment of a generation. Some called it helpful culling of population."

"Oh no."

"What?"

"Here I am hoping they will want to have another sixty mothers in this generation, and we're already having to mine an expansion. How am I going to convince them to change?"

"If Analiyah could win contest while affected, I am betting you will find a way to stop it."

"I don't *want* to kill people. That's the problem…" She sighed. "I'll need to be able to get the profiles to Trae, but I had trouble just getting out the gate today."

"I heard."

"If it's unusual—if I'm the only one with an outside job—that will make it pretty easy to point the finger at me when the profiles come out. Don't you think?"

"Hmmm. Maybe this year I am making groups of girls to help me with preparations for the ball. This will help me, and take focus from you. Write up what you can—we will find a way to get information to Trae, so you are not having to go every day. This is not feasible anyway."

"Crap! You're right. We were going to run the first installment tomorrow, but I've got, um, an engagement. With the Ambassador."

"Hot date, yes?" He chuckled. "Tell me what you know for now, and we will type up a file for him."

She informed him of her best friends first, as they were easiest to remember. Then she tried to think of others who wouldn't point to her at all. As they spoke, though the house blew chilled air throughout, a warm breeze swept gently through an opening in the glass wall and made a big windchime in the corner *bong, bong, bong*—its melody soothing. It helped her think as Turpen typed.

"He is at the Paper, yes?"

"Yes. Trae Skinner."

Turpen pushed a few more buttons and said, "There. I sent to him. You are good for few nights."

"Thanks, Mr. Bello."

"Call me Turpen. Please."

"Fine. Thank you, Turpen. I'd better get back."

"Not to miss hot date?" A long lock of blond hair fell forward when he raised his eyebrows.

She sputtered and he roared with laughter. She put her fists on her hips. "It's *not* a date."

"Uh huh." The man was put together like a marble sculpture, but he had a boyish charm that made Marishel instantly want to laugh, though she tried hard to be defensive.

He was too cute to be mad at for long and she smiled, giving in to the needed levity.

Turpen grabbed a pouch of water for her, and she stepped out into the heat again, ready to trudge back home. *Home.* How easy it shifts when you leave. Home was probably wherever her family went, but right now it was with fifty-nine other girls in a compound of ochre buildings. Each with a target on her back.

The girls were finishing up training when Marishel received a serious whack to the face with Vangie's runaway baton. Lonna had pitted herself against the girl and when she finally managed to disarm her, Vangie's baton flew through the air and landed, quite painfully, on the left side of Marishel's face. Sparring with Shalise—who finally showed her that Lonna had lied from the start when teaching her to fight—Marishel laughed with her head up and never saw the projectile coming. It bounced off her forehead and cheekbone, throwing her head back and knocking her on her behind. Sayra allowed her to finish training so she could stop by the infirmary.

The dorm was empty when Marishel found a note on her bed that said to look under it. More curious than confused, she knelt and pulled out a box. She set it on her bed and took the top off to see pink tissue paper. She looked around.

She gently pulled the tissue paper out, folding it aside to see what looked like a brand-new kaftan. The fabric was a filmy baby pink with sparkling crystals that ran around the neck. She lifted it from the box and the sheer overskirt, with the shimmery colors of an opal, fell to the floor where it curled up at the edges. It felt so light in her hands and looked so delicate. The cape-like sleeves fell from the shoulders to her knees. Vines crawled the bodice in a thin gold thread, with occasional crystal flowers. Golden vines and flowers edged the bottom of the skirt. It took her breath away.

She looked in the box, there was a belt of gold metal filigree with hanging crystals, and in the center was an oval of rose quartz. When she picked it up, there was a tinkling sound. She looked in the box and saw two delicate pink drops for her ears and a note with a big cursive "Q."

Just something I found lying around the house.

~Q

Other girls had received gifts from the Ambassador–small tokens of friendship, or affection, as they hoped. No big deal, really. But something in her mind said that this was more than a small token. It had taken thought and time. Or was she reading too much into it? She wasn't so sure the other girls would agree with its insignificance.

She didn't know whether to pull up her feminist pants and stomp the ground for all her rights to dress the way she wanted or forget all her morality and giggle at the excitement of receiving a beautiful gift. She decided to compromise with herself. Nothing was in her control anymore and she couldn't help that. Maybe she could embrace the feeling for once. She'd wear the dress but let him know she wasn't going to be bought. It was too lovely to refuse.

But she still didn't want to answer any questions about it when the girls came back, so she hurried to shower and put up her hair. She threaded the earrings into her piercings and slipped the light, filmy gown over her head. It fit embarrassingly well. Her cheeks flamed at the thought of his eyes gauging her body long enough to get her proportions correct.

Get a grip, Risha.

Feeling like a princess escaping a ball, she ducked out of the room just before the girls made it back. She heard the group talking as she rounded the hallway out of sight. Marishel wouldn't have minded showing Rena and Shalise. Rena wouldn't mind, but Shalise had been a little testy last night when she and Rena had laughed about the Ambassador's inattention to detail when it came to his hair.

"He's too busy and important for things so trivial. There's a lot he has to do." Shalise crossed her arms as if she were being attacked personally.

"Don't get so prickly, little cactus flower," Rena said, pretending to poke Shalise with her fork.

Marishel didn't think of anything smart or quippy to say, so she just changed the subject.

Now she wondered if Shalise was falling for the Ambassador. She wouldn't be the first. And though every girl dreamed of winning, they all somehow forgot that the Ambassador had nothing to do with who won this Match. The courting was all for the show. The viewers wanted to watch the drama and heartbreak unfold—the wishing, the ambition, the coveting of his gifts, *the contest*—and it suited those at home just fine. But it was really about stealing the hopes and dreams and breath of all your fellow contestants. No wonder they didn't want to think about it.

The lights had dimmed and created dark shadows on the lawn and she walked the long way around the complex, attempting to arrive at the labyrinth privately. She'd managed to escape the girls, but as she neared the labyrinth of eight-foot hedges, she got the feeling she was being followed. She hid around an arbor and waited. Soon, a young man crept forward, darting from shadow to shadow, looking around in confusion. She pulled back and watched him.

He had a mass of light brown hair that was swept to the side. It was a young man in a uniform, but he wasn't dressed as a guard, and not anyone she'd seen before. Suddenly, anger took over. Was someone trying to hurt her, capture her, or frame her? What was he doing? And why was *she* hiding? She'd done nothing wrong.

Marishel jumped out and scared the guy half to death and back. "Why are you following me?" she demanded.

CHAPTER TEN

SECRETS IN THE LABYRINTH

WHEN HE COULD BREATHE AGAIN, THE uniformed young man said, "I just wanted to talk to you alone."

"Hey buddy, I'm not whoever you think I am—"

"Abrielle said you could help." He looked lost. "She said you would figure it out, and now I can't lose my little sister—"

"Tanner Winly?" She stepped forward to meet him.

"Yeah." He hung his head. "I didn't hear from you and—" He stopped.

"I can't help you any more than I already am." She looked around for cameras and listening devices, she knew they were everywhere, but one could generally tell a camera by an accompanying record light, or the hum of electric current. Security couldn't possibly watch every camera, so she doubted she was under surveillance. Still, she couldn't take any chances. She stepped closer to him and took his arm.

"Listen," she whispered, "if I can stop the whole thing, I will. I've got just as much at stake as Veda." She looked at Tanner. "Well, a life anyway."

He leaned down to speak quietly to her. "How can I help?"

"I really don't know. That's why I haven't answered. And I don't know how to get to you anyway."

He chuckled. "Oh, that's easy. I work in the greenhouse. They just haven't put two and two together yet. So, I can see her from far away." Then his face crumpled, and he leaned forward as if she was a pillar of strength, and he could borrow some through osmosis. "I can't watch her die, Marishel. I can't watch her on the broadcast, bloody and broken and desperate to live—and then watch them kill her." His body spasmed with a quick sob. "I'll lose everything—all my family. I'll have nothing left. Along with Veda, Abrielle and I were going to be a family."

"She told me you'd been engaged for six months."

"About a year ago, we discovered she was pregnant. She was five months along when we set the date and told everyone we were engaged. Three days later, she miscarried. A little boy. She named him Adam. She was a total wreck. I spent the last *six months* just getting her back to life. And now … she's gone."

Marishel's heart broke. She had no words. Abrielle's behavior made so much more sense to her now, and Veda's as well. She took his hand in hers and looked up at him with shining eyes. "I'm so sorry."

A single tear fell from his eyes, and she wanted so badly to put Abrielle and Tanner back together—at least she could save Veda. He looked exhausted and she squeezed his hand. He whispered, "Me too. You can't know how grateful I am to you for what you did."

"But I didn't do anything for your gratitude. I'm the one who got her,"—she cringed—"you know."

"At least you tried. No one else has even thought of making a change—making things right." He leaned toward her for support.

Uncomfortable, she stood back but kept her voice low. "I'll tell you what. I have these stories I need to get to the paper. Maybe you can help me find it?"

"Just send Icen for me. He's a solid guy, we go way back."

"Okay. Now you need to go. And don't follow me. It's creepy." She smiled quickly at him, and he stopped frowning long enough for a short chuckle.

"Sorry."

The look on Quin's face when he saw her in his gift was worth the compromise with herself to wear it. His mouth hung open and his brows rose. Part of her hoped he didn't look at all the other girls this way. He stood tall; his dark hair swept back. Broad shoulders filled out a brocade shirt with a short collar in a purple-red shade of wine, but with a similar gold thread embroidery to that on her gown. His jaw appeared to be shadowed by a day or two's worth of growth, and his green eyes were lit from within.

"You look lovely," he said softly. Holding out his arm he continued, "Right this way, Miss."

She took his arm. "Where are we going?"

"Deep into the labyrinth, of course. Where I take all my victims. Mwah ha ha." He led her down the first short row and took a left.

"*Do* you bring all the girls out here? Do they all wear your dress?" She didn't mean to sound snarky, but that bit of female bite in her just wouldn't behave.

He walked in silence for a moment. "Still mad at me, huh? How do I convince you I'm not the bad guy here?"

She sighed and dropped his arm. "I don't know if you can." When her temper flared, she got a hold of herself. She didn't know the plan yet, but this wasn't part of it. She might need his alliance and it was better not to burn bridges, but more than that, she needed to be a better friend.

Marishel took a deep breath. His silent gaze was unnerving, but she appreciated him giving her time to collect her thoughts. "I'm sorry. You're right, of course. You didn't sign up for this any more than I did." And she realized again the truth in it.

His smile was confident. "I guess that's something we do have in common. Can we make the best of the worst situation possible?" He held out his arm again.

"Sure." She took his arm and asked softly, "Wouldn't you rather spend time with one of the girls who might win? One who might be able to make you a happy wife?"

He put a hand on hers, looped through his elbow, and looked down at her. "Spending time with *you* would make me happy. And you're different. I don't know. I can see you are angry and scared; you have every reason to hate me, but you're still here with me, even though I know you want to fight me. I'm hoping that spending time with me will make you happy, too. We could both use a friend."

She smiled sadly and nodded.

They made turn after turn, soft crunches of pebbles rolling beneath their feet. She couldn't see over the hedges, but with all the left turns, they didn't seem to be headed for the middle. She'd been told there was a lovely fountain with benches there, and room for a small gathering of chairs around a table. She'd assumed they'd eat there. "Aren't we going to the fountain?"

"Nope." He chuckled. "When I was little, I used to come out here for hours and read feeds and serials full of stories about heroes and adventurers. Canon and I read together a lot, we'd sync feeds and listen to the books while we read them together. But sometimes I just wanted to be alone, so I came out here. My mother discovered how much I loved the place and one day I arrived, ready to be alone, and she'd put out a mat for me with hydra pillows, and lights. It was magical. I never told her *thank you,* but I knew it was her, and I could always be found out here after that, so I hope she knows I'm grateful."

It was a picture of the First that didn't reconcile in her head. The woman was brutal, ice-cold, a murderer, and fake, as far as Marishel could tell. Could she have been a loving mother once? Marishel didn't like feeling any kind of emotion for the woman save animosity, but she'd better be careful what she said and to whom. "I'm sure she knows. Did you have school out here, too, or did you go to a neighborhood school?"

"Oh, Canon and I were tutored. So yes, I did it out here. Some nights I accidentally stayed so late that the mists came on. The first time really surprised me. I was in little more than pajamas and had snuck out to read after bedtime. My place in the dark ... well, you'll see. Anyway, I was sprawled out on the pillows with my hands behind my head, fully absorbed in the story when the spray rolled in. It was spring—when the crops are budding, and the mist is thickest. I didn't even feel the drops collecting on my clothes until I moved my legs and they seemed ... wet. By the time I'd gathered my things and found my way out of the labyrinth and to my room, I was drenched and shaking cold. It was not a pleasant experience."

Though she enjoyed the thought of him as a normal boy, she was thoroughly fatigued by the green walls of the maze. They all looked the same, but as her eyes adjusted to the shadows, she noticed different colored lights at each turn, so one could find their way out in the dark.

"Here we are."

She saw nothing but dark shrubbery and a glow coming from her right.

"Close your eyes," he said.

She cocked her head and raised her brows at him.

He laughed. "No really, close your eyes."

She did and held out her hands. He took them both and led her forward, then turned a very sharp right. She felt the leaves touch her shoulders on both sides and he said, "Okay. Now."

She opened her eyes to the most magical place she'd ever seen. It was a ten-foot square space with a plush rug-type mat covering the ground to each edge, and little white fairy lights threaded through the thick bushes all around like stars. It had to have taken someone a long time to do this. As he said, there were a plethora of colored hydra pillows in varying sizes around the periphery, and in the middle, laid out on a small blanket was a picnic for two. "Wow." She breathed the word, full of wonder. What would it have been like to grow up here?

As they sat, the light glowed bright enough to see but low enough to make shadows on the far side of Quin's face. He smiled. "I thought you'd like it."

She couldn't imagine him bringing Lonna out here. But that wasn't any of her business. They shucked off their shoes and settled on either side of a woven basket. She leaned back onto pillows filled with water. They were cold against her back, so she pushed the button on the seam behind her to warm one. Quin plated food for them—she couldn't get over real food. She'd never had a real, outside picnic before. He continued to pull food and drinks from the basket.

She nibbled on a roll while he fixed their plates and ran her hand over the blanket. The mist wouldn't affect any of these materials, they were made to withstand mold and mildew, and there was no weather to worry about. She couldn't imagine seeing rain fall from the sky. *Sheesh, she couldn't even imagine a sky.* Looking up and seeing forever? Whoa. Looking up at night and seeing Haumea up in the sky so far away. Just a bit further than Pluto.

The original five colonies had chosen Haumea, Eris, Makemake, and Sedna to mine out and call home. The fifth colony made up the Interspace Travel Station on Pluto. Though now, all the *affected* lived in a colony in Sedna opposite the penal institution. Their families and volunteers took shifts living there and caring for the residents, at least they had until the colonies separated. Now, Eris's people ran the colony. Some of the affected needed full-time care and some just loose supervision. That was about all she knew of the situation.

They'd been taught colony history and politics in school, but once she passed the test, she didn't have to remember it anymore. Not like it would be hard to find out if she wanted. She paused. Not without her *Eye.* She felt absolutely unconnected and floating in space without her *Eye* on, without knowing what her friends and family were doing at any second. Getting immediate answers to questions. She'd heard people didn't know what they'd done for information before Google came along, and she felt the same about her *Eye*. It was more than a tool; it was her lifeline. She felt stupid without it.

Quin handed her a plate and said, "Sudessa Gayne retired today."

"No kidding? I thought Dessa would be an actress until she died." She took a bite of the fish and it melted, buttery, in her mouth.

"You remind me of her. Well, this character she plays. I'm obsessed with the story. This orphaned girl, from another world, is forced to marry her mortal enemy to win back her sister—"

"You watch *To Venus with Love*?" She nearly dropped her mouth open.

"Yeah. Have you seen it?" He gazed at her intently.

"Only every episode since the beginning. Back when Thaelyn buys his first wishes from the invisible entity…"

"You know, they took that character from the religion of the Seafarers. Are you a believer in that?"

"What? The character or the religion?"

"The religion," he said around a mouthful of bread and covered his face. "Excuse me."

"No. We weren't brought up that way. One of the girls has a bracelet with the holy helm on it, though. She must be a believer. My family's more involved in sports. We like the ball games. I think we were religious way back, but not anymore. Oh, my Grammy liked politics, though. You would have loved her. She used to teach me about how to read people and know where they stand on issues. She said politics was more a game—a challenge of wits—than actually making the law fair for people. It's all about interpersonal relationships and knowing the right questions to ask the right people. I think she wanted me to go into law."

"She could teach me how to do all this, I bet." He smiled.

Her eyes crinkled. "She would have thought you deserved more power by now. She was all about finding your potential early in life and not waiting to see what kind of hand life would give you and then figuring out how to deal with it." She made circles in the air with her fork as she spoke.

"Well, getting more power is the idea. You're going to poke your eye out with that thing."

"Oh, I so miss my *Eye*. I feel lost without it."

He gazed at her. "I wish I had the ability to give it back. Or to take you out of all this…"

She cleared her throat. "So, tell me more about these tasks you're figuring out."

Quin put down his plate and pulled out a few books that she hadn't seen behind the picnic basket.

"What are those?"

"Well, you wanted to know more about the new missions." He tapped the cover of one with his thumb. "Are you sure you don't mind? It's not very … um, date-like."

"Is this a romantic date?" she asked, teasing. Enjoying the sight of his unease. She waited a moment until he looked like he was turning purple from holding his breath. "Oh, don't blow an aneurysm, I'm giving you a hard time."

He relaxed with a chuckle. "You make me laugh."

"Now you're calling me funny-looking?" she cried with mock dismay, putting the back of her hand to her forehead.

"Oh, so sorry to offend you, my lady. My lips doth speak on their own, so ignorant to curse your beauty." He reached for her hand.

She laughed when he held it to his lips. "Oh stop, good Labyrinth King."

"Hmm, does that make you the queen?"

"Alright, in this story I am. And our kingdom shall be this space." She held out her arms to encompass their nook.

"Who shall our jester be?" he asked, crunching into a stalk of asparagus.

"Hmmm. Let me thinkest," she teased, tapping her chin. "Who looks funny, tells bad jokes, isn't afraid to embarrass themselves, and dresses like a fool?"

"Lonna." He nodded and she lost herself in a fit of laughter. "She entertains me every night while I eat."

She dried her eyes. "We'll dress her like a clown." She painted her face with imaginary makeup.

He snorted and she tried to smother her laughter. This light feeling, being disconnected from her life, from reality, was so dream-like, the space so enchanting, she gave in to the flirtation. "We have no subjects in our kingdom, though. It is a bit … private."

"Then we can do whatever we want here." He winked and tucked a curl behind her ear, brushing her cheek with the back of his fingers. The curl of his lips made the bottom drop out of her stomach. She'd better be careful how long she played this game. She shouldn't encourage him.

Heat rushed through her chest, and she took a breath. "So, tell me what the books say."

"Ah yes, back to business. Of course. The four areas that he's given me will take some time and need some research. I need to outline some initial steps. The first job is the one I told you before: Inter-colony peace with Eris and Makemake. We aren't worried about Sedna—or the launch colony on Pluto. They're more interested in interstellar travel than us in-fighting colonists. With me as the planet's

Ambassador, he's hoping Eris might be under new rule as well, and that the younger generation may be better able to make an alliance."

"Okay, so we need to find a way to make peace. First, we need to understand what drove them apart. Why is so much of our society's past a secret? Is it just because the leadership doesn't want anyone to know of their mistakes? How can we learn if we abolish our history? If we knew what went wrong and whose fault it was, it would be much easier to fix."

"Okay. Noting that, I'll dig for more facts. The next is something I think has to do with the separation. I've been put in charge of managing the Decennial Testing for next year."

She cocked her head. "Testing for the affected?"

"Yeah. And that's tied to the next one. Apparently, there is a sickness in the Outerlimits? Do you know anything about that? I'm supposed to put together a research team to find a cure if there is one, and if not—"

She took a sip and wiped her mouth to keep it from hanging open in shock. "Everybody knows about the sickness. Tons of miners have it. How did you not know?"

"I don't even know what it is." He threaded his fingers through his hair.

"I thought you guys knew everything." She frowned. "Wow. We don't know what it is. When you get it, you start to cough, then you lose sleep and weight, then the coughing gets bloody and sometimes your limbs give out. That's also why they wear the exoskeletons—not just for extra strength. Then one day you fall over and that's it. We just call it 'The Sickness'—it's all over the Outerlimits. You mean *no one* here has it?"

"No one I've ever known." His brow bunched.

"I always thought you could just afford the treatment and we couldn't." She'd never considered the fact that it was only hurting her people.

"Most Summerlanders don't worry about what doesn't affect them.' His rote answer was over-confident and uncaring to her ears.

"But you work with the homeless. Surely, some of them must have had it."

"Maybe I just haven't been looking at the right things."

Marishel scowled. "And it does affect the Summerlanders. Who will work the mines, if the miners die? Who will be your nannies, when the young women from the Outerlimits die? Who will do all the menial jobs and instruct their children?"

"Good point."

"You said it had to do with the Decennial Testing? How so?" She leaned forward in interest.

"There is a motion, I think by my mother, to send those with the sickness to Sedna along with the affected, in case it's contagious." He took a bite from his plate. "Then, if it spreads through the prison system, and the affected, there will be more space available and save the rest of the population."

"That's the stupidest thing I've ever—it's from the mines. In the air. Don't the miners in other colonies get something like it?"

Quin finished chewing and shrugged. "I wouldn't know. We don't speak."

"Oh my stars, what a mess. That's three, what's the last thing?"

"The last job, I've gotten started on already. I won't need help on this one."

"Oh," she said, a little deflated. "Is it top-secret security or something?"

"No, no." He chuckled and it rumbled through Marishel like thunder. "Nothing like that. I just have all the buyers in place and things are in mid-transaction. And now that I have control of the new construction and private ownership, until they become corporate prop—" he began.

"Wait, what?"

"Oh, well, I'm fixing a mine property issue."

"What happened?"

"There was a policy change, from what I've been told. Individual entities have retained ownership of the mines rather than relinquishing them as public property, and I must make them part of the annual debt and solution."

She looked down at her empty plate. How could she sit here eating with the enemy? She felt like she'd just kicked her father in the gut.

"What? What is it? Was the food bad?" His frown made deep creases between his brows.

"No. It's not that. I—Nevermind. I shouldn't be here." She started to rise, but he grabbed her hand and pulled her back down.

"No," he said. "Please. Just tell me. I want to know."

They stared at one another in the twinkling light of pretend stars. She weighed what she wanted to say.

"I should—well, what's the harm? My father is on the lease for one of the mines, Centra B. He was the one who came in when the mine was on the brink of bankruptcy and solved the problem with the books. He earned his way to the top. We've been saving. He was going to sell it and move us to a farm near my aunt Naidelyn, my mom's sister. Now, because of corporate ownership dissolution, he's going to lose everything he's worked so hard for."

She dared him to push his agenda. She would walk out on him and never look back.

"I'm so sorry." His fierce brows pulled down with sincerity, but it only frustrated her.

"Then make it right. He coughs all night. I want him to be an old man on a farm, not cold and dead in the Outerlimits." She couldn't stop her tears from escaping as the image flashed before her eyes, though she did try. She didn't want to appear weak in front of Quin. It was important to her. She hated being vulnerable in front of people who could hurt her. She wasn't ready to submit yet.

"It isn't—" Quin put a hand out, but she couldn't let it go.

"Only two people in this planet have more power than you. *Use* it," she demanded.

"To give back the mines? Or are we talking about something else?" He narrowed one eye.

"Can you blame me for wanting both? Can you blame me for petitioning for our lives? Especially when you could potentially stop it?" Marishel spread her hands helplessly. "You haven't even *tried.*"

"It's not like I don't want to fight it. You're not listening. The Match is the First's greatest honor. She won't listen to me any more than you. She doesn't think I'm capable of choosing the best match." His voice raised with each sentence. "And she could be right, but it's because of all the ways they hold me back."

Her voice rose, "So show her. We'll show her with these new commissions! Fight it with me."

He paused and her heart leaped with hope. "You realize you're asking me to cross my mother, all the people, our entire history..."

"You're afraid of saying the wrong thing? While I am sentenced to fight for my life?" She knew she was pushing the issue, but she didn't care. Living was worth it. She wanted to evoke a greater feeling in him—engender a response.

"I'm not afraid." He stiffened. "You don't understand my mother. She's been planning this match since my birth. She said she was severely tested, but if she hadn't gone through the fire, it wouldn't have refined her and made her worthy of the position of the First. She will accept no less of a commitment, or proof of passion, or show of determination from my match. This Match is her legacy— she believes that if I got to choose, I would 'marry the wrong one,' and she would be disgraced."

It seemed like an excuse to Marishel. "By whom?"

"I don't know—the people probably. And Eris and Makemake if we ever manage to make peace. I didn't say it made sense. I want to help you, I just don't know how… Yet."

She relaxed a bit. "If Eris is so much better than we are, what's the difference? What makes us less civilized? Have you ever wondered what *they* think of our Match? Maybe getting rid of it would help things." She thought a moment. "You should visit Eris. See how they live. See if they have the sickness and what they are doing about it. If no one in the Summerlands has it, maybe it's the Outerlimits. What about fixing the broken lights, fuses, bulbs, and wires in the Outerlimits so the people don't all freeze to death? Maybe it keeps them sick?"

"I thought they liked the cold."

"About as many as here, probably." She shrugged. "No one is the same. Some do like the cold. Some are used to it. And some hate it—passionately."

"I doubt there's anything you don't believe in *passionately*. Why are you so sure you won't win the Match? You're smart, strategic—" He held up his fingers, counting off her attributes.

She reached out and folded his fingers down. "Don't forget the *sucks at fighting* part. Which is the whole point. I have to find my own way out of this. Someone has to shut this madness down."

He frowned. "It will be an awfully dangerous task."

She ignored his inference. "I'm not altogether sure it's a good idea to let you in on any plans…" She suddenly realized she was sharing way too much and turned her head frantically looking around for a recording device.

He reached out and put a hand on hers. "It's okay. We are totally secluded. This is my exclusive area—no cameras allowed."

"Are you sure? That cameraman is sneaky."

He chuckled. "The guy's a creeper. But no, the cameras will see us entering the labyrinth if we're caught on the scan, and if we'd gone to the fountain, it would have recorded our whole conversation for the viewing public. That's why we came here. We're friends, right? Did you think I'd share this with anyone?" He gestured to the books.

"I don't know—I don't know you." She hunched her shoulders, sad to say it, but unable to call it false.

Quin's hand tipped her face up and she shook it off. "I don't know you either, but I want to," he said softly.

"You don't have much time left. Maybe you can sneak away to Eris and feel them out? See how amenable they are to change and to making peace with us? Maybe if you show your mother—"

"Risha. I don't want to lose you, but we have to find another way. There aren't many who my mother will listen to. If we could convince my father…"

"I'm working on it," she said with a sad smile.

He stared at her for a moment and with an air of resolve said, "I will see if there's anything I can do. We can fight this together. I can't imagine a world without you in it. It's funny, I've gone my whole life in the dark, not knowing you, but you are like a flame. I can see why your friends gravitate toward you … why I am pulled to you."

Her stomach flipped at the way his gaze drank her in and guilt enveloped her at the thought of having feelings for Quin. The other girls would kill her, and she couldn't let her feelings for him distract her from her quest—even if he was offering to help. She wondered for a moment if he was trying to sabotage her, but she had seen the honesty in his expression when he said they would fight it together. She squeezed his hand and nodded to him in thanks. Rarely would a compliment faze Marishel, but coming from this boy, his words made her extremities tingle. *Don't fall for him, Risha.* It took effort for Marishel to shift her thinking.

They ate a heavenly dessert of chocolate and vanilla cream with a vein of coffee and a spongy cake-like layer. She'd never had anything so delectable—and the texture was so fitting. The printer used edible stock of corn and wheat sheets, so the texture of food was always the same, even though flavors differed wildly. Something about the taste of cream with a creamy texture to boot, was like she imagined it would feel to fall into a vat of meringue. To be swallowed up would be the epitome of sweet softness.

As they walked from the labyrinth, she let him take her hand. He drew circles on the back of her hand with his thumb, and his grip was warm and strong. But as soon as they emerged, she dropped his hand quickly. She didn't want anyone to see them intimately together. She already had enough jealous girls questioning her fight. He looked hurt and she knew he didn't understand, but there was no way to explain the female mind to him in the next ten minutes. Speaking of which, it was later than she thought. When they entered the dorm building from the training yard, the wall clock rang out once for eight-thirty. She gasped. Sayra was going to kill her!

"Don't worry," he said quietly in the tomb-like hallway. "I told Sayra you'd be with me."

Oh great. Even better. Sheesh. They rounded the corner and saw Sayra talking to a guard. She looked up and nodded. "Come on, it's time to get to bed."

Marishel turned to Quin. "Thanks for dinner," she whispered, "and the dress."

He squeezed her hand, and she ducked through the door. She changed in the bathroom, folding up the dress into a small bundle that she shoved in her suitcase under the bed. She had to cram it in, and the suitcase scratched along the floor.

"Be quiet, stupid." Lonna rolled over, giving Marishel her back.

She sat on her bed and looked over at Rena, who winked at her and smiled, then closed her eyes. Marishel lay down and surrendered to the heavy pull of sleep.

A ruckus of noise greeted Marishel in the classroom the next morning. She ignored the congregation of girls and made her cup of coffee, grabbing a banana.

"Did you hear about what's in the papers?" Shalise leaned into her and whispered with eyes wide.

What did Trae do?

CHAPTER ELEVEN

BETRAYALS AND LETDOWNS

ONE OF THE FEMALE GUARDS WAS in big trouble. She'd left the paper in the ladies' room where one of the girls found it, and they were all keyed up. Rena left the group and came over to Marishel.

"Did you hear?" she asked.

"No. I have no idea." Marishel peeled her banana and took a bite, attempting to look disinterested. "What did it say?"

Shalise said quietly, "Well, Sayra snatched it away as soon as she saw it. So, no one got a really good look at the article except the girl who found it, but the section had five girls and personal stuff about them, but ... I don't get it. I didn't have any interviews. And *we* were in it. Did you do it?"

Marishel just smiled. "Who else did they feature?"

"It was you, Rena, and me. Then Nahli and Vangie. Everyone's asking me who did the interview, but I don't know." She wrung her hands as they took breakfast to their seats.

"Calm down, Lise. It's okay. You're not in trouble. What else did it say?"

"Oh! That's the important part. It said something about us being murdered in the Match. *Murdered.*"

"Well, what else would you call it?" Marishel asked.

"Not murder. When my parents see this, they're going to flip!"

Marishel grinned. "That's the idea. Do you think they'd be angry enough to speak out? Even to their friends and family?"

"I'm sure everyone in the family is messaging my mother this morning. She won't pretend to be happy about losing me. Even though they told me it was my duty because I'd been chosen, hearing that your daughter will be murdered and knowing you can't do anything about it would surely frustrate her."

"My dad's gonna be fazed." Rena leaned back in her chair and put her feet on the table.

"Watch your language," Shalise said.

"Valorena! *The Ambassador's Bride knows when to act like a lady.*" Sayra nearly growled the words. "And the rest of you—enough nonsense. You all know that what goes on outside this estate is not for you to know. Especially media-related information. I'm sure the reporter will be duly chastised. Now let's get to lessons."

Introducing the Blood Match Contestants

Shalise Mendes

Nickname: Lise

Loves: Dancing with her friends

Hates: When people are rude to their servers

Anyone back home? No

Fears: not knowing where she's going in the dark

Dreams of: seeing her family one more time

Trained to fight? No

Nahline Keegan

Nickname: Nahli

Loves: digging in the garden at her farm

Hates: math

Anyone back home? Yes.

Fears: the future

Dreams of: teaching small children

Trained to fight? No

Evangelea Anish

Nickname: Vangie

Loves: space exploration

Hates: Singers chewing gum while they perform

Anyone back home? Yes.

Fears: Never growing up

Dreams of: Interstellar travel

Trained to fight? Yes

Marishel Vance

Nickname: Risha

Loves: her aunt's farm and reading

Hates: peas made by the printer

Anyone back home? No.

Fears: never getting to find the love of her life and be a mother

Dreams of: seeing her father find his dreams—living to be 18

Trained to fight? No

Valorena Yasuda

Nickname: Rena

Loves: Drawing people in their own cultural habitat

Hates: when people talk with their mouth full

Anyone back home? Yes.

Fears: Never seeing her family again

Dreams of: Being an artist or an architect

Trained to fight? No

Each of these are wonderful girls with bright futures—but all their potential will be lost in two weeks when they are murdered at the Blood Match.

Marishel sat alone in an all-white conference room. It was surreal. One of the walls operated as a screen, and the opposite wall as a whiteboard. The wall at the far end of the room was a window on the top half, and the bottom looked like white plastic. She chose a seat halfway down the long table, not wanting to sit at the end and seem presumptuous. No one explained why she'd been summoned, but when her friends were asked to report as well, she had an idea it was about the Paper.

Part of the tactic, she knew, was to make the criminal wait. Marishel was addicted to crime shows and they always tried to sweat out their perps—give them time to get nervous—and observe them through a camera. She had no doubt the Earth's ocean screensaver across from her was also transmitting her image to someone else—maybe the First herself. She worked to stay cool and kept her expression neutral—or inquisitive—the opposite of the way she was inclined to act.

If she were to look guilty at all— She suppressed a wince.

The door slid open and two men she didn't know filed into the room and took a seat at the end of the table before the window. They were dressed in pressed gray uniforms and black boots, like some type of important people of the law; she wondered if these were Coercitors.

She sat up and perched her folded arms on the table with a non-threatening smile.

They did not return the expression.

"This is Holden and I'm Harris. Miss Vance, why was your picture and personal information in the paper this morning?" They were generic-looking in identical outfits, the only differentiation being their wide age gap.

She glanced out the window. "Oh, was it? We aren't allowed to know outside information about the Match. Could it have been the cameraman I keep seeing everywhere?" she asked as innocently as possible. "That's the only person I can think of."

They appeared to give it thought and one glanced at the other. "Were you interviewed by him, or anyone else? Did you give your information to anyone, not on your staff?"

Marishel played her part, as sweet as chocolate-covered decadence. "No, of course not. It's forbidden to interfere with the Match or push a personal agenda."

"Is that your personal agenda? To *interfere?*" The gruff one with gray in his hair was probably pushing forty. He should have retired by now. He seemed more bored with her answers than anything. Probably the same answers her friends had given.

But the other man, the younger one, was shrewd and just getting started. "Where were you last night? Your friends report not seeing you for dinner and said you came to bed late. Were you feeding information to the Paper?"

"Of course not. I don't know any reporters." She sat back and held her folded arms to her body. *Him* she would have to be careful with. *Don't volunteer anything, Risha.*

"Then where were you?" He smiled like he had her backed into a corner.

She smiled back. "Having a private dinner with the Ambassador."

"We will have to confirm that," he said with malice.

She dropped the pretense and shrugged. "Okay."

The older man, obviously the rule-follower, parted a cylinder into halves and pulled them apart, opening a clear screen that he used to press buttons and fill out blanks. It looked like as far as he was concerned, the meeting was wrapping up.

But the young hound dog, or was that a hot dog? She couldn't remember the term from her show. Top dog? Sniffing out the truth? Whatever he was called, he was tenacious, and she knew he would be the one to watch. She was suddenly incredibly happy the cameras hadn't been recording their conversation last night, but she wondered if there was enough footage of them together to corroborate her story. Of course, the Ambassador would back her up, but they obviously didn't have him on their interview list.

"We will be back." The younger man elbowed the older one.

"Oh, yeah," he muttered. "Stay here."

They rose and gray-hair asked, "Do you need anything?" His partner looked at him like he'd lost his mind.

She cleared her throat. "Some water would be nice."

He nodded and they left the room.

Alone again, she wanted to push the chairs aside and do some stretching, but she stayed cramped in her chair. She didn't want to push it or anger them. If there wasn't validation that she'd been with Quin, she had a feeling she'd be sitting here until things were ratified. She mimed the arm motions of a dance she was learning from the social network. If there had been a whiteboard stylus, she would have been tempted to draw on the wall behind her. But knowing she was monitored kept her vision pointed to the deep sea.

After a while her back started to ache, so she scooted to the edge of the seat and reclined with her neck propped on the back of the chair. She closed her eyes and wondered what her family was doing. What had they thought of the message in the Paper? Would it have an effect at all? Surely after a few days, they would consider joining and ... and what? What did she think they'd do? Call the Coercitors and demand a cease and desist? Surely, she was dreaming if she thought she could bring down the biggest event of a generation. She had to hope the people would respond.

She didn't hear the door open, but when the Coercitors came back to the room and sat down, one of them cleared his throat, loudly.

She snapped her head up and wiped a little line of drool from her cheek. She didn't realize she'd fallen asleep. Top Dog looked quite smug and proud of himself, and it filled her with illogical anxiety. There shouldn't be anything for him to be so happy about.

"We didn't see you on the cameras with the Ambassador, but we did catch something of interest." His smile was predatory.

The other man just looked tired. He was obviously running the show, but his sidekick was the ambitious one.

"What do you mean?" She racked her brain. "I didn't do anything. I met the Ambassador, and we had dinner."

"Please watch the screen." Gray-hair yawned. He wasn't on her side, by any means, but he wasn't determined to frame her, either. She was inclined to trust him more.

She turned back to the screen, and it changed to show a desktop. Top Dog held a remote stick, pointed it at the screen, and then it went dark. She didn't see anything but could make out some leaves in the periphery of the view. A hidden camera. *Ah, Kh'ra.*

She looked at the men, attempting to keep the anxiety from her expression.

"Keep watching." Top Dog smiled viciously.

She watched the dark leaves sway in the breeze, then to the right a spot of light pink. She watched herself slink around in the dark, trying not to be seen by the girls. Then she watched as her image tucked behind an arbor, peeking her head out. In a moment, a male figure entered the screen, looking around. Marishel jumped out and scared him. She couldn't hear the conversation, but she remembered the topics.

Right on cue, the camera caught him laughing conspiratorially with her. This wasn't looking good. She started to perspire around her hairline. She didn't dare wipe it and alert the Coercitors. She tried to remember what came next and her blood ran to her feet. Tanner was telling her about Abrielle losing the baby, but all the camera saw was two somber lovers coming together, holding hands ... and then he awkwardly leaned toward her. *Oh no.* This didn't look good at all.

If she said she was helping him, she would be in trouble. If she said they had a relationship, she'd be in trouble. Even saying they were just friends would sound like a lie confronted with their behavior on the tape. There was nothing she could say. So, she didn't.

The screen flickered to black and then the desktop. Then the ocean reappeared. She had no concept of an ocean. It was all a fairy tale to her. She watched the fish dart around bright orange coral. Blue and red, black and yellow, stripes, spots, fish of all kinds. How did they have room for all those fish?

"Well?" asked Top Dog.

She turned back to look at him blankly. *What do I do? What do I do?* She had to tell the truth. It was the only thing she could do. "He's the brother of one of the girls. I was simply telling him that she was okay and sympathizing with him."

"That's some pretty nice sympathy."

"I hope so," she retorted. "That was the idea." She had to play this very carefully. Give them enough attitude to believe her, but not so much that she became the prime suspect.

Top Dog folded his arms as if he had her just where he wanted. "Does she know you were canoodling with her brother?"

Marishel's eyes widened. *Veda hates me. She wouldn't want me anywhere near him after what I did to Abrielle.* She didn't need to answer by the smile on his face. He had her—and he knew it. She folded her hands on the table. "He was following me, that's why I hid. It wasn't planned—"

"Sure looked like a lovers' tryst to me." He was grinning like a Cheshire cat now.

"Well, it wasn't. Right after that, I met the Ambassador."

"Out in the dark?" Gray-hair looked skeptical.

"We had dinner in the labyrinth." She needed to tread carefully.

"We don't have any footage of you by the fountain," he said.

Did she dare tell them she went to a private, personal nook with the Ambassador? None of this was looking good for her. Maybe she could tell a half-truth. "We didn't go there. He knew of another spot."

"First of all," Top Dog boomed, "there is no footage of you anywhere in the labyrinth or with the Ambassador. Second, all the other young ladies who've had dinner with the Ambassador have met him by the fountain. What do have to say to that?"

I don't know. "All I can tell you is that I was there. With him. He led me to the place; I don't know where it was."

Gray-hair looked sympathetic. "All public areas in the labyrinth are recorded, according to the Blood Match coverage."

She wanted to cry all of a sudden. She hated it. When she got so flustered and frustrated that she didn't know what to do—when she was so mad she could spit—Marishel tended to dissolve into tears. And she hated the way it made her look weak and pathetic. Not that she thought other girls who cried were weak or pathetic, but when it was *her,* she just couldn't see reason. She desperately blinked back tears and by Top Dog's gloating expression, her tears appeared to be an admission of guilt. Anger burned around her ears; she could feel the heat.

"What will the Ambassador say when we tell him you've used him as an excuse to meet your lover?"

Okay, now she was insulted. Marishel was not a liar, but they were treating her as if she was in the wrong, trying to back her into a corner. Her temper flared. "He'll say he was with me. And I already told you, that man is not my lover. He works in the greenhouse—" Marishel slapped her hand over her mouth as the men's brows raised and they looked at each other.

"So, he works in the greenhouse, and he has a relationship with one of the girls?" They looked way too excited about the news.

She didn't answer, but she didn't have to. She'd already said too much.

Gray-hair held up one finger. "Was this young man the source of the Paper's article?"

"Not as far as I know. He's just a young man who wants his family intact. Please don't … hurt him."

They looked at each other again. Top Dog nodded to his partner silently and turned to Marishel. "If you don't mind, we need to confirm a few things. Please wait here."

"So, I can go? I really need to get to class."

"No," Top Dog said definitively. "We'll be back." He pointed to the floor. "Stay here."

Did they think she was a pet?

Again, the nice-mannered Gray-hair asked her, "Is there anything I can get you?"

"Some water?" she repeated.

"Oh right. I forgot. Sorry."

"No problem." She smiled, trying to make herself look more friendly than guilty. This was not going well.

About fifteen minutes after the Coercitors left, she sat with her head on her folded arms, thinking of how this might play out. What if Quin didn't confirm what she said? A part of her felt ill thinking of Quin seeing the video. What would he think? Why did she care? She was thinking about Trae and wondering what repercussions would follow for him. With this kind of response after one article, how crazy were they going to be after one every day for two weeks? Would they fire him? Worse?

The door opened and Marishel raised her head. A young woman brought in a tray of lunch.

"Hi," Marishel said. "Thanks."

No response. She placed the tray in front of Marishel and left, silent as the grave. The tray had a pouch of water, a sandwich, and carrots. It was strange not to put her finger on the pad like usual and have the printer make her something designed for her. At home, they all had a pad on the printer in the kitchen. Mom programmed the meals, and each morning they all pressed their thumbs to their own pad. Though the meals were the same, the portions had the nutrition each member needed for optimal health and bone growth.

It also had small doses of Neupogen to increase white blood cell production, and a cocktail of Prussian Blue and DTPA which bind to any radiation and metals in the body to be excreted, according to the amount each body needed. It supplemented the annual radiation booster they got for living out in space. It blew her mind that the people living on the face of planet Earth—so much closer to the sun—could walk around unaffected by the radiation that sometimes made their hair fall out, gave them headaches, nausea, and ulcers toward the end.

She ate the tasty food, marveling at the new textures with the same tastes. When she finished her water and set down the empty packet, the door opened again, and the girl took her tray away. *Are they waiting on the other side of the door, just watching me?* Before the girl could close the door she asked, "Do you suppose I could use the restroom? I've been in here all morning."

The girl sighed. "Come with me." She followed the girl.

"Thanks," Marishel said in the hallway behind her. But when the girl didn't respond, she muttered, "Nevermind, I guess."

"I'm not supposed to talk to you," she said, facing forward.

"Why not?"

The girl stopped and glared at her. She spoke slowly, like Marishel was a child ... or an idiot, saying again, "I'm. Not. Supposed. To. Talk. To. You." Then she rolled her eyes and turned forward again. She pointed to a door ahead, on the right.

When Marishel reemerged, she wondered if there was any way she could sneak out of there—go back to the girls. Surely, they were wondering what was going on. The Coercitors could find her if they still wanted to talk to her. She thought she knew the way out of the building if she was right. But as Marishel stepped into the hall, the girl reappeared sans tray and led her directly back to the boardroom. She sat two seats over, just for a change. She stretched her legs out before her and bent down to touch her toes, stretching all the new muscles she'd gotten from training. She'd eaten a full ton of bananas to keep them from cramping.

Poor Marishel was back in her chair, drawing circles on the table with her finger, and bored stupid by the time the door opened again. She was even happy to see the Coercitors. They opened the door but stood outside. She heard Gray-hair say, "This way, sir."

Quin filled the doorway. Her stomach warmed at the way his broad shoulders filled the doorway, and the coiled strength that moved his long and lean body. The shadow was gone from his jaw, and he was dressed in State attire. She smiled at him, but he looked somber. Like he'd heard some bad news.

He walked to the end of the table and sat. The men had barely gotten seated when Quin folded his arms across his chest and said stonily, "Show me."

Top Dog looked nervous. Like he'd opened a can of worms he wished he'd left alone. Fiddling with the remote, the ocean disappeared, and the screen showed a dark space with leaves blowing in the wind. *No. Oh please.*

She didn't need to see the video again, so she watched Quin's face. She saw his eyes follow her pink dress across the screen and hide, they opened wider when Tanner entered the frame. He watched in silence—his jaw clenching and unclenching—a little muscle near his ear dipping and bulging. As he watched, his eyes narrowed. When he reacted with a sharp intake of breath, she glanced at the screen to see Tanner leaning into her.

Again, if she said anything, she'd be hurting *someone*. Quin looked at her. There was pain in his eyes. It stabbed her in the heart. She never wanted to cause people pain. "Quin, I—"

He put up his hand. She stopped. He got up, nodded at the Coercitors, and said, "Gentlemen." Then he strode from the room.

Top Dog didn't look as sure of himself as he had before.

"He told you I was with him, right?" She spread her open hands. "Right?"

Gray-hair nodded. "He did."

"So why did you do this?" she cried passionately. "You can't let me die in peace? Do you have to make it as painful for me as possible? You can't just kill me, you've got to humiliate me, too?"

Gray-hair looked sorry for her, but he wouldn't put up with her behavior. Top Dog just sat there. Maybe it hadn't occurred to him that the Paper was right.

"See here, young lady," Gray-hair said, "we're doing our jobs, and you're doing yours. Just try to stay out of trouble. And stay where the cameras can see you. It's for your own benefit."

My own benefit my ass. She nodded and said through clenched teeth, "Can I go now?"

"Yes," he said. "Find your group. And you do not need to discuss this meeting with anyone. It deals with sensitive subject matters."

She nodded again and shoved the table, scooting her chair back. They didn't have to tell her twice. She got up and walked out the door without saying another word. She wanted to find Quin, but she'd been told to find her group and she couldn't risk getting in trouble. There was still so much work to be done. And she wouldn't be able to do any of it if she was being closely monitored. Though she'd have to expect it for a few days. She'd lie low and in a couple of days, when the Paper needed more juicy tidbits, she'd figure it out.

"It's chore time," Sayra announced in the dorm doorway. *Yippee.* Marishel's group headed to the garden again. She peered into the greenhouse windows, needing to warn Tanner, but he wasn't there. Of course, the Coercitors probably had him. As long as Veda didn't see the video… Even though Marishel knew it was innocent, it was hard to see it that way from the recording. It looked like they were looking for each other in the dark, playing a game of hide-and-seek, and when found, they held hands and leaned closer… It didn't look good. To Veda, it could appear as though Marishel had gotten Abrielle killed just to steal her man.

Quin's face flashed through her mind over and over as she worked, his expression accusing her of betrayal. She was partly angry with him for making her feel wrong when she wasn't, and partly desperate to explain. She knew her words held little weight right now. Did he regret taking her to his secret place? The thought pricked her heart and constricted her throat. Why did she care? *She didn't want to.* So why did it hurt?

The time hardly passed before she returned to the dorm to change for training. As Marishel passed Icen by the door, he tucked a piece of paper into her hand, never once looking her way. She was pleased with their sneaky exchange and smiled as she shucked her flat slippers and sat on her bed. There was no way to read the missive without being obvious, so she left to find a bathroom stall.

The paper was light blue and the message cryptic.

RISHA,

I NEED YOU TO MEET ME TONIGHT ABOUT THE ARTICLE. URGENT.

TRAE

How was she supposed to do that? She'd already decided to lay low. But the note said it was urgent. Was he in trouble? Did he need help? Did he want to know something about tomorrow's article? She didn't know.

Marishel pocketed the slip of paper and changed for training. Her mind was on how she could possibly meet Trae tonight. She blindly followed the girls in front of her, letting her mind wander. She'd have to find Turpen. She wouldn't go out on her own. Not now. She needed someone important to have her back if she attempted this.

Outside, she took an electric baton from the training cabinet and a holo-shield that strapped onto her forearm. She was wandering into the group to find a partner when she heard shrieking to her left. What startled her most was that the shrill voice was shouting *her* name.

"Marishel! You defiled, wanton trollop!"

She turned just quickly enough to open her shield and meet the ax in Veda's hand. *Guess she knows.* The ax broke through the partially-opened shield and sliced her arm.

"Ow! Veda, stop! I can explain."

The rage in the normally shy girl's eyes was terrifying. She was unglued. Who would blame her after everything that had happened to her?

"Explain? You can't explain! Tanner is fired because of you!" she cried; her eyes wild as a horse's in a thunderstorm she'd seen on video.

"I'm sorry, Veda, I am. But it's not my fault. It was this video where Tanner—"

"I saw the video! And I'm going to *destroy* you! Screw the Match, you die today!" Veda switched on the laser edge of the ax and charged for Marishel, holding it above her head.

CHAPTER TWELVE

IS NOT GOOD TIMING

THE AX CAME DOWN ON MARISHEL'S shield again and again as she backed up and Veda advanced. She held the electric baton in her other hand but didn't want to hurt the girl any more than she already had.

"Fight me, you lying, cheating, piece of filth! You husband stealer, you dishonest, heap of trash. Fight me!" Veda was nearly foaming at the mouth, spittle flying everywhere, her hair bedraggled, and her eyes crazed. "You've taken everything from me!"

All the girls gathered around them, just watching. Tensions were so high that it seemed a relief to watch two girls beat each other—brimming with aggression—or even kill each other before the match. She could hear Rena and some of the other girls trying to calm Veda, shouting for her to stop.

Veda swung low. Marishel could tell it was coming from the collective gasp of the crowd, so she jumped back, but not far enough. The electric blade of the ax burned through her pants and made a searing cut across her shins and Marishel stumbled backward. She flailed her arms around, swinging the baton wide, but trying to keep the shield over her head. She lost her balance and fell back. She held up her shield as Veda rained blows on it, trying desperately to get around it to Marishel's head and neck. She came close, twice. The second time was too close for comfort and when the side of the ax sheared down her neck, she screamed.

Veda stood back and smiled maliciously. She held the ax above her head with both hands. "This is for Abrielle!" she shrieked, tears in her eyes. Beyond reason, beyond sense, she pulled back her arms, ready to strike her final blow.

"Veda Winly! Drop your weapon!" Sayra stood at the edge of the group holding a stun pistol. *How long has she been there just watching?* Why wasn't she helping?

Sayra held the pistol in both hands—pointed directly at Veda. "That's enough. Drop it. You've had your say and made your point. Now all of you! Find your partners and get to work. Now! Break it up, ladies."

No one moved—they glanced around wondering what would happen next. Then, Veda seemed to lose all her strength. She dropped her arms, nearly cleaving her own leg in two, letting the weapon fall to the dirt of the training yard. The girls slowly dispersed.

Marishel, still lying on the ground bleeding, said, "I'm *sorry* Veda. I was trying to help."

She looked into Marishel's eyes and said softly, deadly, "I hate you." Then she dragged her feet absently to the building, where she slid down the wall into a lump of sobbing despair.

Sayra stood over Marishel and put out a hand to help her up. "Come on, you need to go to the infirmary."

"Why didn't you stop her?" Marishel reached out and took her hand, rising.

"She had to get at least some measure of her aggression out. If she didn't release some of that pent-up rage, it was going to eat her alive. And she'd most likely kill you in your sleep. I had it under control."

Marishel grimaced at the thought. "But why do you care? Why'd you stop her at all? We're all dying anyway."

"I *don't* care. I have one job. To get you all ready, and to the arena, *hopefully alive,* in a week and a half."

"And if we're maimed?" She gestured to her injuries.

"I'm sorry to say, it makes the Match that much more exciting. Trust me, this fight will be airing tonight. Probably along with that unfortunate meeting you had with Abrielle's boyfriend. There will be new wagers: Will Veda seek you out in the arena? Will she find a way to get to you before then? Will you go first, or will she? People will vote for their favorites. You may have gone up on a scale or two, but surely Veda will stir up empathy, and that will earn you a decent amount of new enemies."

"Are the people really so shallow?"

Sayra sighed. "It's all a game. Just a game."

"Not to us!" Marishel gestured around to include her fellow contestants.

"I hate to say it, but in *this*, your votes don't count." She motioned toward the girls as well. "You all are the new sport. The new bridge of possibilities from a life in the Outerlimits and Farmlands to the Gentry." She put a hand on Marishel's shoulder. "No one cares about the ball in a ball game."

Marishel ground her teeth. "I. Am. *Not.* A. Ball."

"You might as well be. Get used to it. If not, when you're in the arena and the crowd is yelling for blood and death, you will stand there with your mouth open, stunned and enraged by their desire to see your blood spill. I've seen it before. And then someone like Veda will see you standing there impotent and strike you down before you even raise your weapon. Then you're not a ball, you're a number. Winnings gained or lost."

Blood dripped down Marishel's forearm, spreading to rivulets crisscrossing her fingers, and dropping from the tips. She inspected her shirt. The blood from her neck soaked the collar, and her shins ran red into her shoes. The sight of so much blood made her a little light-headed. Her eyes rolled.

"Rena and Shalise!" Sayra called, snapping Marishel out of her trance.

"Yeah?" Rena jogged over.

Shalise came from her partner. "Yes?"

"Would you two make sure Marishel makes it to the infirmary? Then come right back."

"Sure." Rena put her shoulder under Marishel's armpit and steadied her on one side.

Shalise looked sympathetic and gripped Marishel's other arm, cradling it like a baby. Sayra took their weapons, and the girls entered the building, leaving a trail of life-giving crimson fluid.

Marishel woke for the second time in the infirmary. Once they'd made it in and removed her sticky clothing, she could see the wounds clearly, and faded out. Which was just as well, as she looked at her arm and saw a wound sewn tightly together with clear stitches. They'd obviously treated her while she was out. Thank the stars. Clear staples zipped up her leg and a taped bandage itched her neck. She was wondering if she'd have to come back to get the staples removed when she realized that the wound wouldn't even be healed by the time they expected her to fight in a little over a week. Melancholy darkness covered her like she was coated in slick, viscous black oil.

It was tempting to sit there and mope, but she had secret things to do. How would she get in touch with Turpen? She decided to leave and sneak out of the infirmary before anyone knew she was gone, and slip out to… To what? She had no idea. The nurse came to give her another shot and before she could think of any more ideas, she was sound asleep.

As luck would have it, Sayra sent Sobia with a bundle of clothes for Marishel to wear for dinner. "Here. These should be comfortable with bandages."

"Thank you," Marishel said, accepting the folded cloth. Was this the dress of a past contestant? She wouldn't fit into one of Sobia's. She still needed an idea for escape. Then it hit her. She whispered passionately, "Hey Sobia! I need to talk to Turpen—to get a message to him—now. Do you have any way to contact him?"

Sobia looked pale and nauseous at the thought. She was shaking like a leaf. "I have my uBand…" She held up her wrist and looked around at the curtains surrounding them, then lowered her voice. "But I don't know… You are not supposed to using media devices."

"I don't have to do it. Can you just contact him and tell him I need to speak with him right away?"

She smiled a little brighter, stood a little steadier. "*Da*. I can do that."

"Thanks. I appreciate it."

When Sobia disappeared, Marishel tried to think of what she would say to him, but again, fell asleep.

The nurse roused her. "Dear, it's almost dinner time. I think you'll be fine. Go ahead and get dressed so you don't miss your meal."

The clinical whiteness in the room was nearly blinding in the fluorescent light. Everything had been so bright since she'd arrived. Technically, the inside lights here probably weren't any brighter than those at home, but her eyes had become sensitive. The *Relax-O* in the medicine cart gave her an idea, but she threw it out. She'd have to find another way to see Trae. She pulled on the ill-fitting dress and quickly re-pinned her hair to leave most of her curls down, attempting to cover her neck. Everyone would know by now what happened, but she didn't need to make a *show* out of it. She chuckled drily. *A show.* That's exactly what she was. In someone's newsfeed, she'd be someone's favorite and someone else's *bête noire*.

When Marishel arrived in the dining room, most were already seated, though others mingled and chatted politely—mostly in circles around the Leader's family members. Marishel was delighted to see Turpen there, sitting one seat away from Canon. She walked up. "May I sit here?"

Turpen pushed the chair out for her.

When she sat and laid her freshly bandaged arm on the table, Canon said, "What *happened* to you?" He leaned forward to see around her curtain of hair. "Gods, your neck! Are you hurt?"

"Shhh. Please keep your voice down." She looked around to make sure no one was listening and told both Turpen and Canon about her day, leaving out the note from Trae.

"That's crazy," Canon said.

"I don't want you to get in trouble, Canon. So don't say anything to anyone," she said.

"What about Quin?"

"What about him?" She cocked her head.

"He's been moping all day. Can't I tell him it was an accident?"

"He won't believe you if you do. Trust me. The way he looked at me this morning…" She shivered at the memory of the coldness in his eyes.

She didn't discuss her intentions or her involvement in any plan; it wouldn't be fair to make Canon lie to protect her. But even saying that to him would be an admission of guilt. She waited until Canon was busy talking to the flirty girl on his other side—in her usual chair—who couldn't stop touching his arm, then she whispered all about the note to Turpen.

"So that's why I needed to see you," Marishel said softly. "I don't know what to do. There's no way I'd risk leaving now, but he said it was urgent. I'm worried something could go wrong. I don't want Trae to suffer the consequences of running the story. It was my decision—"

"Stop." Turpen laid a hand on hers. "He made his choice to do this. If there are consequences for his actions, he earns them himself."

"But what do I do?"

"Hmmm." He bent his head closer to hers and said quietly, "You can *join* the group of young ladies helping to choose fabric this evening. I can tell Sayra you are coming with us, and if anyone asks, I am sending you on an errand."

"What errand?"

"We are hoping no one is asking that." He chuckled nervously. "My husband would shoot me if he knew I had a part to play in this. He was beyond livid this morning when he saw the Paper. I am not sure how much I can helping you. I do not want to compromise my marriage."

"I understand. Will there be anything printed?"

"Yes. Why?"

"Just tell anyone who asks that you sent me off to give a message to the designer. Then it won't be too odd if I go to the Pa—Wait. He never said where to meet him."

"You have met with him before?"

"Yes, but that was in the labyrinth. Surely, he doesn't plan to expose himself to the cameras around here after all that's happened."

"Ah, but he does not know about that, does he?"

Marishel wanted to dissolve into a puddle of despair, but Turpen flashed on his uBand and punched the keypad on his forearm. "I know executive editor at the Paper," he explained. "I will have him give your young man—what is his name?—a message."

"His name's Trae Skinner. If he needs help with the article, I might as well go to the Paper. And if you say I've gone to the printer for a design, it won't seem so suspicious."

"You are sure you want to be seen around the Paper with new articles coming out?"

"Oh. You're right." Marishel registered the end of Canon's conversation with the girl on his other side. They needed to think fast. She leaned a little closer to Turpen.

"I can tell him is not good timing?"

"Yes, please." She nodded. She hoped he wasn't in urgent danger, but there wasn't anything she could do.

Turpen typed his message and waited a moment for a reply, then closed the screen. "He will get message to your friend."

She nodded. "Thanks, Turpen. I had an idea when I was in the infirmary to spike the security team's coffee with laxatives. Not the stupidest idea I've had—but it wouldn't work. I wouldn't know what to do with the electronics once I had the security room to myself. And I can't afford to get caught."

"Do not mention it." He raised his brows to imply that she should follow his directions verbatim.

She needed time to think. She could leave now and take the long way back to the dorms and see if any ideas presented themselves. She saluted him and scooted back her chair, then stood and walked toward the door, but only made it a few steps.

Canon shot his arm out to catch her. "Where are you going?"

"Nowhere," she said lightly. "I'm just taking a walk. I'll see you tomorrow, okay?"

He frowned. "Don't get caught this time."

She didn't *try* to get caught the last time, it just happened. And she hadn't done anything wrong then. She would be more careful from now on, so she nodded to him solemnly and walked out. She looked for the Ambassador and found him watching her, but when she smiled at him, he turned his attention to Lonna on his left. That hurt more than it should have.

As Marishel walked leisurely across the back lawn, she took off her shoes and let the grass tickle her feet. The only lights came from the soft glow of the greenhouse next to her, and the spotlighted training building she was heading to. Her thoughts changed rapidly from worry to fear, to indignation about her innocence, and she chastised herself for worrying about her own skin when Trae had written her urgently. Was he in trouble? *Did he run the story without permission? Was the whole operation sunk?* Scenarios flew through her mind. One after the other, they became more gruesome. As the minutes ticked by her guilt grew. *Did he try to come to the estate? Did the Coercitors catch him? Did his father hurt him—or hurt his mother?*

She stopped behind the greenhouse and watched the guards pacing by the back gate. Should she go find him? How would she get out this time? Where would she start? She dare not go to the Paper. Maybe she could go to his house? She really didn't want to meet—

Suddenly a gruff voice said closely behind her, "You shouldn't be here alone."

CHAPTER THIRTEEN

PUBLIC EMBARRASSMENT

MARISHEL'S MIND SHOUTED "DANGER" AND HER body took control. She went limp and slumped against the figure behind her, sliding toward the ground.

"Whoa there." The burly arms of the maintenance man tightened around her and hoisted her up. "I was just giving ya some good advice. Never know who's out here."

Marishel stood on her own two feet and brushed down her front, irritated. "I'm sorry. I—"

"Don't mention it. You sure you want to be walking around in the dark?"

"Why would it matter? Killing me now would just be a premature relief. And no one's going to kidnap me." She laughed. "I'm not that lucky."

The older man smiled. "No, no. It's what they might think." He nodded his head toward the estate. "Don't want you getting in trouble."

"Thanks. But I'll be fine." She took a step back. "I'm just taking a walk."

Really, she needed to find another way out of the estate. Trae needed to see her. She said goodnight to the man and walked further into the shadows. Under a large tree, she thought she might be able to spot another gate if she got close enough to the bushes without making it look like she was scouting.

Despite the darkness, the sultry wind bathed her skin with warmth. Trying to appear nonchalant, she practiced the new moves from training, swinging a sword and ducking, running quickly, and stopping to turn on a dime. As she darted from shadow to shadow. she searched for telltale signs of a gate behind the bushes. She remembered the trick she was practicing with Shalise and did a run/jump combo, rehearsing the move. She'd catch the weapon, then tuck and roll. She was getting her borrowed dress filthy and sweat-stained. But she continued to sneak around the periphery of the yard, then the training grounds, until she was back at the gate she'd found before. Surely, she'd missed at least one.

Marishel crept back along the wall, trying to be inconspicuous—until she saw it. Another gate tucked behind the shrubbery. She got closer until she could duck between the branches and check it out. This gate didn't appear to be as rusty as the other, but it was hard to tell at night. She pulled on the bars, hoping against hope. Nothing. No movement at all. But when she pulled, an alarm sounded in the yard. She wasn't sure if it had anything to do with her or not, but she wasn't taking any chances.

She'd better get back quickly; it was getting late. At least she could use Turpen as an excuse for where she'd been. Trying to be as quick as possible, but unnoticed, Marishel nearly jumped from one tree's shadow to the next, headed back to the dorms. She heaved the door open with a sigh of relief, and the chilled air cooled her sweat.

In the hallway, before the closed dorm room, Lonna stood, her arms folded across her chest. "Where were you?"

"I was busy." Marishel put a hand on her diaphragm, willing her breathing to slow. "I was with Mr. Bello, as if it was your business."

"Mr. Bello's helpers all arrived *twenty minutes* ago. You weren't with them."

She fought the urge to push the girl aside. "Like I said, Lonna. I was busy. He sent me on an errand."

"What errand?" Lonna narrowed her eyes.

"I had to gather the designs for the printer, for the Blood Ball ... place cards." She hoped it was a detailed enough answer to shut her up, but Lonna was nothing, if not tenacious.

"But why did he send *you?*" she asked as though it was the most ridiculous suggestion.

"I don't know. Why? Did *you* want to go instead?"

"I think I did. Next time, I think, I'll volunteer to be your partner. He shouldn't have sent you out on your own. I'll have to tell Sayra if he's not going to be safe with *his girls.*" Lonna was the image of a cunning apex predator who was assessing her, so Marishel played it cool.

"Sure. I'd like the company." She smiled sweetly.

Lonna's expression registered surprise, but she didn't let that stop her. "Good. I'll let Sayra know I'm your new partner."

Marishel smiled weakly as Lonna opened one of the double doors, strutting, so proud of herself for throwing a wrench into any of Marishel's plans.

The next morning brought more than one surprise for the girls. The three of them sat at their table, peeling fruit and smearing their bagels, and spoke in hushed tones.

"I heard they're hunting for the reporter who made the article in the Paper," Shalise said, wringing her hands.

"Yeah. It must be stirring people up." Rena looked delighted.

"Do you think it will work?" Marishel asked. "Do you think someone out there will get angry enough to cause a ruckus? Or come up with a plan to cease the madness?"

"I don't know." Shalise shrugged.

"That's a good idea, but they may not care. We'd better have a backup plan anyway," Rena whispered.

"I'm working on it." Marishel had explored so many options, from kidnapping and ransom, to tunneling under the wall, to a mass exodus, to paying off the guards, trying to reason with the First, shooting their way out or taking training tools on the offensive, hiding everyone on Match day, setting traps for the ones in power... Nothing feasible. "Someone will think of something. I know I—we—will."

"We believe in you. Right, Lise?"

Shalise nodded. "I'll tell you if I think of anything. But if someone else comes up with a plan, how can we trust them?"

"Sometimes we have to give up control to move forward," Rena said. "It doesn't have to be Risha's plan, even though she's taking it all on herself."

"I'm sorry, guys. That's probably my greatest fault. I wish I could give up the power sometimes, but it doesn't feel right," Marishel confessed. "My grammy said the only fair way, was the way we make for ourselves."

"It's not totally your problem, so it can't be all your responsibility." Rena placed her hand on Marishel's arm.

Marishel sighed. "Well, until someone else comes up with a plan, I will keep trying. But I will try to practice giving up my influence, however foreign it may be. I mean, you guys are helping. I know I need to learn to give up a little control."

Hours later, Marishel sat between her friends, her head propped on her hand, elbow on the table. Sayra instructed the group regarding foreign diplomacy and how to behave as the future First. Then she lectured on the politics of testing and shipments sending prisoners and the affected to Sedna. *Why are they wasting time on this?* Next was the history of dwarf planet colonization—all things she'd been taught in school. She was lost in a dream world of escaping, to the soothing monotone drone of Sayra's voice, when the girls began to murmur animatedly.

She elbowed Shalise. "What did she say? What's going on?"

"Daydreaming?" Shalise asked with a smile.

Rena leaned over and said softly, "The idiots are excited. The dress fitting is this morning."

"But the Blood Ball isn't for another ten days!" Marishel whispered passionately. She felt her time slipping away and needed to get busy with stopping this match *now*. What could they do? What could happen?

"Calm down, basket case," Rena said over her shoulder as she turned to listen to Sayra.

Shalise put a hand on her arm. "It's okay, Risha, we still have time. They just need enough days to make the dresses. That's why the fitting is today."

Marishel thought of the lecture that morning on Sedna. "You guys, if we choose not to fight in the arena, they could send us to the prison station on Sedna and get new girls— just postpone the Match for another month."

Shalise paled and Rena frowned.

"Everyone, line up!" Sayra called.

Marishel sat in a large, stuffy, room with the other girls, each waiting for their turn. Five seamsters stood in front of them, brandishing their measuring tapes with flourishes of the hand. The girls were dismissed to mill about and have tea after their turn, so Marishel scooted to the front of the line, but Sayra decided to go alphabetically, and Vance was at the end. So, she listened silently to conversations going on around her, trying to inconspicuously pick up clues for the Paper. She stared into space as she filled in the gaps in her mind.

She watched as the cameraman flittered around the room, oohing and ahhing over all the girls and their visions of dream gowns, favorite color combinations, etcetera. Soon, there were only five left: Rorie Ullman, Marishel Vance, Unity Wyburn, Pemberlyn Yachowski, and Rena Yasuda.

Rena scooted over to the empty chair next to Marishel and whispered, "Did you get much intel?" *Of course, Rena has it figured out.* Marishel might as well be honest with her.

"Yeah. Did you know Vangie won the all-girls competition for swimming *and* archery? And her parents still weren't happy because she didn't win the final obstacle course. That's crazy. My parents would be ecstatic."

"Everyone has a different idea of what success looks like." Rena shifted in her chair. "My parents are traditional—they want me to settle down and pop out babies. If they knew I had a girlfriend, they wouldn't be mad, but it would change everything. Like when my brother, the scientist, announced he was going to Eris. You'd think they lost a child. My mother cried in his bedroom for a year. All their dreams for his future down the street changed in an instant. And people generally hate change. Not me. I like to shuffle the deck every once in a while for no reason."

Marishel laughed. "I guess that's what I'm trying to do here. Shuffle the deck. Wake them up."

The next open seamstress called Rorie, and Marishel turned back to Rena, but she was called right after that.

Marishel stood on a shiny black pedestal with her arms raised, and her back to a three-way mirror. A young woman with pure silver hair in a tight bun bent before her with measuring tape, judging the waist and length of her hem, when one of the double doors banged open. The Ambassador—Quin—filled the frame with his height and the breadth of his shoulders. He was built like a lean ballplayer. His short collar made his neck look longer and his jaw was clenched and sharp. Lean legs filled out his slim-cut pants with defined muscle. She chastised herself for feeling possessive of him. He hadn't made any mention of exclusivity and there were other girls here with the same thoughts. He scanned the room, obviously searching for something—but he didn't appear happy. He looked concerned, maybe even fearful, by the way his brows were drawn together.

Girls immediately clustered around him, trying to engage his attention or be his next choice for a date, but he continued to stride through the room, plowing through the throng with a scowl, and turning his head in each direction as he went. It looked as though he was a contemplative wolf, dragging his sheep behind him. She suddenly felt silly with her arms in the air. At that moment, their eyes met, and he pivoted in her direction. Whatever it was, it wasn't going to be good.

Oh, Kh'ra.

He stepped up to her.

"H-Hi." She laughed nervously.

"Get down." Not a request, a command. She saw fear in his eyes, though his frown could have been anger. "Please. You have been summoned."

She took his hand and stepped down from the platform. To her utter mortification, he gripped her elbow and walked quickly toward the hallway, nearly dragging her from the room. Quin hauled her through the door and pulled it shut behind them. When they were alone in the hallway, she wrenched her arm from his grasp.

"What are you doing?" she demanded.

He faced her with frustration, and she stepped back. "You have been called by the First. I figured you'd rather not have guards drag you out."

Either way, all of Haumea just watched her get dragged from the room by a scowling Ambassador on camera. She frowned. "Why?"

"Why what?"

"Why does she want me?"

213

"My mother ordered a meeting. It wasn't explained to me."

"Look, I'm really sorry about that tape. I wasn't lying. It was out of context. He was missing his sister and I felt bad for him, that's all. Quin, that's all."

"I know." He sighed. "I listened to the tapes. It's hard to hear, but it was enough for them to catch you saying, 'If I can stop the whole thing, I will.' As of this morning, you're being watched. Be incredibly careful."

"So, you're not mad at me anymore? Why do you look so upset? What do you know that I don't?"

He put his hands on his lower back and looked at the ceiling, taking a deep breath. "I might have questioned having the match—possibly stopping it—and giving me the option of a choice."

"That's wonderful," she cried.

He gently took her elbow again and pulled her several feet down the hall. She followed, taking her arm back and looping her hand through his elbow. After a few steps, she spoke. "So? What did she say? When you asked about having a choice, did she think that could be a promising idea?"

"To say it mildly, she did not."

"She doesn't want you to choose the girl who might make you the happiest? That's ridiculous. She should at least let you narrow it down to ten or something and let the other girls go home. How heartless for a mother to treat her son's future mate."

"She's still my mother. And the walls have ears—tread carefully."

"Sorry. I just don't get it. I know you only a little, but enough to know you're human like me, and we all deserve a chance at happiness. I wish we both had choices."

214

"Me too." He looked forward as they walked. "For some reason, you're the only one who I think would feel that way whether I chose them or not."

"What do you mean whether or not?" She gave him a smile from the side.

He chuckled as they left the dorm buildings and crossed the lawn to the estate's offices. A thought occurred to her.

"Did you mention me? Is that why she wants to talk to me?" Her voice shook. Once she realized Quin wasn't really angry with her, she'd been so relieved, she'd forgotten about the First's temper. "Is she furious with me?"

He held the door open to the office building and waited for her to enter. "I really don't know why she wants to talk to you, but I think she's put my request together with your disappearance and thinks you've influenced me in private. She knows we didn't have our picnic by the fountain. But I can't be sure what's going through her mind."

Her legs were quaking so violently that it was hard to walk. He put his hand over hers to steady her, but it wasn't enough, and she crumbled as her knees buckled.

"Come on. You can do this." Quin pulled her up and guided her to a plush chair in an alcove. He sat her down with a hand on her shoulder. She focused on her breath, pulling air into her lungs and pushing it out. *Here I sit— calm and strong. I am found—safe and sound.* She repeated the mantra her granny taught her to use on the rare occasion when her anxiety grew intolerable. Only this time she wasn't safe and sound. Did the First intend to cane her again or something worse? *What could be worse? Could she end me now?*

Quin knelt in front of her and took her hands. "I'm sorry." With the intensity of his stare, he communicated his regrets, and she understood his meaning. He was sorry for his mother, the lottery, the loneliness, the pain, the fear, the Match—all of it … for him. His jaw clenched with a fierce frown. "I'm so sorry."

She instinctively desired to lean forward, place her hand on his face, and pull him to her. In her desperate fear, she felt out of control. It was like a fire raged inside her and she wanted to live, to love—everyone, everything, she wanted to love all of Haumea before she had to go.

The thought brought so much pain—it crippled her heart. She was relieved to be seated or she would've fallen again. Marishel wanted to sob—and she hadn't even gotten to the meeting yet. How was she going to be able to do this? She had no choice. She was going to have to grow up quickly. It was time to leave behind childish wants and stop desiring things that weren't possible.

Grow up, Risha—fast.

She considered her ideas of adulthood and pulled them on like a suit of armor. *Grownups aren't hurt by silly things, they aren't consumed with boys or fear, especially when they should be thinking tactically.* Adults took things in stride. They stood up when they wanted to sit, worked when they wanted to play, and they found happiness in it everywhere they could, because time just kept rolling, day after day. They made mistakes and tried again— undefeatable—that was her parents.

She sniffed and sat up straight. Marishel wiped her wayward tears and inhaled deeply through her nose. She imagined the air was full of fortifying little microbots that would infect her and make her invincible. She stood regally, pulling Quin to his feet. *Undefeatable.*

But without power. The struggle was at war within her. She needed to be the leader, the one in charge, but against the First? She was woefully inadequate. She had no authority. The best she could hope for was to survive. Rena's words echoed through her thoughts. Maybe giving over command to the First was what she needed to do to win this time?

"Are you okay?" Quin stood over her as one might jealously guard a treasure. "What can I do?"

"Nothing I ... I'm fine. I'll be fine. This is just another meeting, and I can handle it. I will try giving up control to move forward, even if it kills me." She chuckled weakly.

"Everything will work out." He looked at her from the side as they walked toward the First's office. "There is something else I wanted to talk to you about..."

"Can you tell me later? I need my head on straight right now."

"Sure." He led her to an ornate door that was out of place with its finery. The frame was decorated with glass tiles in brilliant colors, and a small fountain bubbled against the wall. They stood silently, staring at each other.

"You ready?" he asked, squeezing her hand.

Marishel nodded and rapped lightly on the door.

It slid open slightly. "Enter, please." The controlled voice from the other side didn't sound as angry or scary as she thought.

When Marishel opened the door, she saw sharp and shiny silver instruments laid out on the First's desk with a pair of cuffs and a cane. Marishel's vision darkened, and the room spun. *Does she plan to beat me, or carve my flesh?*

"Miss Vance, come in. We have much to discuss. Son, you may go."

"I'd like to stay—" he began.

She turned to him and her normally composed, masked expression dropped to show a monster—a killer of girls—and she snarled, "You may go, *now*."

217

Quin, his face frozen in fear, turned wide, terror-filled eyes to Marishel, then he stepped backward with his hands in the Haumean peace symbol. At least he was smart and knew when to cut his losses—only his loss was *her life.*

Marishel was alone with the First and adult or not, she was terrified.

CHAPTER FOURTEEN

PARTNERS OR STRANGERS IN THE DARK?

MARISHEL STOOD CALMLY, OR PRETENDED TO, with her hands clasped.

The two women faced one another, but there was no battle of wills. The First was undoubtedly in control and said, "Miss Vance, the Blood Match is *my* contest. Do you understand? My son's wishes do not matter in this. You disappear and suddenly he is talking about destroying centuries of generational tradition and tearing apart *my* contest. This is a problem. Wouldn't you agree, Miss Vance?"

The First stalked around her opulent glass desk, picking up a shiny instrument of torture. The wall behind her changed and played with shapes of color and light, like a screensaver Marishel had on her *Eye*. It was soothing—or at least it used to be. Right now, it glowed behind the First, casting her as an angel of death.

She didn't know how to answer the First. She could lie and agree with the woman, but the First would think that rude. Or she could say what she really thought and risk any punishment in the whole planet. The First could send Marishel *outside* the planet—with or without a suit. The thought made her hands sweat.

The First continued as if Marishel had spoken, tapping the side of the silver tool in the palm of her other hand. "Right. It would be a most egregious offense. The people would be offended by my lack of tradition and heritage. You see, the colony needs the contest—it elevates the economy and morale. It's a prized tradition and the only way for most, from the sludge to Gentry. Besides, they desire for their future leader's partner to prove herself worthy of the position—and his love."

She motioned for Marishel to stand next to the coffee table before the sofa. "Do you know what this is?" She again tapped the instrument to her palm.

"No," Marishel answered as non-confrontationally as she could. Her legs shook in anticipation.

The First picked up Marishel's hand and turned it over. She appeared to hungrily study each finger and ran her own fingertip along the lines in Marishel's palm. "So dainty..."

"I'm sure Quin agrees with the contest—" Marishel began, but the First cut her off.

"Oh please," she growled. "Spare me the dishonesty. You have been nothing but trouble since you arrived. I don't know how your conscience deals with being the cause of that young girl's death. She trusted you." The First sneered at her. "You are a disease, Marishel. You hurt people."

The water rushed to her mouth and her tongue seemed to swell in her mouth. "I never meant to hurt her. And I never told Quin—"

Again, the First cut her off by holding up her hand and spoke with venom. "I'm going to ask you a question, and you will tell me the truth. Do you understand?"

Marishel nodded. She had a feeling it wouldn't be that simple. *What is coming?*

"These"—the First brandished her weapon–"are my truth-tellers."

Marishel was sweating. "Okay." She nodded.

The First pulled her hand until her arm was fully extended and slipped the end of Marishel's pointer finger through a circular opening until the tip pressed against a cool plate. The device was made of metal and had springs and levers. It looked like a kitchen tool, but she had no idea what to expect. The First tightened her grip on Marishel's wrist and asked, "Are you the one who turned my son against common sense? Did you turn him against the Match?"

Who would answer yes to that? Marishel's mind ran pell-mell considering what her answers might mean. She was stuck. If she admitted to it, what would the device do? Crush her? Electrocute her? Taking a deep breath, she answered, "Of course not."

The First smiled viciously and the pause was agonizing, then she chuckled maniacally and Marishel tensed in fear. She had no idea what was coming.

"Unfortunately—for you—I don't believe you," the First hissed and pressed the lever. The device hummed with power and forcefully chopped Marishel's finger off at the first knuckle, with a crunch like biting a carrot.

Marishel screamed and tried to pull her hand out of the instrument, but it wasn't done. A length of wire, glowing with blue heat, ran over the bloody, now-flat surface and cauterized it neatly. It sizzled as it sealed the skin and acrid smoke rose in the air and curled in the breeze of the air conditioner. She continued to wail as her stomach rolled, and her vision darkened. Bile clawed up her throat and light sparkled in her peripheral vision, the black vignette growing larger. As soon as her finger was released, Marishel leaned back and collapsed onto a chair. She sat there for a moment in a daze and the First allowed her to get her bearings as she rolled the tip of Marishel's severed appendage between her fingers.

Marishel was in shock. Her finger throbbed, sending pain signals to her brain, but there was no more blood. She looked down at her partial digit with a crusty black end. They could just take any body part they wanted. She belonged to these people. Before she could find an emotion for the thought, the First stood before her and picked up a remote. She pointed it at the wall and a feed appeared, looking down on a mob of people swarmed around what looked to be the front door of the Paper. They were yelling and angry. Stones and tools flew at the building, glass shattered and blood ran. The First clicked the button again to show the day's article and the five girls the anonymous writer had chosen for the spotlight. *Better keep sharp, she's setting me up.*

"I'm sure you know what this is?"

"I saw a copy from one of the girls, but the people were different. Is this a copy?" Marishel decided playing stupid was her best option.

The First snorted. She hadn't shared *why* the people were angry and Marishel was wholly curious. They could be mad at the Paper for messing with the Match. *Or they could be against the killing of innocent girls.* Marishel felt it telling that the First didn't reveal the object of their wrath.

Maybe she was affecting them after all. Hope flickered in her chest.

Marishel's cheek suddenly blazed with heat at the resounding *slap!* of the First's hand on her skin. The First smiled viciously like she'd caught Marishel red-handed, and she realized she had relaxed into a grin. She placed a hand to her cheek to stop the sting and felt nauseous as she saw her new left index finger up close.

"The people will not back you up. They *love* the Blood Match. I can't prove you are the source ... yet. But I will. And you will see how fast it ends for you. Standing at the Match without weapons—now *that* would be the best entertainment of the generation." She prowled to her desk and the cuffs jangled together as the First picked them up and motioned with them. "You'll have these on, of course. Here's a tip: tell your family to *bet high* on your death as the first of the Match, and they can probably change their status." Her words sent a sharp chill through Marishel's bones. She'd never seen anyone's hands bound in a Blood Match before.

"Your ladyship, I would never—"

"Save your lies, I have no need for them. This is a battle you will not win." She picked up a scalpel and crept across the room like a predator. Silver flashed in Marishel's vision as the First touched her non-swollen cheek with the end of the blade, her eyebrows raised in challenge. "I am the First around here and you are nothing but a good bet to lose. Oh, I was like you once. I thought I could beat the system, but it will eat anyone who tries."

"I wouldn't—"

The scalpel nicked her skin, and she sucked air in through her teeth.

"You may think you know what you're doing little girl, but you might as well save that spunk for the Match. I hear you're going to need it." She looked pointedly at Marishel's bandaged arm and neck, and Marishel's face burned. If she couldn't stop the Match, whoever won it would turn into this monster next. But how could she do it? Marishel felt the last of her hope drain away.

"Do you have anything else to tell me?" Marishel asked in surrender.

"No." The First's eyes squinted in hatred, her mouth twisting into a gloating smile. "You are excused. Stop filling my son's head with nonsense, or you will be detained until the morning of the Match."

She nodded and left as quickly as her jelly-filled legs would go.

In the hall outside the office, the Ambassador rose from a chair that wasn't there before. *He waited for me.* She couldn't stop the tears that fell, and Marishel felt her strength ebbing away—her adrenaline spike was crashing. *He waited for me...* She stepped in front of him, but her eyes drooped. Quin took hold of her arms as she wilted like a picked flower. She let him lead her numbly down hall after hall—she didn't care where they were going. He held her hand delicately and she chewed over everything the First had said. *She believes I've turned him from common sense? She believes the people's economy needs the Match, and she can't conceive of losing this battle of wills as a possibility.*

Catching Marishel red-handed would bring the First ... joy. Greatest of all, the First knew what kind of chance she had in the coming battle. The conversation swirled through her mind. It was more than a warning; it was a verified threat.

Quin stopped at a nondescript door and pressed his thumb to a pad. The panel slid open, but Marishel stood motionless, lost in thought. He pulled her by the hand and walked into the room backward. Her skirt, edged in pearls, swished the floor of high-pile carpet. It was luxurious, grey, and she wanted to kick off her shoes. She looked around the small room. A chair and matching sofa cuddled around a table of electronics under a half-shaded window. On the other side of the room sat a large desk, cluttered with tablets and screens. Marishel recognized the books from the labyrinth.

"Where are we?" she asked.

"My room." He gestured to another door that apparently led to his private room. She'd never seen a bedroom have an antechamber.

Heat flooded her cheeks at the familiarity, and she pulled her hand from his. "Why are we here? I mean, not that I mind, I just had my life threatened by your mother. I'm sure she wouldn't mind this situation at all…"

"Point taken. You just looked so … fragile. I only wanted to talk to you. But I can take you to the infirmary if you want." He looked unsure. "I have a first-aid kit." It sounded like a question.

"No,"—she smiled and sagged onto the sofa—"I think this is fine for now. I can talk. Tell me anything. I don't like my own thoughts right now."

He perched on the edge of the sofa cushion and pulled out a small kit from the side table drawer. Quin scanned her face, assessing her for damage. His face fell at her swollen, red cheek, then the cut under her eye. He gently dabbed it with a stinging ointment. His gaze roamed over her exposed skin, searching for injury, and lit on her finger, then rage took over for a split second. She watched his face contort as he wound the gauze around her fingertip. His following confusion broke her heart and angered her at the same time. He didn't want to think his mother could be the demon she appeared to be.

She shook her head and huffed a short laugh.

"What?" he asked.

"How did someone as nice as you come from such a sadist?" She chuckled wryly.

"She's still my—"

"—Your mother. I know, I know. I just don't see her ever being warm and cuddly."

"My father didn't have time for us. And though my mother did try, duty always came first with her, never what we wanted. Canon's the only friend I had in person, but I suppose I resented him for it. My spot of sunshine was Gran."

She was intrigued and waited for him to continue.

He wound the gauze around her finger as he spoke. "Gran had my father at age eighteen, so she was only thirty-six when I was born, and I got seven good years of memories to last my lifetime. She won her Match with grace but didn't enjoy it at all. She never showed off her skill in training. In fact, she was considered to be no threat at all, tiny and shy, she circled behind the equipment and twirled throughout the arena, swift and agile, brandishing her blade during the fight and hiding when she could, and in the end, she danced up behind the girl who thought she'd just won and took her in one slice. It was her only kill. Gran was a gentle and kind, soft-spoken woman of great faith. She prayed and sang to me. When her husband passed, she lived at the estate with us and taught me how to cook. Simple things, mostly." He squinted and shook his head. "I'm sorry. I'm sure you don't care about this right now. How are you?"

"It's okay," she said. "I'm fine. So, you're like your gran? That makes way more sense. Tell me what you wanted to talk about earlier."

"Hmm? Oh, I remember. I did what you suggested and started researching exactly why the colonies split. It seems like everyone 'knows' the answer definitively, but all their answers are different." He settled more comfortably next to her, their knees touching.

"How can we learn to make better decisions if no one tells us what truly happened? What do people think?"

"Some believe it was the testing and something to do with Eris not agreeing to the sequestered colony—"

"Well, what do they think we should do with the affected?"

"Live with them, I guess? But as I was saying, others say it was about our controversial gender and marital views, and still more think it was a disagreement of the leaders stemming from the distribution of better equipment and supplies to Eris. That made them feel like the superior colony. And everyone knows Makemake will do whatever Eris does. They had years of intermarriage at one point and most of them are related and still travel back and forth when orbits align. Their sovereign is Eris' king."

"Hmm. So much of our history has been hidden. Have you asked your father? What does he say? The Leader is a smart man; I think I would believe what he said."

"I haven't. I wanted to do this on my own to show him I can do it myself." Quin put his arm along the back of the sofa, and it brushed Marishel's shoulders. She was effectively surrounded by him.

"He might be waiting to see if you're smart enough to ask for help from the wisest and most knowledgeable first," she suggested, self-conscious of the way their bodies fit so well together. It would be too easy to get lost in his embrace.

"Hadn't thought of that."

"Mmmm." She was flustered by his warmth, his spicy scent, his beauty, and his lithe form. But she couldn't fall for him. Besides the fact that she had so much work left to do, it wasn't smart to get too involved with him. He still needed to fight for rights on his own—especially from his own parents. But, if they managed to stop the Match, she could use their collective influence to make real change. She could make people's lives better. A pipe dream. But as of now, he followed orders—right or wrong. Not like Trae. Her duplicitous emotions confused her more than anything.

Quin was the unwilling catalyst for her demise, but an invisible bond tied them together. Trae made her think of happy times, bright Summerland days, all that was good and wholesome—.

He shifted as they sat in silence. She was considering the best way to extricate herself, ready to flee, when he spoke. "I have something—I-I really wanted to tell you … um…"

"Spit it out," she said with a light laugh. "I'm not that scary." Then her face fell. "Unless it's something very bad. Am I in more trouble?" She creased her brow, and her anxiety rose to the occasion. "What did I do?"

"No, no." He held his hand out to placate her. "*I* did something. I don't want—. It was easier than I expected. I guess you were right, I can do more than I thought I could."

"Don't drag it out. Just tell me what you did." A million scenarios ran through her mind. What could he have done? Anything…

But her mind was blank. She had no idea, but it couldn't be good.

He smiled gently and took her tiny shaking hand in his warm palm, threading his long fingers through hers. "I petitioned the judicature regarding the annual debt and solutions, and I proposed they allocate funds from a dwindling department they were holding onto…"

He peered into her eyes with his deep green stare.

She was going crazy. "Well?"

His neck flushed and she could tell he was having trouble finding the words. It was definitely horrible news. She steeled herself, closing her eyes. His thumb rubbed over her knuckles.

"They've reversed the order for corporate mine ownership. Centra B's lease comes up next term, and your father will own it, to do with as he wants. He can sell it, lease it, keep it—it will be his choice."

Her eyes immediately floated in tears. The image of her father in the bright lights, wearing Summerland clothing, was foremost in her mind. He was laughing, rocking in the porch chair at Aunt Naide's—no at his own farm. He would finally get his wish, and in a small way, she had caused it to happen. It made all this pain worth it. For a moment. But her joy mixed with the sorrow of knowing that she'd never get to see it. He would never know it was her doing. Her body jerked and shuddered with a sob that escaped her. The pain was too great, her insides raw and bloody. She clung to his hand like it was keeping her afloat, her body shaking. Emotions roiled within her.

Quin tugged her closer to him, wrapping his arm around her. She latched onto his side, his arm hugging her back, and she cried intractably into his chest. He covered her like a fierce bodyguard and allowed her to weep until the intensity of her emotions sucked her strength and she nodded to sleep on his shoulder.

Marishel drifted on waves of consciousness, distantly registering a warm hand skating over her spine. She snuggled closer to her pillow and murmured, "In a minute, Mom."

"Wake up, sleepy girl," a deep voice resounded in her ear.

She didn't know where she was for a moment. Then she realized she was laying in the Ambassador's lap, curled up like a kitten. A lamp on the table softly lit the room, but the window was dark. Quin set his device on the table. How she longed for a device, or better yet, her *Eye*.

"What time is it?" She covered a yawn.

"Supper time."

She groaned. "Everyone's going to wonder where I was all day."

"Tell them you were with me." Quin helped her sit up but kept her close.

"Do you want them to kill me now?" She chuckled. "No, I really need to think of something."

"Don't tell them anything. It's none of their business."

"Girls don't work that way. They saw us leave together—I'll have to come up with something else." She tapped her tiny chin.

"Maybe say that when talking to my mother, you were given a task to complete, and it took you all day."

"That's good, but what task?"

"Do you think they'll pry that far?" His brows rose.

"Have you *met* Lonna?"

He laughed and shifted his position. "We need to go unless we want to walk in late."

230

She scooted to the edge of the cushion and stopped, turning to him. "Quin? About the mines… I-I want to—. I—" She looked down then peered up into his eyes and said with all her heart, "Thank you."

He touched her cheek with his fingertips. Staring into the windows of her soul, he put the back of his forefinger softly on the bridge of her nose, then drew it down the slope, gently tapping the end. "You're welcome," he whispered.

They leaned closer. Her lips parted. Slowly, so slowly, she closed her eyes and tilted her chin up. His head lowered and she could feel the moist heat of his breath on her skin. She inhaled him, already heady with the kiss-to-come.

Her skin tingled where his fingers brushed along her arm. Her senses prickled and sexuality crackled in the air like the charge right before a lightning strike. Marishel wouldn't have been surprised to find her hair standing on end with the electricity she felt. But she didn't care.

His lips nearly brushed hers—too lightly to feel—and he nibbled at the corner of her mouth like a butterfly alighting on a bloom. A thrilling surge traveled from her lips like a buzz all the way to her toes, and they curled up in excitement. He leaned forward, about to press his mouth to hers in an explosion-worthy kiss when a knock loudly banged on his door.

They jumped apart in surprise.

"Son, it's time for supper." The Leader's voice carried from the hall.

"I—" Quin's voice cracked, and he cleared his throat to say deeply, "I'll be right there."

Silence.

They waited, watching each other's expressions, then they shared a nervous laugh before hurrying out, looking both ways as they ran down the hall.

"Will I be in trouble if the cameras see me coming from your room?" Marishel asked as they slowed down.

"Nah. No one checks the cameras indoors. The, um, guests have open reign inside the estate—they just don't want you to leave without permission. Plus, you're with me and I can take the guests anywhere during the courtship period."

"Oh, so now you're courting me?" She grinned at him from the side.

Quin chuckled with a wink. "Couldn't you tell?"

Marishel felt her cheeks flush with heat. "Well, I don't think it's wise to be seen with you when I enter, so I'm going the long way."

He squeezed her hand. "I'll see you in there."

Quin entered the dining room near his family's residence, and Marishel walked around the library to come in from another direction. As soon as she was seated, she looked across the room at Quin, smirking like they had a secret. He grinned at her, and Lonna glared at them both.

"Hey." Rena poked her in the arm. "Where have you been all day?" she asked just loud enough for Marishel and Shalise to hear.

They huddled together as they waited for their food to arrive. Marishel told them everything … except the almost-kiss. That was hers alone. Besides, they were all here for him, and she didn't want to make anyone feel bad.

She told them about what the First had said during their meeting. "I don't get it," she said. "Why me? I mean, I'm just trying to save our lives."

"Maybe she feels like tradition is more important?" Shalise offered.

"Don't you see?" Rena whispered. "You threaten her. If you succeed and the people decide the Blood Match is killing people and it's wrong, then what does that make her? Would they petition to send her to Sedna? She may be despised by her own generation—openly."

"I hadn't thought of that. This is *more* than personal to her."

"It questions her morality," Rena said.

"It must be hard to make those choices." Shalise looked at the First with pity.

"If it's wrong, it makes her a murderer—a killer. But what's to stop her from killing me for trying to stop her? Nothing, that's what." Marishel sighed. She held up her bandaged finger. "She's already started to hack me to pieces."

"Oh my stars," Shalise whispered. "What happened?"

"The First decided I didn't need my whole finger anymore."

"You'd better be *very* careful," Rena said quickly as someone approached their table.

Lonna stood before them with her hands on her hips. *Joy.*

"Where have you been all day, partner?"

"Partner?" Shalise asked.

"Oh, did Mari not tell you? We're partners now. Sayra said so." Lonna smiled condescendingly with a tilt of her head.

"She doesn't go by Mari. She goes by—" Shalise started, then Marishel kicked her leg and she stopped abruptly.

Lonna waved away Shalise's words like gnats in a field. "So? Where were you?"

"She doesn't have to answer you," Rena said with barely concealed animosity. "Go eat your supper."

"Yes, she does. Or I'll tell Sayra I caught her sneaking in last night."

"What?" Marishel tried not to let the panic she felt enter her voice, but by Lonna's sneer, she didn't think she'd been successful. "But I didn't sneak out."

"I saw your dress sneaking around the lawn last night. I was on the balcony and watched you dart from shadow to shadow, so don't try to tell me that you were on a legitimate *errand*. And I'm betting they believe me. Where *were* you today?"

If they dug into the tapes, they'd see her checking the other gate... Marishel—sweating in her sea-blue gown—tried to behave nonchalantly. "I had a meeting with the First, and she had a list of things for me to take care of for her. I'm sure she would confirm it, but as it's *none of your business*, she might not appreciate your questioning."

Lonna looked like she was going to burst. But Marishel couldn't tell if it was because she didn't believe the lie, or because she did, and was angry at not being called herself. Either way, Marishel had better walk on the thin ice with care. There would be no leaving the estate now.

Lonna went back to her seat by Quin, and they ate. After half an hour or so, people began to roam about, guests leaving for home, girls going to the dorms, and others having coffee or tea and cake, when an usher brought a note to Marishel.

"Thank you." She took the paper and unfolded it to find one word.

PATIO.

She wrinkled her brow. The handwriting was unfamiliar.

"What is it?" Shalise asked.

"Just a one-word note that says, 'Patio.' I guess someone wants to meet me?"

"Do you want us to come with you?" Rena asked, concern etched in the lines on her forehead.

"No. No, I'll be fine." She smiled to herself. *Probably Quin, wanting to pick up where we left off,* she thought. She didn't need an audience for that.

"Okay. If you're sure…"

"Yes. I'm fine," Marishel said smiling, and the other two girls linked arms to leave together.

Shalise touched her wrist. "Don't be late."

"I won't be." *Just a couple of kisses…*

She looked across the room and Quin was nowhere to be seen. It just fortified her assumption that he was the author of the note. She smoothed down her skirts and pulled her hair back into freshly clipped sections. Satisfied that she looked refreshed, she stepped around the room to the ballroom and to the heavy drapes that rustled in the breeze of the open patio arches. Marishel pinched her cheeks, licked her lips, and ducked through the curtains onto the dark patio.

It took several seconds for her eyes to adjust to the dim lighting. She opened her mouth to call out for Quin when a hand clamped over it. "Hush," a voice whispered in her ear. Her eyes flew open in surprise, and she struggled, just to find arms clamped around her like iron bands, pulling her head back, and exposing her neck. She wriggled in vain, the grip around her tightening, and dragging her backward. She couldn't get to her feet.

The assailant was much taller than she and her little feet scraped the ground as she was pulled into deeper shadows. Marishel began to panic. This was *not* Quin.

CHAPTER FIFTEEN

CATCH ME IF YOU CAN

MARISHEL THRASHED AROUND, TRYING TO SLIP from the grip of her assailant. When that didn't work, she waited until they backed up, presumably to a wall, and kicked backward as hard and as high as possible—not that it was relatively high to anything—and she missed entirely. She tried again and hit something soft.

"Kerse it, Risha!" a voice hissed in her ear.

She knew that voice and she stilled instantly.

He chuckled in her ear. "I wish I could have seen your face."

The tiny flame of anger that this contest had ignited in Marishel blazed into an inferno. Trae released her and she spun, fury on her face.

"Aw, Buttercup," Trae said soothingly with a grin. "I was just teasing. You know I didn't mean any—"

She pulled back her arm and punched his shoulder.

He scowled at her. "I was just playing around."

She folded her arms. "It *wasn't* funny."

His face was full of sympathy as he rubbed the side of his arm. "I'm sorry. Buttercup, I mean it. I forget. I mean, I don't—but I'm just so excited to be near you and I didn't want to chance you'd scream if I scared you. I can't be caught here with you. That cameraman sees me and it's all over."

"Why did you send me such an urgent message?" she whispered, distraught. "I was frantic—"

He circled his arms loosely around her. "Relax, Risha. Shhh." His eyes twinkled with the reflection of the glow from the windows. He took her hand and pulled them further into the shadows. "Are you okay?" He rubbed her hands with his own as if they were cold. It was probably the warmest her fingers had ever been.

"Where's your finger?" His voice rose. "Where the faze is the rest of your finger?"

"Sshhh." She snatched her hand back and tucked it into her pocket. "A warning from the First. Don't get involved in this."

He frowned at her bandaged arm, then tipped up her chin to see the one on her neck. "What happened here?"

"Just training. It's been a really long day." She waved it away. "What happened to *you?* You said it was urgent? I was so worried—" she whispered fervently.

"I had to see you. I got you back in my life and we're doing this thing together and then you just sent me the files and I never got to see you." He picked up a curl and smoothed it behind her ear. "I've missed you more than you know. All those months together were … heaven for me—away from my parents and the … screaming."

Embarrassed by their proximity, Marishel stepped back and cleared her throat. "Listen, Trae. I want to collaborate with you, but we have to be careful. I missed you, too, but I can't lose the Match now because I'm taking chances I don't have to. Did you get anything back about the article yet?"

"Did we *ever*. People were hot. The Paper's going crazy. We're stormed with protestors—"

Her head shot up. "Protesting what?"

He grinned. "The Match."

"Yes." She beamed.

"But it was a little surprising." Trae cocked his head in consideration.

"What was?" she asked.

"Well, the people who were maddest were the parents, of course, demanding to know who was going to murder their daughters—"

"What did you tell them?" Marishel asked, her eyes like saucers.

"I said, 'I don't know *which* girl will be the one, ma'am. Fifty-nine girls are attempting to kill yours, but only a few people are making them do it.' And one woman about blew up over the feed. She said, 'That's blasphemy!' Can you believe it? *Blasphemy? Really?* Her face was red and puffy as a tomato. Ha!"

In Marishel's mind, Trae was having just a wee bit too much fun with all this. "You know this is serious."

"You think I don't know that? Whose life do you think I'm trying to save?" He took her chin in his hand. "Kerse it, I've missed your face."

She smiled up at him. "What was the surprising part?'

"What? Oh yeah. Lost my thoughts. The other mad ones were the Outerlimits folks."

"The Needles?"

"No, no. *Our* side's Outerlimits are uprising—but we didn't expect it. They usually play to the underdog. But get this, they were mad because we ran the article that slandered

239

the Match—not from any sympathy for the girls. My boss, Plank, says it's because so many of the lower tier use the Match for their livelihood or to get ahead, plus they don't need sixty-plus more kids running amuck five years from now—"

"But we're mining. There will be new room soon. Right?"

He cupped her cheek. "There's always an alternative solution in your mind, isn't there? Always a way out? You've never believed in destiny."

"I make my own." She thought about it. "Even if some deity knows what decision I'll make before I make it, it's still *my* decision to make. Right? Right."

"Then let's run away."

"What?"

"Let's do it. We could run away to the other side, they wouldn't—"

"That's the first place they'd look, genius. My family is there."

"Your dad works the mines. Maybe they could hide us there?"

"And what of the rest of my family? You know what they'd do. I could never live with myself if I knew my family lost everything they owned, living on the floors and grace of any relatives who would take them in until Mom and Baba could start over." *New clothes, new furniture, new home.* She'd been born in that home. She vaguely remembered the medical personnel and the way her parents' bedroom was arranged when Madi was born. Every holiday, every first event—and now every last—had been in that home.

"I know," he whispered.

240

Stars above, she missed home. The smell of it, the feel of it, the sounds of her family, her comfy room … the perfect place.

Silence hung heavy between them, and she wondered if that would seem like a sacrifice to him, or if he could even imagine being cold and homeless. Would he ever be able to hide in the Outerlimits? For some reason, she couldn't see him there with his tanned skin and open collar, and easy smile… Then why could she picture Quinlan at her table laughing with her family?

She shook the image from her mind. "So how are we going to do this? I thought maybe on the last day of the Paper, before the Match, we could ask the people to storm the arena or something?"

"That could work. Or the Coercitors could get word and be there to arrest anyone who tries."

She grimaced. "Yeah."

"Any other bright ideas?"

"Hey. At least I had one," she snapped.

"Whoa. Calm down, Buttercup. I was just teasing." He leaned back next to her and put an arm around her. "Any more brilliant ideas?"

She chuckled in spite of herself. "No. I just don't have any clue. I guess I'm hoping they get mad enough to call the Coercitors and demand they stop it. What if we had an anonymous line where they could, I don't know … vote against it, or something?"

"We could have a line to the Paper for opinions. That's actually a great idea. We could open up a spot on our feed for video calls…"

Marishel missed her feeds so much. She didn't realize how they had become background noise to her thoughts and actions. She was never without a playlist and music running, or a show she liked. The feeds were where everyone lived. It's where the news was, where gossips twittered, and where you could learn about things beyond your own rocky home. It was where she first saw the oceans of Earth teeming with life and its deserts and grasslands for miles and miles. She imagined lying in the grass, feeling the sun...

"...if they have any, they can leave them for us, and I'll print them alongside the article."

"I'm sorry, what? I missed that last part."

"I'll print them alongside the article?"

"No, before that. What are you going to print?"

"Oh. The opinions people give us about the Match— the unfavorable ones, of course."

She could see the light space where his white teeth shone in the dark as he grinned, and she smiled back. He really was taking a substantial risk for her just by publishing the articles, and she knew he was doing it for her. It made her feel special, but it also worried her that if she upset him, she might lose his help. He was more temperamental here in the city than he was in the Farmlands. It made her nervous. She also knew he liked her a lot, but it felt somehow conditional—but on what, she couldn't tell. She'd just have to be careful with him.

"I need to go," she said. It hit her all at once what she was risking by being here, and with him.

"You do?"

"You're kidding, right?" She tried to see his face in the dark to read it, but she couldn't.

Then his smile dropped.

"What?" she asked.

He ran his fingers through his silvery hair, stress etching harsh lines in his face, making shadowed planes.

"It's just that Client-Paper Privilege is holding for *now*, but the people want to know the source—"

She gasped. "*Me.*"

"I'd never tell on you, but they've been so persistent that my boss is having to take me out of the field, so I'm not harassed any more than I already am." He pushed her away and paced ahead for a couple of steps, then turned around with one hand in his hair.

"Trae, I'm so sorry."

He scowled at her. "The leader is concerned. He wants to look into it."

She felt fear prick like a hot pin at the back of her skull. "What does that mean?"

"For you? Nothing. Like I said: *Client-Paper Privilege.* But they can try to hurt me, or the Coercitors could require my testimony. And I only have one choice." Now he was pacing back and forth—away and back.

"What's that?"

He looked at her like she'd sprouted an extra head. "Well, think about it. If I don't tell them what I know, I go as a prisoner to Sedna… And if I do tell, I'll ruin any and all credibility I've gained—and will never work in journalism again. So, what choice do I have, Risha?"

"Hey. You're acting like this is all *my* fault."

"You asked for my help. Didn't you think I'd be compromising something to do it?"

"I guess I did. But you didn't have to say yes."

He threw his hands up in the air. "What would you have done if I asked you to sacrifice yourself for me?"

She thought about it, really wanted to give it some time, so she could properly empathize, but her silence seemed to irritate him.

"Right. I guess this isn't as two-sided as I thought."

"Trae. I never said—"

"You didn't have to," he sneered.

She didn't like the direction this conversation was going. She didn't like the look in his eyes. And the longer they stayed out here, the later it became, and greater was the chance that Lonna would come looking for her. Surely, she was searching at the moment.

"Look. I know you're upset. I think you should go home and—"

He snorted. "Home? You think *that's* where I need to go? You might as well tell me to go straight to hell, Risha."

She cringed. *Poor choice of words.* "That's not what I meant. I don't want to endanger you any more than I have."

He gripped her by the arms and held tight, like she was keeping him above water. "Do you? What do you want from me? Just tell me. I can't play these girlish games."

She was shocked by the ferocity of his speech. "I-I'm not playing games with you."

"Promise?" His grip tightened. She could see the fear in his eyes.

"I promise." She squirmed. "You're hurting me."

"What do you want from me?" He shook her shoulders.

Tears gathered in her eyes. "I don't want anything. I just want to live."

"So, you knew I'd be the one to manipulate, right?" His voice raised and she was glad no one was around to hear it.

She struggled in his grip. She was not going to be a girl who couldn't take care of herself. She steeled her emotions and looked at him. "Trae. Let me go. I know you're stressed, but this isn't you, you are acting like your father."

In the shadows, she didn't even see his hand coming until it had nearly struck her cheek. *Smack.* She stumbled and he kept her upright. She gasped and reached up to touch the tender and now bruising flesh.

He let go immediately. "Oh, gods. Risha. I'm so sorry."

"You need to go," she said softly. Clearing her throat, she said, "Now."

"You have to know I didn't mean—I never would have done that if—oh gods, it's true." He covered his face.

"I'm sorry, too. But you need to go." She turned for the stairs, ready to descend and cross the lawn when he grabbed her forearm.

"Let. Me. Go," she said, with deadly calm. "And don't come back."

"Risha, please. Give me another chance."

"Don't come back." She felt her heart break with the dissolution of all her childhood dreams as she ripped her arm from his grip and strode down the stairs into the lawn with tears in her eyes. Then it hit her. *What have I done? He's my best chance of beating this.*

Marishel ran back to the patio to smooth things over with Trae, but he was gone.

Laying in her bunk, Marishel stared at the ceiling, listening to the soft sounds of other sleeping girls—and a handful of loud snorers. She knew she needed Trae, but should she give him another opportunity? As much as she loved him and the *idea* of Summerland love, she had to let that idea go. She wanted to forgive him, and every instinct she had told her to give him another chance because she knew the real Trae, and this wasn't him ... except for the fact that it *was*. People weren't what they *said* they were, they were what they *did*. And she knew people like him.

Her uncle was one of those people. Her Aunt Naidelyn would show up black and blue and sometimes nearly dead. She always said the same thing: *you just don't know him, he is under a lot of stress, I made him angry...* Once, Marishel made him angry and he struck her. That was all it took. *Baba told her mother, "Now it affects my family, not just your sister."*

Marishel heard that her father had punched him out, but Baba would never admit to it. He went to visit her uncle and came back with Aunt Naide and her cousin, Prester. They pooled up their savings and moved Aunt Naide way out into the Farmlands where she and Prester could be alone—and safe.

Marishel swore she would never excuse a love interest—or any man—hitting her for *any* reason. And that was that. She could only hope he would still help her, but she shook with the thought that she may be on her own now. Hopefully, the work he'd done so far would be enough to propel a full rebellion from spark to explosion.

The next day in training, Sayra paired the girls, then strode to the weapons cabinet with a frown. Marishel and the other girls watched her, waiting for instructions. Sayra picked up an electronic clipboard and began pointing at each of the girls with the stylus point on the end of her finger. When she got to one name, she circled her finger in the air, going through the girls' faces once again.

"Who was the last to see Nahli Keegan?" she called out.

Vangie raised her hand delicately, like the perfect Ambassador's Bride. "I sat next to her at lunch."

"Did anyone see her after lunch?" Sayra shouted.

"She was with us cleaning the fountain, and then we were covered in grime, so we came back to wash up before training," Veda said.

"So where is she?" Sayra appeared to be asking herself. "I'll go check the dorm and be right back, girls. Choose a partner and warm up with some drills. When I return, we'll go through drills and then run the perimeter for cardio."

Many of the girls groaned, but Marishel was always excited to look for more ways to sneak out *or in.*

Sayra had been gone all of two minutes when an alarm blared so loudly, several of the girls dropped to the ground. Others, like Marishel, stood with weapons out, looking around for danger. She heard the back gate's heavy mechanism clank shut and guards went running to their posts. Icen darted out of the dorm building and over to the girls.

"Come on, ah, contestants. Sayra wants you in two lines. Just pick a line—stand behind these two. Right. Line up here, and here." It was hard to hear him over the blaring tone, but they formed two lines in front of him.

Marishel stood behind Rorie and shouted to Icen while covering her ears, "What's going on?"

He came closer to her, so he didn't have to yell so loud. "Kidnapping ... or escape."

The girls around them gasped and then began a game of telephone down the line.

"What will they do?" Marishel shouted.

Before Icen could answer her, Sayra jogged from the building. "You take that group and I'll take this one. They can help. Head toward the back way and we'll go around the building toward the front. All her things are gone, so look for anyone carrying baggage."

Icen nodded and told his line, "Follow me, ladies." Then he started a mild jog toward the labyrinth. "Keep your eye out for Nahli, or anyone suspicious."

"This way girls," Sayra shouted for her line to follow, waving over her head in the other direction.

Marishel took off, passing the first three girls, and jogged next to Sayra. "So, Nahli just grabbed her bags and took off? And we're looking for her?"

Sayra nodded curtly. "The exits are sealed. Everyone is on the lookout. She won't get far."

"I take it this has happened before?" Marishel breathed deeply to keep her side from stitching.

"Probably once every generation." Sayra looked about methodically.

"So, chances are high she'll be caught?"

Sayra narrowed her eyes. "Are you asking because your plans just fell through?"

"No. Of course not. I was just wondering what her chances are." Marishel waved away the suggestion that she'd even think about leaving.

Sayra slowed down and looked at Marishel. "There is no option but the Match."

Marishel really hoped she was wrong.

"What will they do to her?" Marishel asked.

"I'm not sure you want to know." Sayra turned forward, jogging with her mouth in a grim line.

They ran and walked alternatively around the building, but there was no one to see, other than the on-duty guards roaming in their own search. They passed an outbuilding with gardening supplies and the doors were open. The building reminded Marishel of Roman times because every few feet there was a column with arches leading from one to the other outside the creamy vanilla-colored stone building.

Sayra held her hand up silently and the group halted. She stepped gently to the door—the inside dark—and crept to the frame. Her fingers curled around the opening, and she slowly peered in…

Suddenly her head flew back with a shout as a guard walked out. "Checked in there. It's empty."

"Hmmm." Sayra stood with one hand in her short hair, making spikes, and looked around the area.

Lonna came up to Sayra and whispered something to her.

Sayra whispered back and Lonna nodded.

Marishel followed as Lonna stepped back the way they'd come and, at the edge of the building, pointed.

The space between the columns made shallow alcoves, and down the building of columns, there was a corner of fabric clearly sticking out.

Sayra lightly patted Lonna's shoulder, who smiled triumphantly at the other girls. Marishel rolled her eyes. *What are they going to do?* The girls stood nearby, mostly enjoying the break to stretch or just breathe.

Marishel watched Sayra walk away a couple of feet and speak softly into her comm. She was no doubt showing them the snapshot she'd taken from her *Eye* of the fabric sticking out. Poor Nahli. If that was her, she was probably standing there, scared stiff, waiting for them to leave. She wanted to go to her and tell her to change her mind before she was punished. She unconsciously took a few steps in that direction.

Sharp nails gouged the skin inside her upper arm and Marishel yelled out in pain. She looked back to find Lonna gripping her arm.

"Don't you ruin this for me," she hissed. "I found her first."

"I don't care if—"

"Yes, you do. You want to win as much as I do. I know what you're up to. You're trying to stop the match. I've heard the girls. But you're going to be one of the first to fall. They're lining up to be the one—trust me, you're going down."

"Don't be so sure, *Queen B.* Even you can't count on winning," Marishel said. "Battles aren't always won by strength alone." She pulled her arm from Lonna's grasp, causing the nails to scratch along the inside of her arm. It brought tears to her eyes.

Sayra approached them and whispered, "Okay, girls. Wait for the signal."

"What are we supposed to do?" Marishel didn't want any part in catching Nahli.

"We're going to flush her out, and the guards will get her behind the building."

Marishel was shaking her head when Lonna nodded and said, "Got it." She grabbed Marishel's hand. "You're coming with me, *partner.*"

Sayra crept forward in the shadow between the house and the outbuilding toward the fabric. Lonna pulled Marishel, who resisted her but stepped forward reluctantly rather than fall. Marishel could just make out the color of the fabric in the shade—it was blue—when Sayra took off in a sprint for the alcove. Lonna gave up and released Marishel to take off after her. They rounded the column to a chorus of screams.

"We've got ya!" Lonna crowed, but then her eyes widened.

Sayra had both arms raised like she was trying to scare her to death rather than capture the poor girl.

Marishel was shocked to see Nahli being pulled along and shielded by a medium-sized man and a small, round woman who ushered her toward the back of the building.

"No!" Marishel yelled involuntarily as she imagined the guards taking them down.

The threesome stopped and looked back. Marishel met eyes with Nahli and her father, who knew instantly why Marishel had cried out, and changed direction, pulling his wife and daughter toward the front of the building, barreling through the line of girls, past Sayra and stampeding in Marishel's direction.

"Stop them!" Sayra yelled to Marishel, but she moved out of the way for them.

Sayra started yelling to the guards and Lonna woke up enough to figure out her plan had failed. She pushed off from the place she had stopped, into a TV game-worthy sprint after the trio.

Marishel ran after her, afraid of what she would do.

Girls were yelling and calling to one another and to Nahli, who was being pushed and tugged along by her parents across the massive lawn. *Where are they going? Is there another exit that way?* Lonna was bearing down on them.

The mother kept looking back, slowing them down, and she was mid-stride when Lonna ran around and burst in from the side, tackling Nahli, and knocking her mother to the ground. Nahli's father, not giving up, grabbed Lonna under her arms and hauled her off his daughter, using his strength to toss her to the side. She hit her head on the edge of a large stone flowerpot and lay still. The man pulled up his wife and daughter as Marishel stood there, watching.

"Stop them! Marishel, stop them!" Sayra yelled again. But what was Marishel supposed to do? If she tackled that guy, he'd throw her to the Outerlimits. She stood there impotently, wringing her hands. She didn't want to be in trouble, but she couldn't do anything. She looked for Lonna, who'd been knocked out by hitting the planter—missing her own adventure.

Nahli's dad nodded at Marishel and ran away from her toward the dorm building. Sayra ran up to Marishel. "Why didn't you stop them?" she shrieked.

"What was I supposed to do?" she yelled back.

Sayra shouted her frustration. "Uhh!" Then she followed Nahli's family. "Come on, I might need help!"

Marishel ran behind Sayra just close enough to see Nahli's dad about to turn the corner of the building and skid to a stop with his hands raised.

Three guards walked around the building holding stun pistols pointed at the man's head, heart, and genitals. He backed up but stood protectively in front of his wife and daughter.

"Get down!" the guards yelled, and the man slowly lowered to his knees.

"Don't think about it," another guard said, walking around the group to grab Nahli by the neck.

Satisfied that things were under control, Sayra turned to the girls, all of whom had followed them, except for Lonna. Nobody had gone close to the girl. "Let's head back. I'll have to see to Nahli. You girls are free till supper."

"Why didn't they shoot her like Abrielle?" Rorie asked, pushing sweat-slicked hair out of her face, into a blond ponytail.

"Probably because they'd have to kill the whole family. Now, they will be in cells until the Match."

252

The group dispersed and Sayra went to take Nahli from the guards. Marishel walked over to Lonna on the ground. Her first desire was to kick her, but Marishel wasn't that kind of person. She wanted to do as she said she did, rather than proclaiming to be kind and treating others poorly. She knelt and brushed the hair from Lonna's face. She really was a pretty girl, when her face wasn't screwed up in disgust like it usually was. She'd seen how to do it on her feeds, so she lightly, well sort of lightly, slapped Lonna's cheeks to wake her up.

Lonna opened her eyes, her cheeks bright pink, and blinked a few times, looking confused. "Is this hell?"

"What?" It was hot, but not that hot. "Why did you ask that?"

Lonna looked at her and smiled unkindly. "Because *you're* here."

"Oh, ha, ha. So funny. Next time I'll leave you out here alone."

Lonna sat up and brushed mulch out of her hair. "Where is everyone?"

"We're free till supper." Marishel stood and straightened her shirt.

"Where's Sayra? Did they get her?"

Marishel sighed. "Sayra took Nahli back."

"She's going to be in so much trouble." Lonna smiled.

"You really are a piece, aren't you? No wonder I'm the only one who cared if your head was busted open." Marishel walked backward a few steps. "You're bleeding. You should go to the infirmary."

"I don't need your help," Lonna grumbled, standing up slowly and brushing off her clothes.

"Good. I wasn't offering." Marishel left and went inside to shower and change for supper.

While she was in the shower, Marishel wondered what they'd do to Nahli. That led her to think about her progress with the Paper … and that made her think of Trae and their last encounter. She hadn't expected that from him. She'd never even seen him angry, though he did always have some angst running just under the surface. All those months and years with her he'd been escaping the prison and violent learning ground he'd been raised in. She wondered about his parents. When they met—a lonely mine worker and a girl with a fortune—were they in love? Did he treat her well? Did she have a clue what kind of monster he'd be?

She thought about Quin and how close they'd gotten the few times they'd been alone, and she wondered if he was the same way. Was there a hidden danger behind the Ambassador? How would she know? She wondered if he were tested, *would he hurt someone? Would he ultimately hit her as Trae had?* Baba never hit Mom, but he was the strongest, gentlest person she knew. Was this the kind of thing she should expect? Her aunt surely hadn't suspected it. Was she being unreasonable? Was it more normal than she imagined? It was in so many books and real-life stories. Suddenly, it was important that she know—that she know exactly who he was, whom she was fighting for—whom she'd let in. She *needed* to test him—but they'd have to be alone.

Would he be in his room before dinner? She hoped so.

Marishel dressed in an off-white kaftan that had tiny silver buttons and little silver bells at the hem of her wrap. She hurried down the halls, jingling all the way. A quick rap on his door brought Marishel face-to-naked chest with the

Ambassador. She blushed every shade of crimson there was. "Oh. I'm sorry. I can see you are, um... Is this an inconvenient time? I can go if you—oh, duh, I should go." She turned to leave but he chuckled.

"Come in. I'll grab a shirt."

She followed him into the anteroom, taking in the breadth of his upper back and the way his shoulder muscles moved under his skin like stones under water. She let her gaze wander over his light brown skin, and she wanted to grab his narrow waist and lay her head on his back. She loved how his spine played hide and seek as he walked, rounding in his lower back. He stopped and she bumped into him.

"Oh. Sorry."

"Are you coming with me?" He turned and raised an eyebrow at her.

Marishel realized she'd followed him to the door of his room and was so mortified she wanted to play dead—just drop to the floor and pretend it didn't happen. Instead, she backed up with a chuckle. "No, no. I was just... I'll wait out here." She sat on the sofa and stuffed her hands in her lap.

When he came out of his room, he was pulling a black shirt over his chest, and she greedily watched his flat stomach ripple as he pulled it down. He didn't have to put on a shirt. He could have left it off. Of course, she wouldn't have been able to string together a whole sentence, but what are words when a body is art? What would it be like to run her fingers over his skin? Her fingertips tingled with the desire to skim over his derma with a feathery touch.

Quin sat next to her on the sofa and her heart drummed in her chest.

"What can I help you with?" he asked.

She looked into eyes like dark green glass and her mind wiped. She couldn't remember what brought her here to save her life. She looked at him blankly. "Uh, what are you up to?"

He chuckled. "Just doing some weightlifting."

"That's good. That's good. Um, yeah. Anything you want to talk about?"

He chuckled and leaned back putting his arm on the back of the sofa. "So, you just want to talk? Okay..." He thought a moment, laying his ankle on his opposite knee. "Tell me about the Needles, where you live. What's your job like?"

"Ah, home is much colder and darker than here. I live in a small Moroccan community. Actually, most of it is my extended family. My father's side all live in my neighborhood. My best friend, Yolenie, lives two house rows away. But the homes in the Needles are connected and on top of each other. Yolenie's place is on the top of her row, but I live on the bottom. *Our* house numbers are in chronological order, though, and actually make sense." She raised one brow at him.

"I guess you noticed the Gentry confusion, then?" He laughed and draped his arm across her shoulders. "When were you in the neighborhoods?"

Marishel's mouth went dry before she remembered her legitimate outing. "Ah, I delivered some information to Mr. Bello's house one day."

"Go on." He squeezed her, pulling her shoulder toward him and she felt safe, tucked into his side. "Tell me about being a seamstress."

She had a tough time thinking. "I already told you about my job."

"No, you told me you wanted to take over for someone named Hecate, or something, and that you got an apprentice. That doesn't tell me anything about what you do."

She chuckled. "I'm impressed that you remembered so much. It was, Harlene, by the way."

"Whatever works." His finger drew little circles on her arm and his warm body against hers was heating her delightfully.

She laughed softly. "My job is too tedious to go over now. You tell me something, instead."

"Okay." He reached across himself and picked up her hand, laying her palm on top of his. "Well, my father was pleased with the way I oversaw the mine business. He agreed that it would tamper with morale to take the mines away from the people after all this time, and the implementation I used instead for the budget ended up being more beneficial than the mines would have been. Then he actually *asked* my opinion on something he was working with in the homeless program because he knows I'm interested in it. I'm going to bring up the Match with him. Maybe he'll understand where I'm coming from or could give me a clue on any laws I could find to warrant ceasing the Match. I'll have to feel him out." He bumped against her.

"That's great." She was genuinely pleased for him. If he was going to be the Leader eventually, he needed to get started and figure some stuff out before the whole plate was his. It would help all of Haumea eventually, and she felt proud to be a part of that.

He paused and gently lay his head against hers. "I can't imagine not having you around. The thought of... We have to find a way to fight this."

She smiled up at him in surprise. He wanted to help her? What could he do? She admitted, "That's what I'm trying to do with the Paper."

"That was you?"

Marishel didn't answer. Despite how she was beginning to feel about Quin, fear clamped her jaw shut. What was she doing? He could be against her and drawing out her confession. She didn't really believe that, but she couldn't help her irrational panic. It was best if she didn't answer that out loud. If he was smart, he'd figure it out.

She heard shouting from outside and sat up to hear better. "What's going on? Is that about Nahli?"

"Sort of. News travels fast. The girl's parents tried to 'rescue' her today and apparently a group of their friends and family knew their intentions and had encouraged them. Now that the whole family is detained, the people who supported them have gathered outside the gates to protest."

"Protest? Really? They must be super mad."

He chuckled. "That's one way to put it."

"I hope no one gets hurt."

They sat in silence for a moment while Quin frowned. "What?"

"They came here to rescue her ... from me," he said. "Like I'm a tyrant or a monster who wants to eat her alive. *I'm* the object of their anger."

Marishel couldn't help but feel a giddy success about the protest. It had never been done that she knew of, but of course, it wouldn't have been televised if it had. She felt her emotions war within her; on one hand, she wanted to console his pain, and on the other hand, she was thrilled that more people outside this estate believed the Match was an abomination. Hopefully, more supporters would join them, and they'd raise a coup. Because if the Paper didn't work, she was out of ideas. She prayed that Trae would still help her. Suddenly she remembered why she'd come. *To test him.*

"Whether you want it or not, she will lose her life for you in a matter of days. Can you blame them? They just want their baby to live, and you *are* the reason."

His face fell as if she'd purposely broken his favorite thing. She second-guessed her plan. She didn't want to hurt him, but she had to see what he'd do if she pushed him as far as his limits would go. She steeled her emotions.

Quin pulled his arm back and stood up. He stood in front of the window and braced himself on the sides of the frame, his forearms flexed, his head down. "I am responsible for this," he whispered. "Whether by choice or by force, it is because of me … but I want to fight it—like you are."

She had to make this personal if she wanted to really dig deep. "You can't complain. You get to be the bachelor extraordinaire and do whatever you want while girls are stripped of their feeds and told to wait on your household hand and foot. Then, you can take advantage of whatever girls you want for a month before they all perish for you, and you get to marry the winner—the best. How hard can that be?"

She watched him start to steam as the anger ignited and blazed inside him. "You don't know what you're—"

She cut him off. "Sure I do. I know what's happening here. You need the best of the best to rule. It makes sense. You've got to marry someone who can be cruel, but who can sit next to you and smile as she poisons your dinner party—a liar, a cheater, a killer—someone like your mother."

He turned and stood in front of her shaking with rage. His hands were clenched, and his face was red. Maybe she'd pushed him too far? He breathed in great gulps with difficulty. "I did not make this rule."

"Well, just enjoy it."

He turned around and faced out the window, gripping the frame with white knuckles. Should she push harder? He'd had the opportunity to hit her and hadn't, even though she'd pressed him. She was sure that he was enraged. But was that enough?

"You think I enjoy their pain?" he asked softly.

She thought about it. *No.* She didn't. She didn't think even if she insulted everything he loved that he'd hit her. That wasn't who he was. It shocked her when she realized that she hadn't been overly surprised when Trae had slapped her. It hurt, but from where he came, it wasn't shocking. If she'd heard someone say Quin had hurt them on purpose, she'd wonder if they told the truth. It would indeed shock her to know he had. That's what she needed to know.

Suddenly, she felt remorseful for what she'd said. Marishel rose and walked to stand behind Quin. She could feel the heat radiating off his body. Inhaling his sandalwood, spicy scent, she wrapped her arms around his waist and laid her head on his back.

"I'm sorry," she said. "I didn't mean those things. I just needed to know—"

He spun around and she stepped back. "Needed to know what? Was this some kind of test? Like I'm a liar? You think I've been ingenuine with you? I have gone out of my way to be friends with you, and you think it's a good idea to call my mother a killer? What's wrong with you? What did you hope to accomplish here? What was the test?

To get me so angry I-I—what did you think I would do?" he shouted.

"You're right," she said, clasping her hands. "It wasn't fair. But none of this is. I'm sorry I made it worse. I just wanted to know if you'd—."

"What?" he shouted. "What in Haumea would I ever do to you?"

"I don't know. I just needed to know if you would hurt me, at all." She spread her hands. "You're right. It was stupid. I just needed to know if you'd be the same."

He took a step in her direction, and she quickly took a step back.

"I'm not going to hurt you," he said gently. "Did someone mistreat you?"

She nodded. "Someone I cared about. It took me by surprise. I needed to know if it was normal—if you were the same."

She sighed deeply and Quin reached for her shoulders. He pulled her to him and held her with his chin on top of her head. He inhaled and she was glad she'd just showered. She snuggled the side of her face into his body. The heat melted her, and his arms sheltered her. She didn't think she'd ever felt so safe and warm at the same time.

"Quin?"

"Yeah?"

"I'm sorry. You know that, right?"

He quickly pressed out his breath. "I guess."

"If I can't find a way to stop the Match, what are you going to do?"

"Don't worry about it yet. I'm fighting with you to the end." He stiffened a bit. "Is there some other agenda I don't know about?"

"No. I want to save our lives—and you deserve a choice as much as me." She felt his body relax.

"Yeah."

"Yeah what?" She looked up at him.

"Oh…" He peered down at her. "Yeah, I want a choice. And I'm thinking of a possible loophole. We'll end this somehow. Together."

CHAPTER SIXTEEN

FAUNDA'S CLAIM

THE GOSSIP THAT EVENING WAS ALL about Nahli Keegan and her parents. They'd been taken into custody until the day of the Match, when Nahli was scheduled to enter the arena with the girls, and her parents would be watching by feed.

Sarver and most of the important people for the Match were noticeably absent from supper.

"Where's your husband?" Marishel asked Turpen.

"The production group is meeting for damage control." His voice dropped to a whisper. "You are getting people riled up. You are knowing the plan yet?"

"No." She sighed. "It's up to the First, and I have a feeling nothing I do is going to change that."

"Have you tried appealing to her woman to woman?" he asked.

"Oh, we had a talk, but it was more like her telling me to stop entertaining the idea of survival." She held up her finger, the end bright pink and swollen. The scab had crusted, and bits were falling off, and what was left was angry and sensitive.

"Oh my. Have the other girls agreed to throw down weapons in the arena?"

"Ha. That's laughable. All of the top tier believe they have the best chance of winning." She smiled. "But when we watch the top tier training, my friends and I have been talking to the losers, suggesting that they may not have the odds to win that they thought they did. We've recruited a few, and a few that are conditional."

"What do you mean? What conditions?"

"Well one girl will agree not to fight if another girl will, but she will only cease if another one does. It's like a line of dominos. If the right girls lay down their weapons, we have a chance. But the tension is so high, I'm afraid some of the girls are going to come out slashing everywhere."

"This is a problem. How can I help?" Turpen's eyes were kind and looked at her as a little sister.

She thought about it, but nothing came to her. "If you can't change his mind, just keep Sarver distracted. That will help. Oh, and use Lonna for whatever group you need. She's following me around like a bloodhound."

"I will see what I can do."

The next morning, Marishel arrived in class, yawning, to see five stations set up around the room with divergent backgrounds, each sporting Haumean art depicting their flag. Every station had a huge umbrella light facing a chair in front of the backdrop. The girls murmured about their speculations until Sarver Bello waltzed into the room with a calm smile.

"Today, ladies, we begin a new campaign. With five days left, we need to drum up some more support and squash any—" He stopped with a frown as if he'd almost said something he shouldn't. "We will start an epic campaign for the watchers to follow."

"What do we do?" Vangie asked.

"When it's your turn, you will sit for the camera and read the card you're given. That's all. Simple really."

Marishel didn't like this. It was an attempt to bring the Match back to a game and wipe out the talk of killing. *She wouldn't do this.*

"You'd better say it, or you'll find yourself bunking with Nahli until the Match," Sayra answered when Marishel voiced her opposition to the words on her card. "It won't be a fun time."

"I can't say things like,"—she looked at the card—"*I'm honored for this chance to prove my worth as the future First, and Ambassador's Bride.* It's not true. Surely everyone will see around this?" Marishel sat in front of a colorful depiction of the Haumean flag with five golden-yellow circles for the five colonies, theirs in the middle around the *Sanger Orbiter7*, the ship they'd originally arrived in. The bottom half was blue and the top half, white.

"Just read it." The man with the camera rolled his eyes. "Only don't sound like you're reading."

Marishel tried to do as she was told, but it was impossible to smile into the camera and say, *I'm so happy to be in the Match this generation...* She could almost get through the first sentence, then her smile would drop. "But I'm not happy or honored," she said.

Rorie gasped next to her. "That's pure and blatant blasphemy."

"No." Rena threw an arm over her shoulders and smiled on with pride. "That's just Marishel."

"Does he think people will be dumb enough to fall for this?" she asked Sayra, nodding toward Sarver.

The cameraman snorted. "People will believe anything they *want* to. Has nothin' to do with bein' smart."

"I can't do this," she said again.

Sayra glared at her. "At this point in the game, the pressure is high, and the punishment may not fit the crime. Are you sure you want to find out?"

Marishel remembered her last punishments. Her back had healed in the past weeks, and her finger had oozed a new scab cap, like a little mushroom, but they were not experiences she intended to repeat—ever. Not purposefully anyway. She tried several more times until she was ready to cry. In the end, with tears in her eyes and a wobbly smile on her face, Marishel told the planet how happy she was to be honored for the opportunity to be in the contest—and in the resulting film, she appeared to be so moved by her honor that she was patriotically tearing up at the thought of her happy participation.

When they gaily showed her that part of the promotion, so proud of her, she wanted to be sick. But the editor whisked it away to play on the feeds. Marishel prayed to whoever was listening that it did not reverse her efforts to make the girls into people rather than pawns. *And please, please, don't let Trae do anything stupid in his anger.* She knew she'd walked out on him and she of all people should know how much he needed a friend, but she couldn't be romantically involved with him. No one was going to treat her that way. Not even spiky silver-haired boys with sad blue eyes.

Marishel grunted as the punch landed in her stomach. "Sorry Risha," Shalise said in her tiny voice, laying a hand on Marishel's bent-over shoulder. "You've got to watch for that move. It gets you every time."

"I know," Marishel wheezed, looking to see where Sayra was and who had her attention. She was busy helping a pair of girls involved in a race through the obstacle course, yelling directions. Marishel watched her arms trace the movements as she instructed them on how to move.

"Have you been working on Lonna and Vangie?" Shalise asked softly as she bent down, pretending to adjust her shoe.

"I've been trying with whoever loses the trials, but they both think they're going to win. I know Vangie's started practicing like she's been holding back the whole time. Did you see her run those sprints?" Marishel shook her head. "Her feet were on fire. Even Lonna looked a bit ill. How's the lower tier?"

"Rena and I have it. And most of the rest are following. Those two,"—she nodded toward Lonna, dodging Vangie's side kick—"have pretty big shoes to fill and most girls are smart enough to realize that whether one or the other wins, it *won't* be any of the rest of us. It's easier to fight the system than each other."

"Good."

"They want to know the plan. I told them I'd ask again." Shalise looked up at her through long, black lashes. "I heard that if we don't fight, they throw in hungry fight dogs.

Marishel sighed. "I know." She clasped Shalise's palm and pulled her up. "There are a million slim-chance ideas, and none that stand out as particularly easy or plausible. I've got the paper working for me at the moment, hoping for a public reaction, but beyond that, it's still up in the air. There's not much we can do with our lack of resources or influence. Just tell them that I'm checking out every option and keep those suggestions coming."

Marishel was really sick of only thinking and talking about the same things over and over. It was much more tempting to get lost in the heady pleasure she felt remembering Quin's arms around her. But that was especially why she needed to keep her head in the game and bring her thoughts back to solving this puzzle.

They tossed around a few more possibilities until Shalise said, "What about—?"

"Hit me."

"Huh?" Shalise cocked her head.

"They're coming. Hit me." Marishel put her hands up, and they worked up a satisfying sweat. They worked on their two-man trick; Marishel was just beginning to master it. Shalise knelt on the ground and Marishel ran up to her, jumping to step on her bent knee, and propelled herself higher. Marishel generally caught the weapon Shalise threw to her, then she flipped above her friend and performed a tuck and roll landing. Three times out of five, she succeeded.

They rotated the courses in the training yard. When they were completely beaten and noodle-armed from archery, Sayra blew her whistle, like the sound of a fork screeching across a plate, making Marishel cringe. She was just releasing an arrow when the sound made her jerk to the left. "Hey look at that, Rena," she cried. "I made a bulls-eye!"

"It doesn't count when it's on *my* target, dork." Rena snorted.

Marishel hung back, intending to speak to Icen. To be honest, she'd expected to receive an angry note from Trae after she'd been so curt with him. The girls filed in the door after replacing their training equipment. Marishel laid her compound bow and its quiver of training-tipped arrows in the case.

"Hey," Icen said.

"Have anything for me?"

"Nope. You expectin' something? I can look out for it."

"No, no." She waved away the suggestion. "I was just checking."

She trudged back to the dorm room slowly, giving the first girls time to get out of the shower. Marishel dug through her belongings and found a dress for dinner with dark red draping folds. The bottom was edged with a thin band of golden silk. The hem cut higher across her legs in the front than the back, and gold clasps gathered the fabric at her shoulders. She pulled out a sparkly gold belt and slipper shoes and laid it all on her bed.

"Hey." Rena stood next to Marishel, in a towel, her blonde hair dripping all over the floor. Lines creased between her brows.

"What's wrong?" Marishel asked.

"Shalise is still in there. I don't know what to do. Girls in tears make me nervous."

"She's crying? She was fine an hour ago. What happened?"

"Something about a date, and a bunch of sniffling and sobbing. I didn't get much. I came to find you."

"Okay. I'm going. She's still in the shower?"

Rena nodded and Marishel grabbed her toiletries, then headed for the bathroom. She found Shalise huddled under the showerhead as far away from the door as she could get.

"Hey, Lise." Marishel stepped into the shower stall next to hers and turned on the water. When it was hot enough, she let the water stream onto her back and turned toward the partition. "What happened?"

"It's so stupid. I know I shouldn't care. I know I'm being a total girl, I just—" Shalise tried to stop the new tears, but she was obviously beside herself.

It made Marishel feel protective. She wanted to rage at whoever would say something so hurtful and cruel as to injure a sweet girl like Shalise. She tried again. "I'm sure it's not stupid. If it hurts this much, you have every right to be upset."

"Really?"

"Absolutely." Marishel nodded once, resolutely.

"No. It's stupid. I'm just a dumb girl."

"So? We're all dumb girls. I tried to sneak Abrielle out and made everything worse. Lonna doesn't know she's dumb, and Rena is just dumb on purpose…"

Shalise relented with a small laugh.

"Come on. Who said what? I promise I won't judge or call you dumb."

Shalise hedged. "I'm so embarrassed."

Marishel waited, folding her arms over the silver frame of the frosted partition, but kept her eyes on her friend's face. "Go on."

"Okay. Well, when we got in here, we were all talking about the Ambassador—Quin—and our dates, and Faunda said she had a late breakfast date with him this morning. So, Lonna insinuated that they'd gotten up late, together, for a big breakfast to sustain them from … nocturnal bedroom sports."

Marishel didn't care about all the details—she was about to come unglued out of curiosity, but if she rushed Shalise or upset her, it would take the girl three times as long to tell the story.

"So Faunda got really nasty and said only Lonna would know, but she bet he hadn't kissed *her* yet."

"What?" Marishel's full attention was aroused.

"Yeah. Faunda said they had a romantic breakfast in some secret place, and he kissed her. It's just—he's been so nice to me, and he's … well, the whole thing is about *him* anyway, isn't it? I told you I was dumb." Her voice dropped so low, Marishel barely heard her over the water. "I actually thought he might really like me."

So did I. Marishel struggled to keep her composure. Apparently, neither one of them was as special as she thought. It was a kick in the gut, but what had she expected? He was a bachelor with sixty doting females willing to do anything to stay alive. *How many of them have tried to make deals with him?* she wondered. How many had thrown themselves on him, begging for mercy? She realized she hadn't responded and saw Shalise's sea-green stare gauging her response. Marishel frowned, her brows bunched together comically. "He shouldn't play favorites," she said. "He should have to kiss us *all* now. I'm going to protest! Pucker up, lover boy, here we come…"

Shalise dissolved into a fit of teary laughter. Marishel turned her back to Shalise and ran her hands over her own shoulders like a couple making out. "Oh, Ambassador! You're so … pretty." Marishel laughed. "You should be a model!" she continued, taking pretend photos of Shalise.

"You're so brave and smart, and all the perfect things we want, wrapped up in one boy we can take home to..."

It was getting a little too real and Marishel stopped. Shalise looked like a sad puppy picture that Marishel once taped to her wall. It said: *Missing you is all I do.* It hadn't been sent by anyone, she'd simply seen the photo and the look of heartbreak in the puppy's eyes and thought, *I want someone to miss me that much.*

"I'm going to wash my hair. You finish up, and we'll go to supper. Okay? So what if she kissed him? We knew this would happen, right? And the winner *should* feel something for him. If only we could all have a choice..."

"But I'm not going to be the winner, and I feel something for him." Shalise's expression was of tortured guilt.

"Maybe you wouldn't win in the fight, but if we manage to throw a wrench in the works and he gets a choice, who's to say he wouldn't choose you?"

"You really think so?" Shalise looked like a little girl being told all her dreams would come true when she grew up.

"I'd pick ya." Marishel winked at her friend. "Now, hurry up, this water's starting to get cold."

"Aye aye, captain."

Marishel was decked out in crimson waves and Shalise showed every curve in a black, off-the-shoulder number embellished with bright red and purple flowers traveling from one slim hip to the opposite knee, where the black fabric flared out into folds that swung when she walked.

"Sashay that bunk," Rena said.

"You're not bad yourself." Marishel whistled as Rena held her palms up to shoulder height and turned around. The deep purple of her *Cheongsam* parted on the sides to expose hidden pearly white panels down each leg and matching white cherry blossoms were embroidered on her left breast.

"We're drop-dead gorgeous, girls." Marishel put an arm around each friend and pulled them in close to her. "I will never regret being here with you two."

"Yeah. If I gotta kick it, I'd rather go with you guys." Rena threw her arm over Marishel's shoulders.

"Aww, Rena," Shalise cooed. "Write your poetry for me."

Rena snorted. "You saying I'm not eloquent? Girl, I'm the classiest." She held out cupped fingers. "Just watch. I'll have the Ambassador eating out of the palm of my hand."

"You do that." Marishel released them. "Lise and I have given up on him. Right, Lise?"

Shalise nodded somberly. Marishel knew that she wasn't over it, but the best thing to do was move on, and work harder to find a solution.

"I'll take suggestions," Marishel said, with a scowl.

A few of the girls were brushing their teeth and as excited as they were to be part of a plan, none of them seemed to have one. In Marishel's mind, if you couldn't come up with a solution, you had no right to complain about the ideas of someone else, trying to solve the problem.

"Maybe we could all just grab our things and leave at once that morning? They'd only be able to stop so many of us…" one said.

"It's not like they'd stop running when they hit the gate, stupid. They'd still catch you," another girl sneered.

"And what about the rest of us who don't make it? Will they make us fight each other or get new girls?" still another girl cried.

"What if we kidnap the Ambassador and hold him for ransom until the First ends the Match?" Rena stood behind the rest, who had all stopped brushing and stared at her open-mouthed. *"What?"*

"Nevermind," Marishel said. *"When I figure it out, I'll let you know. And keep those ideas coming."* She looked at Rena who opened her mouth. *"Not you."*

"What if..."

Back in the hall, they reached the dining room but as soon as they entered, Turpen Bello stood and walked over to meet Marishel. Rena and Shalise looked at her questioningly and she smiled, waving them ahead to the table. "I'll be right there."

"Marishel," he began.

"Hi." She grinned, but he didn't return her smile. "What's happened?" Immediately her stomach dropped to her feet. *Who was it? Mom, Baba, Madi?* Her mind flashed to the farm and Aunt Naide, and she thought of Trae. Surely not...

Turpen took her elbow and steered her off to the side of the room, by a wall covered in rich gold fabric that draped in the middle. Marishel reached out to touch it instinctively. The smooth, cool sensation worked to calm her nerves.

"Tell me," she nearly begged him.

Turpen's Russian accent thickened with his anxiety. "Is your boy, Trae, from the Paper. Has anyone told you? No, they would not. He has been taken into custody. Is not good."

CHAPTER SEVENTEEN

STICKY SITUATIONS

MARISHEL GROWLED HER FRUSTRATION. "OF ALL the stupid… Of course, he would go and do something rash and irrational. I knew he would get involved in something— I left him enraged. He strikes out when he's angry—oh— who will run the articles now?"

"Trae's boss is my friend. He believes in the campaign, so *he* will continue to run articles, but you do not understand." Turpen stood in front of her, both of them with a shoulder to the wall. The lighting was low and the room quiet, so they spoke barely above a whisper.

"What? What did he do?"

"He must have seen the new promotion. Sarver pushed it pretty hard. You were brilliant, unfortunately."

"I know. They had me so mad by the time we finished, I looked ready to do about anything to be done. Including being happy to be honored as a future First…" she sneered.

He chuckled and touched the back of her hand. "Careful what you say—ears are everywhere."

She nodded. "Please tell me. What did he do?"

"He tried to fix the mess. He engineered his own channel that came on over the promotions and reminded people that our future leader does not need blood of fifty-nine girls on his hands before he takes office."

"Wow."

"*Da.* He said he cares a great deal for someone in Match—someone better than him, who deserves the life she has—but he could not say so for everyone." He looked pointedly at her. "He said she was worth his life, and he was to fight the Match, calling others to join him, but message was cut off there. So, there is no plan, no meeting place—people who are stirred up are not knowing what to do. They will be louder when they learn he has been taken by Coercitors."

"Oh my. I must have really hurt him."

Turpen lifted her hand and placed his other one over it. "My sister Tamberlyn would have love for you. She would have been a best friend and you two would have beaten the Match together. She never wanted to go... The night they drew her name was first night I'd ever seen my father cry. She left on train the next morning—we watched her every show. We were addicted to catching glimpses of her, trying to read her body language to see if she was miserable. Tamberlyn did not hide things from people. What's that they say? No filter? That was her. We watched her train and she improved, but she was never in top tier."

"Like me. Ordinary."

"Yes, like you—and *not* ordinary. I never got to hug her goodbye. I was a young man then and didn't realize when I patted her back at the train station, that it was my only goodbye. I guess in my head, I always thought I had time." He chuckled. "Such is life? Yeah? We always think we are having more time. Not using time in the moment is our biggest mistake."

"My time is running out. And I don't have any idea what to do."

"What is the best idea you've got?"

"Kidnap the Ambassador and ransom him for the end of the Match."

If Turpen had been drinking, he would've choked. "Sshhh. Are you suicidal?"

She laughed lightly. "You asked for the best idea, I didn't say it was feasible." She saw Turpen stiffen slightly as he looked at someone behind her, and he dropped her hand. Marishel took the cue and said, "Yes, I really thought the promo came out nicely…"

"Hello, partner. I haven't met your friend personally." Lonna stepped up next to Marishel and held her dainty hand out to Turpen. "Lonna Kyrel. Pleased to meet you."

Turpen took her hand and bent over it, pressing his thumb to the back of her hand in the symbol of acceptance. "So pleased am I," he gave the expected response. It struck Marishel that Haumea was all about heritage and tradition. *What they need is a new tradition to take the place of the Match.* She'd think about it.

Lonna released Turpen's hand and threaded hers through Marishel's elbow. "I thought you might want to sit next to me tonight."

Marishel narrowed her eyes. "Why?"

Lonna leaned over to whisper in her ear, "Because I think you're planning something, and I'm going to stop you." She looked into Marishel's eyes and said softly, "I will win." She stepped back and smiled sweetly at Turpen

277

with a little fake laugh. She took in his kilt-like clothing and necklace, being obvious. "Girl business. *You* know."

Turpen's face registered shock at Lonna's blunt statement. Marishel felt like Turpen was a friend and she bristled at the comment. "He's gay, Lonna. Not a girl."

"Yeah, yeah." She waved her hand in the air. "You hungry?" She began to pull Marishel away, but Marishel stood her ground.

"I'll be right there," Marishel said through gritted teeth.

"I'll wait."

Marishel sighed. "I'll talk to you later, Turpen—I mean, Mr. Bello."

"You don't have to stop talking on *my* account," Lonna said with mock innocence.

"Oh no. Of course not. I always like to have my private conversations in front of an audience," Marishel grumbled.

"What is there to talk about that's private around here?" She smiled. "We have no secrets."

Marishel shook Lonna's hand off her arm. The time to be sensitive was over; it was time to be stern. "Lonna, I said I will be there in a minute. You will *not* wait here. This is a private conversation between Mr. Bello and me. Unless you are saying you think Mr. Bello is suspect? Are you accusing Mr. Bello of being *insubordinate?* I'll have to tell Sarver and Sayra."

The edges of Lonna's mouth turned down severely. She pursed her lips and narrowed her eyes, glowering at Marishel. Then, she broke out in a smile so sweet, you'd never believe she knew what a frown was. "Of course not. Don't be silly, Mari. I'll just wait for you at the table."

Lonna turned stiffly and strode to the table to take her seat next to Quin, where she glared holes through Marishel—who ignored her entirely.

278

"Where are they keeping him? I need to help him."

Turpen put his hand up. "Don't worry. I made sure he was alive, if not unharmed. I knew you were going to say this. You cannot do anything right now—is too dangerous. Too many eyes are here." He nodded in Lonna's direction. "Besides, I do not think she is letting you get very far."

"But he's in there because of me."

"He is there because he knew you were forced to make that awful recording and he tried to do damage control best way he knows how. He made his choices—do not waste his sacrifices with impulsive actions. What would he want you to do?"

"Stay here and ... push them all down. The point of training is to get ready. So, what can I do to get ready? How do I plan when I don't know the plan?" She felt a tear of frustration escape from the corner of her eye. "What do I do?"

"I can't tell you this. Is something you must figure out. Not that I do not want to—or have great logic I am leading you to. I do not know. But I have faith that when time comes, you are knowing what to do." He picked up her hand and bowed over it. "I know it. I believe in you, Miss Vance. There is something about you—open, honesty, I do not know. Trust? No, *hope*. You do not give up yet, and you will not."

"I'll try not to."

"For all our sakes, I hope you succeed. These girls need you. I am knowing many of them now, because of you." He flashed a smile at her.

"But why me? I mean, I need a hero, too—just as much as these other girls. What makes me the champion? Why can't there be another warrior—like Vangie or someone strong?"

He chuckled. "Do you see Vangie or any other 'warriors' here fighting for the little guys? Is she doing battle for other girls' freedom?"

"No."

"Why not?"

"Because she doesn't need a luminary? She's her own paragon of strength, for crying out loud. She already knows she can win."

"No. She would rather be home than this contest—just like you. I bet she is not excited about killing any of you, but she will if she must. She is probably hoping for her way out, too. Would you want to being the winner and know you killed other girls to get there?"

"No, but that doesn't answer why it has to be me."

"Is simple. Because you are the one willing to do it— the one girl who is obliging, one who will finally stand up and say, *if what I need isn't here, I will* make *it happen.* This is you. You are the one doing what everyone else *wishes* they could do. Is not a chore, is an honor. When time comes to recognize who was bravest, who never gave up, who won the outcome everyone else wanted, then *you* will be winner. You will finally be happy it was you. And all the other girls will say, *I wish that was me … why can't I be the winner?*"

"They could be the winner. Anybody can."

"Everybody can … but only one will. And the rest will ride the waves of your success. Is the same for all way-makers. Look at bright side—this is Marishel's story. No one can be taking this away from you—if you do the work, you will achieve impossible things."

"Thanks, Turpen. My dad says something like that. And thank you for telling me about Trae. He's got a good heart, I know it."

"Of course. I need to go—you have a lovely meal." He winked at her with a chuckle, and she groaned, remembering her seat next to Lonna. She glanced over and Lonna waved at her, gleefully reminding Marishel that she was always being watched. *How am I going to do this?*

Marishel pushed the food around her plate, listening to Lonna titter away. Quin leaned around her once and tried to engage Marishel in conversation, but though she hated to admit it, she felt a little stung by Faunda's kiss. She'd thought they'd had a moment together, but apparently, he was having "a moment" with *everyone*. It made her peevish, and though she tried to rise above it and smile, she wasn't interested in looking into his eyes and feeling ... well, whatever she felt when he was around. How had she even begun to care for him in only a month?

When supper was over, Marishel got up to leave, but Quin was suddenly in front of her. "Can I talk to you?"

"Sure." She smiled weakly.

"Are you okay?" He squinted his eyes.

"Oh." She laughed it away. "It's nothing."

"Well, I was hoping to speak to you in private..."

They both glanced over at Lonna, kissing the First's feet conversationally.

"I have a new partner. She goes where I go." Marishel frowned.

He smiled. "I have an idea. Be right back." He darted away and came back in less than a minute. "Okay. You remember how to get to my room?"

She nodded. She couldn't help the feeling of excitement in doing something clandestine, even if she had to give up the dream that she meant anything more than any other girl. Really, what did she have that sweet Shalise didn't? Or brave and beautiful Vangie, the warrior goddess? Or the hilarious and spunky Nahli? *Nothing.* She was nothing special and if she wanted to save her heart, she'd better get it through her head.

"I'm going," he said. "Meet me there in a few?"

"What am I going to do with my escort?"

"Don't worry about her. Try to sneak out, though, if you can."

"I will." She breathed deeply. This was what brought her alive. Adventure, intrigue, excitement, danger, risk. It made her heart beat like the rhythm of a freight train, pumping blood through her, whooshing in her ears. She'd just never known it until the Match. Of course, it had nothing to do with Quin's magnetism, or the way she tingled when he touched her, or the thrill of being in his room. Surely, he hadn't taken *all* the girls to his bedroom? She chose to believe this meant something. Maybe he had a new plan to help her fight the Match? The idea buoyed her spirit.

She watched him leave and when Lonna was fully occupied, Marishel crept toward the hall leading to the family quarters. She swayed as she walked like she was dancing to the music that played through the speakers. *Nothing to see here, nothing going on, don't mind me.* When she finally rounded the corner to the hallway, she stopped to breathe a moment. She leaned back against the wall and felt the thumping of her heart with her fingers.

Lonna came running around the corner and nearly knocked her over. "There you are! I saw you leave. Where are we going?"

Kh'ra.

He'd said not to worry about her, but did he mean in the dining room? She didn't know. What should she do? Should she go back into the dining room and wait for someone to draw Lonna's attention, or should she keep going? She had to think quickly.

"I'm just taking a stroll through the lawn."

"You could go out the—"

"I wanted to go this way. It's quicker to reach the greenhouse."

"Who's in the greenhouse?" Lonna asked with a fair amount of sass.

"Why don't you go find out?"

"I intend to. Let's go."

Nervous and sweating, Marishel walked slowly down the hall, hoping for an answer. It came in the form of the Second. She smiled as Canon emerged from a doorway ahead of the girls and walked up to them holding a folder.

"Hi," Marishel called.

"Oh, Marishel. I'm so glad I saw you. Can you take this file and put it in the financer's box, by his office door? It's down that hall to the left." He pointed in the general direction behind him.

"Sure. That's no problem." She took the file. "See you later."

"See you, *Second*." Lonna walked past him with Marishel, but Canon caught her arm.

"Actually, I need you to help me with something important."

She looked incredulous that he would touch her and held her arm out like it was a foreign object. "Thank you, but I'm busy. Besides, why are you working this late? Shouldn't you be in bed?"

"He's *thirteen*, Lonna. Not a child." Marishel shook her head. *People.*

"Okay," he said. "Nevermind. My mother told me to look for you, but I'll find someone better suited to the job."

To his credit, Canon called her bluff and began to walk away.

"Wait." Lonna took a step in his direction, looking back at Marishel, obviously torn. "The First asked for me?"

Marishel waited patiently for Lonna to decide, afraid if she pushed her too far it would backfire.

Lonna heaved a sigh. "Well, if she asked for me, it must be important." She turned to Marishel. "I'll see you in the greenhouse."

Marishel's smile was genuine. *Thanks,* she mouthed to Canon. He patted her shoulder and grinned at her.

Marishel lifted a tiny fist and rapped on Quin's door. She heard a shuffle and then melted at the sight of his smile as he opened the door and grinned broadly when he saw her. He held the door open. "I have so much to tell you."

"Yeah?" she asked, ducking under his arm and walking into the anteroom.

"Yeah." He shut the door and motioned to the sofa. "You're never going to believe this."

She perched on the edge of the sofa and gripped her knees. "Tell me." She was ready for a piece of juicy gossip.

"I did it." He smiled, obviously proud of himself, but Marishel was lost.

"You did it?"

"Yeah, I talked to my father."

"Oh! How did that go?"

"Well, I told him I definitely didn't want to have the contest."

Marishel opened her mouth, but he held up a hand and continued, "He said he was pleased I'd taken an interest and was making some important decisions for the state of Haumea, but that choosing the best woman was impossible to do. 'They have to be tested,' he said."

Marishel frowned, but he smiled and said, "I told him I might like one more than the others…"

Faunda's freckled face played through Marishel's mind—her stray frizzy hairs, her loud abrasive laugh. But then she was reminded of Faunda's smooth accent, brilliant tan, and the exotic tilt of her eyes. He stood there smiling at her like he'd shared a big secret. She couldn't think why he would be telling her this, or why he expected her to be happy about it. Except for the fact that the boys she knew were notoriously dense when it came to the feelings of girls—especially competing girls. By telling her about it, he'd undoubtedly placed her in the "friend" category.

"So, what did he say?" she asked.

His face fell. "He said, 'Then I hope she wins.' Can you believe that? I didn't know he could be so insensitive. He said, 'Maybe you should train her yourself? Sarver would love it.'" He grunted in disgust.

Marishel was imagining Quin on the training field with his arms around Faunda, pulling the string to her bow. She grunted as well. "How is all this good news?"

His brow bunched, but he went on. "My father is concerned about the people's unrest. The good news, I guess, is that he actually took my opinion—and he said he respected my effort. And the people are getting stirred up. He knows how I feel and maybe if I push the issue, I can make a change."

"That is great news. He is beginning to trust you." Maybe they could beat it together. "Maybe you could talk to him—"

"I told him I wanted a choice… He said he understood, and he looked like he meant it, but then he just said he was sorry. Like that was the end of it."

Marishel got up and crossed the room. She looked at the cluttered desk and folded her arms. "He of all people should get it. Killing the competition doesn't make you the best anything. You should have a choice … and I should get to grow up."

"What's really wrong?" He spoke from right behind her and she jumped. Marishel backed away from him. "I can tell there's something you're not saying."

Like what? She'd been pretty vocal that she knew of. How could she possibly explain that she was upset about him and Faunda? They were only friends, after all. She had to know he'd do what he wanted with any of the girls. It shouldn't be a surprise. How could she explain for the millionth time that she was upset about the Match in his name? She couldn't pile that on him again. It wasn't his choice any more than it was hers. "I'm just angry at the whole thing. You know that. I can't stop it." A little voice in her head wanted to shout, *and you don't have a chance of winning,* but she tamped it down and stood on it. She wouldn't admit defeat, though the threat orbited her.

"Hey." He stood in front of her and looked down into her face. "I don't think I believe that anymore."

"What?"

"The more I get to know you, the less I believe you can't win. You're smart and tenacious. Like my Gran. We have options. It would just be so much easier if we succeed. To have my choice…"

She was stunned to hear his praise and answered in a far-away voice, "Yes. I'm sure you two would be very happy."

"What?" It was his turn to appear out of the loop.

"Faunda."

"What about her?"

"The kiss?"

"With you? Well, it wasn't quite a kiss." His lips curled into a grin.

She looked at him like he was a moron. Did he really kiss them *all?* She shook her head and sighed. "No." Suddenly she was very tired, and she wanted to sag. She backed up to the wall and felt the doorframe against her spine.

He stepped closer and picked up a curl from her shoulder. "Tell me." It was more of a question than a command, as he smoothed the curl over his finger.

It was nice—to have someone pay her attention, to touch her hair. But it wasn't her that he wanted. She said with distaste, "Faunda told everyone about you kissing her on your *secret date.*"

He threw his head back and laughed. She was so insulted, her temper immediately flared to life, and she glared at him.

"That's what's bothering you?" he asked jovially.

She scowled and crossed her arms. "It's not *bothering* me. You've made your choice and as your father said, I hope she wins so you can be very happy. Well, if I can stop the Match, then you can choose her."

He pressed forward and her arms pushed against his stomach. She felt silly, so she dropped her arms to put space between them, but he stepped even closer.

"What are you doing?" she asked.

"Were you jealous?"

"Me? Ha." She snorted. "The other girls were jealous. They wanted to skin her alive."

"They should have been jealous of you."

"Why? We didn't actually k—"

He touched his finger to her lips and tilted her chin up with his thumb to look into her eyes. He leaned forward and whispered near her lips, "Because of this," and he pressed his mouth to hers. His lips were petal-smooth. Gentle. Questioning. As first kisses go, it was off to a good start. She threaded her fingers through his dark hair, soft as his mouth. "Forget Faunda."

She smiled and kissed him back. He held her face, pulling her lips with his, confidently, insistently, passionately.

She did what felt right and boy, it felt right. Marishel Vance—the *never-been-kissed*, no more. Quin's hands pressed hot against the skin over her spine, left exposed by the open-backed bodice. The crimson gown displayed dark red beadwork from the gathered shoulders, where his fingers traced the edge of the fabric down her V-neck to her waist, where his other hand grasped the skirt, flaring out in chiffon waves to the ground. Two sashes of deep, bloody red chiffon streamed from her shoulders and wound around her upper arms, edged in thin golden strips like her hem.

His palm smoothed up her back to her neck, where he held her captive to his mouth. She was overwhelmed, and for once, speechless. It was the best first kiss ever. She pulled back with her arms looped around his shoulders. She could just make out his features in the dim light. It was a magical place. She was glad she'd come. Why had she come?

"But … what about Faunda? She said you kissed her, too." Her dinner soured in her stomach at the thought.

"I have only kissed you," he whispered. Had he been talking about *her* all along? Surely not. But this was hard to argue with. "You're the only one."

She kissed him this time. A kiss of overwhelming appreciation—a kiss that said *thank you for seeing me,* and an offering of her lips in lieu of the life she could not give him. Even if he had a choice, the First would lose her marbles if he picked Marishel. Could she make that work, too? She'd worry about it later.

They banged up against the door jam in their loss of control and traveled through the doorway into his room. She released him to breathe, and they stared into one another's eyes—each asking questions that no one could answer.

At that moment, the door to the antechamber flew open and the First called out, "Son? Where are you? We must talk."

Marishel's eyes were twin pools of silver, wide and terrified. They could hear her coming toward the open door, and Quin yelled out, "Wait!" He shoved Marishel under the bed unceremoniously as he yanked off his shirt and dropped it to the floor.

Marishel was no sooner under the bed when the First walked into the room. Although the swirling dust was irritating and attempted to force its way into her nose, she pinched it shut, holding back her sneeze. She could see the First's heeled shoes—fancier than any she'd seen from the Outerlimits—walk toward Quin's bare feet. *Click, click, click.*

"Mother," he chastised, "I was changing."

"Oh, son. Please. I am your mother. Besides, I don't have time for silly diffidence."

"I don't lack self-confidence. It's decorous."

289

"Pfft. Don't insult me." She stepped closer. "I need to know. What do you know of the girls' plans?"

"What?" He sounded genuinely confused. *He's a good actor.* Marishel didn't know if the thought made her feel better or worse. Anyone who could act that well in front of another, could be acting in front of her. "I don't know what you're talking about."

"If you do, or if you learn anything, you must come to me immediately. It's that Marishel. She's trouble. I want you to try to force it out of her."

"Mother, I will not force the girls to do anything."

Her shoes stopped directly in front of his toes and Marishel heard a slap. "You will do what you are told. Your part in this is no greater than the girls until the day your father retires. You will play the part, and you will find out who this informant is. If it isn't that girl, she knows who it is. And when she tells you, I'll be ready."

"You can't—" Quin caught himself. "I don't want you to hurt her. She should get the same chance as everyone else."

"Oh, I won't need to hurt *her.* I have someone she cares about in custody. She'll do whatever I instruct. We might be able to turn this around. She did give us the best spot on the new promotion. They've played it practically non-stop." She tittered a little laugh. Then her voice lowered. "Did you have anything to do with the Paper?"

"No."

"You need to be honest with me. I will punish all those involved when it comes to light. I just need to know if you will need damage control."

"I said I didn't." Quin sounded angry, but not altogether unafraid. The woman was terrifying.

"That girl is involved somehow, and you're going to discover how she's doing this."

"Doing what?"

"Sabotaging *my* contest—*your* Match. Ruining everything I've worked for since the day I—" She stopped and Marishel waited in the silence. "Since the day—"

It was like she was trying to finish the sentence from any direction, but the rest of the memory was so awful, she couldn't find a way to get there. Marishel imagined the First as a teenage girl in this very estate all those years ago, lying in her bunk at night, crying for her parents and the life she was fighting for, and she almost felt sympathy for her. It didn't last.

"You will find out what she's up to and we will stop her. We need to catch her soon. There's a faction that's appeared calling themselves the Rebellium. I don't know who is feeding the Paper, but if it's one of the girls, my bet is on Marishel Vance. If they find a way to get to her, or she hears of them, she could cause trouble. Set her up if you need to." The urgency of her voice made Marishel tremble under the bed. If that woman knew she was under there... The First spoke slowly, and with a low timbre that vibrated in Marishel's bones. "If she gets in my way, I will crush her." She spewed the words with so much acid anger, Marishel knew if she'd been standing where Quin was, she would've melted on the spot.

Quin sighed. "Okay, mother. I'll speak with her. I doubt I'll find out much—"

"You are an attractive boy, I'm sure you can woo her into a confession."

"Woo her? Really mother?"

"Whatever you kids call it now. Bat your eyes at her. That's all it seems to take with the others."

291

"Marishel isn't like that."

"Oh really? What *is* she like, son?"

"I don't know." He was flustered.

Just don't give me away, Marishel begged silently.

"I haven't been able to talk to her since you assailed her with your watchdog, Lonna," he said.

"What could you mean? I didn't have a thing to do with that. However, I can assist if you need to find some time alone."

"It would be helpful."

Her voice softened. "I'll see you tomorrow, son. Soon this will all be over, and you'll never have to think about this unpleasantness until your own son's Match."

The way her ankles were bent forward, it appeared the First was giving him a hug.

Very softly he said, "Mother, there will be no more Blood Matches when I am the Leader. My son will choose the best candidate by a set of standards, not cunning and murder."

She gasped and stepped back. "How could you?"

"The Match isn't who you are. Not anymore. You don't have to perpetuate this."

"You are too young to understand."

"Maybe you're too old to see clearly."

"I can see we are at an impasse. While your father and I still rule, though, you will do as you are told or there will be consequences you aren't prepared for."

"That sounds like a threat, Mother."

"Oh, believe me, Quinlan, it is." She spun on the ball of her foot and strode out, the sliding door vibrating in its frame.

Quin followed behind the First and Marishel lay paralyzed under the bed, her hair caught in something above

JENNIFER HASKIN

her. She dare not move, though, until the coast was clear. *Kh'ra.* It was time to go before she was missed. She needed to hurry.

Quin's long, tanned feet came to stand before her. "You all right?"

"Mmm hmm. Is she gone?"

"I think so. I doubt she comes back tonight. I upset her pretty well. I shouldn't have said that."

His doubt gave Marishel strength. "You absolutely *should* have said that. Who else do you think she's going to listen to? Not me." She untangled her hair and pulled her body forward, trying not to think about the dust and dirt she was wiping with the front of her dress. Her head poked out and he leaned down to help her up. She held his hand, using her other one to brush off her front. She sneezed. "Oh, that felt good."

"I hate to hurt her," he continued.

Marishel looked up at him. He stared back. "And I hate to do this to you ... but it's her or me," she whispered.

He cringed and said softly. "I know. I don't want to hurt you, either."

"I'll figure it out," she said resolutely, chin up.

"What did she mean she can hurt you now? Do you know who she has?"

"Yes. It's a boy I grew up with. His name is Trae. I think he's locked up where Nahli is, but I don't know where. I wanted to find a way to release him, but I was told to lay low."

"The guy from the Paper?" Quin looked confused. "You know him?"

"Yes."

"That was you?"

293

"Yes ... I'm the one who fed him the information. I had to. I couldn't—"

He cut her off and said slowly with a frown, "No. I meant *you're* the girl he was talking about. The one worth more than his life." He stepped away from her. "So, what's your plan to get him out?"

"I don't have one. Maybe you can help? He means a lot to me."

"I'm sure he does." He looked toward the window. "Is he the guy from that video the night we had our picnic?

"Quin, no. It's not like that. I mean it could have been once, but not now."

He narrowed an eye. "What changed?"

"Well? You, I guess."

He sighed. "You changed my life, too, Risha," he said with a slow smile. "I'll try to find out about this rebellion."

Her spirit swelled with hope. "We'll figure it out together."

"My hero." He chuckled and reached out to wrap his hand around the back of her neck and pulled her face to his, meeting her lips with soft caresses. The pull and release of his lips was dizzying, and she leaned against him. Just when she was almost too dazed with feeling, he pulled away and smiled. "Goodnight," he whispered.

"Yeah," she whispered with a sigh. She didn't even care if he chuckled at her. Tonight was more than Marishel had hoped for with this horrible situation. The thought of her dated Match fought to bring her back to the present. She'd be doomed to an even uglier death if she'd gotten caught tonight. And for what? *Kissing? Really, Risha? What a stupid risk.* She needed to get her head in the game and get herself back before bedtime. Surely the others were all quietly preparing to sleep.

The next morning, Marishel was lost in her mind. Running scenarios. Rerunning scenarios. Then she'd remember Quin's kiss and the way he dove into her like a crystal-clear pool, never wanting to surface—and she happily jumped in with him…

Whoa, Risha, she told herself, *resist it.* He'd merely kissed her, not declared intentions or anything. Nothing had changed.

In class that morning, they were allowed—told rather—to write a goodbye letter to their families, to be sent home with a standard monetary amount if and when they perished. It broke her heart to say goodbye to her parents and Madi all over, to pour her heart out on a page that they'd probably frame when she was gone. She had to accept it was a possibility. It was harder even than leaving them at the station. She would give anything to go home.

She sat at a long table with other girls, sniffling through their letters. Marishel sighed when she was done, lay her head down, and listened to the soft conversation.

"—didn't you date back home?" Rorie asked the girl across the table. "You have met other boys, right?"

"Well o' course I did." The girl, Joany, smoothed her paper out flat. "I'm just sayin', he's cute and has a lot o' power. Who wouldn't want him?"

"Not me. I don't go for prissy boys. I like them straight from the Outerlimits, all rough angles and dark broodiness," Rorie said with an overdramatic sigh.

Joany's eyebrows squeezed in frustration. "He's more'n just a prissy boy. He has a job, an' helps people—

he's smart, sweet, kind, an' loves his family. He's a little dark an' brooding."

"I just don't see the appeal." Rorie folded her paper.

"You jus' don't know him."

"And you think *you* do? Get real. It's all an act put on for the show. He's vapid." Rorie's volume increased with her words.

"Is there a problem over there, ladies?" Sayra looked up from her tablet.

"No," Rorie said, bowing her head in respect.

"All I'm sayin'," said Joany, "is that ya could do worse. An' I think he's a catch." Her voice lowered to a whisper. "An' I don't think *he* likes this contest, neither."

Shalise nodded.

"Who are they talking about?" Marishel murmured, poking Shalise in the side.

"The Ambassador, of course."

Marishel spoke up. "Whether he likes it or not, he can't do anything to help us." She leaned forward. "He's bound by the law—and his parents. Best to let that thought go."

"Was jus' an idea." Joany shrugged.

"A stupid one," said the girl on her other side.

Then the bickering began. The girls were so stressed out that they were turning on each other. How was she ever going to save them? There seemed to be only one answer, but it wasn't a good one.

Marishel walked from lunch to her job for the day, the skirt of her royal blue kaftan swinging, and she pulled Rena and Shalise into an alcove in the main hallway. "We're going to have to come up with a plan amongst ourselves for now. We have to agree not to fight when we get to the arena. Tell the girls."

"Do you think it will work?" Shalise asked.

"No, but it's all I've got," Marishel said softly. "And they need to have *something* to plan on—as a backup, at least."

"What about Lonna?" Rena whispered.

"I will talk to Lonna. Maybe her partner has some pull." She grinned. "Nah, I'm not that stupid. But I'll talk to her."

"We only have three days left," Shalise said, twisting the fabric of her blouse, colorful flowers embroidered along the ruffle falling from her shoulders.

"A lot can happen in three days," Marishel said with a wink.

CHAPTER EIGHTEEN

SELF-INFLATED SPACE DOLLS

MARISHEL STOOD IN FRONT OF THE targets, waiting for her turn, her bow slung over her shoulder.

Since it was their last day of training, the girls were evaluated on skill once more, for Sarver to run the rankings in the final winner's pool, desired by the voting/gambling public. Instructors and girls stood scattered around the training yard in small groups.

Vangie took her place in front of the archery line. Standing tall, she was a formidable force. She lined up her shot and pulled back the bowstring ... she closed her eyes briefly and slowly exhaled. Just as her fingers were releasing the arrow, Lonna—next in line—managed to trip over her own two feet and dove into her back, head-first.

The arrow flew, luckily toward the right target, but it missed the bullseye she had planned on and landed in the farthest ring, barely on the board. Vangie was furious as the judges typed and scribbled on their electronic clipboards. She spun around with a murderous glare.

"You self-indulgent, cheating, piece of trash!" Vangie began. "I'm going to pull your—"

Sayra was immediately in front of the livid girl, with hands on her shoulders. "Brush it off, Miss Anish. Brush it off." She walked Vangie off to the side.

"She did that on purpose!" Vangie stabbed a finger in the air toward Lonna.

"That's the nature of this game," Sayra soothed in a motherly voice. "Whoever shoots first, wins. She'll win the trials today, but it doesn't mean much. Anything goes in the arena. Hold onto your anger until then. It will help."

"Vangie," Lonna sweetly called as she took her place at the front of the archery line. "This is how it's done."

Lonna pulled back her arrow and let it fly, hitting just to the right of dead center.

Marishel stood a few girls back in line, watching with rapt attention. She viewed the next events in slow motion as Vangie roughly pushed Sayra aside and plucked a new arrow from her quiver. She pulled back the string on her bow and aimed for Lonna.

Marishel didn't hesitate. She didn't know what came over her, in fact, it was probably the stupidest thing she could've done. If they'd asked Marishel if she cared for all of humanity or the rights of combat, she would have said *not especially*, but for some reason she ran for Lonna, barreling into her and driving her into the ground. The arrow sliced through the air above them, embedding in a beam on the obstacle course.

Sayra tackled Vangie and wrestled away the bow as Vangie screamed for another shot.

"You should have left it alone, Marishel." Vangie's growled words echoed throughout the training field as the other girls stopped to stare. "Now you're my second target." She continued to yell threats as Icen helped drag her into the building.

"Get. Off. Me." Lonna pushed Marishel with a scowl.

"You're welcome." Marishel grunted as she tried to lift her body while Lonna shoved her over. Marishel fell to the dusty ground with a thump. She was nervous about Vangie's threat for a moment but brushed it off. It didn't matter what number target she was, Vangie would get her, or she wouldn't. Marishel had no control over that. She could only stick to the only plan they had and hope a better idea came along.

"I didn't ask you to throw me on the ground." Lonna stood and brushed off her form-fitting, matching workout wear. "I don't need your help."

"You ungrateful snob," Rena said to Lonna, reaching down to help Marishel up. "She saved your over-priced life. Buy a conscience."

"What are you talking about?" Lonna faced off with hands on her hips.

Rena walked up, inches from Lonna, and pointed to the post she'd been standing next to and the still-vibrating arrow about chest-high.

"She was aiming for my heart!" Lonna's complexion paled. Her prank had almost cost her life ... prematurely. For just a fraction of a second, Lonna looked at Marishel with something akin to gratefulness mixed with shock, but then it disappeared under her regular mask of perfection. "If I'd seen where she was aiming, I would've moved."

"Right." Rena drew out the word. "Uh huh."

"Oh, shut up, tribade. Nobody asked you."

300

Rena turned five shades of deep red, almost purple. She called out to Sayra, "I have an HR complaint against Lonna."

Everyone stilled. A crime worthy of the greatest sentences, an HR complaint was like saying someone had committed a grave personal assault, an unforgivable sin, and the felony punishment that Human Rights gave was rarely one that didn't involve severe repercussions to one's everyday life. Calling an HR complaint was like yelling "fire" in a crowded space—if you could help it in any way, you did not do it. It wasn't a meaningless threat. Lonna paled.

Sayra strode over to them, suddenly all-business. Marishel stood next to Rena, half scared, and half proud. She wasn't familiar with the word Lonna used, but she knew that Rena had called Lonna's bluff in a big way.

"What's your complaint, Miss Yasuda?" Sayra pulled out a card from her pocket that folded open to a twelve-inch screen. She attached the tip to her finger and began to click on the fields.

"I didn't mean anything by it," Lonna said with a little laugh. "All joking among friends, right? It's supposed to be funny. I wouldn't say anything like that and actually *mean* it. You know that. Right?"

Rena ignored Lonna completely and said calmly, "Decalogue number ten: *I have the right to be who I am without prejudice and harassment.*"

When anyone called on the HR department of Haumea, people panicked. One who is reported for contravening the unalienable rights of another could have any or all of *their* rights taken away. If the offense was great enough, they could lose their right to live inside the planet. And everyone knew you didn't live *outside* it for very long.

It was not an idle intent of prosecution and even Marishel was surprised but glad to see Rena stand up for herself. Especially against Lonna. It was a little late in the game with only three days left, but it would go on Lonna's record if she won, or they managed to stop the whole thing. It was crazy to Marishel that her planet could be so liberal and yet blind to the heinous nature of the deadly contest due to tradition and a sick desire for blood.

Lonna launched into a self-condemning philippic but realized her rant wasn't going to save her and sealed her lips before she got into hotter water. The cameraman nearly danced around them in glee at the drama.

"Marishel saved your rotten life, you know." Rena stood with arms crossed while Sayra filled out the necessary fields on her submission. "Why don't you try living a life worthy of being saved?"

Lonna opened her mouth to argue and cocked her head, then just stared ahead.

Marishel didn't like being the focus of the argument and felt like she was intruding on a private moment, so she patted Rena's shoulder and walked over to where Shalise was learning with a trainer. Most of the girls had begun to disperse and go back to their training once Vangie was led inside, and the archer after Lonna stepped up to shoot.

"This is a variation based on the ancient Eagle Claw technique," a trainer said to Shalise and a few other girls who joined them. "The Eagle Claw took years of practice, but we don't have that kind of time." He had the grace to look upset about it rather than pretend this was a contest of worth.

"It took strength and skill, and the study of human corpses, to discover the technique. Yong Sool Choi, from

Hisashi-Japan, learned from the bodies where the chest muscles were connected, to pull them right from the body with just his hand, causing the opponent instant excruciating pain *and* disabling their dominant arm. In effect, it wins the fight." He smiled at the group, but as he'd spoken, he'd mimed the ripping of chest muscle for them, and a few looked a little green.

"I will *not* tear off a boob rather than just stab a girl. I don't need to know this." The girl speaking and her friends left. The day had been emotional for everyone. Most of the girls were in their heads, thinking about killing each other, and fuses were short.

The trainer just shrugged. "Their loss. I wasn't finished."

Marishel chuckled inwardly. *Rule: The Ambassador's Bride must not be too hasty when making decisions.* They should have paid attention in class.

The trainer continued, "Since we don't have time to gain the strength and learn the skill, and since we—you—are, ahem, ladies, the technique I will teach you is a little different but simple, and just as effective at disabling someone trying to kill you."

He reached into a bag and brought out a pair of mechanized claws that were wickedly shaped and cool as hell. Since he was originally talking to Shalise, he handed them to her. "Just put your fingers in here, it's really easy—right, and strap this to your wrist. Tighten it here. Now the thumb. Be careful."

He bent over her hand to attach it. The thumb of the contraption had a longer, deadly-sharp, and slightly hooked, bladed claw that attached to the frame over her hand. She looked like a harbinger of death, but on shy Shalise, it made Marishel worry for the girl. If she didn't come up with something better than tackling the fighters, the girls weren't going to make it.

"Now,"—the trainer lifted his head to speak to the other girls listening—"the concept is the same. You want to grab a major muscle group—the chest, of course, but also biceps, shoulders, back, thighs, calves, you get the idea—and pull. First, you push four of your fingers in under one side of the muscle as best you can—the pistons will help you with strength as well as grip—and when you activate the thumb..." The trainer stopped and stood up, then said to Shalise, "Go ahead."

The thumb seemed like a spring trap. When she moved her four fingers into a grip position and flexed her thumb, it lasered on and almost too quick to see, curled in like a talon, searing whatever flesh it would have grabbed, and as soon as the thumb closed, a hiss shot from the back of Shalise's hand and her fist shot back toward her, nearly popping her in the face, but she moved her head in time. *Quick reflexes.* Maybe Marishel should worry more *about* Shalise and less *for* her.

The girls gasped in awe. Not only did the tool help one grip and pierce the muscle, but it also pulled the whole thing out for you automatically.

"There are ten of these," the trainer said softly to the group who leaned in to hear him. "If you are ever allowed the option of choosing a weapon, get this one. Got it?"

The group nodded en masse. None were in the mood to talk about the purpose of the weapon, *or what might happen if they met someone in the arena with one*, Marishel supposed.

The trainer kept his voice low. "You get caught, or disarm someone, or get into hand-to-hand—you grab for anything, you hear me? You grab for whatever you can. This baby will do the rest."

"What do you call it?" Marishel asked.

"The Hawk Talon," he said.

She nodded. "Thank you."

Suddenly she was exhausted. It had been a long day. The weight that she felt for the responsibility to stop this Match was wearing on her. *I can't do this alone.*

She thought of Trae, locked up for her sake. She was angry with him for making it all about her. She already knew he was sorry about losing his temper, but saying his sacrifice was for her, meant that she was now at fault for anything that happened to him because of it.

Then her mind flashed to Quin. Would he join her in the real fight when it came down to it? She remembered their quiet times together and couldn't help the out-of-control feeling that surged through her. It certainly wasn't giddy love or anything, but she wanted him to want her as much as she was overcome by him. She'd never felt like merging, uniting, with any other person her age—not truly. But something about Quin made her want to know all his secrets; she wanted to give him what he wanted, spend time learning about him. She wanted to hear his favorite songs, and to know what his hair looked like when he woke up. She wanted to know what he thought about things that were important to her, to see him interact with her family. It was a pull that she wasn't prepared for, and it scared her.

No, it terrified her, because he made it seem like he felt some special way for her, and that made the chance of her failure so much more desperate—it raised the stakes in the game for her. It gave her something to live for, but it also gave her something else to lose. She had to win this, somehow. And she had to give Quin options—whether he chose her or not—but she hoped he would. It was just another part of the plan she couldn't control.

She'd told Rena, Shalise, Unity, and Rorie that they were to divide the girls into groups to pass on information—Shalise sorted that out—then the four became her personal crew. There were too many girls to have to talk to each one. Up till now, Marishel told Rena and Shalise everything she could and the three of them told the others only what they needed to know.

In the empty bathroom that afternoon, before heading to training, the five new group leaders spoke quietly.

"We'll split up the girls in the winner's tier and assign a group to each of the top ten if we can. Then, when they call us to fight—usually the whole assembly is there in the arena—each of our circles will surround their top-ten girl, separating the top tier from each other, and disarm them as quickly as possible, then hold them down, no matter what it takes," Marishel said.

"That doesn't sound too hard. But then what?" Rena asked. "You can't take on everyone by yourself."

"Well ... I will petition the Leader. Surely with all the unrest and the Paper, if the girls refuse to fight, hopefully, he'll take the reins and put a stop to it. He knows—" She almost said the leader already knew Quin wanted to choose, but saying that to this group might get her into hot water. Tempers were high. People were looking for cheaters, and everyone was suspicious of everyone else.

"What?" Rorie asked.

"I was just about to repeat myself. He knows the people are unhappy. But is the noise loud enough?"

"Hmmm." Shalise tapped her crossed arms. "Does that mean we need more people or more volume?"

Marishel shrugged. "Either would be great with me If we could all contact our families, we could ask them to join anyone protesting the Match—but we're running out of time. I wish we had current outside information. Gods! That would make things so much easier. I would imagine if the people were angry enough, they would try to find each other and group up. But what can they do? If I knew any of them, I could try to coordinate plans, but my contact is locked up."

"Sorry." Rena touched her arm.

"It's okay I guess he knew what he was doing. But part of me wonders if he expected me to go get him out. Was that part of the plan? Did he figure it out and he was planning to infiltrate from the inside? I just don't know." Marishel's heart thumped a hysterical beat.

She wanted to pull her hair out. She didn't want to inform them of the rebel group she'd heard the First telling Quin about. It was too much of an uncontrolled variable. When she knew more, she'd tell them. If she could only contact the Rebellium... Trae could've done it, she was sure. Maybe Quin would?

"You can't risk it." Shalise was all business today. "We need you. The girls need you. If anything happened, they'd lose their heads thinking the plans were scattered. Tomorrow is the Blood Ball. You have one day to get ready—and that day is going to be packed."

Marishel forgot. She thought she had more time. But the primping for the Blood Ball took nearly all day. Girls would be watching live from home, having their own spa parties, and doing one another's hair, pretending to be their favorite girl.

"Pray girls. And let your team know everything we have planned so far."

307

"I believe in you," Shalise said. *"I fight who you fight."*

Marishel pulled her into a quick hug and squeezed her with the deepest thanks.

Now, back in the training field, she had an idea. She wanted to talk to Quin. Training was nearly over, so Marishel went to help put weapons away, trying to memorize the various weapons she'd been taught and what they did, and to place the location of The Hawk Talons—just in case.

"Would you sit with me tonight?" Quin stood in the hallway with the exhausted, nervous-chatting girls, waiting for the dining room to open. He looked resplendent in one of Marishel's favorite fabrics—brushed cotton—in her new favorite color, the green of his eyes, now open and questioning. He hadn't asked her to sit beside him since the night she'd rebuffed him out of necessity.

She understood that he risked wounding his own pride by asking a second time, so she smiled and looped her hand through his elbow. "I'd love to," she said just loud enough for him to hear.

Content to sit and eat, Marishel enjoyed the relaxed environment and the warm pressure of Quin's knee resting against hers.

"Well, I think these rebels should be brought to justice." Lonna sat on Quin's other side. Of course, she wasn't giving up her seat. Especially for Marishel. *Partners* had a shallow meaning in Lonna's personal dictionary. But Lonna's words now caught Marishel's attention.

"What rebels?" she asked.

Lonna went on as though Marishel hadn't spoken. "I mean, if they're going to interfere with matters of state. ."

"What rebels?" Marishel asked again.

She rolled her eyes at Quin. "You tell her."

"There's a Rebellium that's formed. *You* know—that boy from the Paper?" He raised his brows at Marishel. "They formed from his articles but have just now started to make demands."

"Like what?"

"I can't tell you." He looked ahead and wouldn't meet her eyes.

"How does Lonna know about it?"

"My opinion is highly regarded by the Leader." Lonna looked proud as a peacock.

Marishel turned to Quin who explained, "She overheard my father talking to me and he asked her thoughts on it, that's all."

"Ah." She understood. *Self-inflated space doll probably actually believes herself.*

As Lonna regaled them with her opinions on all things, Quin slid his hand over to the side of his chair and inch by inch traveled over to the side of her seat to find her fingers. Quin's grip felt strong, immovable as steel itself, and as alive as the far-away sun—their living, lava-churning, life-giving home star. Long, smooth, tanned fingers caressed the back of her hand and Marishel wished Lonna would talk forever.

"Did you even hear me Marishel?" Lonna leaned forward with an expression of disgust, and Quin squeezed Marishel's hard.

"Not a word." *No sense lying to her.*

Lonna gave a short shout of frustration. "You're going to wish you'd paid more attention in two days."

"To what? You? The Match is supposed to be in two days. Once everyone's dead, it won't matter what you said tonight." But she would remember Quin's warm, safe, stabilizing grasp, and the way it made her feel so worry-free for a few moments.

"What do you mean, supposed to be? Are you with the Rebellium? What's their plan, Marishel?"

"Lonna." Quin's voice was low and firm.

"First of all, it *is* supposed to be in two days, second, when would I possibly meet with a Rebellium with you tracking me all day, and finally, do you really think if I knew the plans, I would tell *you?* Over supper?"

Lonna sniffed. "Well, you don't have to be so nasty about it."

Marishel shook her head as she exhaled.

Supper that night was a fancy cut of meat smothered in a brown sauce with onions and mushrooms piled high, and sides of rice pilaf and shredded carrot salad. It was tasty, but when they were told it was specially made because tonight was their last night in the dining room, there were a few silent tears around the room. The mood remained somber, despite Lonna's lively conversation. She was excited to win the Match and be with Quin, or so she thought.

With dismay, Marishel realized something Trae had said was true; she *did* always believe there was another way—a solution must be possible. She needed to admit to herself that there may not be a way to stop this horrible thing.

She could be leaving the planet in two days as her spirit floated out into space. What would that be like? Would it be cold? *Not the cold again.* Marishel hadn't shivered in weeks, but she shivered now as she felt the icy finger of death draw up her spine. It was right behind her, but she wouldn't look. She still had two days. No, she couldn't give up yet. *I can't believe there is no way out, I can't.*

After supper, Quin exchanged a few words with his mother, who called Lonna over to her. Then he came back to their table and whispered with a smile, "Come on, let's go."

"We going somewhere?" she asked, rising.

"Anywhere you want to go?"

"Let's go to your spot in the labyrinth." She smiled.

"Done." He nodded. "My mother knows you're with me, she'll tell Sayra. Make your excuses from the girls and meet me at the labyrinth as soon as you can."

Her excitement was a cosmic contrast to the others in the funereal space. She attempted to look grave once more. What should she tell the girls? They might want to talk together tonight. *Man, this stinks.* She wanted this time with them, too. What were the sayings? Fries over guys? Sisters over misters? Her feminist side said to ditch him for the girls, but her feminine side said this was her time to say goodbye to the boy she had grown confusing feelings for.

As she walked Rena and Shalise back to the dorm, Marishel told them she was going to think and be alone for a while—*I need to meditate,* she said.

"Aww, Risha. We understand. Right, Rena?" Shalise threw her arm around Marishel's shoulders and Rena grabbed her from the other side.

"Yeah. Faunda wants to play some horrible group games or something else equally torturous," Rena said with a moan. "You were supposed to make it bearable."

"I think she said we were going to play hide and seek, too … and charades," Shalise said with childlike joy. "What should we tell them?"

Marishel hadn't thought of the other girls wanting to talk to her. But of course, tomorrow would be chaotic, and the next morning, who knew what would happen then?

"Well, just tell the girls I went out to the labyrinth to be alone for a while. I'll play when I get back."

"Good. I know some of them want to let you know they support you."

"Hey," Marishel said. "That's not a bad idea. Tell your girls in the morning to have anyone who's with us for the Match, give me a wink sometime in the day or at the ball—nothing too conspicuous, but that way I'll get an idea of who's with *us*, and who we need to watch out for if it gets that far."

"You got it, boss." Shalise saluted.

"Wrong hand, land lubber." Rena showed her the proper salute. The only bodies of water big enough to sail on would be the ponds in the Farmlands, but nothing bigger than a rowboat would be necessary. The main water reservoir was agreeably *not* for swimming or boating as it was eventually drinking water. Suffice it to say, Rena had never been sailing in her life.

They laughed together down the hall. Marishel was going to miss these two ... one way or another. She felt like *kh'ra*.

"If I come back early, we can talk."

"Okay." Shalise was obviously excited to play. She probably missed playing with her brothers.

"We'll see you later," Rena said, grabbing Shalise's hand and swinging it.

Marishel watched them walk away, then walked down the next hall, and pushed open the door.

"Marishel!"

She turned to see Icen running her way. "I hoped I'd catch you." He took several gulping breaths and held out a note.

She took it. "Are you okay?"

"Yeah." He panted. "I was just … waiting to give you that … and when the girls came back, they told me … you were headed this way to be alone … so I ran."

It was only down the hall. She raised one brow and narrowed the other eye. "Hmmm. Either you are seriously out-of-shape, which I doubt, or it sounds like you've been running for a while."

His dark complexion paled momentarily, but as if he suddenly remembered who she was, he calmed with a smile. "Let's just say I brought you that one personally and keep it at that. Tanner and I go way back."

She was intrigued. A note from Tanner? "Thank you Icen. I'll read it when I'm alone."

He nodded and she stepped from the cool dorm building into the heated evening. The lights were dim and the smell of the First's garden was a heady scent on the breeze. She stood alone in the training yard and opened the note.

Marishel,

I trust Icen with this, so don't worry. The leader of the Rebellium wants to meet you tomorrow night. He has a plan. I can't tell you what it is, but he'll share more then—at the Ball.

Was the leader someone she knew? She couldn't think of anyone who would organize something like this.

He will have a Sanger Orbiter7 shield. His first name is Blayk. Be prepared to leave with him. You will meet the rest of the team at an undisclosed location. Be safe, and thank you, Marishel. For fighting for Veda and my Abrielle. I can only hope to repay you through this.

Tanner

CHAPTER NINETEEN

FIRST DATE NERVES

MARISHEL TORE UP THE NOTE FROM Tanner and deposited it in a waste bin on her way to the labyrinth.

When she arrived, Quin was waiting just inside the arbor for her, leaning casually. When he didn't respond to her standing directly in front of him, she realized he was watching the feeds on his *Eye*. She was inordinately curious. Was he watching a feed about the Match? Suddenly he smiled in a way that made her instantly jealous of whoever had his attention. She cleared her throat. *He can watch it another time,* she thought peevishly. This was *her* time with him. She cleared her throat.

"Oh! Marishel. Hi. I was just watching your new spot on the promo. You were very convincing."

He was watching her? She was suddenly flustered— and irritated, though she didn't know at whom. "You mean I was so convincing that no one believed I was exasperated with the words and livid at being in the Match enough to nearly cry, being forced to say it?"

He chuckled and held his hands out. "You mean there's *nothing* redeeming here?"

She knew he was teasing, but she was suddenly in the mood to bite someone's head off. There was too little time, and too much she didn't know. What if this Blayk guy—*nice name, bozo*—had a terrible plan? And what if she didn't want to bow to the leader of the Rebellium? (Blayk must have named that one. *Highly creative.*) Marishel scowled at Quin. "Are you fishing for compliments?"

"Yes. Yes, I am. And I'm not ashamed to say my feminine side needs reassurance. Don't you find me beautiful?" He tossed a fake headful of hair. That just happened to be an oft-parodied line from Madi's favorite shampoo commercial, and she used to go around the house, flipping her tiny head of shiny hair, and asking everyone, *"Don't you find me beautiful?"* The picture of Quin flipping long shiny locks made her sputter with laughter.

"Ah, there it is. Risha's smile." Quin softly tapped the tip of her nose. "Boop."

"I don't want to say goodbye yet," she said, her lips twitching, the corners dropping. She felt tears gather and tried to blink them away.

"You don't have to. Just sit by me—I want to be with you."

"Lead the way."

He offered his hand, and she held it—not like a lover, but she gripped it like a frightened child—a lamb being led to her slaughter. She didn't know what was to come, but could she be happy trading thirty minutes of magic with Quin, for her future, in his honor? Her heart pulled inside her chest and her lungs tightened.

She immediately hated the girl who was going to win. With a deep unfettered rage, she felt the heat bubble up within her, spewing poison. She walked alongside Quin imagining him sitting in the stands regally, ruling next to Vangie, or Lonna.

She had to admit both girls would probably make a more suitable leader than a seamstress who'd never even left her side of the planet and *looked* like she came from the Outerlimits. But she had faith that she could fake it until she learned. She just didn't want to have to assassinate anyone to get there.

They reached Quin's hideout and Marishel softened to see that he'd added a fluffy-soft blanket, and several of Haumea's popular candles were strewn about. They were flameless but emitted a trail of vapor that caught the light of the colored laser within and reflected its glow as the mist undulated in the air before evaporating, and they smelled so good. It reminded her of home—when family would come by and Mom would "light" the candles, then the whole house smelled like a garden, or a sweets shop, or whatever scent she chose.

These candles were streaming pinky-orange flames like an Earth sunset and smelled like coffee. "Mmm. It smells like a café in here."

"I thought you'd like a night 'out' before … well, before things get complicated. But we're not going to think about that. Not tonight." He motioned for her to take a seat in a nest of pillows he created for her. "Tonight, we are two kids on a date."

"We are?" She settled her lilac skirt around her legs.

He sat facing her in another pile of pillows. "Yes. I met you in class. I'm new and you were so nice, you helped me on my first day."

317

"I *am* nice."

"Some time has gone by, and we've become friends." He picked up her hand, surrounding it with his long fingers.

"Mmm hmm?" she said with encouragement. "I think enough time has gone by."

"So, in math class, I asked you out on a date."

Marishel gasped. "Oh my. What did I say?"

"Well at first you were afraid because you're moving in a few days and I might not get to see you, but then you remembered how much you like me and how much we laugh and how it feels when I look at you—I mean, how handsome you think I am—so you said yes."

Her eyes danced with laughter. "And then?"

He lifted her hand and kissed the end of one dainty finger. "Let's see. I picked you up around six-thirty and your father answered the door." He shook with mock fear.

"Ooh," she said through her laughter. "Scaaary. Did he rough you up? Tell you to be a gentleman?"

"Oh no. He didn't need to do that. I'm always a gentleman." He winked at her and kissed another fingertip. "But he did tell me your weakness. Which is,"—he paused to lift the cover over a platter she'd seen to the side, and in the middle were two plates topped with a decadent creation dripping with sticky drizzles and topped with—"chocolate-covered strawberries on caramel cheesecake."

Her mouth dropped open. "How? How could you know that?"

"I have my secrets and you have yours. Let's not ruin the mystery, shall we?" He settled himself in his pillow nest opposite her and handed her a plate and a utensil.

She unfolded the prongs and slid her fork through the creamy cheesecake, into the moist graham crust, then shoved the whole forkful into her mouth, closing her eyes. "Mmmm…" She sighed.

He brought out a carafe—*where was he hiding all this stuff?*—and poured her a cup of coffee. Then he added *almost* a spoonful of sugar—or what they called sugar but was really stevia they planted in lieu of sugar cane—and a little disposable cup of double creamer.

Whom had he spoken to? Who knew her favorite things? She was baffled as she tried to remember talking about it but couldn't. She must have said it to someone. And how she took her coffee? She racked her brain. Had she said something to Canon? He'd seen her fix her coffee many times.

He chuckled looking at her expression. "I can't tell if you are happy about the dessert, or so confused you've forgotten about it."

"It's exquisite," she said. "Have you had any?"

He lifted his plate but looked at it doubtfully. "The idea of cheese and cake together never appealed to me. And caramel on cheese sounds disgusting. But some of the weirdest combinations are good together, or at least have an interesting taste for a few bites. I'll try it."

She smothered a laugh at his face. He appeared to be a child in front of a spoonful of cough medicine. Quinn wrinkled his nose and cut off the tiniest piece with his fork.

"You won't even taste that!" she protested.

"Okay, okay. Don't push me." He got almost a bite's worth on his fork and screwed his face up, putting it in his mouth. He frowned as he moved his jaw very slowly, taking in the creamy texture.

It was the best cheesecake Marishel had ever tasted, and she scrutinized his reaction. He moved his mouth faster and a smile beamed across his face like a lightbulb before it burnt out, when it surged in a brilliant flash before winking away.

"You like?" she asked coyly.

"Mmmm. Wow. It doesn't taste like cheddar, or mozzarella, or brie! It's-it's—"

"Cream cheese ... and lots of sugar."

"I see why you like it so much." He grinned.

"It's not an everyday thing, of course, but on special occasions ... it's perfect." She looked meaningfully at him.

"I think so too," he said softly, scooting closer.

Her lips curled into a smile. "So, after the café, where are you taking me? I'm sure my father told you to have me home at a decent time." She took another bite.

"I bought us tickets to a show."

"Really? What kind of show?" Marishel licked the caramel oozing down the handle of her utensil and Quin watched her.

He squeaked, "What kind would you like?" then cleared his throat.

"Comedy." She nodded. "Definitely a comedy. I want to laugh and laugh—like I never will again."

"Risha." His eyes shined when she looked at him. Then he smiled. "Comedy it is."

Quin pulled a basket from behind his pillows where he'd been hiding everything. He picked up a small, clear square, a translucent plastic stand, a cord, and what looked like a ring box. The basket, he set to the side of them and closed the lid. Marishel watched while he set up the stand, but when he unfolded the screen, she understood. Quin plugged the cord into the screen, and into the small, square speaker, which he opened like a ring box to send the volume their way. With his *Eye*, he selected a comedy she had never seen from the old world, back when movies were just beginning the big dome theater age—around the end of the third millennium.

The movie was so funny, it made her forget her situation entirely for a while, and it was also a love story. When the hero kissed the heroine, Marishel glanced over at Quin and found him watching her in the darkness, the white twinkle lights glowing on his face. She turned back to the screen and laughed until she cried.

When the show was over, Marishel helped Quin pack up the basket with their plates and the tech. This time, he straightened out her pillow castle and rebuilt one for two. He sat back, put an arm along the back of the mound, and curled a finger at her with a devilish grin.

She would've tittered if she didn't fear appearing vacuous. The spot under his shoulder—curled up next to his side—was heavenly and Marishel silently claimed it as her spot. *There.* If anyone else sat in that spot, they'd be trespassing. So says Marishel.

When her head rested with her cheek nestled against his neck, she said. "Now what?"

"Are you tired? Do you want to go home?" he asked, brushing a curl behind her ear.

"Never."

When he chuckled, it rumbled through his chest and all the way to Marishel's belly. She almost shivered, it was so delicious. "Here, let's walk." He didn't make a move to get up but held out his hand, so she took it.

"Are we walking now? Hand in hand?"

"You're so smart. After we ride the sidewalks there, we'll come to a big gate that says, *Stay out!*"

"But we won't, will we? So, I'm assuming we are at a driveway or a path?" There were one- and two-manned vehicles around Haumea, but they were used by the Gentry, and many vehicles were used as utility vehicles, delivery and emergency transportation, and shipping—that kind of thing.

"There is. *Hey.* Have you been here with another guy?" He feigned indignance and wrapped his arm around her, squeezing her tightly to him.

"You know I haven't. I'm new at all this," she said in a silly high voice.

"Don't worry. I'll protect you. You have nothing to fear with me around." He puffed his chest out.

She snorted her laugh. "Mr. Valiant. What's at the end of this path?" She traced little circles on his chest. He was so broad, she felt completely safe in his arms.

"When the grass levels out there's a terrace—"

"There's grass?"

"Yes?" Quin pulled his chin back to look down at her with confusion.

"I love grass. Go on."

"Okay." He relaxed and rubbed circles into her lower back. "If we go to the middle of the terrace, and turn our backs to the water, directly ahead is a hidden path through the trees. It isn't marked, and the entrance is strategically covered, but my tutor and I found it one day and he let me pretend we were explorers or pirate hunters—"

"Pirate hunters?"

"Well, it's by the water…" he said. "There's no railing here and the bank goes right from shore to the deep end, so we stay back and watch the waterfall."

"You can see it from there?"

"Yeah. It pounds into the main reservoir like they say in school, melted from ice out on the surface. It's really pretty … and loud." Quin drummed his fingertips along her spine.

"Really? But it's water. What does that much water sound like?" She didn't imagine that it sounded like the trickle of the sink or the hiss of a hose.

"It sounds like *ruusshhh* ... like ... pouring rice from a huge bag."

She spoke into his neck, "Like *ruusshhh?*"

"Risha." He looked down at her.

"What are we doing at this secluded park near the waterfall?" She tapped his chest with her finger lightly.

"I spread out a blanket and we watch the water until—"

"Until I have to go to the bathroom." She chuckled.

"Hush." He bopped her nose. "We talk. You tell me your favorite color..."

"I like them all, but lately I've been appreciating a particular shade of green." She looked up at him. For all the coldness he showed the world, she'd seen him through the crinkle in his eyes long before she realized it. He wasn't prissy or sweet, he was determined, brave, thoughtful, and a romantic.

"And your favorite music?" He watched her face, smoothing her hair back behind her ear.

"Twenty-seventh-century jazz." She hummed the melody of one of her favorite tunes.

He ducked his head to hers and hummed the tune back against her lips. It tickled and she rubbed her lips together, laughing. "That tickles."

He kissed her softly and pulled her chest toward his. Quin's hands roamed her back, kneading, searching. He found her skin and she sighed with pleasure. His fingertips skated over her flesh and her iron core melted, lava boiling in her ears.

"Favorite school subject?" he asked close to her neck.

"Science," she said breathily.

"Me too." He kissed her quickly. "After school?"

She smiled. "That's when I work as a seamstress." She brought her hands between them and mimed sewing with needle and thread. "But you knew that."

"Aha." He picked up her hand in his and turned it over in the shadowy darkness. "So tiny. Fragile."

"You know, I *am* breakable. Quin, we need to accept the fact that this might not work out—"

"No. Stop."

"I can't, Quin. I have to force myself to say goodbye to you." She gave a wry laugh and looked around. "The perfect spot. Right here by the waterfall. I'll be thinking of it when they—"

He captured her mouth with his to stop her from saying more. She would have pushed him away and insisted they accept reality, but she wanted to forget it as much as he did. She wanted to be right here, or even at a real waterfall, as long as Quin was next to her. She clutched the fabric of his shirt like she was drowning, and the kiss deepened passionately.

She grabbed the back of his neck, and he dove his hands into her hair, holding her lips captive to his kiss. He desperately explored her, and she inhaled deeply, memorizing his touch, his scent, the sound of his breath, the taste of him, the feeling of bliss, of being wanted.

Quin pulled her closer and she threw her leg over his hips to sit on his lap. Never breaking their kiss, they gripped and pulled at each other like two people drowning at once. They held each other as the planet exploded around them. Fire, stone, ice, erupting, searching, accelerating … detonating. Desire pumped through her veins.

"Gods," she breathed heavily. "You make me…"

"What?" His voice was husky in her ear.

"Forget. You make me forget … everything. All the bad."

"What about the good?"

"What else is good? All I can think of is you."

He took her face in both hands and his lips pulled hers in a deep kiss. "How is it you've been on that side of the planet for all these years, and I never knew it?"

She laughed scornfully. "It's funny, isn't it? To know how close two worlds apart can be."

"When I'm with you I feel like I've been given a gift that I didn't know I needed. Have you ever felt like that?" He pulled back to see her face.

"Yeah." She put her head back on his shoulder. "You know what's really messed up?"

"What?"

"If I can't convince anybody to fight with me against the Match in two days, you will be ordered to marry my murderer."

"Marishel." He sounded angry and she knew she'd gone too far.

"Sorry, but it's true. I can't unthink it."

"So, you thought I needed to think it, too? So, *I* can't unthink it? *Think, Risha.* If that awful thing actually happened, now I have an almost-beautiful memory of you to keep me company with that marvelous thought." He held her away from him like he might push her off and get up.

She pounced on him, wrapping her hands around his shoulders. "I'm sorry. You're right. I'm so sorry. I-I— Can we go back to the waterfall?"

He sat in silence, peering over her shoulder.

"Please? Oh please, Quin. Don't leave me this way. I couldn't stand it." She held his face and tears sprang to her eyes. Deep, shadowy green irises measured her, and his lips tightened with no expression. "Quin?"

Inside an exhausted sigh, he said, "Yeah?"

"What's your favorite thing to do after school?" she asked timidly.

"I run." He frowned. He was going to make her work for it. *Fine.*

"What kind of music do you like?"

He relaxed with a little smile. "Syntheticks, to the public, but secretly—the Martian Symphony."

"Are they the one with the bells?"

"Yeah, that's their song. You've heard them?" His brows rose.

"A little. They're good, but I like their string music better. Okay, favorite color." She held up first one finger, then two.

"It used to be blue, but it changed."

"And now?" She gazed into his eyes. They were translucent, like his father's.

He caught her stare and said softly, "Silver."

"Kiss me?" She leaned forward, pressing their hearts together, and hunched to bring her face to his. Tentatively, her lips met his, pulling them as she tilted her head deeper into the kiss. Warm emotion coursed through her veins. It magnified her anxiety and the floating sense of being wrapped in Quin's arms. He enveloped her, squeezing them closer together, and she was melted butter. Her lips sang under his, making music to the tune of her heart breaking. She needed this. Gods, she needed this. It was all she clung to, and when he pulled back to check on her, he was kind to the desperate sorrow she tried to control. The pain overwhelmed her, and she started to cry.

"I'm sorry." She sniffled.

"Don't be." He pushed her head to his chest and held it there with his warm, strong hand. She sobbed. After a few minutes, he breathed deeply, and she followed.

"I don't want to tell you goodbye." She hiccupped. "I can't—" She couldn't finish the sentence as a fresh wave of tears followed.

"Sshhh." He smoothed back her hair, running his fingers through her mass of curls. "I'm here."

"Will you be at the Match?" She clutched fists of fabric from the front of his shirt, wrinkling the cotton fibers.

He stiffened just slightly. "I don't want to be, but I won't leave you to face it alone."

"You don't want to come?"

"I don't want to see—"

"I want to know you're there." She clung to him. "If I don't figure this out … I need you there."

"Hey. You're shaking. Risha. Aw, baby."

Then she really lost it. No one had ever called her that—other than her mother—and that didn't count. To be honest, no boy had even called her Risha besides Trae. Fleetingly, she was remorseful about leaving him locked away when here she was canoodling.

It made her cry for the hurt she was causing him. It would hurt her friends, too, to know she was out here with Quin alone. Shalise had taken the fake-kiss with Faunda much harder than she would have expected. And she was close to Shalise, she should have known. Surely, some girls would have been devastated by it, had they known he really had kissed one of them—especially her, the leader to some, and yet, the apparent antagonist for others.

She could have spent the night with him next to their pretend waterfall, but reality came crashing through her glass house like an elephant. "What time is it?"

"Getting late," he said, his voice laced with disappointment. "Maybe we can stay a while longer."

Suddenly she was grateful that the First had ordered him to spend time with her, but even more so, that she had cleared the way with Sayra. It must have been well past ten-thirty. She would slip in quietly, all the girls sleeping, and go to bed. She'd talk to the girls in the morning.

Tomorrow would be a fair amount of interviewing by Sarver and primping in front of vanities, extra stitches added and taken out of dresses, and makeup artists volunteering their skills to the Match in hopes someone would like their "style" and hire them for something else. And those who *weren't* engaged by the staff—the producer, the cameraman, the beauty teams, and such—would be milling around bored to death, talking about everything they could think of, other than why they were getting ready, or the next day's Match.

Marishel sniffled and dried her eyes. Quin reached across her and handed her a napkin. "Thanks," she said.

"Sure." The way he looked at her, she would have thought he was pitying her, but she didn't think so.

"What?" she asked.

"It's just my luck to find you now."

"If it weren't for the Match, we never would have met. So, I guess I'm glad for that." She straightened her spine and leaned back, blowing her nose, but tears continued to fall.

"You're thankful for the Match?"

She wiped her face. "No. For this. You are my spark of amazing at the end of a brief lifetime of drudgery." She reached to pull his lips to hers.

Quin whispered against them, "You're my reward for any good karma I've sewn, and so much more than I deserve. I can't lose you. Is there anything I can do to help your plans?"

"No," she said softly. "I know you tried, and I appreciate you. But it's up to the girls now. They will either join our protest or battle us. But I will continue hoping for a better solution. Ultimately, I have to pray for some time to convince the people to rally. Maybe I can plead from the platform into the stands. If I stir them enough, they may have been swayed by the Paper to take action. It's all I have."

"I don't want to let you go." Quin held her with fierce protectiveness. "I'd take your place if they let me."

Marishel chuckled softly. "That really wouldn't work." She gazed at Quin with all the hope she could muster but her voice shook. "This is my trial—my mantle of misery." She laced their fingers together. "But I can conquer it if I know you're with me."

"To the very end." He captured her mouth once more.

When they drew apart, Marishel lay her head on his shoulder, resting her hand over his heart. She could feel the steady thumping through her fingertips. She yawned and snuggled in closer. He propped his chin on her shoulder and rubbed her back.

"You're tired," he whispered.

"No."

He laughed. "It wasn't a question. You need to get to bed."

"I don't need sleep. I can stay awake,"—she yawned—"for days."

"You'll be sorry." He was joking of course, but it occurred to her that if she was dragging on her feet, she wouldn't have any chance in the Match. With all her strength, she at least had a chance to protect herself for a while—which might be all she needed. He was right.

"Okay. I'll help you take this stuff back. All the girls are asleep, so everything will be dark."

Marishel sat up and moved off of Quin, holding out her hand. He grabbed it and nearly pulled her down. She shrieked in laughter, and he stood on his own with a grin. They packed the basket, but the carafe didn't fit, so she carried it while he took the heavy basket. Marishel didn't want to be responsible for breaking the tech inside, which was likely if she carried it.

They walked leisurely through the labyrinth, swinging their hands and smiling at each other in the dark. Halfway back, they cut through the center of the labyrinth where the fountain was. They were walking past the stone pool when they heard a voice.

"Marishel?" Shalise's face fell when she saw Quin holding her hand.

Oh no. She nearly threw his hand from her own.

"We came to make sure you were okay, and not lonely, *all by yourself,*" Rena said with admonishment.

"Guys—"

"I think I *am* tired now," Shalise said to Rena.

"Wait. Why are you here? I mean, awake?" Marishel was trying to make sense of it.

"Disappointed?" Rena asked. "Sayra gave us a late curfew since we're supposed to die and all. Did you two come up with a plan for yourselves, or did you include the rest of us?"

"Rena. Shalise. You guys know I didn't—"

"Didn't what? Didn't *mean* to lie?" Shalise asked. Rena took her arm, and they brushed past Marishel.

"I'm sorry," she called after them.

CHAPTER TWENTY

PRIMPING

MARISHEL WALKED THE PICNIC BACK TO the kitchen. Quin said a quick goodnight and she hurried to the dorm. She arrived as the last girls were winding down and the lights were low. She got into bed and said quietly to Rena, "I'm so sorry. I needed—no. No, I was selfish. I wanted a few minutes of someone from the outside telling me that my life would be wasted if I lost it in the Match. I didn't—I lied because I *didn't* want to hurt you."

"Go to bed, Marishel. I'll be fine in the morning, but I don't know about Shalise," Rena mumbled, her face pressed into the pillow.

"Did you talk to her?"

"She used me like a human tissue. It was disgusting. I told you I don't know what to do with crying girls. You were supposed to be on *our* side."

"I am. I promise. I'm sure you did fine. I don't know what to do."

"Well, she's cried herself to sleep, so there's no more damage you can do tonight. Go to bed."

"I'm sorry," she said again.

"I know." Rena rolled over and went to sleep.

"Good morning, ladies!" Sayra sang out. "Everybody up! There is a table set up in the classroom. It will have breakfast, lunch, and snacks throughout the day; if you're hungry, just help yourself. If your name is called or you are given a scheduled time, pay attention. Be where you need to be, so we don't have to go looking for you and waste everyone's time. Otherwise, you are free today. Dress comfortably in something you can change from with your hair and makeup done. The dresses will be here at about four and we'll head to dinner about six. Okay, let's get going! Sobia has the first list of names, go see her right away if your last name starts with A, B, or C."

Shalise was still lying in bed when everyone got up. Marishel looked over at Rena and raised her brows. Rena motioned for her to go over there. Acid churned in the pit of Marishel's belly, she hoped she wouldn't get sick. Being the cause of her friend's unhappiness wrapped her in a straitjacket of shame, pulling tighter and tighter around her middle. A hive of bees in her stomach would've been less painful. She stepped carefully across the tile, willing Shalise to get up, but she didn't. What was she going to say?

Kh'ra. She was terrible at apologizing. She got nervous and babbled so much that she usually stuck her foot in her mouth and made whatever she was apologizing for worse with stupid dialogue. She wished she was a character in a fairytale book and the author could write some eloquent, heartfelt, clever, and effective apology that Shalise would magically listen to and accept. But this was Haumea and fairy godmothers didn't make appearances at the Blood Ball.

She sat on the edge of the bed. "Lise?"

"Go away, Marishel. Just let me die in peace."

"You're not going to die if I have anything to say about it." She rubbed her friend's back. "And no boy is worth dying over. I'm sorry I lied to you. I wanted to tell him … goodbye." She heard the tears in her voice and cleared her throat. "We became friends. But I should have told you. I didn't want to hurt you and I ended up making it worse. Please forgive me, Lise."

"Did you make a plan together?"

"What? No. We didn't. He can't do anything about the Match, and I'm still—wait! I got a letter from Tanner last night." She spoke low. "I forgot to tell you after—well, you were asleep."

Shalise sat up, smoothing down her bedhead. "What did it say?" Her eyes were red and puffy.

"Hang on." Marishel looked at Rena and motioned her over.

Rena approached with caution. "Yeah?"

Marishel looked around but most of the girls were engaged in dressing or getting toiletries ready to shower. She spoke just for the three of them. "Tanner sent me a note last night. There's a rebellion that's gathered."

Shalise looked around as well. "Really?"

"Yes. And the leader of the group wants to meet me tonight at the ball. Tanner said I should be ready to leave with him to meet the team and discuss the plan. I'll come right back. If they can sneak me out, I'm sure they have a way to get me back in."

"What is it?" Rena chewed on a ragged fingernail. "What's their plan?"

"I have no idea. He said they'd tell me tonight. So, I'll need you guys to cover for me, if you have to. Or at least play stupid. I don't want either of you in trouble the night before the Match."

"Not that I care right now, but what about you?" Shalise asked.

"Yeah, genius. What are we going to do if something happens to *you?* Maybe you shouldn't risk it." Rena spat the fingernail out and it landed on the bed in front of Shalise, who glared at her.

"I don't have a choice," Marishel said. "I haven't come up with anything better than refusing to fight and that could backfire on us in a big way. I have to go with them. Any plan they have has got to be better than the one I have."

"Be *careful*." Shalise brushed the nail onto the floor.

"So, do you forgive me? I'm really sorry. I promise I am."

"No." Shalise sighed. "But, I know I will eventually. Doesn't really matter if we're dead, I guess. I'd rather he was with me than you—but to be honest, I'd rather he was with you than Faunda."

"Hey, what about me?" Rena said in mock despair. They ignored it.

Marishel nodded. "He never kissed Faunda. She lied."

"How do you—ooh. Did he—?" Shalise's eyes were wide.

Marishel felt the hot blush that she knew covered her cheeks and throat.

Rena took one look at her and barked with laughter. "Yes, he did."

"Hush." Marishel folded her arms and frowned.

Rena laughed at her. Shalise brought her knees up and wrapped her arms around them defensively.

"We're still a team. Let's shower and get breakfast. We're at the end of the alphabet,"—Marishel nodded to Rena—"and Lise is halfway through it. We have plenty of time."

Rena looked up at the number of girls heading to the bathroom and said, "Better yet, let's go eat and shower when they're all done."

"Deal," Marishel said. "Come on, lazy bones." She squeezed Shalise's arm gently and offered her a smile, but Shalise couldn't form the expression. One more thing Marishel was responsible for. *Great.*

Rena and Shalise must have mentioned their after-supper conversation to the girls the night before, because while they piled their plates with pastries—*who cares about her figure in a situation like this?*—three girls winked at Marishel. At first, she didn't remember the conversation and thought the first girl was being a little overly friendly, or maybe joking. The second one made her wonder if there was something on her face, but by the third girl, it occurred to her.

"Did you tell your teams about the wink last night?"

"Yeah," said Shalise.

"We thought it would travel faster through the groups if we started telling them last night." Rena bit a sausage patty.

"Okay. Let's see, that was Anora, Harley, and... What's her name?" she whispered. "Over there. The one with the armband. That's pretty."

Shalise looked quickly. "Oh, that's Kosie. The armband is part of her family's religious belief. It symbolizes the deity Architus from the Church of Universal Verity."

"Really. Huh." Rena narrowed her eyes. "I mean, I do believe there be magic, but what some people believe... Wow."

Shalise ignored her. "Believers now say that Architus' spirit came to Haumea with the *Sanger Orbiter7* and exists here telling them how to live so they finally learn not to make the same mistakes as the Earthens."

"That would be pretty hard out here." Marishel stuffed the last bite into her mouth and licked her fingers. "I would not agree to be an explorer, for any amount of credit. It's been awful not having my *Eye* for the last month. I miss my feeds. I'd never make it in a mining-only society. Though I do crave real food now. I think when I get home—"

They all stilled. Did she really still imagine she was going to make it out of there? Marishel changed the subject. "So, who do you guys think the cameraman is going to swarm today?"

"I heard Rorie's dress is really pretty," Shalise said softly. Marishel wanted to shake the life back into her.

"People are going to be betting all day. Who's wearing what color? Who drinks too much champagne? Who falls out of her dress?" Rena said. "The cameraman is going to be everywhere, taping everything, like a kid with credits in the sweets shop."

Marishel laughed at the picture she saw of the cameraman in too-small kid's clothing with his big glasses, face pressed to the shop's window, his mouth watering for rows and rows of sweets.

It was late in the day when Marishel's name was called. Shalise had been facialed, made up, and then moved on to the stations for hair. She hadn't seen her since. Marishel entered one of the large conference-type rooms set up with stations around the periphery. She looked for an empty place. To the left, one woman wiped off an empty barber's chair in front of a mirror surrounded by lights. The woman's ruby lips framed a radiant gap-toothed smile.

"C'mon over lass. Have a seat and take a load off." She swiveled the chair around to face the middle of the room, and Marishel walked over to sit facing her.

The woman's hair was a wild nest of pumpkin-colored corkscrew curls held back with a blue kerchief. She wiped her hands on a towel and stuffed it in her apron. "Now, let me get a good look at'cha." She took Marishel's chin gently in her thin fingers and turned her face in all directions. "Hmmm." She narrowed an eye and leaned back to hold Marishel's face at arm's length.

"What?" Marishel asked without moving her jaw.

"Ah. Just lookin' at your colors, luv. I think we'll do a royal purple on the eye. Pink rose for the cheeks—just a dustin'. Mmm hmm. And,"—she tilted Marishel's face up to the light— "mulberry for the lip color. Ah yes. That'll be right pretty. Won't clash with your dress, will it?"

"Oh. No, it won't."

Marishel hadn't thought such care would be taken. She figured they'd all get blue eye shadow, hot pink cheeks, and red lips. That's the way she felt in makeup anyway. She might as well be a clown. She was grateful for this woman—small mercies and such.

"Okay." The woman let go of Marishel's face and stood back with arms crossed, tapping her lip with one finger. "Where do you come from, lass?"

"What?" She was confused.

"Different places we live, we each have different needs for the skin."

"Oh." She thought she understood. "I'm from the Outerlimits. The Needles—on the other side."

"Och yeah. Shoulda known. Little bit dry, yeah? Does it itch you?" she asked, smoothing a hair away from Marishel's face and brushing her cheek. It felt like a mother's touch and Marishel was suddenly more homesick than she'd been so far. Her eyes swam in unshed tears. "Ah, lass. I know it." She looked around and then leaned forward, hugging Marishel to her breast.

Marishel tried not to cry, but instead, she worked to suck all the strength she could from the moment. She fought to gain control of her emotions—to absorb this woman's support. She imagined an outpouring of rose-colored comfort and bright yellow encouragement flowing from the woman in waves, filling Marishel's body. She took in more, and more, so greedy for it. When the woman stepped back, Marishel exhaled rose-gold relief into the air and watched its vapors curl away and dissipate.

"What's your name, li'l one?"

"Marishel."

"I'm Elmora Lenicks. I've a sister there, in the neighborhood over from the mines—name of Bonney, her husband Ulu's got a store there, I hear."

"I might know him."

"Good. Feelin' better?" She turned Marishel's chair around to face the mirror and stood before her, arranging unfamiliar items on the vanity. There was a remote camera

338

in front of every mirror. *Of course.* They wouldn't want to miss a second.

"Yes. Thank you, ma'am."

"Call me Elmora. Now, let's work on your skin a bit first."

Marishel sat patiently letting Elmora administer pastes and serums to cleanse, tighten, pucker, and plump. She felt fresh as a daisy when Elmora started her cosmetics. It was a shame to put makeup on after cleaning her face so well. But she supposed it was better to have makeup on clean skin, than sealing in the grime that was apparently already there.

"Wow, Elmora. I look like someone else—I mean, I still look like me, just so much better. You have magic hands."

"Don't tell me husband that." Elmora chuckled. "But thank ye. You do look quite lovely, dear. I wish I could see ya all done up."

"Well, watch the feeds tonight. I'm sure you'll see me."

Elmora put her hands on her hips and smiled. "You're done with me. Now go through those doors at the far end of the room, and ye'll find the hair stations." She looked at her uBand. "The dresses should be here by the time you're ready. Now off wit' ya." She smiled as she shooed Marishel with both hands.

Marishel hugged her quickly. She didn't want to get emotional and smear her makeup. On her way to the door, she passed Rena, just coming in. They shared a secret smile and brushed palms. In the next room, several stations were closing down and cosmetics artists packed up their supplies.

It didn't feel real yet. Marishel's head was a balloon, not attached to her body, not in reality. No innovative ideas flew through her mind, though she tried to strategize in her fuzzy thoughts. The rebel group must have a great plan, with adults putting their heads together. She perked up a bit. Marishel wouldn't admit defeat until they speared her through the heart. She would continue to believe that this Blayk guy had the answers she'd been seeking. She expected some mucilaginous Summerland businessman who thought he had life figured out—young and blond and tan, lanky, with stylish glasses.

It's okay, Risha. Any plan is better than mine.

Girls winked at her as she found her place in the stylist's chair, and she tied their names and faces to her faction—noticing those who made eye contact with only the most genteel smiles and bland, meaningless pleasantries—one point for the iniquitous. Luckily, Marishel was winning the majority so far. She prayed it stayed that way.

Marishel was lost in her mind, but it didn't matter. She was a Vance, always end of the alphabet. She was used to being chased out by the cleanup crew. So, it didn't surprise her when another stylist—done for the day—sat in the chair next to Marishel, swiveled it around, and proceeded to chatter away in Spanish with the beautiful, young Latina so painstakingly curling and pinning, and curling and pinning Marishel's hair. When she was finished, the woman tapped Marishel on the shoulder.

"All done," she said. "Thee dresses came half an hour ago. So, thee fitting room line will be long. You are welcome to sit here for a while if you don't want to wait in line."

"Really? You think they'll still be busy?" Marishel asked.

The woman in the other chair barked a short laugh. "They don't tell you girls nothing."

"Shut up." Marishel's stylist shook a curling wand at the woman, nodding toward the camera on the vanity. She looked at Marishel through the mirror. "Thee girls get their dresses one at a time."

Marishel was confused. "Of course."

"No. I'm not saying this right." She squinted her eyes and looked at the other woman who shrugged. Her eyes widened. "Ah. There are only one fitting room."

"What? Why? There are stations all over the place."

"Maybe you're not remembering the old shows? But all girls stand in line outside the back of thee fitting room, coming in one at a time. Helpers make adjustments or problem with the dress. They come out on other side, in front of a six-way mirror and camera, seeing each girl's first time viewing herself. A table of sandwiches are there to get you to dinner. By thee time *you're* done, it might be time to go. Grab a sandwiches now while you are waiting."

It was the most the woman had said to Marishel in hours. She was grateful, though. She liked to be informed. It was one of the reasons she missed her *Eye* so much. She always had her finger on the pulse of her family, friends, and community. She even had a program that connected to her cochlear dial with an auto-translate feature to follow any conversation, but without it, she only understood English. She was absolutely starving for information. *Even a little gossip would be welcome*, she thought frivolously.

She wondered at her lightness of mood under the circumstances and deduced that it was a combination of girly joy in looking professionally pretty, and an up-till-now unrealized relief that the burden of a plan out of this mess was no longer fully on her shoulders. It was on Blayk's. She smiled. For once, she allowed herself to fully give up control. Let somebody else worry about it for a while.

Surely, he had a huge following and a team dedicated to coming up with the best solution. He had resources, connections, money, and time. She was happy to help in whatever plan they'd come up with. It was the first time she felt like it wasn't all up to her. She had an abundance of help, but everyone still expected *her* to be the leader ... until now. She hoped she still had a useful part to play.

The snack table itself was dressed to impress with finger sandwiches, *petit fours*, and tea, with crystal glasses and tiny silver forks. She wondered if they were afraid of theft, but then realized they'd soon be leaving all their belongings here if Blayk's plan failed. She lost her appetite and decided to just wait in line. No sense in letting more people join the line when she could be moving ahead.

The line moved surprisingly fast. There was an overpowering amount of excitement and anxiety in the air, and the girls were fairly bouncing with anticipation. Marishel kept shifting from one foot to the other, trying not to clench her teeth.

"You look pretty, Marishel," the girl behind her said.

She turned to look at the girl, Freda. Her hair had been colored a beautiful shade of blue. Her face was enhanced with a deeper shade of indigo, almost violet. She looked...

"Stunning." Marishel pointed to Freda's head. "You ready?"

"For tonight or tomorrow?" she asked.

"Either." Marishel laughed.

"Tonight should be fun; we've earned it. And tomorrow?" Freda winked at Marishel. "I'm ready."

Marishel was so happy the girls were going to lay down their weapons. It was still a good backup plan. But she wasn't worried about it anymore. She'd just wait to say something until she could confirm it later. She hoped Blayk wouldn't keep her out too late. She also hoped he didn't show up before she had a chance to dance with Quin a few times.

Marishel was nearly asleep on her feet when it was her turn. Freda nudged her.

"Hmmm?" Marishel turned.

"You're up." Freda nodded ahead of her.

"Oh. Sorry." She laughed lightly and entered the fitting room.

Two small, older women wrapped in lengths of measuring tape, with pins in their mouths, and gray-streaked hair slipping from their hairclips, ushered her into the small cubical space. They were a tiny, round pair and they chattered gaily while they worked. One helped Marishel take off the loose clothing she wore, and the other stood on a step stool and held the dress over her head.

Marishel reached up to put her arms through straps or sleeves, or whatever held the thing up. "Just a moment, dear," the one holding her dress said. Then she called over to her friend, "This is the Arteggio Bali."

"Oh!" The second woman clapped her hands together. "You're going to love this," she said to Marishel. "Let me help."

The first woman pulled over her head a cylinder of fabric made from a webbing of crystals that flowed over her curves like liquid. The crystals sparkled in the room's light. The bodice covered one breast and fell to pool on the floor like a puddle of mercury. The other side of the dress, from the thigh-high slit up the bodice, trailed an intricate vining over transparent silver mesh that continued over the other breast and up to circle her neck. The second lady fastened it behind her like a necklace.

"Shoes!" she shouted near Marishel's ear, scaring her to bits.

"Shoes!" the other woman got down from her stool and went to the hanging bag Marishel's dress had been in and produced delicate, strappy, low-heeled sandals, then bent down to slip them onto Marishel's feet.

While Marishel tried to balance and put on both shoes without falling over, the second little granny poked crystal teardrops on wire from her earlobes, then crowned her with a headpiece of leafy metallic swirls, adorned with crystals that hung from the sides.

"There." The first woman stepped back and folded her arms with a smile.

"You go get 'em," said the second one, blowing a string of hair from her face.

This is nerve-wracking. She was more afraid to go out that door and onto a stage than she was to enter the arena. What if they didn't like her? What if Quin didn't think she looked good in makeup? What if she fell, or ripped the gauze of her bodice? What if Blayk never arrived? When Marishel continued to stand there, the ladies glanced at one another with concern.

"This way, dear," one said as the other took her hands and led her to the next door.

Marishel took a fortifying breath. What if—? *No,* she shook off the unanswerable questions. This was nothing. This was just a mirror and a camera. No big deal.

She pushed through the door and passed through a set of violet velvet curtains that were held back at the sides. She emerged into a bright light but tried not to come out squinting. Before she could see. Marishel heard gasps and "aahs" and "ohhs" of appreciation.

She froze in amazement at the woman that stood in front of her in the mirror. The sparkling gown of crystals clung to her figure and dragged a small train on the carpet, her leg playing peek-a-boo through the slit. The stylist had pulled her hair up, sweeping up the sides and back, with curls dropping down her neck, and the headpiece held it regally in place, the dangling crystals twinkling. The makeup still impressed her, and she marveled at how well the deep purple and wine-stain on her lips complemented the iridescent crystals.

"Awww." Sobia's brow wrinkled and she managed to smile with a frown. She clutched her fist at her chest. "She is beautiful, yes?"

"She cleans up pretty good," Sayra answered next to her.

Marishel was so happy to see them. The two women were familiar and made this not as strange. A gaggle of contestants stood around with teacups, watching their friends come through the curtains. Marishel stood uncomfortably as the cameraman skipped around her, calling out directions.

"Look here … Marishel, is it? Yeah. Good. Now smile. Good. Wait there. No, don't turn. Stand right there and pull back your shoulders a bit. Okay… Great. Now … turn that way, no—just your head. Now frown. Oooh, fierce. I like it. Now turn around and—no, no, your whole body, like this— put your leg out through the slit … yeah, and … turn and look at me over your shoulder, but don't smile. Yes! Yes. Marishel, you are all done. Thank you."

She stepped down from the platform but didn't know where to go or what to do. Suddenly things felt very out-of-place, and she wanted to go downstairs, wash her face, brush her teeth, and climb into her bunk for a nap, at least. The realization that their evening hadn't even begun yet, made Marishel feel instantly exhausted. She decided to get a drink, use the restroom, and come back to find Shalise and Rena. She couldn't wait to see what they looked like.

CHAPTER TWENTY-ONE

THE BLOOD BALL

WHEN MARISHEL EMERGED FROM THE RESTROOM, girls were passing the door, heading *en masse* from the dorm building to the banquet hall where they would eat, before moving to the ballroom for dancing, drinking, and dessert until no one could stand anymore. She didn't have time to find her friends. She joined the group and when they arrived at the great hall, gave her name card to the dining room usher.

Marishel sat at one of at least twenty extremely long dining tables, laid with china and the old kind of silverware with fork, knife, and spoon, rather than their singular utility utensil. *Who are all these people?* The hum of chatter throughout the room soothed her a bit, but she was frustrated at not being able to locate her friends. She tried to look around the room, but her place setting was hidden behind one of the tall golden urns that adorned the tables every few feet, each stuffed with a mix of pink, fuchsia, and wine-red roses, peonies, and other large blooms amid their greenery and white baby's breath. Ribbons hung in curls, tied with loop over loop in baby pink.

She sat between two complete strangers—a woman with a comically long neck, and a man with a humped nose. He was dressed in the uniform of an official, though she didn't have a clue in what capacity. He'd introduced himself as Politician Hinkle and attempted to draw Marishel into conversation, but her mind was stuck on finding Quin and—hopefully later—Blayk. But she couldn't see a thing around the giant urn sitting right in front of her. No doubt planned by the First.

Everything down to monogrammed napkin holders for visiting attendees was laid out according to her plan. Marishel was certain it was no coincidence that she was placed at the farthest table from the dais, at the farthest corner of the room—next to these painfully boring people.

"So, have you had a nice time at the Leader's home?" Politician Hinkle asked obtusely.

She tried to erase the incredulity from her expression, but she was sure she was unsuccessful. "Well, it hasn't been tea parties and sleepovers. Do you watch the feeds? Did you bet?"

"Oh. Ah, no. I don't gamble." He had the grace to blush and wince. "I don't suppose they do much of what I was expecting."

She laughed lightly. "Probably not."

They ate in silence for a moment. Politician Hinkle glanced over at Marishel's hand, and she hid her disfigured manus under the table.

"What *did* they have you do?" he asked, his face a mask of curiosity. If he'd looked at the least interested in a sadistic way, she would have told him off, but she saw this as a teaching opportunity, so she explained their rigid schedule … and what was to come.

"They make it sound like a wonderland of dating and excitement." He was quiet for a moment. "Do you think it very distasteful of me that I don't wish to support this after all?"

She turned to him in surprise and said softly, "That's not a very popular opinion around here."

He pursed his lips and nodded. "All the same, I don't think it was fully explained to me when I agreed to invest."

"People invest in the Match?" The thought hadn't occurred to her.

"Oh yes. The girls' meals, their housing, the extra staff, the newest training equipment… There's a whole list of options, or you can sponsor a girl of your choice."

"Really." She put down her napkin. She'd lost her appetite. The food was too rich anyway. After a few bites, she'd been full. She just continued to eat because it tasted so good. But now there was a bad taste in her mouth.

The banquet hall was packed, and the heat made her skin dewy with perspiration. There had to be hundreds of people present. To be fair, Marishel wasn't very good at estimating numbers of people over a hundred. But how many of them were investors? How many times over had they been paid? Surely the girls had done a staff's worth of cleaning in the last month. And she herself had helped harvest food from the gardens. Of course, some things must be paid for, but she didn't think they were lacking any funding. The First began a presentation up front that they could hear clearly due to the sound equipment but had no hope of seeing.

Marishel wondered where Rena and Shalise were. Were they together? Close? For the hundredth time, she leaned around the planter and tried to see the leading family's table on the platform to get a glimpse of Quin, but she could only see their heads, no clear faces. She squinted. He was wearing something green. She remembered telling him it was her favorite color. Had he remembered? She allowed herself to believe it was for her. Nobody else needed to know.

When the meal was over, people carried their drinks and moved in slow lines toward the adjoining ballroom where they heard a group of musicians finish their tuning and begin a jaunty melody. Marishel joined a line and looked around the banquet hall to find someone familiar, but there were no girls around. The Leader's family had been the first to leave, so she didn't bother looking for Quin.

Suddenly she wanted to cry as a feeling of abandonment swept over her. *Get a grip, Risha.* As Rena would say, *Don't lose it on me now.*

Politician Hinkle held out his elbow. "Would you like an escort, young woman?"

She took the sweet older man's arm and walked next to him down the long aisle.

The mass of people bottlenecked at the double doors to the ballroom, so they stood patiently, waiting to move forward.

"Risha!"

Marishel heard a voice from several tables over. She turned to look and had to do a double-take. Rena laughed at her expression and Shalise smiled wearily. Marishel could tell that Shalise was trying to forgive her, but it wasn't easy.

"Would you excuse me, please? Those are my friends."

Politician Hinkle smiled and patted her hand. "Of course. Friends are good right now. Spot of sunshine in the dark and all that."

She laughed inwardly at his attempts to be friendly, though they failed horribly. "Thank you," she said and walked over to meet the girls.

Shalise's stylist had changed her hair color to a deeper pink than her gown at the ends of her brown barrel curls, and braided bits held back with pink flower clips. Her dress had the full skirt of a sparkly princess's ballgown.

"Shalise. You look like royalty." Marishel gave a little bow, holding one hand out to the side, and circling the other one near her belly.

"I know. Mucho sexy, right?" Rena ran a finger over Shalise's bare shoulder, making her shiver.

"Stop that. You know it gives me goosebumps," Shalise reprimanded.

"Speaking of sexy, Marishel ... va va voom." Rena made a feminine outline in the air with her hands.

Marishel laughed. "I've never worn anything like this in my life. It's an adjustment."

"I bet the Ambassador's going to need an adjustment, himself." Rena guffawed.

A high-society woman nearby sniffed at them, which made Rena exhibit even more-inappropriate hand motions, and Shalise and Marishel sputtered laughter till they were light-headed.

Rena's stylist had left her fine, straight hair bleached blond, though it was touched up to be a bit brighter and cut in a pixie style that made her look fierce. Her nails were golden talons. and her dress was a simple, shimmery peacock blue fabric covered in strands of varied lengths of shining peacock crystals, with oval-shaped cutouts in the

351

bodice. The back was open, and sparkly shoulder pads dripped hanging crystal strands that swung back and forth as she walked.

When they made it through the doorway into the ballroom, the mass immediately dispersed. Marishel looked over the heads of the crowd.

"Have you seen him yet?" Rena asked.

"Who?" Marishel asked.

Rena rolled her eyes. "Who *else* are you looking for?"

Quin came into view and Marishel's face lit up, but he was soon lost in the crowd again.

"I bet I know," Shalise said with a weak smile directed at Marishel. She was trying hard. Marishel was glad Shalise was taking it so well. Not that she had much choice. But she could have made a bigger deal of things if she'd wanted to. Shalise wouldn't stand in Marishel's way with Quin, though—and she wouldn't have with anyone else, either. She was just that kind of person—she knew when to call it quits and move on. Still, Marishel knew she was wounded and tried to treat her tenderly.

"Let's go dance, girls." Marishel pulled them.

The three girls linked arms and entered the dance floor as a united force.

Marishel scanned the ballroom. She hadn't seen Blayk yet, but she wanted to know who he was.

"What was the thing Blayk was supposed to have? So you'd recognize him?" Rena asked. "We can help you spot him."

"The note said he'd have a Sanger Orbiter7 shield, whatever that means," Marishel complained.

"What kind of shield? Wind shield? Heat shield?" Rena laughed at her own joke.

"Magnetic shield?" Shalise joined her. "Whipple shield, electric shield, deflector shield, ion shield?"

"Holy crow, how many shields did the ol' Sanger have anyway?" Rena lifted a glass of champagne from a passing tray and gulped it down.

"Slow down," Shalise said, pointing to her empty glass. "I don't want to be hanging in the bathroom all night while you puke."

"Really? You're going to deny me this? With what could happen tomorrow?" Rena looked at her incredulously.

"I didn't say *stop*. I said, *slow down*, dummy. Or you'll hurl on Karthik's shoes or something even more embarrassing."

"If she looks ill," Marishel said just for the three of them, "point her at the First."

Shalise gasped and looked around. "Marishel!"

"What's she going to do tonight?" Marishel took Rena's second glass and sucked it down.

"Oh great. Not you, too. I can only manage one of you by myself—"

"Don't forget—she's going to find out the new plan from Blayk," Rena interjected. "I still don't like it."

They'd traveled to the center of the floor and moved to the beat of the dance music.

"What am I supposed to do?" Marishel held her hands out.

"I don't know. But couldn't he just tell you the plan? Why take you with him?" Rena's mouth pursed.

"I don't know. Maybe he doesn't trust me. I don't trust any tool with the name Blayk, either." Marishel laughed. "Listen, girls, if anything goes wrong, stick to the original plan. Okay?"

"What's going to go wrong?" Shalise looked a bit panicked.

"Nothing, nothing," she soothed, with a hand on Shalise's arm. "I'm just saying, you guys can do things by yourselves if you have to."

"What are you planning?" Rena narrowed one eye.

Marishel heaved a sigh. "I already told you. Nothing. I just don't know what tonight will mean. I don't know the plan or where I'm going, or how to get back. I just want to know that if anything happens to me, you guys will take care of it."

"It sounds to me like she's planning something. You think so, Lise?"

Shalise screwed her mouth over to the side and wrinkled her tiny nose. She scraped back a wayward curl with one baby pink fingernail. "I don't know."

"Guys…" Marishel fought tears. "I told you. There's no plan that I know of."

"Is Quin going with you guys?" Rena asked, sneaking a shorter glass with brown liquid in the bottom. When Shalise turned to look for the leading family, Marishel chuckled as Rena took a sip and puffed her cheeks, blowing out an imaginary candle. She shook her head and grinned at Marishel.

She didn't care if Rena drank all she wanted. It wasn't her right to judge, and she certainly didn't begrudge anyone their vices on a night like this.

The music changed and the lights lowered. This would start the organized dancing of groups and pairs together. "Whew!" Marishel fanned herself. "It's getting hot in here. You guys want to step out for a while?"

"Sure," Shalise said, holding Rena's arm to keep her from wandering off in a state of tipsy bliss and getting injured or worse. Surely the place was ripe for predators— they'd been warned by Sayra to keep a buddy system tonight. There were too many empty halls and wealthy benefactors who enjoyed the company of young ladies.

They stepped out on the patio and saw groups of girls walking around the lawn among the guests, heading for the bathrooms or the library, or the art gallery. Tonight, the public areas of the estate were an open house, and people who'd never visited before roamed the grounds, touring. One whole group of girls winked at Marishel, and she had trouble remembering all their names and faces. It was becoming a muddle in her brain, and she was terrified she'd forget who needed to be watched for. Luckily, Rena and Shalise were also watching.

"That's most of them, don't you think?" Rena asked.

"I counted at least forty-two," Shalise offered.

"It's most everyone except the winning tier. Vangie has them all convinced that the winner will be one of them. So, none of them would even listen to the possibility that they might lose. Between them, there is a great amount of skill." Marishel wiped her forehead. "I wish I was that confident."

"About what?" Shalise asked.

"About anything." There was a difference between taking control of your circumstances and feeling like one had the power to win. Marishel didn't have any problem taking over a situation, but knowing she would be successful? Another story. Though she failed more often than she wanted to admit, she was currently surrounded by a blanket of security. She had too many roles to fill and she was happy to be giving control over to Blayk. She prayed it wasn't a false sense because she was relieved to have help. It was a foreign feeling, but for the first time, she welcomed it.

As they were leaving for the ballroom, Rena gripped Marishel's elbow, holding her back. Shalise walked ahead of them, not noticing the exchange.

"What's wrong?" Marishel frowned.

"I got a little something in case the Blayk situation gets … sticky." Rena reached under the split in her skirt and pulled out a small, thin dagger. Marishel gasped and Rena said quickly, "I just want you to be safe." She handed the weapon to Marishel.

"Where did you get this?" Marishel whispered, but Rena just put a finger to her lips and shook her head.

Then, looking around them, she said, "Hurry up and hide that before someone sees it."

Marishel quickly tucked the sheathed dagger down the front of her dress. She barely had it hidden when Shalise turned and said, "Come on, you guys."

They returned to the ballroom, but the music had just turned soft again, so they sat in the front row of a set of chairs lining the room, three rows deep. Plenty of the guests were sitting and talking, taking a rest during the quiet song. A swirl of blood-red organza caught her eye and Marishel saw the First on the dance floor, being led around the polished parquet by her eldest son. Marishel beamed, taking him in.

Quin looked regal with his straight posture, the shadows from the candelabras casting deep shadows under his cheekbones and jaw. He smiled, but he did not look happy in the least. It was like when she saw him on the vid screen at home. He glared at people like a caged animal, plotting the death and consumption of its captor. Marishel shivered, subconsciously imagining that angry stare directed her way. *Yikes.*

She sighed watching him move with grace and a commanding presence. He often glanced around him. Why couldn't his parents see that he cared about more than just impressing people with his frostiness? Why didn't they give him the right to train and the ability to use his power for the people? Why hold him back this long? Why didn't they trust him with his decision on a mate? She felt indignant for him, and the tension in her belly grew with each lap he took around the floor. He was turning around and around. Weren't they getting dizzy? He continued to scan the room.

The First misstepped and tittered a little laugh telling Quin to slow down, but he continued to spin her around the square floor with a speedier tempo than the music required. He looked frenzied. *What's wrong with him?* Marishel was immediately concerned and wanted to help him. He was looking around the room as he turned a box step, looking first left, then leaning right. *What does he need?*

She stood involuntarily as he came closer, and she caught his eye. When he looked at her with recognition, she smiled, and he tripped. He lost his footing and overcorrected, with his shiny black shoes on the floor, polished to a shine, and threw the First to the ground. She fell on her hip and cried out. The Leader was there in a moment, offering her a hand.

She stood, looking confused and concerned for her son. As soon as she was up and his father had relieved him of his post, Quin walked away from them without another word. He walked directly toward Marishel, who was instantly the focus of everyone who had witnessed the accident. Marishel squirmed under the speculative glances flying at her like darts from every direction.

She remained frozen as Quin stood in front of her, speechless. He took in her newly made-up fanciness, looking from her sandaled feet to her pile of spilling curls.

"You are stunning," he said.

Marishel vaguely heard some whispers nearby, but she couldn't form a full sentence. The emerald green of his jacket made his eyes stand out in his face like stars in the sky, lit from behind and clear as a wish.

Rena stood and poked Marishel in the side.

"What? Oh. I'm sorry. You're quite handsome—especially in my favorite color." Her eyes crinkled, and she hoped he was feeling better now.

He smiled. "It just so happened to be one of my choices."

"It suits you." She looked at his shoes. For some reason, she couldn't stop staring at the white spot of shine on the toes, and the shiny fasteners on the side. Her tongue was tied and the fiery arrows of hate and speculation coming from around her, burned through to her insides. She wanted to shrink away from the attention.

He held out his hand. "Would you dance with me?"

Aware of the glares directed her way, she hedged. "I don't know if…"

"I'm sure Lonna would love to," Rena said in Marishel's ear, which had its desired effect.

"I'd love to." Marishel smiled.

He stalked regally to the center of the floor, with his hand out and her fingertips lightly resting on his palm. He stopped and stood in one place while she walked around him in a circle, following his hand. He bowed and she curtsied as an old folk dance played, then he reached around her waist and put his hand on the small of her back, holding her other hand in his.

Quin pulled Marishel so tightly to him that she felt like she was going to walk on his feet, but she didn't. She kept thinking she was going to trip, but every time her ankle rolled, he lifted her off her feet and swung her around, her right hip and his interlocking. She pointed her toe as he swung her, touching down lightly with a few skips before the next step.

They stood apart and clapped twice over their left shoulders, then spun in place. He stood still and crossed his arms while she did a walk-skip around him, touching his leg with her instep every turn. Marishel quickly readjusted the falling dagger before putting one hand on her hip and the other palm up like she was holding a serving tray. They spun and dipped, twirled and clapped, laughed, and shuffled two steps at a time. Finally, the music came to the lilting sweet strains of strings, winds, and bells. Quin pulled her close and she hoped the blade wouldn't fall from between their bodies. Trying to remain present in the experience—which might be their last—she concentrated on the music.

"The Martian Symphony. Your favorite," she said with a tilt of her head.

"Yeah. Mother knows I like it. Maybe it's her apology, but I doubt it." He looked down at her and smiled subtly.

She doubted that very much, but she let herself move to the music. It was taking her back to a happier time. "Why would she apologize?"

"She was angry that I couldn't *woo* your confession." He chuckled.

She grinned. "You can try again," she said. "I'm down for some more wooing."

He threw his head back and laughed. Then he looked down at her and his features morphed into a gaze of desire.

"You look beautiful tonight." His thumb rubbed her hand, and his other hand caressed her waist intimately.

The bottom of her stomach dropped out.

She inhaled the warm fragrance of sandalwood and let her emotions go. She was just a girl, in lo—*was she in love?* She didn't know. Just a girl in *like* with a boy, on a date.

"So, is this our second official date?" she asked. "After the dessert, of course. My father was proud of you for being such a thoughtful gentleman."

"About that—did you work out the problem with your friends?" His concern was evident in the wrinkle etched across his forehead.

Marishel glanced toward the chairs where she left the girls and saw them watching her. Shalise clutched one fist to her chest, squeezing Rena's hand with the other. Rena made kissy faces and rolled her eyes at Marishel who laughed despite her attempt to play it cool. Quin followed her gaze and laughed—a great booming bass that rumbled through Marishel's chest deliciously.

She lay her head against him, and they slowed their movement to a sway. She didn't care what face Rena was making … she was home.

When the music changed, Rena and Shalise joined them in a hip-swaying fast dance. A couple of young men in attendance also slid into their circle and one tall and skinny guy kept making eyes at Rena. When she ignored him, he stepped closer to Shalise who seemed flattered by the attention. Marishel was having the best night of her life and tried to push thoughts of tomorrow from her head. She wanted to imagine that she and Quin were normal people with a future and hopes of happiness together. They didn't talk much, but all made faces and bumped each other, Rena

JENNIFER HASKIN

wrapping her arm around Marishel as they danced the same steps to a popular song from the social network.

When the waltz played, the other guys asked Shalise and Rena if they'd like to get a drink. They agreed and as they left, Rena put a hand on Marishel's arm and smiled. "We'll keep looking for you-know-who. You guys enjoy the dance."

When they were gone, Quin asked, "Who are they looking for?"

"Oh! I didn't have the chance to tell you. Remember your mother speaking about that group in rebellion?"

He nodded.

"The leader is here somewhere and wants to meet with me. I'm sure they have a fantastic plan."

"That's great news. Do you know what it is? Can I help?" His brows rose.

"I have no idea. We're looking for a man with a *Sanger Orbiter7* shield."

"Well, let me know if you need me."

She grinned. "I always need you."

Quin opened his arms and Marishel stepped into his embrace, pressing together, and swaying to the beat. She didn't care about propriety tonight. No one knew what tomorrow would bring, so she lost herself in his arms. They stared at one another, communicating with their gaze, the emotions they had no words for.

As she realized how much she'd grown to care for him and how uncertain her future was, the black and heavy weight of despair squeezed her insides. She drank in his presence, wishing they had a solution. She never wanted things to change, and she felt out of control. It was a feeling she did everything in her life to avoid. Instead, Marishel

361

concentrated on the present. She was right where she wanted to be, and she clung to Quin desperately.

"Are you okay, baby?" His brows lowered in concern, and it was her undoing.

Tears filled her eyes. "I want to stay like this forever."

He hugged her tightly. "Me, too."

"Can we pretend tomorrow will never come? Let's run away."

His brows scrunched in curiosity. "Really? You'd lose your freedom, and your family would lose everything. Are you sure you'd want to do that?"

"Right now, I don't care. As long as I have you."

"Are you serious?"

She thought about it, even as she knew she had no choice but to complete the task ahead of her and sighed. "Just hold me?"

"Absolutely. I'd do anything for you. Just tell me what you want." He appeared so sincere.

"I want you," she whispered.

He bent his head toward her like he was about to kiss her, his expression filled with passion. She tipped her head back and parted her lips. Their eyes were half-closed, their lips nearly touching, when a throat cleared loudly nearby, bringing them back to the present. The Leader approached them with Politician Hinkle, an amused half-frown contorting his face. "Ahem. Son? Miss Vance?" He put a hand on Quin's shoulder and the couple parted.

What could he want? she wondered peevishly. Politician Hinkle stood there with another man one could only describe as tall, dark, and handsome. Unfortunately, it was apparent in his stance and cool smile that he knew it. Marishel was immediately turned off. She hoped they didn't have much to say.

"Yes, Father. Politicians. How can I help you?" Quin sounded so responsible; she was proud of him.

The men smiled at them, and Hinkle said to Quin, "I have something of importance I need to discuss with you." Then he turned to Marishel. "Miss Vance, I'd like to introduce you to a very dear friend of mine, Politician Kyrel. He's happy to keep you company while we chat for a moment."

"Oh, that's really not necess—" she began.

"I'm afraid I must insist. There are time-sensitive matters at hand." Politician Hinkle put a hand on Quin's back, and they began to walk off, Quin glancing back at her.

"I'll just be a moment," he said with a wink. "Stay here."

She nodded to the Leader and Politician Hinkle, but as soon as they left, she attempted to beg out of the dance. The problem was, if she wasn't dancing with Quin, she needed to look for Blayk. She'd forgotten herself, and suddenly, it was of vast importance for her to find the man as soon as possible. She couldn't risk missing out on his plan. The Match was approaching quickly, and she began to panic.

"I'm sorry, Politician Kyrel? Are you related to Lonna Kyrel? Though I am quite pleased to meet you, I really must go." She turned to leave and took a step.

The man grasped her arm just above the elbow and she gasped and turned back to face him with a glare. It didn't hurt, but the grip was firm. He was letting her know he wasn't taking no for an answer. She expected him to be angry, but when she shook off his arm, he was smiling but tense, like a frustrated salesman.

"Not to be redundant, *Miss Vance*, but I'm afraid I insist. Would you like to dance, and I can explain?"

She didn't want to, but it was apparent she needed to humor this politician for at least a few moments. Marishel accepted his hand and allowed him to lead her around the room in a waltz.

He tried to engage Marishel in conversation a few times, but she was too preoccupied to answer. She searched the room for Quin, but he was gone from sight, and no one she saw was carrying a shield. Would Blayk have a literal shield with the *Sanger Orbiter7* on it—or something else? What else could it be?

"Are you looking for someone, dear?"

Marishel hated it when older men called her "dear." It made her skin crawl. "Yes, actually. I am." She knew she was frowning when he began to spin her around the floor. Politician Kyrel led her steps so quickly, she didn't have time to stop and plant her feet and insist that he stop right now. Her feet barely touched the floor. His shoulders were massive, and he sported a square jaw full of light stubble. Very old-world Superman—if Superman were a smarmy salesman. "I'm expecting someone, and I can't spend my time, well—"

"Dancing?" He raised one brow at her, calling her bluff, and she liked him even less.

She followed his steps, panting with the effort to keep up. "Fine," she said breathlessly. "You win. Just slow down."

He flashed a very self-satisfied smile and she wanted to sneer back at him—or slap him. His look of superiority and pomp was probably all just a cover for some major inferiority complex. When she narrowed her eyes at him; he looked just like *her*. She stiffened.

"You're Lonna's father, aren't you?"

"Yes."

She pulled her arms, trying to extricate herself from his embrace. He'd prepared his daughter to win. What had she told him about Marishel? Did she tell her father that Marishel was threatening her success in the Match? Was he here to stop her? How? With a blade across her throat like Analiyah?

He held her tightly. "We are going to talk ... privately." His voice lowered so only she could hear him.

"Look Mister—ah, Politician Kyrel. Don't take this the wrong way, but I'm not going anywhere with you." Marishel planted her feet, and he jerked back when she stopped cold and stood still.

"Don't make a scene. Just step out on the patio with me."

"Why can't you talk to me here?" She put her hands on her hips.

"There are too many eyes and ears here," he said through gritted teeth.

Every bell went off and every red flag raised in Marishel's mind. Lonna's father could not mean good news for her in any way. The man was a cold-blooded politician. She refused to move, though his fingertips were digging into the soft flesh of her arm. That was going to bruise.

"Let go of me," she said with deadly calm. "Right now."

He sighed and rolled his eyes. "Fine. Have it your way. You're waiting for a man, right?"

She looked at him warily. "I'm not saying you are right or wrong, but what business is it of yours?"

He held out his arms in a dance pose and she relented, allowing him to draw her around the floor. Marishel looked for the girls, but the chairs were abandoned, they were nowhere to be seen, and Quin hadn't come back. As the music played, they circled the room and came closer to the arches leading to the patio. She didn't know if she was shaking and sweating from the dance or from her sudden unspeakable fear. He couldn't be happy about her plans if he wanted his daughter to win. He would need to eliminate Marishel for that plan to work. What would he do to her if he got her alone?

He looked at her. "Well?"

"Well, what?"

He growled softly—actually growled. "The man you're looking for. Look here." He pointed to the left, near the main doors, but his shoulder was in her way, flashing about five hundred pins for rewards in service on his jacket. No one that faithful to Haumean politics could have her best interest in mind. If he didn't plan to assault her, she couldn't imagine why he would want to get her in private.

She stood on tiptoes and looked over his shoulder, then around his arm, and narrowed her eyes at him. "He's not here yet." She didn't know what she was looking for, but she hadn't seen any blond jerks yet. No shields.

"When we go outside and get to know each other better, I'll show you whatever your little heart desires."

She was appalled at the man's forwardness—even for a politician. Marishel ripped away from him but didn't want to go outside where he wanted to abuse her in the dark, so she sprinted for the hallway to the next building.

"Hey! Wait!"

Marishel could hear him running after her.

"Come back here you pain in the ass," he called after her.

Not made for running, her sandal heel twisted and broke off and she stumbled forward, putting her hands on the ground and pushing herself back up as well as she could do in the sheath dress. She rose and took a step when the man's hand squeezed around her arm tightly.

"Enough," he said, panting. "Marishel Vance,"—he straightened up and held out his other hand—"I'm Blayk Kyrel."

CHAPTER TWENTY-TWO

KH'RA

MARISHEL'S MOUTH HUNG OPEN IN THE empty hallway, the buzzing of the lights overhead like a wasp nest in her ears. "You're Blayk."

"I was starting to think you'd never get it."

"But what about the ... thing he's supposed to have for me to recognize him?"

He sighed again, like maybe she *was* stupid. "I already showed you." He pointed to his left lapel and poked one of the pins that was in the shape of a shield, with a generic-looking spaceship in the middle of five gold circles.

She felt stupid. "I'm sorry. It's been a crazy day. So, if you're leading the—"

"Sshhh. Let's go outside."

"Okay."

As she turned toward the door, she saw him kick something, but she didn't know what. It pinged in the hallway. Blayk followed her out to a shadowed sidewalk before taking the lead. He strode with purpose, and she nearly ran beside him taking three steps to his every one. "So, if *you're* the leader, how does that work? How can we trust you?"

"You can't." He stopped and looked at her. "You don't have a choice." He began to walk again, and her stomach dropped. She had a bad feeling about this. They crossed the back side of the lawn, away from the other guests.

"So why do this if you've trained Lonna to win?" Marishel leaned down and flipped her shoes off, tripping a few steps and hurrying to catch up.

"Lonna's mother died right after she was born." He stopped again and stood looking up at the dim lights above and Marishel waited.

"Lonna came out just like her—the love of my life. *Loves.* The Ambassador had just been born. I'm a politician, but even that wouldn't save Lonna if she got called for the lottery. I couldn't stand the thought of losing her—in a way, losing my wife twice. I did it out of weakness." He sounded angry about it. "I trained her so that if she was ever chosen, I wouldn't lose her."

"What changed?" Marishel asked softly, and he began to walk again. She jogged to catch up, holding her sandals by her fingertips.

"Vangie." He spat her name like poison. "Or any one of those worthless girls. The so-called 'winner's pool' is a joke. All the footage is edited. It's impossible to tell who's actually winning. It's skewed for the blood-hungry public." The more he spoke the faster he got, and consequently the faster he walked. "Vangie is slated above Lonna. Has been for a week. Plus, accidents happen. Anything could happen, and I'm not prepared to deal with that. I refuse to deal with that."

Marishel tingled with an unexplainable nervous feeling. Anxiety crawled her limbs like spiders building acid webs. She had confirmed that Blayk was indeed mucoid, but the words he spoke agreed with the cries of her spirit for freedom—for fighting back.

"What's the plan?"

"I'll explain it to you on the way there."

"Where?" she asked.

He looked at her like she might be affected and turned forward again. They walked behind the buildings and cut through an alley between the kitchen and the wash building. They emerged to a cacophony of sound. The kitchen staff, finished with their duties and allowed to feast on leftovers, were having a raucous party of their own with music *not* First-approved. The song was loud, and drunken revelers stumbled about chasing skirts and fist fights.

"Just keep your eyes forward," Blayk said quietly as they cut between parties and the joint attendees. "And take this off." He pulled off her headpiece and threw it like a flying disc, but she didn't have time to be offended, he was moving too quickly.

The whole area smelled like a still, mixed with vomit and urine. They headed to a little parking lot off to the side, lined with small delivery vehicles.

"You're the last part of the plan. My people have been working while I came to fetch you. I hope they didn't run into any trouble."

Marishel didn't answer that but asked, "Are they waiting for us?"

"The last of 'em is in the van." He pointed ahead. "Or they should be. If not, plan's off."

Acid burned up her throat. She cleared it and swallowed. Her legs weakened and felt jelly-filled. It couldn't backfire now. But what were they doing? What was the plan? She needed to know what was going on fast. Or she was going to have to back out. She got the feeling Blayk may not be entirely hinged correctly. The feeling surrounding the whole thing was uncomfortable, to say the least. She was thankful now, that Rena had pilfered the dagger, *just in case.* She resisted the urge to touch it.

As they walked up to the white van, she thought she heard screaming, but then a girl flew out the kitchen door, shrieking wildly while a young man grabbed her around the waist from behind. Marishel smiled, jealous of the young lovers and their freedom, their ability to play guilt-free. The boys banged on tables as several pairs held arm-wrestling competitions. They were surrounded by laughter and gaiety. Blayk walked up to the back of a white van and pounded on it with his open palm. Three bangs, pause, two bangs. Then an echoing set of thuds came from inside the van.

"Okay," Blayk said. "All set. Let's go."

"Look, I'm not sure about this—"

"Gods, you kids are difficult. Not like I give a bunk, but you might want to look in the front seat—where you need to hide—right now. We need to get out of here."

Marishel peered into the cab of the vehicle and saw a figure in a dark coat and hood. She squinted her eyes and ducked her head to see under the hood and she gasped as she recognized the pearly white teeth and sparkling blue eyes.

"Trae!" she cried, slapping her hands over her mouth, and looking around.

"Great. Now get in the kersed van," the politician grumbled.

Marishel climbed into the small cab and threw her arms around Trae's neck. "I'm sorry about— I was so worried about you. What happened? How are you here?" She pulled back to see his bruised face and frowned. "Are you all right?"

"Yeah." Trae grinned. "This Rebellium group came and busted me out. Said they had a plan to stop the match and they needed a reporter who was sympathetic to cover it. They knew I was locked up from my 'special announcement.' I didn't know they were with you."

"They're not."

"Who broke me out, then?"

Marishel pointed across him to the driver. "Meet Blayk Kyrel. Lonna's father. He's the man with the plan."

Trae turned to Blayk. "Thanks, man. Where we going?"

Blayk looked sideways at Trae, measuring him. "Warehouse behind the Yind building. Know it?" He maneuvered the van out of the parking spot in a three-point turn and headed for the gates. "Hide her."

Trae helped Marishel down to the floorboard where she tucked under the glove box in a little ball. Trae's dark cloak covered her, and his legs pressed against her side.

"The Yind building," Trae repeated. "It's a set of warehouses if I'm thinking of the right place. There a good connection there for the feeds? I'll need a one-twenty-one-bit connection."

"All good. It used to be a functioning assembly plant and has a hot spot. What else do you need?"

"Do you know what I'm supposed to say yet?" Trae's narrowed eyes and focused expression said he was ready to work.

"Yeah." Blayk was silent for a minute as they passed a pair of guards guiding people for the ball. He rolled his window down and Marishel could hear him jovially chatting with the guard as they waited their turn to file out the gate. When they were clear, he spoke again. "It's a promo setup that goes over the Blood Match coverage feed, like the one you did before." After another minute, he said, "Okay, she can get up."

"So why do you need me?" Trae asked as he pulled on Marishel's arm, but she couldn't find her feet, so she shook him off and maneuvered her way into the seat by herself.

"I'm a politician. I can't be on camera. We need you to be the Rebellium's mouthpiece."

Marishel imagined the hungry camera feeding on Trae's energy, recording his desperate plea to stop the match.

"What's our reassurance?" Trae looked like he trusted this guy, maybe she was wrong.

"Huh?" she asked.

"It's a motivator for the people to make a certain decision and prompts the public to know we're serious," Blayk said. Then to Trae, "Oh yeah. We've got a doozie of a reassurance. Wait'll you see."

Now Marishel was certainly confused.

There was a bang from the back of the van, followed by yelling, and Blayk chuckled. "That's probably them now."

"In the van?" Marishel heard alarm bells echo in her head.

The men were laughing congenially while Marishel looked out the window and chewed a nail. She hadn't agreed to kidnapping anyone. Who was back there? Did he have Vangie? Rena and Shalise? Did he plan to hurt them?

373

No, no. This wasn't good at all. She wanted no part in a plot that would cause someone bodily harm. That was the whole point.

"They're fine," Blayk said with a chuckle. "Probably scratching my guy's eyes out."

"I didn't sign up for kidnapping." Marishel crossed her arms. The air in the cab was cold and her dress wasn't made for keeping warm.

"Did you sign up to die tomorrow? To kill your friends?" Blayk sneered.

Trae put his arm around Marishel, rubbing her bare arm briskly.

"No," she said. "But that doesn't mean I want to cheat. If we threaten them, they'll only see us as terrorists and refuse to negotiate, then we'll be tried for any crimes committed—on top of the Match."

"Don't worry so much. With what *we've* got planned, they'll listen." His maniacal smile was faced forward, but Marishel saw enough of it to confirm he wasn't playing with the right deck, let alone a full one.

This isn't going to turn out well. Would she need to use the weapon hidden inside her dress? She hoped not.

Trae tightened the arm around her when her body tensed with apprehension and concern. He said to Blayk, "I'm happy to report and be recorded, but I don't want any part in someone getting hurt. That's not journalism it's—"

"Would you two settle down? The hard part's done. All you have to do is read the cards we give you and you,"— Blayk looked over toward Marishel quickly—"all you have to do is stand there, next to our *reassurance.*"

Trae narrowed his eyes. "Everyone will assume the message is from her."

"Exactly," Blayk said. "We don't have to say who we are. We don't have to lie. She's done enough on her own to show she's against the thing. It's the natural assumption."

"No…" Marishel said the word in a near whisper, then again, louder, "No. I'm not going to be the *only* one to take the fall for your crazy plan."

It was the wrong choice of words and the van nearly swerved off the road and into the glass railing panels of the moving sidewalk, as he turned to look at her. "It's a well-designed plan! Fool proof."

Marishel kept quiet. She shook in her seat, and Trae's arm squeezed her shoulders. When they pulled behind a dark warehouse building, a garage door opened and Blayk drove the van inside, shutting off the engine and hopping out with the keys.

"I'll talk to them. See what I can do." Trae swept back her hair with his other hand. "You won't look very at fault if they have to tie you up in the shot."

"I'm scared," she said, seeing him in the light for the first time and noticing the bruises all over his face. What had they done to him? What would they do to her after this? "For the first time, this seems real. I've assisted in a kidnapping and I'm going to be seen as a terrorist. The Match will go on and I'll be hunted. They won't stop the Match just because he has the girls—or maybe Vangie or Veda—it would certainly make me look guilty."

Trae squeezed her. "No. I won't have any part in that. We're a package deal. If they want me to report it, they'll have to leave you out of it."

"Get out." Blayk stood just outside Marishel's window and waved toward himself.

Marishel refused, folding her arms. She wasn't going to be his savior.

Blayk opened the door and gripped Marishel's arm. She growled, "Let me go. I'm warning you. I want you to take me back, this instant."

He roughly pulled her from the vehicle, and she reached for her dagger ... but it was gone. Alarmed, she realized it must have tumbled from her dress when she'd fallen and now that she needed it, it was gone.

"Looking for your child-sized weapon?" Blayk sneered, then raised his eyebrows. She knew then that it must have been her dagger that he kicked away in the hall. She gave in—she had no other choice—and Trae scooted out behind her.

Blayk pointed to Trae. "You come with me, and we'll fill you in on the essentials. You"—he pointed to Marishel—"stay here with Ghaty and guard the prisoner."

Marishel wrinkled her brow. "The prisoner? Now Politi—"

"Oh, blow it out your ass, Marishel. You're the scapegoat. You don't have a say."

"I never should have come with you," she said.

"Always trust your instincts," he said with his upper lip wrinkled nearly to his nose.

"Point taken." She folded her arms.

They were in a vast, dimly lit concrete space with huge concrete pillars lined up like chess pawns on a board. To her left, a floor of rooms stood in the middle of the warehouse created by black beams and half walls in white, topped with paper-thin panels, where she could see silhouettes moving in the rooms.

Blayk and Trae headed in that direction. Then, Blayk looked back at her for a moment and yelled out, "Ghaty!"

"Yes sir!" a young man not much older than Marishel hopped from the back of the van. He was dressed in the uniform of one of the servers from the Blood Ball. *We have been infiltrated.* Marishel felt a bit of ownership with the Leader's family and entertained the notion of personal offense as one of the household—however temporarily.

Blayk pointed to Marishel. "That's her. The girl. See that she stays here with you or it's your job. Got that? If she tries to leave, bind her." He looked at Marishel with raised brows.

She tittered a fake laugh. "I'm sure that's not necessary, Politician. We'll be just fine."

He narrowed one eye, and she wondered if she'd overplayed her hand. But he put a palm on Trae's shoulder and restarted his previous conversation, walking toward the offices.

She was going to have to play this safe until she knew what to do. Of course, she couldn't let them blame her, but she had faith that Trae would make good on his promise to back out if they tried it. Plus, she really did need his plan to work. If, for some reason, they could even postpone the Match—even just long enough to look for Blayk and Marishel—it would give more people more time to come up with a better plan. It would work. She just needed to know a little more about what was going on.

She wasn't unhappy that she hadn't come face to face with the furious captives yet, but she knew the time was coming. They'd definitely blame her. Might as well get it over with.

Marishel turned to Ghaty. "Do you need help? What are you doing back there?" She smiled her most friendly, inviting smile and he blushed. She was delighted. *He's putty.*

"The tie came loose, and with all the thrashing about, I had to use sedation," he said.

377

"Oh." *They are going to wake up furious,* Marishel thought. "How long will they be out?"

"I only gave three-point-five cc's." He peered into the van. "They're starting to stir now."

Great. She'd better help the poor man, or he was likely to get a face full of fingernails. If it *was* Vangie, Marishel really was lucky to see the great presence tumble from her pedestal. Couldn't happen to a nicer girl... Suddenly she hoped he'd taken Lonna to throw the suspicion from himself. Marishel chuckled. That sounded like *Blayk*. At least she'd be comforted that her instincts had been dead on.

"Sure." He smiled widely. "I could use a hand."

Marishel walked to the back of the van and gasped with her hands to her mouth. Even with a bag over her bent head, she knew the dress that sprawled out on the hard bench—had watched it sweep across the floor. She turned to Ghaty. "You took *the First?*"

He grinned. "All by myself." A frown flashed across his face. "Well, almost. But we got her through the window and past her entourage, then I took over."

"Are you—" She was about to question his sanity—but remembered her position. She certainly couldn't get tied up now. *Kh'ra.* What was she going to do? She needed to think. She started again. "Are you going to keep her bound? Where should we take her?"

Marishel stepped in the van, hunched over, and helped Ghaty half-drag the First out to the back gate. She wasn't heavy, rail thin in fact, but the van had a low ceiling, and the process was unwieldy. The poor woman wasn't unconscious, but she wasn't aware of the living in any capacity. She didn't deserve this. Well, yes, she did. As misguided as she was, she was a mother trying to do the best for Quin. Still, Marishel couldn't help but feel a tiny bit of glee at her power over the First. She couldn't let them kill her—it would all fall on Marishel's head. Maybe if she rescued the First, she'd get a reward—like leaving the contest? She doubted it.

Ghaty hooped down and scooped the woman up under her knees, and the First lay her head on his shoulder.

"Karthik?" she said. "So tired."

Marishel watched her, so vulnerable, so breakable. If Trae got on the feed with the First as a hostage, they would kill him ... and her. Talk about thinking they were terrorists... They'd just proved it by playing their ace first. Karthik would do what was needed to get his wife back, but then he'd annihilate them all. Quin would hate her. *Quin. Oh no.* She made up her mind in a split second. She had to do whatever it took to get the First out of there. As awful as she was, Quin had reminded her more than once that she was still his mother. Marishel couldn't do this to him. And she couldn't bear to see hatred in his eyes when he looked at her.

She followed Ghaty around a concrete pillar and saw a stage set up as the inside of a room, exactly like the one at the state news department. It was the backdrop to any planet-wide official announcement, reproduced up to the widely criticized flag of Eris in the background. It would appear that they were broadcasting live from the law offices. *Clever.* Ghaty sat the First gently in a chair, letting her upper body rest on the desk in front of her.

"How'd you carry her so easily? You're not much bigger than I am." Marishel noticed.

He chuckled. "It isn't that hard if you distribute her weight evenly, and it helps that she's so light. Even if she wasn't, I could use specific muscle groups to lift a heavier patient."

"You seem to have some medical knowledge."

"I'm in the medical college." He smiled kindly.

"Don't take this the wrong way, but then, why are you here—with them?"

His face reddened with emotion, his lips turned down, and she was afraid she'd angered him, but he said, "I have a twin. A sister also in medical school. We are a surgical team."

"That's, that's, amazing. I've never met a doctor so young."

He laughed. "You're not the only one. We developed a technique that needs four hands and one mind to complete. The timing must be exact, the hands moving concurrently."

"I'm not following."

"You might know my sister. Her name is Kosie Anada. She is scheduled to fight and lose tomorrow, *and all her talent will be wasted*," he quoted the Paper. "The procedure won't work with anyone else. Even if it could, I can't allow her life to be taken… There is so much we planned to do."

"So, you joined the only people with a plan. Makes sense. I did the same thing. Look, Ghaty, I want to stop this as much as you do, but this is a terrible idea. The girls have agreed to lay down their weapons tomorrow. They will refuse to fight. I planned to appeal to the Leader and the First. But if we let them try to ransom her life for the end of the Match, we may sentence ALL those girls to death if they call our bluff. Either way, you will never practice medicine again. When Blayk goes down, do you think he won't take you with him? Everyone here will be a walking target if it happens."

He paled.

"Don't you realize I'm telling the truth? Think about it Ghaty. I know you're a smart guy. Surely you were acting passionately, out of love for your sister, but stop and think. Where is this going?"

"They could kill her anyway?"

"Wouldn't you? If someone threatened your wife's life for something you were set on doing, wouldn't you be a little tempted to retaliate? Call their bluff? To show your power—if you're a leader? People will be watching what he does, Ghaty. This isn't a private affair."

They were silent a moment and she let him think while she wondered where they were and how to get back. *Why didn't I pay attention to how we got here?* She would have to go back an alternate way no matter what, but if she didn't know the route, how could she stay away from it?

The First was stirring. Her wrists were bound, and her arms lay on the desk. She rolled her head around on the flat surface.

"What should we do?" Ghaty asked. "We don't have much time. 'Ten minutes tops' is when he said he wanted to record."

Marishel thought. "Do you want to come with us? Help me get her home?"

He shook his head. "I can't let you leave. The politician will hunt me down and break my fingers. He told me so. Then I'd lose my job."

"That's what he meant when he said it's your job at stake? What an unimaginable jerk." She smiled kindly. Though he wanted to help, Ghaty was now an extra hassle. She'd have to get around him somehow. *Think, Risha.* "Okay. I'll help you. We need to untie her and get the bag off her head. But she's coming around. Should we give her some more of that sedative?"

He frowned. "Yes, but only a little."

"Where is it?" Marishel asked.

He pointed to the vehicle. "I have a case with syringes in the—"

"I can get it. You cut her loose. I'll be right back." Marishel ran back to the van and under the bench, she felt a small case. She heard his blade flick open, and she slipped one syringe from the case, tucking it in her bodice, and zipped the case up. She brought it to him, and he motioned for her to set it on the desk while he cut the First's arms free. Marishel put the case down and removed the First's hood. Then, when Ghaty bent down to slice the zip tie at her feet, Marishel moved behind him, plucked out the syringe, and stabbed the needle into his neck, pushing the plunger all the way. *Was that too much?* She hoped not.

Ghaty put a hand to the back of his neck and faltered before slumping over onto his side. The First's head lolled on her shoulders; her eyes closed. Marishel had a little too much fun slapping her cheeks.

"Wake up." She tapped the other side again. "Wake up, Gioia. We need to take a little walk. Come on. Wake up."

The First roused enough to rise from the chair and collapsed on the floor next to it.

Marishel bent down and used Ghaty's zip ties to bind his ankles to the chair. She nodded, then stood looking down at him. *Time to go.*

The First moaned on the floor.

"Okay, you. We need to get going quickly. Come on," she said, grunting with the effort of pulling the woman to her feet. "Gioia. Wake up. Work with me here. One foot in front of the other. Come on."

Marishel settled herself under the First's shoulder and wrapped the woman's long arm behind her. The First leaned on her and Marishel pushed the woman forward with her hip. They took a step. Oh, this was going to take a long time.

She had no choice. She had to run, or they'd catch her before she was off the premises.

Distribute her weight. Marishel got in front of the First and knelt, so the wobbly woman leaned across Marishel's shoulders. When Marishel stood, she held the First's arm over one shoulder and her leg over the other while red organza flowed behind them. It fluttered like a bull's flag as Marishel used all her new muscles, stamina, and the rest of her adrenaline to step quickly for the door. The First was light enough to carry but heavy enough to make Marishel pant with the effort. Luckily, she only needed to get to the first place where she could hide them both.

It was a grueling pace, even as insubstantial as the First was, and Marishel had long sweated off her makeup when she found a street she recognized. At once she knew where she was and the best way to get back. Her spine ached and her bare feet trailed bloody spots from the sharp rocks–her sandals still on the floorboard of the van.

Marishel, exhausted and teetering, entered the residential street and sneaked into the closest backyard. Attached to the house was a utility and bike shed. She unhinged the creaking door and stepped inside. Using the wall, she lowered herself to the ground and carefully rolled the First from her shoulders. She still hit the ground with a thud and a moan. Marishel sighed. She couldn't go any further.

Though she'd thought she heard voices yelling and saw headlights flash in the distance, the chances of them knowing where she was now were pretty small. She would rest here in the dark until the First could wake up enough to walk. Then they'd run home. *Home*, she chuckled.

She rolled her shoulders and stretched one arm across her body, holding it there, and then reached around her back to pull her shoulders taught. Marishel's fight-or-flight hormones had kicked into action mode and allowed her to carry the First to relative safety, but now she was crashing hard, and it was getting late. Without moving, Marishel leaned back onto the First and slipped out of consciousness.

"Get off me, you maggot!"

Marishel heard the words from far away, but as her body was pushed upright, she woke suddenly and turned. "Oh! I'm so glad you're awake! Are you okay?" Marishel looked at the First, holding her hands out, but the woman glared hatred back at her.

"You!" she spat. "I should have known *you'd* have something to do with this."

"What? No. I saved you. Someone else kidnapped you. Don't you remember?"

"All I know is that I was at the ball, and now you are laying on me in a dark room. Where are we? I demand to go back to the ball at once. I will see you caned this very night." The First pushed herself up and looked around in confusion.

Marishel sat on the floor. She'd thought the First would see reason and be thankful Marishel saved her. All she wanted was an answer—a way to stop the Match—but everyone was out for themselves. How had this gone so wrong?

CHAPTER TWENTY-THREE

CAN'T TRUST YOUR INSTINCTS

THE FIRST STRODE OUT THE DOOR and Marishel hugged her knees, waiting. The woman returned to the shed and pulled the door behind her, leaving a crack of light to see each other. "Where are we?"

Marishel sighed. "I told you. Some rebel guy—Lonna's dad—had you kidnapped, and they were going to ransom you to stop the Match. But I saved you."

"Lonna's father is a politician," the First said with her nose in the air.

"Yeah. I know. And a father who doesn't know if his daughter has a chance to live or not. There are a lot of people who want the Match canceled."

"Who?" she scoffed. "Your *friends?*"

It wasn't worth it to implicate anyone else, so she didn't answer.

The First stood with hands on her hips. "Well? Let's go."

Marishel hung her head. She would be at fault either way. "I'm not going," she said. "Take yourself back. You can sic the Coercitors after me."

The First cocked her head and regarded Marishel for a few minutes gauging her level of commitment to the assertion, but Marishel did not back down, nor did she move a muscle. The First strode to the other side of the shed and back a few times.

"Fine. I won't harm you. I understand what you're saying. Someone from the outside must be responsible. You couldn't have done it on your own, and I know you didn't carry me out in front of everyone. I don't know how you got me *here*, but I believe you. We will find the real criminals and deal with them later. Thank ... you. For ... helping me." The First nearly choked on the words, but she looked so out of her element next to the shovel and purple bike. Her face dropped all malice. She actually appeared fearful. Marishel had the smallest spot of pity for her—she'd been through a lot, too. "Can we go back now?"

"No." Marishel didn't believe her for a minute.

"I said I wouldn't hurt you. If you don't get up, I will wait here with you until the Coercitors find us, and then you'll wish you had." Her voice was menacing.

What should she do? She could run from the Coercitors, but they'd strip her family of everything they owned—and she could never go back. If she went with the First, maybe the woman could explain that Marishel had saved her. At the very least, the girls had a game plan. She decided to trust her instincts this time.

"Okay," she said, standing. "Let's go."

JENNIFER HASKIN

They walked side roads. The First had no idea how to navigate the neighborhoods. Even though Marishel knew where she was, she explained that the kidnappers could be out looking for them right now, ready to throw them into a moving van and knock them out. The First paled and nodded. They walked most of the way back without saying a word, occasionally checking the area for lights or the sound of a motor.

When they crossed a side street with a fountain on the island, the First exclaimed, "I know where we are."

There's no feeling like being lost and realizing you know where you are. Marishel appreciated the First's enthusiasm and the woman gathered speed.

"Come on, hurry up," the First called back in her excitement and Marishel jogged, stepping lightly on the balls of her bare feet, trying to avoid any sharp pebbles.

The First was walking quickly when they rounded the wall to the rear of the Leader's complex, but Marishel was right by her side. There were guards stationed at the gate and Marishel thought there must have been quite the ruckus when they were found missing. The guards watched them approach, and suddenly the First broke out into a run.

"Oh, it's so good to be home," the First cried. "Guards, guards!" She ran up to the men who came together to meet her—hair bedraggled, dress torn and stained. She grabbed one by the shirt, pointed back to Marishel, and said, "Guards, arrest her. She has attempted to kidnap me. She threatened my life, and I escaped."

"What?" Marishel yelled. "Why would I *do* that?" She asked the guards, "If I kidnapped her, why would I walk her home?"

They looked at each other but shrugged and moved to either side of Marishel, each grabbing an arm. Tears of frustration sprang to Marishel's eyes.

"But—I helped you. I saved your life from the real kidnappers. Why else would I bring you home?"

The First smiled kindly at her. "You know what my mother used to say?"

Marishel shook her head.

"Ignorants are ignorant of their ignorance."

"What?"

"Don't expect me to feel bad because you didn't know me well enough to guess this outcome. You will be detained until the Match. No more plotting for you." She pointed to Marishel with an over-exaggerated swirl of her finger.

"What about the girls?"

"What about them? You'll see them in the arena. And they'll be ready for you after I explain how you brainwashed the Ambassador into running away with you. And how, when I caught you, you said the other girls could take your place in the arena—that you didn't care about their fate as long as you could be with Quinlan. They'll be so hurt by your betrayal."

"But I didn't— That's awful. I'd never do that."

"Do they know you that well?" The First crossed her arms. "I've been keeping tabs on a few of your conversations. Everything in this estate comes through me first—and you haven't been very subtle."

"Why are you going to so much trouble to frame me?" Marishel tried to think of anything that might connect them in a safe way. "Your sons care for me, and I ... am fond of them, too."

The First screwed her face up with sarcasm. "Nice try with the mommy card, but I've been waiting too long for this. I've always known there'd be an adversary. There is every time. And I get to win the day of the Match—my second win—and then it's over."

"But if I win?"

The First smiled viciously. "You won't."

"I imagine it had to be very difficult after you won." Marishel changed tactics.

"Oh, please. I don't want your sympathy. And I don't want *you* thinking you understand me, because you don't. You don't know." The First was flustered. Marishel had gotten under her skin. *Good.*

"You're right, I don't. But I know the one thing you wanted that you didn't get—the thing your own sons deserve the most."

The First turned to walk away. "I'm not playing your games."

Marishel called after her, "A choice."

The First stopped but didn't turn around so Marishel continued. "Do you think Karthik would've chosen you? Do you think the Leader would have seen all the good you could do in your future? He would have seen how smart you are. Wouldn't you rather have been selected?"

When the First turned around with a purely murderous glare, Marishel knew she'd gone too far.

"You stupid little girl. You live in a world of black-and-white fantasies—shadows of real life. Fake. Lies. *You will perish tomorrow.* Just look up to the stands when you're struck—I want the last thing you see to be my smile."

"Then why not kill me now?" Marishel whispered with her chin up. The guards looked at one another as the First advanced.

She walked up to Marishel and stroked her cheek. "Patience, child. The time will come soon enough. Besides, for my win, I need to make sure things are fair."

"Fair?" Marishel cried out. "You call this fair?" She wiggled her arms, causing the guards to pull them tight.

"No. But that's not what you really want. You don't want to fight. You want to be saved. Why even ask me for death as if you want it? Don't you want to bargain? Don't you want me to spare your life?"

"What's the point? Sure, I want to live, and I want Quin's freedom, but you're going to hurt both of us either way."

The First scoffed. "You know nothing about my son."

"I know more than you think," Marishel said with a smile. "There aren't cameras everywhere."

"Don't threaten me. Things are already not going your way. You *failed*, Marishel. I don't know your plans—I don't need to—but whatever they were, they're over now. You will show up in the arena and die—fighting for my son. Then I will send a donation to your family ... and forget you." The First spun on her toe and took a few steps. "Oh, have fun down there, it isn't a *picnic in the labyrinth*. And trust me, Nahli did not adjust very well, either."

Marishel's voice shook. "What have you done to her?"

The First tittered like she was at a tea party, and gently swatted the comment out of the air. "She's spunkier than I gave her credit for. She didn't even give *you* up. And believe me, she was motivated. Let's just say, even you will have a better chance in the Match." She turned to the guards. "Now get her out of my sight." She strode away.

The three of them were silent, watching her go.

"You guys heard that, right?" Marishel looked at the men who hardened their faces and erased any surprise they might have had at hearing their boss's cruelty.

"Come on. You're going to a cell for the night." The guards gently, but firmly, led her through crowds of late partygoers milling about, tipsy and gossiping.

Marishel hung her head. It didn't matter what she said. They'd believe she was guilty. Why wouldn't they? The public didn't know her. In fact, if she didn't know better, she would have considered the First as a foremost authority on factual reporting. The girls *should* know better, but even Rena and Shalise had doubted her lack of a plan after catching her in a lie with Quin. And Quin ... the First would force him to choose between them. He didn't have a chance. His mother would order him to pick *her*—and she had the power to back up unfavorable opinions with consequences. He was right. There was nothing he could do. At least she knew he was trying.

She didn't pay attention to where they took her—only that it was *down*—down stairs and more stairs, halls, and more halls. Marishel walked numbly. The First was right— she *had* failed. She did see things in black and white. And why shouldn't she? There was truth and there were lies, were there not? So what if there were shades of gray? That didn't mean wrong wasn't wrong and right wasn't right. *Don't give up,* she told herself. But she hadn't even gotten to the cell yet.

It was easy to forget, with all the civility around them, that before there were walls and plastic partitions, their world was carved out of rock. Keeping more of the structure intact helped with the strength and integrity of the planet overall, and there was so much rock to carve. Many homes had old basements that had been carved and never finished with the rest of the house. The Leader's estate was apparently one of them.

A locked door led to the final set of stairs—they were cut rock and felt like ice on Marishel's bare and swollen feet. The guards had put a zip tie around her hands, and they went down the stairs with one guard in front and one behind. She thought, ironically, with her hands tied together, she was probably more of a threat to the guy in front than before—but she decided not to mention it. So Marishel descended the final stairs with her arms held out before her, to keep her balance.

They filed down a sparsely lit stone hallway of doors until the first guard stopped in front of one. He fished a metal ring out of his pocket and flipped through the keys. Marishel held her bound hands out to the other guard, who snipped the tie with his pocketknife.

"Sorry," he whispered. "You really saved her life?"

"Yeah. I listened to my instinct to give her a chance. And I should have known she isn't trustworthy. Now I'm going to die."

"Weren't you anyway?" the first guard asked, having heard the whole thing.

"I was hoping—if we could even pause the Match—I could make the Leader see it's wrong."

"Well, I got twenty-seven credits on Lonna, so I hope you don't. But I wouldn't wish to be you," he said. "Go on in." He motioned for her to pass him.

She bent over to get through the door, and she tried not to think about any creepy crawlies that might have found their way down to the cold and damp tenebrosity. The hallway was dimly lit, but the cell was like a glorified closet—nothing on the rock floor or walls of the cubed cutout, and only a barred hole in the door. She shivered and moved to the wall, but it was sweating, and the dampness chilled her skin.

The guards closed the door, and she heard the heavy *thunk* of the lock, then she was alone in the darkness, staring at the rectangle of light from the hallway. At least they hadn't shut it off and left her in the total blackness of space. She was grateful for it and made a point to breathe in her indebtedness and blow out her gratitude. She was alive, inside the planet. She still had her rights, but she didn't belong to herself anymore. That took her mind in many directions, but not anything she wanted to think about now.

She wanted to hope that the girls would rescue her, but knew the possibility was slim. Maybe the girls would—*no*. She couldn't count on the girls anymore. They were going to believe the First. Lots of girls go nuts the night before the Match. The First would say this time it was Marishel who'd gone crazy, and the girls would nod somberly, secretly glad it wasn't them, and yet jealous for the break in reality that bogged them down.

This was it. She inhaled deeply. Soon she would do this for the last time. She exhaled. Tomorrow, her breath would leave her body and she imagined she might float overhead and watch the battle, and then she would fly home and see Mom, and Baba, and sweet Madi. Tears gathered under her closed lids and slid effortlessly down her cheeks.

She would be no more. Would it be dark and cold and damp, like this? Or would it be like training under the lamps—torridly oppressive and sweaty? Or could it be Heaven, like the farm? Would she leave the planet to get there? Or was it really here where her spirit belonged?

She suddenly wished for greater wisdom—or religion. What was out there? She wanted to know the secrets of the universe. There were many manuals on how to live. Was there a manual for *leaving* life? She was terrified of what she didn't know.

Marishel couldn't turn her brain off to sleep. She kept thinking. What if she'd done things differently? What would have happened? What if she'd jumped from the train? What if she had actually convinced Quin to run— could she have done that? What would happen now? What would happen next? She lay on her side with her arms curled into her chest, her knees tucked up, and her ankles crossed under her behind. Compared to being stabbed by people you cared about, lying on the floor was just not that painful. *Relatively speaking, of course.*

Her original solution had never been realized and with Blayk's plan having bombed, she realized all hope was lost and accepted defeat.

The night dragged on forever, but the second Marishel heard Sobia saying, "Good morning," it faded as if it had only been an instant. Her stiff muscles bunched and screamed at her when she sat up.

The door lock clanked open, and Sobia bent as she entered, holding a bundle of cloth.

"It's good to see your face," Marishel said and immediately burst into tears.

Sobia set down her bundle and soothed Marishel, hugging her and running a hand over her hair, now fallen around her shoulders. At some time in the night, she'd been poked by the last hairpin and pulled them all out, throwing them about the room; Sobia stepped back on one and frowned.

"There is no bed for you here? How are you supposing to fight properly?" Sobia's accent was soothing. And her indignance on Marishel's part warmed her heart.

"What are you doing here?" Marishel asked.

"Getting you ready—I am helping." Sobia picked up the cloth bundle and shook it out to unroll it.

"Are the other girls getting ready now?" Marishel asked softly. Sobia nodded and picked up a hairbrush. She brushed Marishel's hair to a sheen and smoothed it back into a ponytail. She fixed it with a band but then pulled another from her pocket. She moved between Marishel and the door, facing her, and held out the bumpy silver band.

"What is it?" Marishel asked softly, reaching to touch it. It was cool to her fingertips.

Sobia whispered, "Is secret weapon—like zip tie, but metal ball joints. You use this, girls cannot escape, cannot cut or open it."

"Like handcuffs that don't open?"

"Is like that. You can twist, make loop for two hands, feet, whatever." She smiled.

"What are you whispering about?" A different guard—older, heavier—spoke from the doorway.

"We're just talking." Marishel ignored him. Really, what was he going to do? There was nothing he *could* do. So, she didn't feel bad about taking out some aggression on him with sass. "I'm getting dressed. Can't a girl have some privacy? I mean, if you're there, where am I going to go?" She motioned to the room around her. "Unless you plan to watch?"

The older man grumbled something unintelligible as he shut the door.

"You are ready for the Match?" Sobia attached the silver band to her ponytail, and picked up the cloth, shaking out socks and shoes. She held up a gray uniform. The Haumean flag was embroidered on a patch on the back.

When Marishel had the form-fitting one-piece suit on, gold stripes circled her biceps and thighs like Aztec bands, and she felt like a warrior. She had to sit to put on her socks, then Marishel put on one shoe while Sobia put on the other.

"Sobia? Do the other girls hate me? Did the First come talk to them?"

Sobia frowned and nodded slowly. "She came late to the girls and told them you are running away with Ambassador. She said you did not care about girls."

Marishel dropped her head into her hands.

"Your friends tell them do not listen. They whisper at many girls, but most were not looking happy." Sobia held out a hand and helped Marishel stand.

"I guess it was too much to hope they'd believe in a nobody like me." Marishel hung her head.

But Sobia tipped her chin up. "Stop this. You are wonderful girl—thoughtful, kind, friend to all. Did Turpen tell you of our sister?"

"Yes. I'm sorry. Is that why you offered to assist us?"

"*Da.* I am wanting to see what she went through. What is Match really like for girls? I need to know this to understand. I was baby when she was in contest and have no memory. But as a child, I am feeling her ghost around me. I am expected to be her by our mother and father. Yet, I know not how to be her. I am thinking she felt much like you on this morning."

"I know everyone is afraid today. All their plans have fallen through, and the person they trusted to lead them has betrayed them—or so they've been told. The winner's tier hates me for wanting to stop the Match, and now everyone will be racing each other to spear my heart."

"Have hope. You must always have hope."

Marishel looked at her incredulously. She'd *tried.* She really did. But there was nothing left. "There is no more hope, Sobia. I've run out."

"Mother used to say, *When you feel like rope is at end, borrow hope from good friend.* I let you borrow my hope for today." Sobia smiled at her with such acceptance, she couldn't answer. The small woman's blond hair fell forward like a silk curtain as she put her hands together and pressed them to Marishel's heart.

Marishel gave her a watery smile and they clasped hands. It was the anchor Marishel needed. She would fight. She would defend herself as best she could. She'd find Rena and Shalise and hopefully, they'd fight back-to-back until they couldn't hold their weapons anymore. Then someone, a small group, would overtake them and wear down their strength. Marishel would die today in Rena and Shalise's arms. She would pay the price, though it wasn't fair. And if she could do anything about it, she would.

Maybe she could climb up the wall to the stands and speak to the Leader face-to-face? Or, more likely, she might get halfway up and try yelling to him. Marishel wasn't sure if she wanted to see Quin today. She told him that she wanted him there, but she didn't want that picture to remain in his mind when he held his new wife. The thought irritated her like sandpaper toilet rolls, though there was nothing to do but get used to the idea.

She'd smile at him and that would be it. She'd forget him and fight for her life. Only the girls would matter after the presentation.

Marishel nodded at Sobia. "I'm ready."

Out in the hall, Marishel waited while Sobia gathered up the dress she'd left on the floor. Another door opened

397

down the hall and an attendant walked out carrying a bundle of cloth. She spoke to someone in the room and nodded.

Nahli slowly emerged from the cell and immediately limped swiftly to the next door. She banged on it with her fist. "Mama! I'm going now. I love you." Her hair was roughly shorn close to her head, chunks almost bare between dark brown tufts. The girls' uniforms were identical, but Marishel was horrified to see that Nahli was quite thin and now missing her right hand. Her face was dirty and tear-streaked and Marishel's chest ached, imagining what it must have been like down here in this cave after all this time.

A withered pair of hands stuck out the opening high in the door. Nahli held them with her only one.

"We are so sorry, darling. Daddy and I tried, but—" the voice inside the cell warbled.

"No. I don't blame you. Not at all." Nahli gripped the hands frantically, ignoring Marishel.

"You be brave," a voice came from the next door down and one large, brown hand hung out the opening.

Nahli ran over to the door and gripped the hand in hers. "I will Daddy. I'm going to win. Then I'll be back for you. I promise."

What would happen to Nahli's parents after the Match? A ball of anxiety in Marishel's stomach grew long needle-like spines. Every way she moved she could feel them poking her insides. *Enough*, she told herself, *stop being a baby and go be a warrior.* She turned to Sobia and motioned toward the stairs. "Let's give them privacy to say goodbye."

A shuttle waited for Marishel, and she didn't know how long Nahli would be, so she hopped in, and Sobia said something to the driver in a language she didn't understand. Marishel leaned her head back on the seat and listened to the foreign words as the shuttle rocked side to side. She felt the lights on her skin and inhaled all the way to the bottom of her lungs. The heated air felt good expanding in her chest.

When they arrived at the training center attached to the arena, Marishel stepped out. A woman with a tablet stood at the door and asked her name.

"Marishel Vance," she said.

The woman slid her finger down the list of names and stopped at the bottom. "Here it is. This is for your left wrist." She pulled a stack of multi-colored bracelets from her pocket and chose a black one. She pulled Marishel's outstretched hand and secured the band to her wrist.

"This is new," Marishel mumbled.

"Everyone else got ready in the locker room. They've lined up to be presented, so you need to hurry. When you enter the arena, keep going to the left and follow the line of girls. One at a time, you will stop on the platform, directly in front of the Leader's family, and bow gracefully. Across Haumea, once each girl steps off the rostrum, the voting for that girl is closed—all bets final. Do you understand your instructions?"

Marishel rolled her eyes. "Enter arena, follow line, stand on platform, bow to Leader's family. Got it."

"Don't get smart with me, please. Do you have any questions?"

"No, I don't." She sighed deeply. "Oh. When does the killing begin?"

"Young woman. Such language is not necessary. The contest will begin when all are in place and a tocsin sounds." The woman, in a gray uniform with gold stripes at the shoulders, held her device to her chest. "Do be a good sport. We won't tolerate unsportsmanlike conduct."

Marishel barked a wry laugh. "What would that entail?"

"Harming the staff—guards or cameramen—for one. And cheating, of course—gouging out one's eyes without 'finishing the race.' Leaving a contestant to merciless natural consequences, leaving one in great pain, or abandoning them to the next opponent without the chance for a fair fight—that type of thing."

"You realize we're not out there to *race,* right?" Marishel's stomach dropped. They wanted her to "finish off" an opponent she wounded or caused pain. She didn't know a girl there that she wanted to run through with a sword—not even Lonna. This was going to be a bloodbath. Pure and simple. She didn't want to be there anymore. Every instinct said to turn and run, but she had a responsibility.

Sobia pushed Marishel from behind. "Let us go. We will find entrance to arena. Come, Marishel."

She moved of her own accord, but her feet grew heavier with each step. As they traveled through a concrete locker room used periodically by ball players and other large competitions, Marishel tried to grasp the dream of ever winning this ordeal. She heard the hollow clunk of Sobia's shoes in the vast empty rooms, and it echoed her heartbeat.

"Remember," Sobia said. "Use *my* hope. Do not lose it."

"I'm sorry Sobia. I don't know if I can do this." Marishel dropped her shoulders. "Nothing I do will stop this. I have to prepare my head. I need to think of my family. They wo—"

Sobia stopped her. "They would not like to be seeing you go out there without hope. They cannot watch you giving up. You must be strong—you must fight every way you can till it ends. Do *not* let them have you." Her eyes shone with tears, and she narrowed them in anger. "Make them take it from you—only when you are gone."

Marishel threw her arms around Sobia's neck and held on as tightly as she could, absorbing all her hope like a sponge. Sobia was right; her family couldn't see her like this. She stood back and wiped her eyes, then took the tissue Sobia offered. Standing tall, she squared her shoulders. The First would be surprised and that gave her a guilty glee. There would be a winner today all right, and it was going to be Marishel. The First couldn't have her until she was dead and gone—and then it wouldn't matter.

Sobia threw away the tissue and placed Marishel's dress on a bench near several clothing items left by the other girls. Since they were going through the line—she'd better hurry. They neared the arena door and the two of them could hear a man speaking over the loudspeaker. It was attached to a huge screen in the back of the arena. There would be cameramen wandering around among the girls to get the best shots, putting themselves in mortal danger for the click or moment of a generation.

The shots were split and shown on the screen two or three at a time. There would be pandemonium when the starting alarm blared. The Blood Match always began with an introduction and premium shots of the girls from the past month in training, laughing while clustered around the sinks brushing their teeth, talking during supper with forks in the air, and sitting in class like proper ladies, learning about foreign diplomacy. Oh, it looked like the funnest Summerland camp ever.

She was glad she missed the next part. It used to be her favorite compilation of before-the-Match coverage. The screen would focus on private shots of the Ambassador on dates with different girls. A scene shot from over the bookcase in the library where the Ambassador spoke softly to one girl, or a half leaf-covered shot in the labyrinth where he splashed another girl by the fountain. Picture after picture of the Ambassador playing his part as bachelor of the generation would fade across the screen while the girls stood in front of the platform, shifting from foot to foot.

They'd seen it in the training videos. It was the same every contest. But now, Marishel heard the man and realized he was calling names near the end of the alphabet. She looked at Sobia with wide eyes, and they ran toward a gray door with a rounded bar handle that was nearly vibrating with the loud bass from the arena speakers.

"Rorie Ullman." The man's voice made an echo across the arena when Sobia flung the door open and pushed Marishel out.

Marishel stood there, blinded by the glare from the arena's VitD lamps, and she put her hand up to her eyes. Ahead of her, the few girls left waited at the bottom of the platform in the narrow band of shade from the arena sidewall. She dashed to the end of the line, shielded from the stands by a tall, white-painted wall, covered in smears of mud and old blood. Rorie's face filled the jumbo screen, a tight smile stretched her mouth and abysmal fear widened her eyes. In the middle of the arena stood a massive and more complicated version of their training yard obstacle course.

Half a dozen traps were rigged around the imposing structure, sharp-toothed jaws that would snap shut on anything that landed on them, and posts were stationed at intervals with dangling chains. Rope nets hung from ten-foot-tall frames where girls could climb up and battle on horizontal ladders resting between them, forming a precarious walkway.

Marishel knew Rena would be the last person in line, so she kept her head down. She couldn't handle Rena's frown or the blame in her eyes, accusing Marishel of betrayal. There was nothing Marishel could say that would make them believe her, and she didn't have much time left.

"Unity Wyburn," the voice called, and Unity climbed the platform stairs as Rorie stepped down on the other side, beyond Marishel's sight. Unity's face appeared on the screen, much the same as Rorie's, full of barely concealed fear.

Marishel stood behind her friend as they inched forward, but she must have made a noise because Rena spun around in shock, unaware someone was behind her. When she turned and saw Marishel, tears sprang to her eyes. Rena smiled broadly at Marishel and flung herself against Marishel's chest.

"I thought you were dead," she whispered.

"I thought you'd hate me." Marishel squeezed her and stood back. "I didn't—"

"We know. We knew as soon as she came. Shalise and I told the girls not to listen. But they were afraid you were dead, and morale went down the toilet. We tried to organize them, but no one would listen to us." Rena smiled. "You should have seen Shalise. She got fierce."

Marishel grinned in relief. A weight the size of their entire planet lifted from her shoulders, and she stood taller, lifting her chin. She had hope to spare. Her strength and resolve bolstered, she knew that brains, heart, and courage were required to face her fear. She was awakening to see her world differently. If she could somehow organize the girls…

"What did you tell them to do? What's the tentative plan?"

"Pemberlyn Yachowski," the speakers boomed.

They stepped forward again. Rena was next. "We told them to stand in groups of about five to each one in the winner's tier—or anyone they know who's not with us. The idea is to subdue the winner's tier first, but we didn't agree on anything after that. We were hoping—we didn't have a clue what was going to happen. But you're here." She laughed softly and shook her head. "Shalise is going to lose it when she sees you. She was so worried."

"I've got it. I have an idea. First, I need to eliminate the girls who are a threat, long enough to get a word with the Leader. If it doesn't seem to work, I have another idea. A last-ditch effort. It's a long shot, but I have hope." Marishel smiled genuinely.

"Valorena Yasuda."

Marishel squeezed her hand, and Rena disappeared up the stairs to loud applause. She was obviously a fan favorite. Of course, she was. Marishel was waiting for her turn when Nahli burst through the side door and stumbled trying to run over to her and dragging a foot. She was panting as she reached Marishel.

She watched as Nahli leaned over, her hand on her knee. "You okay?"

"No." Nahli didn't look up.

"Look, don't fight. Find a girl you know on the bottom tier and do what she does. I'm going to stop the Match." Marishel smiled. "Don't worry—it'll be okay."

"Marishel Vance."

She walked up the stairs regally, posture straight, shoulders back, head held high. The crowd erupted and she smiled joyfully at them and waved. Marishel looked ahead into the private box and met eyes with Quin. Her eyes swam and his were wet as they stared at one another. He stood and stepped toward her, reaching out his hand. He tried to come to her, but the First grabbed his arm, said something to the Leader, and they both pulled him back to his seat. He struggled to escape their grip. He was still fighting for her. Marishel smiled sadly, but with determination. No, she wasn't beaten. Not yet.

Her gaze slid over to the First, who was clearly in shock from her expression. Apparently, she had expected a much more demure, joyless, and fearful girl, and a much more obedient son. So Marishel beamed at her and gave a little bow. The First frowned deeply, but then a slow grin took over her face and it sent a chill down Marishel's spine. What did she have planned?

Suddenly, she knew she had to get through to this crowd, and she had to raise the girls' morale. "Watchers of the match!" she shouted with her arms raised, but the clear screen in front of her muted her voice. There were no microphones here, no one could hear her. She didn't have much time, so she spun around and faced the girls in the arena. She tried to meet her friends' eyes. "This isn't over yet! We don't have to do this! We can—"

"Nahline Keegan."

"—fight this!!" Marishel finished. "Remember what we talked ab—"

A mountain of a guard stepped up to the platform and yanked Marishel by the wrist, pulling her toward the stairs. She saw guards with rifles posted high along the arena walls, above the spectators, raising their weapons, aiming them her way.

Marishel stepped down and Nahli took her place. At the bottom of the steps to her right, a pair of guards stood next to the training cabinet full of weapons. The girls in her periphery all carried a weapon in each hand. *Good.* She could deal with those odds. She crossed to the training cabinet and went directly for the drawer where the Hawk's Talons were stored.

A young guard stepped in front of her, and she almost ran into him.

"Your bracelet."

She stared at him in confusion.

He held up his wrist and said, "Let me see your wristband."

"Oh." She held up the black band. There was a collective gasp from the crowd and Marishel looked up to see what it was, but the crowd was blocked by the wall, so she looked over the arena and saw herself on the huge canvas screen, with her bracelet held up for all to see. *The crowd must have a program that tells them what the colors mean.* But why that response?

She was confused once more, and the guard said, "Come here."

She assumed she would have a choice of weapons, but they must be given randomly. Marishel reached out, waiting for the guard to hand her weapon.

"I need both of your hands." The guard said, his voice deep and angry.

She held out both hands, expecting a larger weapon, and peered out into the arena looking for large gear held by the other girls.

The guard took her outstretched arms and slapped a pair of linked cuffs on her wrists. "Now, move along."

"What?" she asked, scrutinizing the chain between her hands.

He repeated more sternly, "I said, *move along*. The black band means you don't receive weapons, you get restraints." He motioned for her to leave.

She stood frozen for a moment, not sure what to do. Well, she couldn't stand there thinking about it. She attempted a non-bothered smile, but she knew she was failing horribly. She decided to stand as far out of the way as she could and try to think quickly.

Marishel stayed close to the wall and walked toward the middle of the arena. As she passed the first girl though, Binty Something-or-other, Marishel looked into her face and Binty winked with a little smile. A grin of relief. The girl was standing with a small group next to one of the course's pillars. The girl next to her winked as well. It took her aback. The support pumped life into her heart and body as she hugged the wall facing the structure, and almost every girl she passed, winked like a salute. The groups were spread out, many along the upper levels of the obstacle course. She nodded her head to each one. Rena had disappeared—probably to find Shalise—but Marishel couldn't see either one.

She felt suddenly vulnerable. There were not only cameramen in the arena, but guards were also stationed along the perimeter—though most looked disinterested, and a few leaned a shoulder against the wall. She prayed for a miracle. *Please, please ... all I need is a moment of distraction and an opportunity...*

Knowing the girls believed in her was the reward she'd wanted for doing the hard job—being the one responsible—and it felt good. Maybe she didn't fail after all. As Nahli chose her weapon—she was allowed only one—the girls nervously inched toward members of the top tier. Nahli walked over to Binty and whispered to her. Binty nodded and tilted her head toward Marishel, who looked back with an inconspicuous nod.

A shrill screech echoed in the arena, and this time the clinical voice of a computerized woman filled the air. "Ready to begin Blood Match... Five. Four. Three. Two. One."

A synthetic horn blared over the loudspeaker.

Each of the top-tier girls came alive swinging in all directions. Blood sprayed on the constructed course to a chorus of grunts and screams. Weapons flew and girls fell. The girls who were the least able to fight had a tough time subduing the most powerful girls who showed not only strength but skill with their spears and axes. Blades met muscle and bone. It was apparent to Marishel that at least a few of those who winked at her had been lying, as they slew their comrades closest to them. Confusion reigned.

A hand arced through the air to land near Marishel's feet as she hugged the wall, trying to stay out of the way. She was completely vulnerable and saw Lonna glancing at her as she hacked at the girl nearest her with a spiked wand, and held a shield in her other hand, deflecting blows of less talented girls.

With so much activity at once, it was difficult for the girls to coordinate anything. Two of the top-tier girls had banded together and stood back-to-back, spearing anyone who got close to them, and they moved gradually in Marishel's direction.

I can't just stand here, they need me, she thought, looking for an opening, or some way to help. Kindel, the girl Marishel knew from school, balanced at the top of a support and aimed her bow down, into the throng of girls, and began to fire. "Binty!" Marishel shouted. "Get Kindel!

Up there!" Marishel pointed to the beam and Binty notched an arrow in her compound bow, aiming at Kindel.

Two arrows flew—one after another—and missed. Kindel turned and aimed at Marishel. She jumped from side to side to make a more difficult target, but just as Kindel was pulling the string back, an arrow went through her hand, piercing her neck. She pulled the tip out swiftly and as blood spurted from her artery, she fell from the beam into the throng of fighting girls. If Marishel didn't do something, she would soon be a target. She shouted to another girl and made some progress and got an idea.

A few looked to Marishel, standing next to the wall in view of them all, and she spun into action like a conductor to an orchestra, calling instructions. She pointed at one group with her cuffed hands. "You guys, grab Faunda!" To another girl, she yelled, "Look out for Freesia!" An arrow arced high above the platform through the air, and she shouted, "Unity, move!" Then, back to her other side, Marishel called, "Quick, Anora—get Lonna! Her arm! The baton! Watch out, watch out. Kosie get down! Anora, *now!*"

A cameraman came to stand next to Marishel. He moved up close to her face and she frowned at him, pushing for him to give her space. She needed to help the girls first. Soon, her voice echoed over the arena, and she realized they were piping in the feed from the cameraman next to her. It was obvious she was leading the debacle and Marishel saw nearby guards push away from the wall and walk in her direction. She quickly spoke into the camera to the crowd, "Don't you all see how wrong this is? Have we lost the value of human life? Your children are killing each—" The feed stopped, and the crowd began to rumble.

She wasn't ready yet—they didn't have all the "top tiers" subdued. Marishel cautiously walked away from the guards, leaving the safety of the wall and coming closer to the fight. She still called out to the girls, holding her connected wrists over her abdomen.

As the majority fought for control, the entire top tier, plus a few she hadn't suspected, fought off one teammate after another. Girls were lying on the ground, the course, and one bent backward over the edge of the walkway, eyes open and her mouth dripping blood, just like Marishel's vision.

The crowd in the stands erupted with boos and lively chants to "stop the hate, mediate," and "voices for choices." The stands showed signs of coming chaos and violence as one man threw another into the arena, but the figure on the ground didn't move. A guard ran over to him and Marishel noticed the close proximity of the other guards headed her way.

Please, she thought, *I need some time...*

To Marishel's far-right, three sets of double doors burst open with a crashing boom. Heads jerked to see a flash of yellow-orange fire, and smoke billowed through the doors into the arena. She watched as a group of civilians wearing matching red clothing stormed into the arena with who she thought was Trae in the lead, shouting with fists raised. They carried staffs and batons and what appeared to be the chains from the door. A few of them dragged guards. As soon as they made their way into the arena, they spread out. It was pandemonium. The guards instantly changed course and attempted to round up the herd of rebels when one began the chant, "Stop the Match! Stop the Match!" and everyone wearing red, as well as revelers in the stands, joined in.

Many protesters entered the fray of murderous girls, trying to help defend some, but not knowing who was whom, they were more of a target than anything for the girls who were determined to win at all cost. And a few red-shirts were lost as bullet shots whizzed from above like deadly rain, drops pattering on their targets.

A guard held one man—who appeared to be Ghaty, dressed in a long red *kurta*—pushing with his arms behind his back. She was glad he was all right, and fleetingly hoped they didn't hurt him. *Wait.* This was her distraction—it was now or never. The platform was empty, but even if she could get up there, she couldn't speak right to the Leader. *I need another camera.* She hadn't noticed anyone after her but looked behind her anyway.

She saw the closest cameraman and took off. In her peripheral, she saw Vangie plowing through the girls around her, eyes locked on Marishel. Without weapons, she had no chance against Vangie. Her only option was to make it to the nearest camera first and say her piece before she was struck, but their paths would intersect before then. There was no time to think. Marishel tucked in her arms and dug the balls of her feet into the thick dust, pushing into a sprint, pebbles spraying everywhere.

Vangie decimated three girls who gave their lives trying to stop her. Time slowed to a crawl. Like a pedigreed racehorse, Vangie's perfect skin slid over her bunching muscles like copper-brown silk. She jumped over fallen girls as she ran and held a sword with a blue energized blade in both hands, making a figure eight in front of her. The distance between them narrowed. Marishel wasn't going to make it. Vangie would surely intercept her before she reached the screen. She had a split second to decide her options and Marishel hoped she had time to either jump or duck the swing. She geared up as Vangie ran from the right, straight toward Marishel's path.

Suddenly, a body jumped between them. Marishel knew instantly from the pink-tipped braids which beautiful girl had stepped in to protect her. And she knew the trick they'd been practicing was going to work. She would catch Shalise's blade and roll, standing to battle Vangie, hoping for others to join her. Shalise knelt and held up a shield of orange laser squares, humming with energy, and faced it toward Vangie. Marishel ran up to Shalise. She jumped high and her foot pushed off Shalise's knee, propelling her even higher.

Marishel soared through the air and flipped above Shalise. At that moment, Shalise tossed her sword up to Marishel, who grasped for it with both hands and missed completely. She flew over the shield and tucked her body to roll under Vangie's advancing sword, but when she had reached for the weapon, she lost her sense of balance. Her feet flipped over her head, and she landed flat on her back. Marishel gasped for the air thrown from her lungs as she lay on the ground, rolling from side to side, at Vangie's feet. Vangie raised her weapon, but Rena charged toward them with a battle roar brandishing a hand-scythe, and Vangie readied to defend herself. Shalise lowered her shield, but Vangie spun back, plucking a curved dagger from her waistband, and threw it at her.

"Shalise!" Marishel screamed as the dagger slid across the top of the shield, creating a shower of orange sparks, then lodged in Shalise's shoulder. The girl tumbled to the ground.

CHAPTER TWENTY-FOUR

BLOOD MATCH

THEY MET IN A CLASH ABOVE her and Marishel watched a crimson line run from Vangie's skin. But Vangie beat down on the scythe, nearly forcing it from Rena's hands. As she scrambled out of the way, Marishel's fury erupted, so hot she couldn't form rational thought. How could she help? There was nothing she could do. *Wait.* She ducked for the sword she'd missed in the air and picked it up with chained hands. The sword was top-heavy, but she pushed the anger into her limbs and turned to find Vangie racing toward her. *Where is Rena?* She barely had time to lift her blade when the swords met with a clang, then zinged as Vangie's cutting edge slid along Marishel's, knocking the weapon from her hands.

What am I doing? I don't want to kill Vangie. This is the whole point.

"You don't have to do this, Vangie. We can fight *together*." Marishel backed up and held her linked hands out, pleading for a stop to the madness.

"I don't want to fight with you!" Vangie lunged and Marishel jumped back. The crowd booed.

Marishel glanced over at her friend, lying injured on the ground. Her heart skipped a beat and her eyes filled. She wanted nothing more than to run over to Shalise, but Vangie advanced.

"You're fighting the wrong opponent. We can stop this. You don't want to kill all these girls," Marishel called and again, heard her words echo through the arena. "This is not how we evolve, how we get better. We are supposed to make things better for the next generation. Things *need* to change."

Vangie twisted back to attack Unity who ran up to help Marishel, but Marishel yelled, "Stop!" Unity held her sword still and backed up. Vangie, shocked at the surrender, stopped, and turned back to Marishel who continued, "For all the rights we have, this—quencher of blood lust—must stop. No one wants this anymore. We must grow out of this hate. Don't you want an honest life? Don't you want to be *chosen?* Selected by love?"

"Love is overrated." Vangie raised her sword and pointed it straight at Marishel's heart. "Besides, it's tradition."

"It's murder," Marishel countered.

"It proves the one worthy to rule!" Vangie yelled and swung, but Marishel let herself fall backward, tucked herself in a ball, and rolled away from her. The sword cut across her ankle and the crowd booed again.

"It *kills* innocent girls," Marishel said to the cameraman as she tried to maneuver herself from the ground. A few girls stood behind Marishel, ready to assist her.

"It's what everyone wants." Vangie looked less sure of herself.

"No, it isn't. Listen to them." Marishel cocked her head and waited for Vangie to hear the words of the crowd and realize that their violence and protest were not blood lust, but a call to cease the Match.

"It's the way we do things," Vangie cried, flustered and unhappy with the lack of support from the crowd.

"It's wrong!" Marishel yelled before they could cut off her feed.

"No." Vangie's eyes shone. "*I* am worthy. I am a winner."

"You are a puppet."

Vangie growled and lunged at Marishel, who threw herself to the side to avoid the hit, but Vangie's blade sliced through the material on her arm. Blood pooled at the edges of the fabric as she hit the dirt on her side. "This isn't going to end well, Vangie," Marishel warned from the ground as Vangie raised her sword and the other girls closed in. "Are you sure you don't want to join us?"

"Ha! Join your circus?" Vangie motioned to the confusion around them. Girls on the obstacle course still battled each other, and guards chased and detained red-suited heroes. They were beginning to outnumber the top tier and were ganging up together to pin the flailing girls down and disarm them. "You can't talk your way out this time."

Marishel pushed herself up to a sitting position—an idea formulating in her mind. "I warned you, *Evangelea*," she said.

Vangie barked a laugh at her. "You just don't give up, do you? It doesn't matter what you say, *Marishel.* I will kill you."

As fast as she could, Marishel flattened out and rolled toward her opponent. Vangie backed up in surprise—not quite fast enough—but raised her sword to strike, the blue light sparking as she gave it maximum power. Marishel rolled right into Vangie's legs, and her rival worked to keep her balance and swing. In seconds, Marishel pulled the metal zip tie from her ponytail and clamped it loosely around both of Vangie's feet as she shouted, "Last chance!"

"Never!" As Vangie yelled her battle cry, Marishel gave her a little push when she swung down. The movement forced her to back up a step and as her foot caught, refusing to move any farther, she froze, her mouth in an "oh" shape. Her feet remained tethered together and she fell backward—her sword arm flinging out to the side—and the blade went flying. The other girls advanced on her as she sat swiftly, and held weapons to her throat.

According to the rules, Marishel was required to "finish her off," and not leave her there, helpless for other contestants to come along and torture her. And the girls pressed into Vangie as if they meant her harm. Marishel yelled out, "No!"

The girls took a step back and Marishel stood, looking into the lens of a cameraman who had chased her across the arena. "No more blood spilled."

She glanced over at Vangie, whose hands were up in surrender. The cameraman motioned for Marishel to go on, and she realized this was her chance. This was it. *Finally.*

Marishel looked around her at the girls subduing the top tier and turned back to the camera. "Karthik Porter!" she shouted, and the Leader's name bounced from the concrete walls. "You are a good leader, and you listen to the people. Hear them now—this tradition needs to change. What was done in the past is not your fault, but today you have a choice. A choice the Ambassador should have. I have learned through this process that sometimes, even when you have control, you must believe in the ideas of others.

"As our Leader, you have the right to choose our fate when we break the rules, but what about these faithful citizens? Will you kill them as well?" She held her cuffed hands out and swept them from side to side to indicate the girls around her. "They've done nothing to deserve this punishment. None of us deserves execution."

She looked toward the Leader's box but couldn't see it. She faced the camera. "For the contestants' families, and friends, for the rebels and the girls—and for the Ambassador, who deserves to have the mate he finds worthy—please let the girls go. Let us all go and find a different way to choose the Ambassador's Bride... A hierarchy built on blood cannot stand."

Marishel waited for the Leader to trump the First and agree with her. She waited for him to see things her way, the way they made sense. But no call came to stop the Match. The crowd began to chant, "Stop the Match! Stop the Match!"

The top-tier girls struggled against their captors and screamed for their weapons and the chance to end it all. Vangie yelled to the Leader through the cameraman's microphone, too, "Let me finish her, Leader! She's standing in the way of our heritage! Allow me to end her and resume the Match!" The crowd erupted in matching cries of agreement, drowned out by booing, calling for an end to the Match. It seemed like chaos was taking over as the seconds clicked by. Marishel's nervous sweat was pungent to her senses. Her hands shook. *Why won't he answer?*

Rena ran up to Marishel. "It's not working. What do we do?"

The other girls around them echoed their rising panic at the failure of Marishel's plea. They shifted from foot to foot like skittish animals of prey downwind of a predator. Red-shirted traitors to the monarchy shouted as they were rounded up into groups under the watchful eyes of guards with loaded weapons powered up and aimed.

Marishel needed to think fast. There was one last-ditch effort she could make. It would backfire if he didn't care, but it was the only shot she had left. Whether it mattered to the Leader or not, would remain to be seen. If she could get *all* the people to agree with her—the Leader was known for his equitable logic—he might grant her wish if she could show him that he was utterly wrong in the eyes of everyone.

Marishel looked at the cameraman and asked if he could do her a favor. A shrill tone beat their eardrums from the speakers—a system warning. Bars of color lined up across the screen while the sound screeched, and the crowd silenced as Marishel's face appeared on the big screen and the vid screens at home. She removed her fingers from her ears and smiled at her family as she imagined them at home facing the screen, then took a deep breath. This was her final option.

"Leader? I call a Human Rights Complaint against the Match."

The crowd in the stands gave a chorus of gasps and murmuring hums. Marishel waited until it was quiet again and began her speech. "You can't give us human rights and just ignore the ones you choose when it's 'tradition.' The government has no right—even to satisfy the desires of the people—to take a life. If I have the right *to live in peace, without slander, abuse, or exploitation inside the planet* ... the Decalogue says that I—we—have the right to *live*. And we have committed no crime, so the state cannot take our rights away. *We have the right to be compensated for our work, to make future family decisions about our future children*—you can't take our future families. *We have the right to be who we are without prejudice, without harassment.*"

The people hushed and the arena vibrated with the hum of a multitude of murmurs.

"And the last one: *I have the right to live without bodily harm*. If you cause my death, great Leader, you will be breaching the Decalogue. An added charge for every girl in this arena. And I guarantee there are people here who would hold you to that."

No one moved. Marishel didn't even know if the Leader had been present to hear her speech. She waited while the rumble of people in the stands grew in volume until they were once again shouting, "Stop the Match! Stop the Match!" And a new chorus of, "Human Rights! Breach of Decalogue!" rang out in agreement.

Seconds passed slowly and Marishel perspired, fear clogging her throat. Then the Leader's flushed face flashed onto the screen, filling it with his displeased presence. He cleared his throat and the people settled. "There are times when a rebel speaks and outlaws need to be punished,"— the crowd booed loudly and the Leader raised his voice— "however, sometimes a revolutionary comes along to show us things we might have ignored, overlooked, or forgotten, that need changing. Your next leader will be Quinlan Porter. I have conferred with him, and we would like to make a change in policy. The Blood Match is canceled—indefinitely."

The girls cheered and groaned, sagging in relief. Most of them. Marishel ran to Shalise. Her head lay in Rena's lap and her complexion was pasty, sweat beaded on her forehead. Tears fell from Rena's lids as she pressed her palm to the wound. Blood dripped from between her fingers, and she cursed. "Can somebody get a medic?" she cried.

The "cleanup crew" in black coveralls, already prepared to remove fifty-nine bodies, rushed into the arena to claim their dead and a handful of emergency techs followed, half of them carrying medical bags to treat injured girls. Their group waved over one tech to help Shalise.

Marishel dropped to her knees beside them, laying her hand on Shalise's shoulder. Within minutes, the public stormed into the arena, families looking for their contestants. Marishel saw Ghaty running through the mass of people to swing Kosie off her feet and through the air. She smiled sadly. Was it worth it all if Shalise sacrificed herself? A dark pall fell over their little group when Shalise's breath rattled.

Suddenly, Marishel was lifted to her feet from under her arms. She spun to see her parents and Madi.

"You came!" she exclaimed.

"Of course," said her father.

"Of course," her mother said in the sweet voice she'd missed every night.

Marishel's face crumpled as the weight of the whole Match fell on her shoulders and she found she could no longer hold herself up, let alone hold the responsibility for Shalise's life. She collapsed into her parents' arms and put her bound hands around Madi.

"I missed you all so much." She could feel her eyes water, but she had a feeling it would be a regular occurrence for a while.

As her parents pulled her from the blood-spattered arena floor, Marishel craned her neck, searching for the Leader's box above the platform. *Where was Quin?* Was he coming for her? Should she stay and wait for him? Her parents tugged her toward the arena doors. Surely, he would contact her as soon as he could. As she resisted their pull, she perused the crowd looking for Trae, as well, but the crush of people in the arena made it impossible to find anyone.

Back at the Leader's estate, the training center was bedlam with girls and their families gathering items to leave as quickly as they could, taking advantage of their ability to escape before anyone in the government could think to detain them. No one bothered to ask if they could, they just quickly packed their things and rushed out. Baba gathered Marishel's luggage and, thinking fast, asked Sayra to restart her feed. The staff was flustered and confused, the Match not turning out the way they had expected at all. Their previous instructions null, they stood impotently while chaos reigned.

Marishel expected to see Quin at every turn, to grin and congratulate her, and maybe even kiss her goodbye. It seemed to her that people were everywhere, even going to the tube station en masse. The gamblers were pleased that their bets were still valid—there was a first and last death, there was turmoil and fighting, and so much gore.

Hopefully, the Blood Match junkies could find something *new* to bet on.

They rushed home as if they would be forced to stay if they dallied. Marishel was so exhausted she slept all the way home on the aerotrain but her sleep was plagued with nightmares of spraying blood and flying body parts. More than once she was jolted awake by the movement of the aerotrain and she nearly jumped from her seat, ready to battle. The anxiety clenched her insides like a coil being wound tighter and tighter.

Warily, she trudged home from the Outerlimits' tube station with her family. She jumped at loud noises, so Marishel's father kept his arm around her shoulders, radiating pride for his little "revolutionary." She arrived home, climbed the stairs, snuggled into her own bed, and slept the rest of the day.

People spoke downstairs in hushed tones during the evening.

"Marishel?" Her mother stood in the backlit doorway, with her head poked into the room. Marishel startled, thinking she was in the dorm, her heart pounding. "Baba's family is here. Granny Elspeth, Sootsie and the twins, Uncle Bo and Uncle Hixon. I made your favorite. You want to come down and say hi?"

The sounds of laughter and gaiety relaxed her body and she remembered she was blissfully, happily, home. She attempted to tell her mother that she'd missed her so much, and she wanted to talk to her parents. There were so many things she needed to know about life before hers was over. But when she rolled over and her cheek brushed the cool fabric, she was gone—catching up on missed sleep and rewinding after a prolonged period of constant anxiety.

Marishel woke with a shiver to the lightening of the morning and pulled the covers up over her shoulders. She tucked them under her chin and reveled in the feeling of comfort. She never thought she'd be back here. The day lights were now fully on outside, but the dim shadows in her room were unfamiliar. They must have been there all along, but she'd never noticed them before. They'd been part of life, but now that she'd lived in the bright, hot, Summerlands, the darkness depressed her. She felt like if she waited long enough, the lights would brighten and get warmer, but she knew they wouldn't. She thought of the girls and wondered where they were right now.

Suddenly, she saw a vision of Quin, sitting in his bed in the warm air. Was he happy that he would finally be allowed his own decision? *Would* he get a choice? Or had the Leader merely placated the crowd and played his hand with no options after she'd called him out in front of everyone? She vaguely wondered if the First would hold her grudge and come after Marishel.

She decided she couldn't worry about it. She couldn't live her life thinking of all the "what if's." Life was meant to be experienced to the fullest degree, without worry and fear. No trouble was as bad as dying. She knew her life was about to change; she no longer believed the problems in her life couldn't be solved. There was nothing impossible, and no reason to wait for what she wanted.

Just as suddenly, the idea of her previous safe future no longer appealed to her. She wanted to travel—see everything. The planet wasn't that big, just one-fourteenth of the Earth. In school, she'd learned that if the Earth was the size of a nickel, Haumea would be about as big as a sesame seed. But surely, there was so much she hadn't seen yet. She wondered if they would allow Quin to go with her.

The cold draft assaulted her feet when she stepped on the hard floor. The house was quiet, but she smelled something wonderful and sweet. She pulled on her favorite pants and sweater, tucked her feet into soft, warm socks, then lightly stepped down the stairs. The table was set with coffee and juice glasses, and a platter sat in the middle, stacked high with French toast. Her mother must have overridden the nutrient system.

Sometimes it malfunctioned when she missed too many meals without being deleted from the program. It warmed Marishel's heart that her family hadn't the heart to delete her information from the housebot. As far as Nex was concerned, she'd been at the farm, as usual—though she was rarely gone this long, and she didn't plan to be for a while.

When she sat at the table, once more her thoughts turned to Quin. How was he? Did he miss her? Was he happy when she stopped the Match? Was he thinking of her? Why hadn't he called? Though she had her *Eye* back, she'd kept it off as it seemed like too much noise in her subconscious—but she'd left her message alerts on. And ... *nothing.*

She'd meant it when she said he should be able to make a decision, even if it wasn't her, but she'd hoped he would choose her anyway. She imagined him picking one of the other girls and she sighed in disgust.

Baba put his screen down and looked at her, squinting his eyes. "You okay, Seashell?"

"Yeah. I just—I don't know what I expected after the Match, I thought so much abcut ending it, but I never thought about what came next."

"Do you miss it there?" Her father looked alarmed.

"No. Not the place so much. Though there were moving sidewalks, and fountains inside, and real food—not N-I printed. We learned about how to deal with foreign diplomats, and we trained with the coolest weapons—"

"Did you go on dates with the Ambassador?" Madi asked with her mouth full.

"Ew, Madi. Gross. Close your mouth. And yes, I did "

"Alone?" her mother asked, a brow raised.

"Yes. But the other girls did, too. And we weren't *that* alone, there are cameras everywhere."

"Good. I'd hate to think he had opportunities with so many young ladies."

"Mom!" Marishel felt a hot blush creep up her neck. "He did not have *opportunities.*"

"Betcha he kissed her, though." Madi winked at their mother who laughed lightly.

Marishel blushed eight shades of tomato and her family laughed at her.

"So, do you have any clues as to who the Ambassador's going to opt for?" Her mother took a bite and washed it down with her coffee.

"What?"

Her father looked at his screen and said, "It says in the Paper this morning that the Ambassador made his choice, and he plans to announce it this afternoon on the vid screen."

Anxious sweat slicked her palms. She hadn't heard a thing from him. He did mean *her*, right?

"So? Do you know who he chose?" her mother asked again.

"No. I guess I don't." The color drained from her face and Marishel felt light-headed. Her heart cracked.

After breakfast, she sent him a message, *Hey. Just checking on you. How are you doing?* There was no reply.

All morning, neighbors and friends stopped by, keeping Marishel's mind busy and off the announcement that she was growing increasingly certain she was not going to like. Everyone told her congratulations.

Yeah, congratulations on being alive. What an accomplishment.

"What's wrong with you?" Yolenie sat on her bed.

Marishel related the story in short form and Yolenie's eyes filled.

"Oh, Risha. I'm so sorry. He will regret not choosing you. Are you sure he didn't?"

"Would you expect him to pick you if he was going to make an announcement to the whole planet, but he hadn't contacted you at all after you threw a wrench into all his parents' plans? And *said parents* hated you, not only as a romantic potential but as a human being? Otherwise, he would've called. Right?"

"I see your point."

"They could have set him up with someone. Or maybe they forced him to make another choice, after all." She imagined that the First could have forbidden him to choose her, out of all his options.

When Yolenie was gone, Marishel's mother appeared in the doorway. "I have a new dress for you, Risha. It came in while you were gone. I thought you might like to wear it."

"I'm not going anywhere," Marishel said.

"You might change your mind. You never know. Yolenie mentioned something about trying to get your mind off things. Anyway, here it is." She pulled out a brand-new kaftan. It was a gauzy salmon-pink color with an open back. A little racier than her mother usually made them. The front of the dress, after curving over the chest like a heart, swept fabric over to one side, where it passed through a golden circle connected to a necklace piece. The long strips of chiffon would flow from the ring across her shoulder and down her back to her knees.

"It's beautiful, Mom. I'm sure I'll wear it soon, but I doubt I'm going anywhere for a while," she said with a yawn. The shadow of depression loomed over her, and she was suddenly exhausted.

"Risha! Mom said to call you down here!" Madigan hollered upstairs from the living room.

Marishel chuckled as she heard her mother's exasperated voice saying, "Thanks, Madi. I could have done *that* myself."

Madi ignored the sarcasm and sang brightly, "You're welcome."

Marishel trudged down the stairs.

"What's wrong with you?" Madi asked.

"Nothing," Marishel tried to say with more energy than she felt.

"It's a big announcement, Madi," her mother said. "Risha is probably just nervous about what he's going to say."

"You mean *if* he picks her?"

"Madi!" Marishel ducked her head and took the vacant spot on the sofa next to the side table. Her mother sat next to her, curled up into her father's side. Baba's arm encircled her protectively and Marishel was jealous of her parents' relationship for the first time. They were so happy just to be together. They wanted to spend every minute they had with each other.

She thought of Trae and wondered if he'd gotten away from Blayk for good? Did he escape that night, or was he still wrapped up in Blayk's plan? Or was that him in the arena? Did he see her on the feeds? Know she was all right? She hadn't heard from him, though he'd never contacted her at home before. He might not know where she lived. She'd just have to hope that he was okay.

"I'm not even sure watching what's-his-name is important. Maybe I'll just go back upstairs," Marishel said, getting up from the sofa.

"Just come sit with me," her mother pleaded. "I missed you so much."

Marishel nearly flew into her mother's outstretched arms. "I missed you, too." She snuggled into her mother's side, making the three of them like nestled dominos, having fallen over. "Maybe I'll watch a little bit."

Madi collapsed in a giggle attack on the floor. Marishel narrowed an eye at her, asking her mother, "What's with her?"

"Beats me," her mother said, settling back into Baba's shoulder.

Her father manned the remote. He said it was one of his few rights as King of the house. To which the females of the house chuckled and let him amuse himself with the idea that he had control over anything.

The screen switched to a view of the Ambassador standing behind a lectern. She was immediately drawn to his hair. He must have just taken a shower because his hair was in shiny brown curls around the edges of his collar. The microphone in front of him was turned off and he spoke to someone on the side, off-camera. Quin smiled sweetly to whoever was on the outside of the frame and Marishel thought that must be the girl he'd chosen, waiting there with him to make the announcement. She was already disgusted.

The Haumean anthem played instrumentally, and Quin stood up straight, shuffling note cards and then stuffing them in the opening behind the podium. The music ended and the Ambassador cleared his throat. He tapped the microphone and someone off-camera spoke.

He nodded to them and turned back to the viewing public. Marishel's nerves were tight as a bowstring. Whose name would he say? Who had stolen his heart and rendered all of her dreams with him sour?

"My dear people… I am Quinlan Porter, your Ambassador—and the next leader of Haumea. Yesterday, we decided to cancel the Blood Match. Many of you have come forward with concerns about our traditions and what we choose to do in lieu of the Match. We will be discussing whether a contest of any kind will remain in the future. As of now, the position of Ambassador's Bride will be won by the decision of the Ambassador.

"The time has come for me to announce my choice, and I realize you are concerned with how this is to be done. I understand your desire to know who I will choose today as the future First. I know many of you are tuning in tonight to hear good news. Please understand, even as a leader, having a choice doesn't always mean we like our options." Was he talking about the girl he was forced to choose?

He didn't appear upset. In fact, he had a teasing glint in his eye that was only caught by knowing him and the expressions he made. Quin's dimpled smile on the screen made Marishel's heart beat faster. *Who is she?* Anger flashed through Marishel like a jolt of electricity. It buzzed in her ears and heated her core with hatred for anyone he might pull to stand beside him.

"Therefore, I've chosen *not* to make a choice. I am *not* choosing a bride … yet. The time allotted for my selection will be extended. I haven't made any final decisions, but I hear time is irrelevant once you *know*. And, because knowing generally takes some time, I am excited to learn about the process of dating and will enjoy being able to court my intended mate."

Marishel's shock was the only thing that held her fracturing heart together. He wasn't choosing *anyone?* Of all the scenarios she'd imagined, this one hadn't entered her mind. And what of their time alone? Did that mean nothing to him? Did *she* mean nothing to him?

Quin lay his palms on the podium. "I am taking over extra responsibilities while the First takes a leave of absence to rest in the Farmlands. The Blood Match was a very traumatic experience for her. If you encounter the First as she travels, the Leader and I expect nothing less than your displays of kindness, thoughtfulness, and respect for privacy during this time—the experience will take time to heal from."

It was traumatic for her? Marishel thought with a snort. She wasn't angry. Not really. She felt … raw … and tired. It was like nothing she'd been through had been worth it—not without Quin. Maybe she was being a bit of a romantic about it, but she thought they'd had a connection.

At that point, the Ambassador's grin widened, and he looked like a child who'd been let in on a big secret. "I know that as a servant of the people, you are all interested in my well-being, but I ask for privacy with my budding romantic life, just as you would appreciate the same thing. Please remember to give space to those I care about and do not be offended, but I am not interested in suggestions for a pairing."

Marishel felt sick and wanted nothing more than to take a nice, hot bath and read in bed until she fell asleep—for a week. But the Ambassador wasn't finished and since she had no plans to see him for the foreseeable future, she just wanted to watch him for a few more minutes. His eyes sparkled and his even, white teeth made her think of his smile in the dark, surrounded by hundreds of tiny twinkling lights. She imagined running her nails over his scalp, letting his hair curl around her fingers. She sighed.

"This is new territory, and I will not be disclosing any personal romantic information to the public after tonight, but in case you vid screen watchers and faithful gossips would like to know, my new girlfriend's name is"—he paused, and her head snapped up—"Marishel Vance. I'll be there at 6:30, Risha, we have a date." Quin winked and the screen turned black.

Marishel's shrill scream was only matched by the cry of her mother and Madi's contagious giggles. Baba's laughter boomed over them all. "Tell that gentleman to have you home on time."

Marishel looked at her father in shock. "What did you say?"

"Who do you think told him you like chocolate strawberries on caramel cheesecake?" His eyes crinkled at the edges.

"And who do you think sent us the dress?" Madi shouted.

"You knew?" She looked blankly at her family.

"You were his Match after all," her mother said.

Marishel sat back and smiled, imagining their date to come.

The End

EPILOGUE

"I FEEL LIKE I'M LOSING YOU all over again," Marishel's mother said in her doorway with a sniffle. "I've only had you back for six months."

"I know, Mom. But this time there's no threat to my life. It'll be okay. I'll visit—I promise." Marishel stopped folding clothing and put the last piece in the box on her bed. "I'll be home at least every other weekend."

"But, but—" Madi sputtered from her place on the bed, snuggling Marishel's pillows.

"I was going to be growing up soon and leaving anyway. I won't be far. Just an aerotrain ride away." She patted the box flaps closed and ran the tape roller over it.

"Is Rena going as well?" Her mother handed her an empty box. "I like her. She's spunky. Make sure to bring her back here to visit."

"Spunky?" Marishel laughed. "That's a good description for her. Yeah, she's coming, too. She's apprenticing with the fitness programming. She learns fast and will be a good asset to the team."

"Just like you," Madi said. "You learn fast."

She smiled at her little sister and reached over to tug her pigtail. "So do you, little scholar. Mom told me about your grades. Good for you."

Madi beamed. "So, what will you do in the capital?"

"Well, I'll live at the estate—"

Madi's eyes were round. "With the Ambass—"

"In her own little apartment," their mother clarified.

"Well, it's not an apartment. There's no kitchen or anything. But I will have my own room and a sitting room for entertaining, with my own bathroom, and an office near the legal team." To Madi's blank stare, she summed it up. "I'll be working as an advisor. Or learning to be the advisor to the next ruler."

"Ambassador Quin," Madi said, obviously proud that she was following anything to do with politics.

"Yes." Marishel chuckled. "One day I will be his advisor. If everything works out."

"There's no reason why it wouldn't," her mother soothed.

Suddenly, the bottom dropped out of Marishel's stomach, her mind plagued with doubts. "Are you sure? I mean, what if I say something stupid? Or he decides he doesn't like me? Or—"

Her mother pulled her into a hug. "Nothing is going to go wrong. You're right. It is time for you to grow up and be on your own. I'm just going to miss you." She smoothed Marishel's hair. "You are good at this. Politics is all about psychology, and you know how to work with people, and you have fresh ideas. Who else beat the Match?"

Marishel sighed and took in her mother's strength. "We all beat it, Mom. Quin, me, Rena, Shalise, the people... It wasn't just me alone."

"But everybody else says it was you." Madi squeezed the pillow and put her chin on it.

"Yeah. I'll probably get that for a long time. But it wasn't just me, Madi. The thing is, any smart girl could have realized what I did, and done what I accomplished, and they all could have said what I said. The only difference is ... *we* did it."

"How's your other friend?" Marishel's mother gave her a squeeze, then let go of her and sat on the end of the bed.

"Shalise? She's back in the Farmlands, healing up. Vangie's blade caught her right shoulder, luckily. Her heart was safe. It nicked her lung, though, so they had trouble with that, but from what Rena's told me, she's healing up well now. I'd love to visit her, but Rena said it's not a good time yet."

"Why not?" Madi asked.

"It's complicated, Madi-bug. I hurt her feelings." Marishel picked up her toiletry bag and paused. "I didn't mean to, but I did."

"And she's still hurt?"

Marishel nodded. "She just needs some more time."

"Like the First?" Madi picked up a paper 'zine with the ruling family on the cover.

Marishel looked at her mother, not sure how to answer.

"Yes," her mother said. "She will be in the Farmlands recovering for a while—until she's ready to lead again. Same thing."

"So, when she said those things about Risha and what she would do to her friends, she was just sick?"

"Again, Madi, it's complicated. But Risha will be fine." Her mother paled. "None of those things will happen. The Leader assured us."

"But she said she would send Risha to Sedna with Trae and that snotty girl and her dad because they kidnapped her. She said—"

"Yes, Madi," Marishel said. "We know. But she was having—a nervous breakdown. Her mind was sick. That's why she needs some time. Don't worry. When she comes back, I'm sure everything will be fine." An alarm pinged through Marishel's cochlear implant, her *Eye* flashed the time, and a message scrolled along the bottom of her vision.

>*Quin/ You ready, sweet girl?*

<*Risha/ Almost finished packing. :^D What time will you be here?* ♡

>*Quin/ I'm leaving now. At the station. It should be half an hour from here.*

<*Risha/ How's your mother?*

>*Quin/ Same.*

<*Risha/ I'm sorry.*

>*Quin/ Don't worry about it. She's tough, she'll make it. See you soon. xoxo*

"Was that him?" Marishel's mother asked.

"Yep. He'll be here in half an hour. I've got to get this finished."

"Can I come to visit?" Madi asked.

"Of course."

"Maybe I'll find my blood match there, too."

"One Blood Match was enough for this family," her mother said, and they laughed together.

Thank you so much for reading! I would love to hear what you thought of Hierarchy of Blood! If you would like to leave a review, please click here:

www.amazon.com/review/create-review?asin=B0B66H85VS

ACKNOWLEDGMENTS:

I always thank God first, for life and love, for the time, the patience it takes to write books, for my family and friends, and for everything I have that makes authoring a book possible. I'd like to thank fans of my first trilogy for giving my new book a shot, and the early critique partners, like Ela Mishne, Keira Wattus, and Aurora. Thank you to my writing partners for reading every line out loud and making Monday writers' tea parties fun: Alisha Davis and Zachary Drummond, thanks for believing in me throughout each chapter.

Thank you to my family for putting up with coffee breath and mood swings, all-nighters, and online conferences that last for days. I love you all: Mom and Dad and Morgi, Huckleberry, my bright star, my mighty mountain, my shining jewel, my little warrior, and my lovely rose.

Thank you also to my reviewers, I appreciate you and get so excited to read your reviews. I realize that I rely on your level of love for my fictional worlds and your kindness to share your thoughts on Amazon for the readers who aren't sure if my book is for them yet.

Thank you to my fellow authors for all the advice and support along the journey.

Finally, thank you to my readers and fans. You make the entire process worth it.

Photo Credits for The Paper:

Shalise: Matt Moloney

<a href="https://stocksnap.io/photo/woman-portrait-ZG1SST226T">Photo</a> by <a href="https://stocksnap.io/author/mattmoloney">Matt Moloney</a> on <a href="https://stocksnap.io">StockSnap</a>

Marishel: Matheus Bertelli

<a href="https://stocksnap.io/photo/girl-lights-8A4E0ECYK3">Photo</a> by <a href="https://stocksnap.io/author/matheusbertelli">Matheus Bertelli</a> on <a href="https://stocksnap.io">StockSnap</a>

Nahli: Matt Moloney

<a href="https://stocksnap.io/photo/girl-outdoors-VKWHNQ8HUU">Photo</a> by <a href="https://stocksnap.io/author/mattmoloney">Matt Moloney</a> on <a href="https://stocksnap.io">StockSnap</a>

Vangie: Alesia Kazantceva

<a href="https://stocksnap.io/photo/people-humans-QLGW2QSEI2">Photo</a> by <a href="https://stocksnap.io/author/50563">Alesia Kazantceva</a> on <a href="https://stocksnap.io">StockSnap</a>

Rena: Cottonbro

Photo by cottonbro: https://www.pexels.com/photo/light-fashion-people-woman-6531476/

ABOUT THE AUTHOR:

  Jennifer Haskin has a passion to help authors with their writing journey, as well as achieve their publishing goals. She spent a few years learning the ropes of the publishing world as a literary agent, and then a publishing consultant, helping authors ready their submission materials to get the best shot at the contract of their dreams. An author, both traditional and indie, she markets her YA fantasy romance trilogy while helping authors perfect their books as Associate Editor for Touchpoint Press. She blogs her own journey weekly with writing, editing, publishing, and marketing advice. Books are pretty much her thing. Jenn lives in Kansas with her hubsalot and five teenagers, who provide plenty of YA angst to help her writing come alive. When she is not drinking a grande iced white mocha and writing a book or editing manuscripts, she's running a weekly writers' workshop and is honored to be a judge for the annual writing contest Ink & Insights. Come find her on social media and say hi @haskinauthor.

For more information, or to read Jenn's blog:

www.jenniferhaskin.com

For information on hiring Jenn as an editor:

www.frontpageediting.com

ALSO BY THIS AUTHOR:

The Freedom Fight Trilogy:

Princess of the Blood Mages
www.amazon.com/dp/B07XWVSH2B

The Queen's Heart
www.amazon.com/dp/B07XWTH6ZB

The Final Rescue
www.amazon.com/dp/B07Z5PFYVW

Printed in Great Britain
by Amazon